Angel tried to break her weapon free, but Nicoli's strength and her own fatigue made it impossible.

"Yield." Nicoli's quiet tone hinted at more than just the sparring match.

"Never." Feeling for the small button in the grip of her sword, Angel pressed it. The hilt separated from the blade and with a last burst of energy, she quickly raised her hand and placed the dagger's sharp edge against his throat.

Suddenly her feet were kicked out from under her. Unable to get her arms back in time to cushion her fall, Angel hit the ground hard enough to knock the wind out of her. In the nanosecond it took to catch her breath, Nicoli pinned her down with his body. She brought her hands up to beat at him, but he caught them easily and held them trapped beneath one of his, using the other for support.

A grin spread across his face. "Lesson number one, Baby Girl. Don't pull it out unless you intend to use it."

She struggled against him, but the effort did nothing more than rub their bodies together. The earthy scent of crushed grass and dirt rose to mingle with the aroma of virile male, filling her senses. Her mind begged her to resist, but her body refused. Beneath his weight, her pulse quickened.

"Yield," he whispered, his breath fanning her face. Again, she twisted beneath him, a futile attempt. When a groan escaped his lips, she froze, noticing for the first time his arousal pressing against her stomach. For what seemed an eternity, their eyes met—searching, assessing. Anticipating. Then his mouth captured hers.

TOO CLOSE TO THE SUN

ROBIN T. POPP

LOVE SPELL NEW YORK CITY

*To Corky Sandman, who read every word of every
version I ever wrote. Your faith in me and this story
was sometimes greater than my own.*

LOVE SPELL®

July 2003

Published by

Dorchester Publishing Co., Inc.
276 Fifth Avenue
New York, NY 10001

ISBN 0-505-52547-X

Printed in the United States of America.

Visit us on the web at www.dorchesterpub.com.

ACKNOWLEDGMENTS

I would like to thank:

Mary O'Connor and Georgia Ward, for being the best critique partners. Your advice is invaluable; your friendship is irreplaceable. I could not have gotten here without you both.

Adam Popp, my husband and personal hero, for providing the encouragement, time and support that allowed me to follow the dream.

Dakota, Mihka and Garrett, for the hours of entertaining themselves and occasionally scrounging up their own meal so I could write—and most especially, for never once thinking that someday their mother might not be published.

Kate Seaver, my editor, for giving me this chance.

TOO CLOSE
TO THE SUN

Chapter One

West Coast Beach
Las Vegas, Nevada
Earth, 2503 AD

"You're not afraid."

It was more observation than question and Nicoli Alexandres Romanof did not bother to respond. Though he could sense his friend's unease, short of changing his mind, there was nothing he could do to lessen it.

There were others on the beach, enjoying the night-fishing, the stars, the moonlight, each other. A couple sat watching as the incoming surf chased their young children up the shore. Their peals of laughter floated to Nicoli on a salty breeze and mingled with the soft crash of waves. For a moment he paused to watch, conscious of his lack of happy childhood memories. A pang of guilt assailed him and he wished he could warn them all, send them away to safety. But he couldn't. He wouldn't. If the beach were empty, then *they* wouldn't come, and it was imperative that *they* show up. Even knowing that some of the

1

others on the beach would die horribly tonight did not alter his resolve. He tried to find solace in the knowledge that what he was doing was more important than the loss of these innocent lives; that the good of many often comes at the sacrifice of a few. Failing, he forced his attention back to his task.

"This will do," he said softly, selecting a patch of beach somewhat away from the others.

The older man merely nodded and reached into his inner jacket pocket to remove a slim silver disc, no larger than the palm of his hand. Next he took off the chain he wore around his neck, at the end of which hung a clear crystal tube, about four fingers' width in length. He stared at them, doubt clearly in his eyes.

"It'll work," Nicoli reassured him, nodding to the disc.

"This is not your best idea, Alex."

Nicoli smiled at the use of his middle name. Only Yanur Snellen persisted in calling him Alex because, in Yanur's words, "Colonel Romanof was too military and Nicoli sounded too formal." Nicoli tolerated it, not because Yanur was the most brilliant scientist he'd ever met, but because Yanur was his friend. In a universe full of people, he only had one of those.

"If the Harvestors do show up tonight," Yanur continued, "and this plan of yours works, it could be days, even weeks, before your life essence is returned to your body." He paused before quietly adding, "I don't know if I'll be able to put it back."

"I'm not going to change my mind."

"This whole plan is crazy. What if I run into problems tracking your body? What if I never find it?"

"Let Richardson worry about tracking my body. That's why I hired him."

"Okay, let's say we find your body, but can't put *you* back? Are you prepared to live the rest of your life in this?" He held up the tube.

Nicoli sighed. "If you can't put me back, then have my body programmed for sex and give it to your maiden aunt as a present. Don't think I haven't seen the way she looks at me. This way, the old girl can do what she wants with my body and I won't be around to care."

"This is no time to joke."

"I'm not joking." He looked up and saw the concern in his friend's eyes. "Okay, I'm sorry. Look, I have complete faith in you, Yanur. You'll do your best."

"What if my best isn't good enough? You may actually succeed in killing yourself this time."

"I'm not afraid to die," Nicoli assured him.

"That's what worries me."

"Yanur, the Harvestors must be stopped. Their systematic annihilation of our people cannot be allowed to continue." Nicoli gazed out across the horizon, his patience wearing thin.

"I agree. But who made it your responsibility to save the universe?"

"I did."

"Why? Why you?"

"Because I have the military experience. Because I have no family to leave behind." He turned to face Yanur and looked him directly in the eyes. "And because I figured out how." His tone left no room for further argument. "Now let's get on with this. The night is getting old."

Nicoli lay down on the beach, raising his arms to place his hands, fingers interlocked, beneath his head. He crossed his legs at the ankles and for all appearances seemed to be resting peacefully. Further down the beach, other "moon-sleepers" lay in similar poses.

Resignedly, Yanur knelt and placed the silver disc on Nicoli's forehead. He stood the tube on the disc, then ran his finger along the side to activate a hidden switch, but hesitated at the last moment.

"Are you sure there is no other way?" he asked, voice gruff with emotion.

The answer was in Nicoli's grim expression. "Remember, once the transfer is complete, leave. It won't be safe. Come back at the first light of dawn. If my body's been taken, go to the ship. Richardson will be waiting for you. If my body is still here, we'll try again tomorrow."

"But—"

"Don't argue with me. Just do as I say." Nicoli suffered a

moment's hesitation as children's laughter floated to him once more. He cursed himself mentally for being weak, knowing that despite a lifetime of practice, he had failed to rid himself of all emotion. How many great plans failed because emotions got in the way? At thirty-eight, he was getting soft. "One more thing," he said softly. "When you leave, take that family with you."

Yanur nodded and then, with their gazes locked, he pressed the switch.

Immediately, Nicoli's eyes went blank and a wispy, amber light seeped out of his body. The light grew stronger as it formed a cocoon around the prone figure. The top of the tube opened automatically with a quiet hiss. Yanur watched, with some satisfaction, as the light gathered and was then sucked into the tube.

When all the light was contained inside, the lid lowered, making a slight clicking noise when the tube was properly sealed. Yanur placed two fingers against Alex's neck and only removed them when he felt the strong, steady beating of a pulse. It had worked! Alex was still alive, or at least his body was. Even the worry of what lay ahead was not enough to squelch a moment's elation for an experiment gone right.

He picked up the tube, now brightly glowing with Alex's life essence, and secured it to the chain before hanging it around his neck. He returned the silver disc to his pocket and lifted his gaze to the night sky for a quick check. All was quiet.

He walked across the beach to talk to the young parents, then stood by and watched as they gathered their children and belongings and headed for home. Once they were gone, he returned to his friend's side and, ignoring the earlier order to leave, settled down to wait.

Less than an hour later, an isolated portion of the night sky began to shimmer and, like a hologram taking on definition and substance, an alien spaceship appeared. Caught dozing, Yanur scrambled to his feet, looking fearfully upward. Clutching the tube hanging from his necklace in a death grip, he studied Alex's body one final time, offered up a silent prayer, then turned and ran from the beach.

*   *   *

Skeeter's was the last remaining icon of an era gone by. Situated at the remote end of the Las Vegas Coastal Airfield, the Old World pub offered sanctuary to world-weary travelers down on their luck. The ale might be watered down, but it was cheap. The meals weren't gourmet, but they were hot and the portions filling. The rooms upstairs were small and lacked the amenities considered standard fare at even the low-end hotels. But they came free of pests (of all species) and could be inexpensively rented by the hour, day or month with no ID and no questions. The gaming that went on twenty-four/seven in the dank side rooms was just this side of legal. The activities that took place in the back rooms weren't. The regular clientele was rough and settled differences without benefit of legal intervention. All in all, Skeeter's was a place best avoided by self-respecting, law-abiding citizens and the last place one would look to find a young woman of good breeding and affluent family. Which was precisely why Angel Torrence called it home.

Sitting now in the cockpit of her Falcon XLT, she studied the pub's lights shining from across the tarmac. It had been a safe place to hide these past two years. Given the circumstances, she'd almost been happy here. But two years was about a year and a half too long. She needed to move on.

This time would be different, though. She ran a hand lovingly along the console of her ship. Now she had the means to go anywhere she wanted. With the money she'd earned from this last job, she could make the final payment. This ship represented freedom.

Freedom. She'd been on the run since she was fifteen. Running from those who wished to control her, use her for their own purposes. Running from those who refused to let her go. There had been times along the way when she hadn't known if she would survive. But she was tougher than she looked. And luck had been on her side, for the most part. Now she worked as an independent galactic courier. She wasn't a certified pilot because that required registration and a background check. But her lack of certification mattered little to her clientele. Transporting illegal goods wasn't always easy, but it was lucrative.

Right now, she had a job to finish and the sooner the better.

Dugan would be waiting to hear how things had gone on Felinea. More important, he'd want his money.

Angel obtained final clearance for the Falcon with the control tower, verified that the stasis field was in place and prepared to disembark. She stopped by the small onboard cabin to retrieve her things. Gathering her waist-length hair into a braid, she shoved it beneath her shirt. She should have cut it a long time ago, but being tall and lean, with curves so subtle they went unnoticed beneath a few layers of clothes, her long hair was her most feminine feature. In a lifestyle of sacrifice, leaving it long was her only concession to feminine vanity.

Taking a cap from the closet, she pulled it low over her head, casting her face into shadow. She checked the gun in her shoulder holster, knowing it would be well-concealed beneath the flight jacket. When she reached for the satchel containing Dugan's money and hefted it over her shoulder, pain lanced through her side, reminding her that the gash there was still raw. Sneaking a look beneath the jacket, she could see that blood had soaked through her homemade bandage to her shirt. But the stain was small and dry, so she figured the bleeding had stopped and she wouldn't need stitches, after all.

Moving cautiously, she left the ship.

The sun was just beginning its ascent across the eastern sky, painting the airfield in grayish blues and pinkish yellows. The field was in decent shape, considering it was routinely subjected to terrorist attacks. Now, despite the early hour, there was a steady drone of activity. At least a hundred ships hovered over designated landing pads, stasis fields holding them in place while maintenance crews ran through pre- or post-flight checks. At the head of the tarmac stood the control tower, from which all launches and landings were coordinated. Even this far away, she smelled the familiar pungent odor of Tyrillium fumes and inhaled deeply, watching as pilots and other personnel rushed back and forth, taking care of business. She would miss all this.

Turning to her own ship, she gave it a cursory once over. Everything appeared in order. As much out of habit as curiosity, she took note of her neighbors. Most of the ships she knew by sight. On the left hovered TJ's derelict cruiser, the kind typically used for common trade. On the right was a sleek little number she'd not seen before. A real beaut. A small three- or four-person craft designed for high speeds and long distances. She wondered if it handled as well as it looked and ignored a twinge of longing to find out. Drawn by peculiar openings on either side of the nose, she stepped closer. Smartly embedded in the outer paneling were PCPs: pulse cannon portals. Definitely not your standard aircraft. It looked like Government Issue, but that didn't make sense. The United System of Planets' Security Forces had its own airfield not far from here.

Bold blue letters across the side spelled the ship's name, Icarus. The name sounded familiar to her. She searched her memory of ancient Earth folklore and remembered a character from Greek mythology who had fashioned wings out of wax and feathers to fly. Unfortunately, he had foolishly flown too close to the sun, causing the wax to melt. He had plummeted to his death. Angel couldn't help but wonder if this was an appropriate name for a starship. Maybe the ship's owner had a sick sense of humor. Which negated the government theory, seeing as how the government had no sense of humor, sick or otherwise.

Turning from the ship, Angel scanned the tarmac once again before starting across. The sense of foreboding that had started last evening, before she left for Felinea, was getting worse. If what happened there was any indication of what was to come, the sooner she left, the better.

Inside Skeeter's, things were quiet. Only the die-hard patrons were still up and about at this hour. A few heads turned briefly at her entrance. Across the room, Martin stood behind the bar, cloth in hand, wiping down the counter. Ol' Joe was passed out in his usual spot, head down, a thin stream of drool leaking from the corner of his mouth to pool on the countertop below. Over by the stairs, Pixie was finishing "business" negotiations with a potential client. Angel had to admire the older woman's stamina. This was probably her tenth customer tonight. Others sat around gaming tables, wagering and drinking ale. It was the same scene as a hundred times before, right down to the outsider sitting in the corner.

He looked out of place drinking coffee, but he was minding his own business. Angel could respect that.

She gave a mental shrug as she moved into the room. She had her own problems to worry about. The door to Dugan's office was closed and she knew better than to knock. Martin had no doubt pressed the button under the counter alerting Dugan to her arrival, so she headed over to the bar to wait.

"How ya doin', Angel?" Martin's smile was warm and friendly. She was afraid her own came across looking more like a grimace as she tucked the toe of her boot under the bottom rung of a stool and pulled it out. Hiking a hip onto the seat, she left one foot on the floor for balance. With some effort she lifted the satchel off her shoulder and onto the countertop.

"Jeez girl, what happened to you?"

Angel looked up and saw Martin staring at the place where her jacket gaped open at the side. She quickly pulled it closed. "Nothing."

"Don't give me that. I know blood when I see it. You run into trouble on Felinea?"

"Nothing I couldn't handle. You should see the other guy." As a joke, it didn't work.

"Yeah?" He sounded skeptical. "Maybe I should take a look at it. Clean it up. Do a little sewing?"

"No, thanks."

Martin didn't press her further, but instead reached under the bar to pull out a double-shot glass, which he filled with an iridescent sky-blue liquid.

He pushed the glass toward her. She downed the icy cool liquid in a single swallow. Martian Ale went down cold, but arrived hot. As the warmth spread throughout her body, she felt the pain in her side ease.

Angel pushed the empty shot glass across the counter, indicating with her hand that Martin should fill it again.

He gave her a questioning look. "You never drink more than one. That side of yours must be hurting."

"I'm celebrating," she said, watching him fill the glass again.

"Really? Care to share the good news?"

"As of tonight, I am the proud owner of one Falcon XLT

spacecraft." *Tonight, for the first time in my life, I'm free.* But she didn't say it out loud.

"And at such a young age, too." Martin smiled. "Well, I guess congratulations are in order." He pushed the refilled shot glass toward her, then poured a smaller one for himself. They raised their glasses in a silent toast and downed the contents. This time the icy burn wasn't as startling to her system.

"What's the story on the stiff in the corner?" Angel wanted to change the subject.

"Don't know. He doesn't talk much, just sits and drinks coffee. Every now and then, he'll look at his watch and go outside. I followed him once, just to see where he went."

"And?" Angel prompted when he paused.

"And nothing. He walks over to that sleek little number on the field, you know the one I mean, and just stands there for a minute like he's waiting for someone. Then he comes back here and orders more coffee."

Angel lazily pondered what the man was up to. Thanks to the Martian Ale, she felt almost as good as new. Her hands absently played with the empty shot glass as her attention wandered down the bar.

"I miss something?" She nodded toward the images flitting across the vid-screen.

"Harvestor attack, not far from here. West Beach."

Angel absorbed the news in shock. She'd just flown over that area not an hour ago. "Damn."

"Yeah." Martin nodded. "It's getting so decent folk aren't safe going out at night."

Angel shot him a look, eyebrows raised. How long had it been since either of them had been considered "decent folk?"

"Point is, no one is safe anymore." He focused his look at her injured side.

"I can take care of myself."

"Torrence!" A male voiced bellowed. "Get your ass in here."

"Then again . . ." She pushed the empty glass toward Martin and slid from the stool. "Been nice knowing you." This time she hardly winced when she hefted the satchel onto her shoulder. With more calm than she felt, she walked into the back room.

Alistar "Skeeter" Dugan, underground boss of the West Side, was in his mid-fifties and sported an athletic build just starting to go soft. His commanding presence gave him the stature his average height could not. He was overbearing, unforgiving, and his sense of humor had died along with his wife and daughter ten years earlier. He was not a man to be messed with, and Angel had no doubt that if she irritated him enough, he would forget how much she reminded him of his daughter.

"It wasn't my fault," she said, walking across the room to his desk. She slid the satchel off her shoulder and let it fall to the desktop. "Here's your money."

"Not your fault?" Dugan shouted, slamming the door behind her. "You shot the son of Felinea's leading crime boss!"

"Give me a break, it's not like I killed him. It was just a scratch."

"You shot off his—"

"I know what I shot off," Angel interrupted. "Look, the guy was all over me. I told him I wasn't interested, but the more I said 'no,' the more he heard 'yes.' I didn't have any other choice. Besides, what's the big fuss? He's Felinean. It'll grow back."

Dugan stormed up to her, causing her to step back. She wanted some distance between them, just in case. His hand shot out and grabbed her arm, wrenching her around. Pain shot through her side with the sudden movement, and she couldn't hide her reaction fast enough. Distracted from what he was about to say, Dugan pulled back her jacket flap.

"Explain this," he said when he spotted the blood.

"Like I said, Tony didn't like hearing 'no.' Things got a little rough before I got my point across."

Dugan studied her for a moment, and she saw some of the anger drain from his face to be replaced by something else. Resignation, maybe. "If you were anyone else, I'd have your head on a platter, literally, and see that it got delivered to Felinea with my deepest apologies."

Angel swallowed hard because she knew Dugan meant what he said. "I'm sorry, but the guy had it coming and it's not like I did any permanent damage."

"Yes, you did."

"No way. I purposely used a narrow beam so I could isolate the damage to that single area. Now granted, there was some confusion and it was a small target, but—"

"Oh, you hit what you aimed for. But you don't get credit for originality. You do, however, get credit for being number nine, and as they say, the ninth time's the charm with Felineans. No more regenerations for that particular organ, and folks over there are upset. Tony, in particular."

The news hit her with the force of a physical blow, but she tried to cover it with flippancy. "He's a slow learner. They should thank me for taking him out of the gene pool."

"The Tom's not laughing. He wanted grandkids. Now he wants revenge." Dugan went to stand behind his desk. He pulled the satchel closer and opened it. Reaching inside, he dug out the bundles of currency and counted them. After counting them a second time, he looked at her. "It's not all here."

"No, it's not. I took out what you owed me, less the final payment for the ship, as per our agreement." She refused to look away, waiting for his reaction. Then, to her relief, he nodded. Picking up one of the bundles, he stared at it for a moment, as if trying to decide what to do, then held it out to her.

"Take this," he said. "You'll need it where you're going."

"Which is where?"

"I don't know and I don't care, but don't take your time getting there."

Angel shook her head. "I don't need your money. I'll be fine."

Dugan walked around the desk and shoved the stack of bills into her jacket pocket, being careful not to touch her injured side. "Don't be so damn stubborn. The Felineans will be here soon. For political reasons, I won't stop them, but I sure hate the thought of you dying, so I think it'd be better if you weren't here when they arrive. I'll ship the stuff from your room to you later, if you want."

"That won't be necessary." Angel had learned long ago not to accumulate more than she could carry. So her "stuff" included the locket hanging around her neck, a gift from her mother, and the laz-gun resting in her holster, a gift from Dugan. Everything else could be replaced.

11

"How bad is your side? Do you need Martin to look at it?"

"No, I'll be all right."

"Then you'd better go."

And just that easily, her moment arrived. Angel knew she had to leave, had even planned on it, but somehow it hurt to be told to go. Sometime over the past two years, despite her best efforts to remain distant, she'd developed a fondness for these folks. They'd become her family. It shouldn't be that hard, she told herself. She'd left family before. But as she looked at Dugan, a feeling of such loneliness stole over her, the weight of it was suffocating. Emotion rose unbidden to choke into silence any words she might have muttered.

As she struggled to compose herself, a commotion in the outer room distracted her.

Curious, Angel joined Dugan behind the desk so she could see the security camera monitors. Out front, six men, looking serious and extremely tough, stood with guns in hand. Tables lay overturned around them while most of the clientele stood waiting against side walls.

"Terrorists?" Angel asked hopefully.

"Felinean Avengers," Dugan corrected.

"Damn." This just wasn't her day. She could see Martin with one hand under the counter, no doubt with his mini-Mag trained on the group. But he'd only be able to take out two, three at best. The rest of the patrons wouldn't interfere and, as Dugan had warned her, neither would he. That left three of them to one of her. She didn't like the odds.

"Take my private exit," Dugan said, pressing a button under the desk. To her surprise, an opening appeared beside her in the wall. "This comes out two doors down, behind the trash Dumpster."

Angel stepped into the opening, but couldn't bring herself to just walk off. She had brought trouble to Skeeter's and to her friends. She couldn't just leave them to fend for themselves.

"Dugan . . ."

He nodded as if he understood, then reached into his own jacket and pulled out an impressive Smith & Wesson Destroyer. He gave her a slow grin. "Better hurry."

She smiled, turned and left. Despite what he'd said, Dugan wouldn't make the Felinean Avengers' job any easier. No one came into Skeeter's to start trouble without getting a little in return.

She went swiftly through the tunnel, exiting behind the trash Dumpster. She skirted the side of the building and gazed across the open stretch of tarmac separating her from her ship.

There were no Avengers outside waiting for her, but the hairs on the back of her neck started to prickle anyway. The sense of impending disaster weighed heavily upon her as she started the trek across the landing field. Her feet felt leaden, but she forced herself to move quickly.

She hadn't taken three steps when the explosion came.

The shockwave caused her to stumble, while gravel rained down on her, peppering her head and back. Instinctively, she turned to see the scorched spot on the ground several meters off. She tried to locate the Avenger responsible, but none was visible, so she scanned the rest of the airfield. Everywhere, people stood frozen as they, also, tried to figure out what had happened.

Into the quiet came another explosion, this time on the opposite end of the field. The Avengers wouldn't take out the entire airfield just to get to her. It had to be a terrorist attack. As if to confirm her thoughts, the terrorist alarms began to wail and total chaos broke loose. For Angel, it was a blessing in disguise. If she survived.

People scattered aimlessly in an effort to get away from the unseen attackers. From around the field's perimeter, patrons flooded out of pubs and restaurants, desperate to get to their ships. Angel was soon lost in the crush. Sneaking a look behind her, she saw the Avengers leave Skeeter's and head her way. She turned and let the moving crowd carry her in the direction of her ship.

Halfway there, another explosion came almost from behind and knocked her to the ground. She tried to get up, but a weight pinned her down. Twisting her body, she looked up to find the stranger from Skeeter's lying on top of her.

"Get up," she yelled, but he wouldn't move. Exasperated, she tried to shove him off but to no avail. She looked around for help, but people were too concerned with saving themselves to offer assistance. Then she noticed the blood on her hands. Had her wound reopened in the fall? She didn't think so. Concerned, she searched for the source of the blood.

And found it. A large piece of shrapnel stuck out of the stranger's back. Judging from the quantity and color of the blood, she feared the metal was deeply embedded. She looked again at the stranger's face and this time registered the blank, lifeless eyes.

Overhead, a distinct whistling sound distracted her. She covered her head with her arms as the missile arced past her, praying she had misjudged its trajectory. Please God, she silently pleaded, let its target be TJ's junker.

Chapter Two

When the explosion came, she was too close. Intense, blistering heat rode the shockwave and blasted her full force. Ironically, the dead man's body protected her from projectile pieces of debris and certain death. When she finally lifted her head, she saw what was left of her ship, and freedom, going up in flames. It was almost more than she could bear. Despair filled her and she cried out. When her vision blurred, she angrily wiped the unwanted tears from her eyes and defiantly vowed that she would not let "them" win.

Still trapped, she fought to free herself and with a final, desperate effort, rolled the body aside.

Standing up, she looked around for another means of escape, her mind racing through the possibilities. Involuntarily, her eyes returned to the lifeless stranger at her feet. She noticed one of his hands clinched tightly in a fist. Unsure why she did it, she pried open his fingers. And removed a key-card.

A key-card to a spaceship. She turned to look at the Icarus, standing unscathed and in need of a pilot. She took off running.

At first, she didn't see him as she fought to insert the card into the hatch lock. An older man hid behind the ramp, eyes staring wildly at the chaos all around, his hand keeping a death grip on a necklace charm hanging from his neck. He was obviously in the wrong place, at the wrong time. And he wasn't her problem.

Angel glanced around. Everyone else had the good sense to run for cover. Only this man remained motionless, seemingly in fear. If she left him here, he'd be killed, either by the terrorists or by the thruster-fire of the ship as she took off. With a silent curse, she tugged the sleeve of his shirt to propel him forward.

He seemed oblivious to her, rooted to his spot, a wild desperate look in his eyes. In the background, Angel heard the explosive sounds of pulse canons discharging. She quickly pulled open the ship's hatch and lowered the ramp. Turning back to the man, she grabbed his arm hard enough to get his attention.

"Come on," she urged.

"But . . ." Several distant explosions muddled the man's objection.

"It's okay," she tried to reassure him as she pulled him along. They had reached the top of the ramp now, but still the man hesitated. Angel couldn't leave him behind, but they were out of time.

"Get on," she ordered, releasing him so she could bolt for the bridge. Climbing into the pilot's chair, she strapped herself in.

"Are you the pilot?" she heard the man ask in a shaky voice.

"Yeah. Now come on. Things are a little crazy out there." That was the understatement of the year. "I think you'd be safer with me than out there. Your choice, of course, but make it quick," she stated calmly, while madly flipping the switches necessary to warm up the engines. She spared a look over her shoulder and found him standing just outside the entrance to the bridge, near the hatch.

"Are you in or out?" Angel shouted over the noise of the ship's engines. "My personal advice? Choose in!"

At that moment, another ship blew up, so close they felt the concussion. The explosion seemed to galvanize the man. He rushed to the empty chair behind the pilot's and secured the safety straps around himself. "I'm in!" he shouted. "Go!"

"Roger that," Angel agreed, noticing a definite accent in the man's speech. Tourist. Hell of a time for a visit, she thought, pressing the button that closed the hatch automatically. Knowing the protocol was a waste of time, she opened a channel to Flight Central. "Tower, this is Icarus. Request permission to take off."

"Icarus, permission denied," a voice crackled across the open comm-link. "The pattern is full. Delay your lift."

Delay? Were they kidding? All around, ships were lifting off, desperate to escape the dangers of remaining grounded. Not far off, terrorists stood, their long coats pulled back to reveal bucking pulse cannons with muzzles blazing. Wherever they aimed, destruction followed. Less than ten meters from the ship, she spotted two of the six Avengers and even as she watched, they turned toward her. Her eyes locked briefly on the eyes of one of them and in that moment, Angel saw her own demise if she didn't act quickly.

"Tower, no can do." She switched on her perimeter view screens while increasing the power to the upward thrusters. "Hold on!" she yelled to her passenger. "This bird's gonna fly!"

"But there are too many ships," he protested. It was true. She saw that pilots everywhere, in an effort to save their own lives, were breaking protocol and taking off without proper clearance.

"They'll make room for one more." Her voice carried more confidence than she felt.

"What if they don't?"

"Then I guess it'll be a short trip." She shut off the stasis field and the ship, suddenly released from its anchor, shot upward. She kept the ship in a barely controlled ascent, using the upward momentum to gain a height advantage over some of the other ships whose pilots were more cautious.

Angel left the ship's outer sensors off and relied on her own senses to meet the challenge of getting the ship out safely. She learned a long time ago to trust her instincts, as well as her skill. When an Orion Stellarcruiser materialized suddenly in front of them, Angel slammed the guidance stick sharply to port. The ship responded immediately to her touch. Seconds later, she

17

sent the Icarus into a dive to avoid an out-of-control stealth cruiser, resisting the urge to duck when it shot over her bow.

She pulled back on the stick, bringing the ship level again, only to notice a Talbar't freight cruiser lumbering into their path up ahead. Because of the highly explosive nature of its cargo, the freighter had one speed, even in a crisis—slow. And the Icarus hurtled forward on a collision course!

A T-150 Star Fighter, too small to blaze its own trail, followed close behind in her wake, cutting off retreat. A gigantic Sonic battle cruiser blocked her path off to port while several private shuttles emerged above and to starboard. The Icarus was boxed in. Escape seemed impossible.

She pushed the forward thruster lever to its maximum position, fighting the slight pull of gravity as they accelerated toward the freight cruiser at an alarming speed. With a final quick glance at the ships falling behind, she hauled back on the directional stick as hard as she could, forcing the Icarus into a vertical climb and shot above the other ships.

Once the Icarus safely cleared the freight cruiser, Angel leveled off and proceeded at a somewhat reduced speed. They may have missed the freight cruiser, but traffic had not diminished. Her adrenaline never stopped pumping as she dodged ship after ship. This was the kind of flying she hated, and loved. One wrong move could be her last.

When they finally broke free and entered the peacefulness of open space, Angel increased their speed to put distance between them and the chaos left behind.

Now that they were safe, Angel noticed her muscles starting to ache and she forced them to relax. Swiveling in the pilot's chair, she turned to her passenger. His face was beginning to regain a little of its lost color.

"Sorry about the rough take off. Couldn't be avoided. Are you okay?" Her voice came out scratchy and rough. She'd breathed in more smoke than she realized.

"I think . . . yes." He gave her a slight smile. "Impressive flying. You saved my life. Thank you."

When she didn't answer, he rose and moved to take the copilot's seat. Turning to face her, he shook his head and gave a soft chuckle. "You're certainly not what I expected."

Angel shot him a questioning look.

"Your age," he added, as if that explained it. When she continued to look confused, he elaborated. "I was expecting an older man, not a boy your age. When I was told the arrangement, I assumed it would be a more seasoned pilot working with us. But obviously, with your flying skills, it makes sense."

"I'm sorry, but I'm not who you think."

"You're not Richardson?"

"No, I'm not." She thought of the man from Skeeter's lying dead on the landing field. "Your pilot didn't make it."

"What happened to him?"

She tried to come up with a kind way to phrase it and gave up. "He died."

"Oh." There was a moment as he seemed to absorb the news, then he held out his hand to shake hers. "My name is Yanur Snellen. And you are?"

"Michels," she lied, shaking his hand. She never gave her real name to strangers.

"You can't be very old. How long have you been with the S.F.?"

The thought of working for the government's Security Forces brought a smile to her lips. "I'm not exactly with the S.F."

"You weren't sent here to meet me? In Richardson's place?"

"No."

"But you had the key to the ship."

"True."

"I see." He gave her a parental look of disapproval. "Stealing is against the law."

"Yeah, I'm all broke up about it. I'll turn myself in at the next space station. In the meantime, where can I drop you?" Enough of this, she thought.

"There's no time. We'll just have to adjust our plans. Alex won't be happy." He removed the glowing amber tube from his necklace and leaned over the ship's console, sliding the tube into a concealed opening. Before she could stop him, he flipped a switch on the console.

"What is that? What did you just do?" Angel reached out to

remove the tube, only to have her hand firmly shoved away.

"Yanur, is that you?" A deep male voice boomed from the com-system. "Are we on schedule?"

"Who is that?" Angel asked, confused.

"Not exactly," Yanur answered, ignoring her. "We ran into a problem at the airfield." Quickly, he recounted the turn of events out loud. Angel was still trying to make sense of what was going on when an alarm started ringing.

"What now?" She searched the ship's console for a clue to the problem, wishing she were in her more familiar Falcon XLT.

"IGT-Beacon," the voice said. "Adjust our course and speed accordingly."

"Excuse me?" She never took orders well, especially when she didn't know who was giving them.

"We have less than a minute to get within range of the target. Use the beacon!"

"What beacon?" Angel asked, exasperated. "What is going on?"

"Look at the navigrid." The voice sounded as if it was speaking through gritted teeth. "You should see our target at the edge of the screen."

She looked at the screen. "The red, blinking light?"

"That's it. Let's go," the voice ordered.

"Look, I'm piloting this ship and I'm not doing anything until someone tells me what's going—" Suddenly, the ship altered course.

"What the . . . ?" She examined the console readouts for an explanation of the malfunction.

"We're not going fast enough" the voice announced. "Make the jump to hyperdrive. It's imperative that we reach the target as quickly as we can. Do it now."

Angel was beyond frustrated. "What in the hell is going on?" She glared at her passenger. "Who is that giving orders?"

"It's Alex."

Angel shot him a look. "That doesn't tell me anything. Where is he?"

"In the computer."

"The computer?" Angel waited tensely until he nodded. "Are

you telling me that the computer is giving the orders?" Her disbelief must have shown on her face, but the old man only nodded. She was about to say more, when the hum of the engines changed pitch.

Oh no. "Hold on!" Angel shouted just as the ship made the jump to hyperdrive. The resulting g-force crushed her into her seat. The accompanying wave of nausea passed quickly as the life support system kicked in and stabilized the internal pressure.

After a moment, the alarm ceased its incessant pealing and the bridge grew unusually quiet. Angel stared out the front view port, watching reflected light from the stars race by and swore under her breath.

"Are you okay?" She turned to look at her companion. His complexion had a greenish hue, but he nodded. She turned her attention back to the ship, hoping something as simple as a malfunction explained their unscheduled jump.

"Computer," she said aloud. "Identify ship's malfunction."

"There was no malfunction," the computer replied. "I made that jump."

"What?" Her voice came out barely a whisper.

"You took too long."

"Too long!? Without the correct coordinates, a jump to hyperdrive can be fatal."

"I had already calculated the correct coordinates. There was no danger."

"Excuse me," she bit out, "but I am the pilot."

"I think not. Since you are obviously incapable of following directions, I have assumed control of this ship."

"Over my dead body," Angel muttered. The thought of a freethinking computer taking over scared her. She wanted to end this now. She typed in a command to override the computer, but the ship failed to respond to her. She glared at her passenger. "Disconnect it."

He shook his head at her request. "No."

She grabbed the tube and pulled, all the while enduring her passenger's quiet stare, as if he were a parent waiting for his child's temper tantrum to subside.

"Is there a problem?" the computer asked patiently.

"Yes there's a problem, you self-absorbed, mutant computer chip. Disconnect from my ship immediately."

The damn computer had the nerve to laugh at her! It was a full-bodied male laugh that sent shivers of awareness tingling down her spine, despite her anger. "First of all, this is *my* ship. And from now on, I give the orders and you'll do as I say. If that's a problem, get over it. Or get out. Your choice. Shall I open the hatch?"

As if she could leave, she thought furiously. With a last yank on the tube, she gave up. It wouldn't budge.

"It seems you win," she addressed the computer. "For now."

"Clearly. Now be a good boy and sit back and relax. I don't know how far we have to go or what type of space we'll travel through to get there."

Boy? Even the computer thought she was a boy! Surely Yanur would have mentioned she was a woman if he had finally noticed. She lifted a hand to the back of her neck, under the pretense of rubbing it, and discovered that her braid was still hidden down her shirt. With the hat shielding her face and her voice rough from breathing all the dust and hot fumes from the attack on the airfield, she probably did look and sound like a boy. Well, maybe that wasn't so bad.

"Computer, how long do you intend to hold me hostage?"

"Until I complete my mission."

"What mission?" When her comment met with silence, Angel narrowed her eyes to stare suspiciously at the old man, who, in turn, watched her closely, his expression unreadable. "Exactly where are we going?"

"Harvestors' home planet." He spoke the words slowly.

"That's impossible. No one knows where it is. Myths and legends, but nothing factual."

"That's not entirely true," he pointed out.

"Well yeah, but even if you could find a Deep Space Trader, you'd never get one to spill that particular location."

"True. But we don't need them to tell us."

"Why?"

It was the computer that answered. "Because the Harvestors will take us there themselves."

It took Angel only a moment to make the connection. "That signal we've been following? That's a Harvestors' ship?" She rubbed her forehead, hoping to ease the pressure building behind her temples. "Just how did you manage to get close enough to tracer-tag one of their ships?"

"Actually, the tag is implanted in one of the victim's bodies."

"Come again?"

"We had a volunteer implant a tracer-tag into his body and then make himself available for the Harvestors' last raid."

It was suicide, pure and simple. "Who in God's name was crazy enough to do that?"

"I was." The computer responded.

"What do you mean, you were. You're a computer." There was silence. "You're a computer." She repeated, only this time she wasn't as sure of herself, and the statement came out more like a question.

"A temporary interface. But I assure you, I am quite human."

"Impossible."

"On the contrary. My name is Nicoli Alexandres Romanof. I'm a colonel with the United System of Planets' Security Forces."

"I've never heard of you."

"You wouldn't have. I specialize in covert assignments."

"Oh." A distant ringing in her ears made it difficult to follow what was being said, so she shook her head. "And this is one of your assignments?"

"Yes. My mission is to locate and destroy the Harvestors."

"This is crazy." She shook her head. "You're not real. You're a computer with a programming glitch. And you," she pointed to the old man, "might want to help me shut it down before we end up on the Harvestors' planet for real."

"My destination is the Harvestors' planet whether you like it or not," the computer said in that irritatingly sexy voice.

"And what? I'm supposed to hang out while you go annihilate these aliens?"

"Of course not." The computer said, allowing Angel to breathe a sigh of relief. "I expect you to help. And you'll start by getting back my body."

Chapter Three

"No. Absolutely not." Angel shook her head as if to reinforce her words. "I refuse." Unlatching her safety harness, she stood up. "This is ridiculous. You," she stabbed the air in front of the old man, "and your computer buddy are certifiable. Crazy. Whacko. Do you hear me?" She ignored his bemused look and walked off the bridge.

She stormed past the hatch and down the short hallway until she found the sleeping quarters. Since she couldn't leave the ship, she might as well have a look around.

The first door she came to was unlocked, so she walked in. While it definitely was *not* a Vista 250 luxury suite, it wasn't bad. Soft beige, tan and coral tones gave the room a calm, spacious feel. Immediately to the right of the doorway was a small table with two chairs. Above these, set into the wall, were the intercom and recycler. The small bed stood against the right wall and opposite that was the door to the decon-closet.

It was a small room with a bio-waste unit and lav on one side and the shower stall on the other. It used the standard super lightweight solution known as Superclean to deliver a fine, cleansing mist that dried quickly. It wasn't as relaxing as soaking in a warm-water bath, but served its purpose.

Angel stepped out of the decon-closet and saw the door to the clothing closet. Curious, she looked inside and found various shirts and pants hanging neatly. She rummaged through them, catching the faint musky odor of the owner still clinging to them. It was a distinctively masculine scent that made her think of dark forests and high adventure. She took another deep breath and sighed before reluctantly shutting the door.

She would take this room. At least until they reached a space station or someplace where she could escape. It was just a matter of biding her time.

Having made the decision, she left to explore the rest of the ship, making sure to check out every nook and cranny as she went. When her stomach growled, she remembered that she hadn't eaten and went to find the galley.

It was as small as the rest of the rooms, but definitely state-of-the-art with its Cosmos Food Genie and pre-set menu selection pad. She typed in her selection of a Holwraith meat and Zantl cheese sandwich on whole-grain bread, and a glass of Aldenberry juice. Less than two minutes later, she was back in her quarters, eating her food and letting her thoughts wander. So much had happened—the encounter with Tony, the terrorist attack, losing her ship, stealing this one. And then, the coup-de-grâce—being taken prisoner by a computer that claimed to be human? Her head hurt.

Thinking of the computer made her wish she had taken time over the years to learn how to hack into computer programs. That skill would've come in handy right now. But she hadn't, so now what did she do?

It claimed to be this man, this colonel. What had it said his name was? Romanof? She'd seen a lot of weird stuff in her life, was it so hard to believe the story they were telling? Couldn't it be real? Couldn't he? The computer certainly didn't sound like any computer she'd worked on. Not with that velvet-edged, pure sex quality to it.

"Michels, report to the bridge."

She forgot to include overbearing and authoritative in her description.

"I'm busy." Irritated at the intrusion, she finished her sandwich and swallowed the last of her drink. She didn't take orders well, and the sooner the computer/Romanof understood that, the better. She waited in the brief silence that followed.

"Michels, an uncooperative pilot is as useful to me as a dead pilot. Report to the bridge."

She executed a salute using a gesture more commonly found on the streets than in the military, stood up and disposed of her plate and cup in the recycler. Then, in an admittedly childish act of defiance, she turned down the volume on the intercom so he couldn't bother her again and crossed over to the closet.

She rummaged on the floor until she found an old boot. Taking the money Dugan had given her out of her jacket, she stuffed it into the boot. There was no point in carrying all that cash around with her, for now. She hid the boot in the very back then closed the door.

Then the events of the last forty-eight hours caught up with her, along with the lack of sleep, and she yawned. The bed beckoned her and she had no will to resist. She lay down, only to rest a bit, and fell fast asleep.

Nicoli considered his current situation. His plan was little more than a calculated gamble. He'd had no doubts the Harvestors would take his body from the beach. Tall, well-muscled from years of rigorous training and, if what others said was true, attractive, Nicoli fit the physical profile for desired sex slaves. It wasn't vanity; it was fact. A fact that made the chances of recovering his body at one of the Harvestors' nefarious black market auctions better than good. That was the crux of his plan.

Losing Richardson had been a blow. Nicoli had personally selected Richardson for his piloting skills and vast field experience. He needed someone seasoned in battle by his side as he infiltrated and destroyed the Harvestors. While Yanur would do anything for him, Nicoli refused to let the older man endanger himself. Now he was short one man and stuck with a boy. But not an ordinary boy, that was apparent. This young upstart had kept his head during a terrorist attack, shown resourcefulness in stealing Nicoli's own ship, demonstrated charity by taking Yanur aboard rather than leave him behind and then piloted a strange ship through a near impossible course into open space with skills Yanur claimed were exemplary.

But all the guts and raw talent in the universe were useless if the boy couldn't accept and follow orders. Whether Nicoli could change that or not remained to be seen.

He checked the ship's progress. They had entered The Forty-Five, a wormhole discovered decades ago. Wormholes provided shortcuts across the fabric of space and this one led to a lesser-known quadrant.

From inside the wormhole, there was no way to judge their proximity to the target. They were gaining on it, but not fast enough to suit Nicoli. To increase the ship's speed would seriously tax the ship's engines, which were already straining. Not to mention the potential dangers that awaited at the other end.

Nicoli hadn't lied to Yanur when he'd said he didn't fear death. But the thought of living forever scared him considerably. *Eternal life as a computer? No thank you.*

He increased the ship's speed.

It was her fifteenth birthday and life had never been so good. She and her parents gathered around a picnic and while they ate, her father told more of the wonderful stories that made her laugh, and made him smile.

Suddenly, his body jerked and the smile turned into a grimace as a red stain spread across his chest to soak into his shirt. He began to fall and Angel reached for him. Clutching a handful of clothing, she pulled with all her might. But when she looked down into his face, it was no longer his. Instead, the scowling face of her grandfather appeared.

Shocked and confused, she released the shirt and looked about. Her mother, wearing a black mourning robe, appeared beside her. The yard where they stood dissolved into a cemetery and she was left facing a fresh grave site. The headstone bore her father's name.

She screamed, but there was no sound. In disbelief, she watched her mother walk away. She tried to follow, but her leaden feet refused to move. Her grandfather loomed before her, a wicked smile upon his face. He held out his arms, talons reaching to claw at her. Terror banished her paralysis and she ran, not daring to look over her shoulder. Before her, a house materialized from nowhere.

Seeking refuge within, she fled down the main hall, the sound of heavy footsteps following her. She must get away. He'd killed her father and now he was after her.

The doors along the hallway stood closed. Trying one at random, she found it locked. She moved to the next. Locked also. Again and again she tried, until finally one opened. Sanctuary at last. But to her horror, the room was bare. No closets. No furniture. Nowhere to hide.

She ran to the window, but found it barred. Trapped. Turning in horror, she stared at the door. The footsteps outside grew louder. Sweat dripped down her face, into her eyes. It was so hot. Wildly, she looked around. There! A door appeared where before there had been none.

She rushed forward and tried the knob. It opened.

She ducked inside, pulling the door shut. There was no lock, so she gripped the knob with her hands. Trying to quiet her breathing, she listened for the sound of her grandfather's approach. His footsteps sounded louder, just outside the closet door. He had found her!

Beneath her clinched hands, the doorknob moved, but she held on tightly. He pounded on the door and her body shook with each strike. The inside of the closest grew hotter and she felt smothered. She dragged air into her lungs, unable to get enough. The banging on the door grew violent. How much longer could she hold it shut?

Angel came awake with a start. Covered in sweat and shaken from the dream, she sat up in bed and tried to regain some semblance of calm. The nightmares were coming more frequently and getting worse each time. And more realistic.

Even now, as she took a couple of deep breaths, she found it hard to breathe. No, it wasn't the effect of the dream. The room really was hot.

Something was wrong.

Something hit the ship, jolting her in bed. It sounded like a radon torpedo.

She jumped to her feet and tore, barefoot, out of the room and headed for the bridge. It was empty.

"What in the five Hells is going on?" She yelled, knowing the computer could hear her.

"We're under attack," the computer responded, sounding stressed.

"No kidding." She didn't try to hide her sarcasm as she took the pilot's seat and studied the status reports scrolling across the screen.

The autoshields were in place and holding, barely. She didn't know how much of the attack she had slept through, but it obviously had been long enough for several damaging hits. The rear port shield had sustained damage and was showing signs of buckling. She wasn't sure how much more they could take.

Then she noticed their coordinates on the navigrid. "How'd we get to the Darwin Zone so fast?"

"I increased our speed."

"This zone is dangerous." Now that she knew where they were, she had a better idea of who was attacking them. "Why didn't you call me when we first entered it?"

"I did." The tone was cold and hard.

"Oh." Belatedly, she remembered turning down the intercom.

"I altered the environmental controls in the sleeping quarters, hoping that would wake you."

"That explains why it was so hot. I was afraid life support had been damaged." She paused long enough to look quickly around the bridge. "Where's your friend?"

"Who?"

"The old man."

"His name is Yanur. And I don't know. He's not responding to my summons." The computer sounded worried, but there was no time to think about it. She decided to get a positive ID on the attackers.

She activated the all-angles view screen. It was a much larger ship than theirs, one capable of housing a crew of twenty or more. That alone did not make it unusual. But the paint job did. Only one group sported black ships with red criss-crossing lightning bolts. Free Rebels. Space pirates that "sailed" the heavens, attacking the unfortunate ships that crossed their path. They took what they wanted—cargo, supplies, even the ships themselves.

But they never took hostages.

Angel checked the status of the on-board weapons system. It seemed they had sustained more damage than she realized. The weapons on the port side were disabled, and the rear propulsion tube was inoperable, rendering the ion torpedoes useless. That left the single remaining starboard electromagnetic pulsar and the pulse canons mounted at the front of the ship. What a mess.

The ship bucked as the Free Rebels sent another volley of pulse cannon discharges their way, just to let them know they were still interested. Angel took the controls and tried to change the ship's position, but there was no response.

"What's the problem? You're a computer, for cripes-sake. Get us out of here."

"You try dodging bullets while maintaining all systems, weapons and shields."

"Let me pilot the ship."

There was a tense moment of silence. "Take it."

Angel tried the controls again and this time they responded to her touch. She readjusted the position of the Icarus, putting the stronger shields toward the attacking ship. A defensive posture, she thought disgustedly.

"I don't know if we can outrun them," Angel said, thinking aloud. "And I'm pretty sure we can't outgun them."

"I have a plan."

It was more than she had. "Let's hear it."

But at that moment, the Free rebel ship drew closer and a short burst of light momentarily illuminated the sky. Almost immediately, Angel felt the impact of the hit. The bridge lights flickered, then went out, leaving the emergency lights to cast an eerie green glow over everything. She strained to hear any little noise in the sudden silence, and realized the engines had died. Was this the end?

"Romanof?" Even at barely above a whisper, her voice seemed loud.

"Quiet." She could barely hear his voice. "I'm overriding the ship's diagnostics. When the Free Rebels scan us, it will appear that we're totally disabled and all life forms have expired. They may lose interest and go away."

And if they don't? Angel sat and looked out the viewport. The longer the rebel ship sat and studied them, the tighter the knot in her stomach became.

A sound from behind drew her attention. The old man leaned against the entryway, blood streaming from wounds on his head, left arm and leg.

"Oh!" She rushed to help him into one of the passenger seats.

"Quiet," Romanof hissed.

"How bad are you hurt?" She asked, keeping her voice low. Momentarily distracted from the Free Rebels, she bent over the older man to get a better look for herself.

"I think my leg is broken," he said, causing Angel to look at him in surprise.

"What happened?" She took a sterile wipe from the first aid cabinet located on the bridge and dabbed at the cuts on his forehead.

"I don't know. I was taking a nap. I didn't know the ship was under attack until I felt it rocking. One moment I was asleep, the next I'm on the floor, buried under the table. When I tried to stand, a horrible pain shot through my leg."

"Looks like you cut your arm in the process." She took another wipe and carefully cleaned around the ripped flesh in his shoulder. Studying his pupils as she worked, she noticed that he was suffering from shock.

"Quiet," Romanof said more insistently. "Not one more sound."

Angel turned back to the cabinet to take out a blanket and when she did her peripheral vision registered a sickening sight.

"I don't think the plan worked." In horror, she gazed out the front viewport as a Free Rebel ship moved toward them. With the engines off, the Icarus had started to drift. There wasn't enough time now to restart the engines and make a run for it.

Angel strained to see out the side viewport as the Free Rebel ship pulled alongside them. Then something started coming out of the ship. Terrified, she watched as a space tunnel elongated until it reached the Icarus, completely covering the outer door.

"Turn on the autoshields," Angel ordered.

"I can't. The systems sustained damage. It's going to take approximately ninety seconds to code and fix the problem."

The sound of a metal drill drifted to her. "That's ninety-one seconds longer than we have. They're drilling through the lock on the outer door!" Angel tossed the almost forgotten blanket across the old man and raced from the bridge. If the Free Rebels disabled the lock, the door would open without a problem. In that event, it would be twenty or more bloodthirsty Free Rebels against a computer, an invalid and her. Not great odds.

She went to the supply closet and prayed it would have what she needed. Luck was with her. Selecting a T120 fire-gel and a timer, she headed for the air lock. Halfway there, she stopped, disgusted with herself, and rushed back to the closet. She couldn't afford any mistakes. She grabbed an oxygen mask, a docking-harness and a tether, then took off again.

"Are they through yet?" She shouted as she ran, knowing Romanof could hear her.

"No."

Time was critical. Taking a deep breath, she opened the inner door. Her luck was still holding. Once inside the air lock, she shut the door behind her, sealing herself in. She put on the docking-harness and pulled the straps tightly across her chest. Then she connected one end of the tether to the harness and fastened the other end to a wall hook. She strapped the oxygen mask to her face and took a few breaths to regulate the flow. Finally, she connected the timer to the fire-gel. Now came the real fun.

She set the timer for thirty seconds. With a quick mental count to ten to calm herself, she started the timer and set the fire-gel on the floor in front of her. She palmed the control to the outer door.

Caught off guard, the Free Rebels paused as the door started to rise. When it had cleared less than half a meter, she kicked the fire-gel under, and slapped the control again, to lower the door. That was when her luck ran out.

One of the Free Rebels shoved his drill under the door, to

prevent it from closing. In horror she watched as he squirmed his way through the opening. When he stood up, Angel got her first good look at a Free Rebel. He was humanoid, but resembled nothing human.

Fathomless black eyes peered at her out of a chalky, cadaverous head. They studied each other for a moment, but Angel knew when the Free Rebel gave her a humorless smile revealing rows of sharp, canine-like teeth that he had found her wanting as a worthy opponent.

Just then, the gel bomb exploded at the entrance of the tunnel. The impact knocked the drill out from under the door and it slammed shut, trapping Angel with the Free Rebel. He wasn't much bigger than she was, but the tether securing her to the wall held her hostage. Angel grabbed the fastener on the harness and tried to free herself, but it wouldn't open. She looked up just as the Free Rebel launched himself at her.

The first blow caught her in the side of the head and she fell back. Blinded by the sharp sparks of light brought on by the pain, she lashed out with a front kick that connected with the Free Rebel's stomach.

He doubled over, falling back a step and Angel tried again to free herself. Her fingers fumbled unsuccessfully with the buckle and too soon, her unwanted guest straightened, this time holding a knife. Angel jumped back as he slashed at her, but the wall stopped her retreat. With the next sweep of his hand, the tip of the blade sliced through her harness. The cloth of her shirt fell open where the blade caught it and Angel bit her lip when the sting from freshly cut skin washed over her. Fortunately, it was little more than a scratch, but the gaping fabric left her exposed in more ways than one. She could tell when the Free Rebel's eyes widened and his smile grew feral that he had discovered her secret. A new fear gripped her. Assault was one thing; rape was another.

"Michels, report in. Michels!" In the background, Romanof's voice called to her.

The Free Rebel fell against her, pinning her against the wall. She struggled against him, but he laughed at her efforts. Dropping his knife, he placed one hand against her throat and grabbed her breast with the other. She gasped when he squeezed it painfully.

"Michels, are you all right?"

"Open the outer door," she screamed, pushing herself into the Free Rebel and forcing him back a step. The outer door opened and immediately everything not anchored down was sucked out into open space, past the mutilated remains of what had once been the Free Rebels' tunnel.

Fighting the pull, the Free Rebel grabbed for anything he could hang on to, in this case, Angel. As he lost to the drag of outer space, he slid down her body until he clutched her ankle. Angel watched her cap sail across the room and disappear. Her feet came out from under her and the suction lifted her off the floor. She felt the broken harness slip and quickly crossed and locked her arms in front of her, holding on for her life.

They were at a stalemate. The Free Rebel held on to her ankle with both hands and all she could do was dangle at the end of the tether like a streamer in a fan. Outside, she saw the tunnel break free of the *Icarus*, pulling the rebel ship with it as it drifted away.

Risking a look behind her, Angel saw that the wall hook was pulling loose. She was on borrowed time. Looking down, she saw the Free Rebel smile. In his eyes was the promise of death—hers. It didn't sit well.

"Not today." She gritted her teeth and brought her free leg up. She slammed it down sharply on the Free Rebel's face. The sound of breaking cartilage inspired her to kick again. The Free Rebel's grip loosened and Angel delivered a third blow. Weakened, the pull of space proved too great and he lost his hold. Sucked out of the ship, his eyes, devoid of any emotion, held hers until he disappeared completely.

Then she felt herself slip. Looking back again, she saw one of the bolts securing the hook sticking out of the wall, wobbling precariously. In the next second, it popped loose and sailed past her into space. Angel knew it was only a matter of seconds before she followed it.

"Shut the door!" She screamed as a second bolt slipped farther out of the wall. She desperately clawed behind her, twisting her body, trying to find something to grab.

Her mind screamed in frustration as the door failed to move. Then the last bolt burst from the wall and Angel was airborne.

Chapter Four

Angel sailed toward the black void of deep space, body-slamming into the outer door as it slid into place just in time. She slumped to the floor and lay there, trembling, disgusted with her reaction. The sudden roar of the ship's engines sounded faint and distant. Somewhere in the corner of her mind, she realized Romanof had the ship moving. She doubted the Free Rebels would follow. She didn't think there were any left alive; it had looked as though the tunnel explosion had destroyed most if not all of their ship.

"Michels, report in." Romanof's voice boomed over the intercom. She ignored it as she took a few more steadying breaths.

"Michels, damn it, report in! Are you all right?"

She peeled off the oxygen mask and harness, letting them slip to the floor.

"Michels, answer me!" It was interesting, she mused, how his voice sounded so human-like—concern mixed with irritation.

"I'm okay." It took effort to sound calmer than she felt.

"Good. Get back here. Yanur needs your help."

She let her head drop forward in resigned disbelief. It wasn't as if she was lounging around in a thermal pool. But Yanur was hurt and she wasn't, so she pulled herself together, gathered the mask and what was left of the harness and tether and left the air lock.

If she wanted to maintain her disguise, she'd have to do something about her clothes. So before heading for the bridge, she stopped by her room. Catching a glimpse of herself in the mirror, she absently smoothed down the many strands of hair whipped to a frenzy about her head by the wind. This would never do.

She found her boots and put them on. Then she removed the knife hidden there and used it to slice through the fastening securing the ends of her hair. Returning the knife to its boot-sheath, she walked into the decon-closet and found the wall cabinet. A quick search of its contents yielded both a brush and a replacement band for her hair. She didn't have time to work through the tangles properly, so she brushed her hair just enough to get the top to lie close to her head and then secured the rest with the band. Again, she tucked the length of it down her shirt. She found another cap in the clothes closet to replace the one she'd lost. She pulled it low over her head and then looked around for her jacket.

It lay on the end of the bed, where she'd discarded it earlier. She put it on over her torn shirt and zipped it closed. Then she studied her reflection in the mirror and hoped that the old man wouldn't look at her too closely.

When she reached the bridge, a quick glance out the viewports confirmed that Romanof had everything under control. She moved to Yanur's side, wondering where to start. Gingerly, she felt his leg, trying to assess the extent of the damage.

"How bad is he?" Romanof asked.

"I don't know."

"I'm fine, Alex. I keep telling you." Yanur smiled, reaching out to pat her hand. "If you'll secure a brace to my leg and help me to my room, I'll be fine."

She went to the first aid cabinet and removed one of the larger braces. She stretched his leg out straight, placed the brace behind it and secured it in place with the self-adhering tabs. Not bad, she thought, stepping back to scrutinize her work, considering that her medical training was limited to what she'd figured out in taking care of herself over the years.

Next she cleaned the cut on his shoulder. After closing it with a butterfly bandage, she helped him to his feet.

Together, they made it slowly to his room.

"You are very brave." Then he added softly, "especially for a woman."

Angel turned startled eyes on him. "How did you know?" she whispered, not wanting Romanof to overhear.

"My dear, I may be old, but I'm not blind." They were in his room now and he waved his hand, silencing her when she would have spoken. "No, I know what I thought and said following the terrorist attack, but I was confused and you were a mess. Since then, I've had time to study you."

She shrugged. So her disguise hadn't been as good as she'd hoped. "Can I ask you a question?"

"Of course."

"Is he for real?"

"Romanof? Yes, he is."

"Then how is that possible?"

"I beg your pardon?"

"How is it possible for Romanof to be alive, without his body?"

"Oh, that. Cyber-hosted biopod."

She looked at him blankly.

"The tube. The one I was wearing around my neck?" He looked at her to see if she remembered, continuing after she nodded. "It's a cyber-hosted biopod, currently housing Alex's life essence. The cybernetic nature allows him to interface with the ship's computer, which in turn, allows him to communicate with us, and—"

"And control the ship," she finished for him.

He smiled. "That's right."

She shook her head. "Unbelievable. Why would he do it?"

"The answer to that is complicated. Let's just say that it's because he could."

"But it's crazy." As soon as the words were out, she regretted them. She didn't want to offend Romanof, or his friend. "I'm sorry, I didn't mean to be insulting. It's just that it's so . . ."

"Crazy," he finished for her, his smile very understanding. "Over here." He pointed to the bed.

Angel eased Yanur down until he sat on the edge of the bed. As she did, her mind wandered to thoughts of mortals playing at God. When Yanur was settled, Angel started for the door. She made it halfway there before she stopped and looked back. "How often does he do this whole extraction of life essence from the body thing?" She tried for a casual tone, but failed.

"We've done it a couple of times, but . . ."

"But what?" She knew there was something he wasn't telling her.

"This is the first time we've done it for any extended period of time."

"Meaning what, exactly?"

"We've done the transfer three times, with two hours being the longest period of separation."

She knew her face reflected her shock, because Yanur smiled. "We've already been gone a lot longer than two hours. How do you know you can put his life essence back? You know, into his body? This whole mission might be a waste of time."

"There's no reason to believe it won't continue to work." His tone wasn't nearly as convincing as his words.

"Well gosh, very scientific. I know I feel better about this whole thing." Her voice dripped with sarcasm. "Assuming for a moment that it *will* work and we find his body, how does Romanof know the Harvestors haven't done something to it? Like hack it into pieces. They sell replacement organs as well as slaves, you know."

"Alex is willing to take that chance. But there is reason to believe that his body will be intact when I go to purchase it at the auction."

"What happens if you're wrong?" she asked.

Yanur hesitated for the briefest moment. "Then he spends eternity as a computer."

"Eternity's a long time," she said softly.

"Too long, I'm afraid, for someone like Alex."

Angel wasn't exactly sure what he meant by that, but she had a pretty good idea. She wouldn't want to be stuck in a computer for all time, either.

She walked to the door, then stopped with her hand on the doorknob. "Will you be okay?"

He smiled. "Yes. I'm just going to rest for awhile. Maybe you should do the same."

If only she had that luxury, she thought, returning to the bridge to run another diagnostic. She compared the results with the readings she took from several gauges. Romanof must have fixed the program because the results matched. When she was satisfied that the gel bomb had not adversely affected the Icarus and Romanof was making the needed system repairs, she let her mind wander to the information Yanur had shared with her. She didn't know which bothered her more: that a man's living essence had been placed inside a computer, or that this particular computer was really a man.

"The auto-repair program won't be able to fix everything," Romanof's voice broke the silence. "But I've managed to reroute the programming to the extent I can. You shouldn't notice any differences in the handling of the ship."

"That's good." A tentative silence descended as Angel struggled with what she needed to say. "I want to thank you for what you did back there. Closing the hatch door when you did. For a minute there, I thought I was about to be just so much space debris."

"I didn't want to lose you." The warm, deep voice washed over her.

"Yes, well." She felt uncomfortable, still coming to grips with the knowledge that the sexy voice actually belonged to a man. "I'm just glad it's over."

"Not yet, Michels. We still have the Harvestors to deal with."

Angel let out a sigh. Of course he would still want to complete the mission. "In that case, I'm going back to my room."

"Why?"

"I want to take a shower and change clothes. That attack was a little rough on this set."

"You said you were okay." He actually sounded concerned.

"I am. Just a few scratches." *To go with the gash at my side, which feels like it might be bleeding again.*

Angel didn't wait around to see if he said anything else. The walk to her room seemed to take forever and once inside, she fell back against the closed door, exhausted. Shutting her eyes, she took deep breaths and forced herself to relax. Then, with what felt like the last of her energy, she walked across the room and kicked off her boots. The jacket came off next, tossed to the floor in front of the closet. The cap followed it. She peeled off the jumpsuit, taking extra care around the bloodied scrapes across her chest and at her side. The fabric was irreparably torn, so she wadded it up and shoved it down the recycler. Almost as an afterthought, she reached over and turned up the volume on the intercom.

This time, she was careful in removing the band from her hair. She laid it aside and retrieved the brush. Starting at the bottom, she carefully worked through the tangles until the brush easily glided through the long strands. When her hair felt smooth to the touch, she laid the brush aside and walked into the decon-closet. What she really wanted was to soak in a pool of hot, fragrant water. But that would have to wait until she was back home.

Home. She had no home. The depressing thought depleted the rest of her energy. She stepped into the shower and turned on the fine superclean spray. After adjusting the temperature, she rested her forehead against the wall and let the steamy hot mist envelop her.

Yanur sat on his bed marveling over Michels. He had thought her nothing more than a common thief, but in the past twenty-four hours, she had shown there was nothing common about her at all. With unsurpassed flying skills, a quick intellect and unwavering courage, she reminded him of a young man he had once known; a young man who had risked everything to break a political prisoner out of jail during a time of war.

Thinking of the young man Alex used to be made Yanur smile. The smile turned into quiet laughter when Yanur considered the fireworks that lay ahead when the flesh and blood Alex came face to face with the woman calling herself Michels.

Careful not to put too much pressure on his broken leg, he pushed himself to a standing position and limped over to the table where he'd left his medical bag. But when he got there, it was missing and he knew a moment of panic as he looked around. Finally, he spotted it lying in the corner of the room, where it must have been thrown when the table overturned.

He moved as quickly as his damaged leg would allow and bent to pick it up. This bag contained his most precious scientific inventions and he was afraid of what might lay broken within. Then a more horrifying thought hit him. What if the transfer disc had been destroyed?

A cold fear gripped his heart as he looked inside.

He found the disc close to the top and after turning it over several times and seeing no damage, he breathed a sigh of relief. Replacing it, he noticed a vibration coming from deeper within the sack. Searching for the source, he found the Cellular Reparator. Somehow when the bag had been tossed about, the Reparator had been activated. He took it out and flipped it over to read the crystal battery gauge. As he feared, the power level, already low, now showed the crystals to be almost completely drained. There might not be enough left to mend his broken leg.

He undid the self-adhering tabs securing his leg to the brace and propped the brace against the small table. Taking a scalpel from his medical kit, he slit open his pant's leg to the knee and pulled the fabric aside. Running the warm beam of the Reparator over his bare leg, he felt the tingle of increased molecular activity as cells began to mend themselves. But before the bone and flesh could do more than lightly knit together, the Reparator died.

A feeling of defeat consumed him. Alex was counting on his assistance when they reached their destination. But he wouldn't be much help with a broken leg, and he couldn't mend his leg without replacing the power crystals. And if that wasn't bad enough, replacing the crystal wouldn't be easy. The Reparator ran on pure tyrillium, not the less potent, refined rocks so readily available.

Michels. The thought came unbidden and Yanur knew with certainty that Alex would suggest that Michels take his place for the rest of the mission.

But he couldn't let that happen. Going into a closely guarded black market environment was dangerous. What if she found Alex's body but had to fight to secure it? She had survived the Free Rebel attack, but could she fight the Harvestors? They could prove to be a far worse adversary. What if she was injured? Or worse, what if she was killed?

Which lead Yanur to his final objection. Alex. Althusians were very protective of their females—Alex even more so. He would rather suffer a thousand deaths than allow a woman to suffer the smallest of injuries.

Yanur had merely to reveal the truth about Michels and Alex would refuse to let her help. But in doing so, what cost would Alex pay?

With a heavy heart, Yanur set the Reparator carefully back in the bag and strapped the brace around his broken leg.

Straightening, he heaved a sigh and squared his shoulders. Then he headed for the bridge.

Ruling House of Scyphor
Planet of Coronado

Sitting behind the desk where he conducted most of his business, the high counsel of the House of Scyphor, the dominant region on the planet of Coronado, confronted the soldiers standing before him. His three most trusted advisors stood silently by his side.

"High Counsel, we went to Earth as instructed," the first soldier began. He was the older of the two and battle worn, with scars criss-crossing his face and bare arms. Both men were tall and muscular as most Coronadian males, with warring blades hanging at their sides.

"Where is she?" The elderly man's tone was cold and as sharp as glass shards.

Neither warrior allowed any emotion to cross his face. "We tracked her to the airfield," the older one said. "Felinean Avengers were after her and she ran. Before we could intercept her, Colossus Disrupters attacked the airfield." There was the barest hesitation before he continued. "We lost her in the confusion." He fell silent. He had failed his mission. It was a blemish to his personal reputation, and to the reputation of the legion of warriors he represented.

"Am I to understand that after fifteen years of carefully tracking her and letting her think she has eluded me, that she has finally succeeded?" The high counsel's hand slammed down on the desk, his face darkening with rage. "Is that what you're telling me?"

"Yes, High Counsel."

"And the Felineans? I suppose you allowed them to escape, as well?"

"No, High Counsel. I executed them."

"Very well. Leave me." The high counsel growled and waved a gnarled hand toward the door. After the soldiers left, he turned to his advisors.

"Contact our emissaries. When she resurfaces, I want to be the first to know. She—" He fell into a coughing paroxysm, temporarily overcome. The young men moved closer to offer assistance, although they knew nothing could be done. The old man was dying. It was just a matter of time.

When the spell subsided, the high counsel raised his hand and the men retreated. "Find her and see that she is brought back. Now leave me. I wish to be alone."

Behind his back, the men exchanged glances, but nothing on their faces revealed their thoughts. They bowed and left the room. None of them spoke before parting to go in different directions, presumably to carry out the high counsel's directives.

As each walked away, one considered how best to execute the high counsel's orders. One fantasized about the young kitchen maid whose charms he plotted to enjoy in the very near future.

And the last thought about plans to save his people and take over a planet.

* * *

Angel lost track of time as she stood directly under the shower's spray and let the warmth seep into her pores and loosen tight muscles. Lulled into a dreamlike state, her thoughts wandered to Romanof.

What kind of man was he? Dangerous, she decided, her mind conjuring an image of a darkly sensuous man, his face hidden in shadow. Moving with the grace of a panther, his sleek, powerful body slipped close to hers. Rough hands caressed her, leaving highly sensitive skin tingling in the wake of his warm touch. When he whispered words of passion into her ear, it was Romanof's full, masculine voice she heard. *Oh yes, very dangerous.*

She'd been alone too long if she was starting to fantasize about a computer, she thought abruptly, shaking off the last remnants of the daydream. As for Romanof, he was probably an old man like Yanur, just one with a great voice.

She turned off the shower's mist and stood for a second or two as the last drops of moisture evaporated. Such daydreaming was absurd. Her No. 1 concern at this time should be getting back to Earth where she could enlist Dugan's help to get safely to a location of her choosing.

Getting out of the shower, Angel went in search of clothes. Again, a pleasant musky scent filled her senses when she opened the closet door, reviving briefly the image of her dark dreamlover. Then a new thought occurred to her. Not every ship came equipped with a slot in the console for a cyber-hosted biopod. This had to be Romanof's ship. And these were probably Romanof's clothes! Unable to stop herself, she leaned farther into the closet, inhaling the musky scent and letting her hand trail lightly across the garments while she enjoyed the feel of well-worn cloth against her fingertips.

Tightening the leash on her imagination, Angel pulled out a uni-fit jumpsuit and put it on. She found the brush and ran it through her hair, trying to focus all her attention on the mundane task.

She was back in control by the time she finished arranging her hair. She didn't bother trying to hide the long strands now. What was the point? She put on her boots, picked up the supplies she had discarded earlier and walked out of the room.

She replaced the items in the closet where she'd found them and, as she shut the door, the sound of voices from the bridge caught her attention.

"I'm sorry, Alex." Angel detected an apologetic tone to Yanur's voice.

"What's up?" She walked onto the bridge and sat in the pilot's chair. Her question met with silence, so she looked at Yanur, but his expression was unreadable.

"Yanur has just informed me that he will be unable to assist me when we reach the Harvestors' planet," Romanof said.

"Because of his broken leg?" Angel asked.

"Correct. Therefore, I require your assistance, Michels."

"What?" Angel asked at the same time that Yanur said, "No."

"Is there a problem?" Romanof asked.

Angel looked at Yanur, curiosity momentarily distracting her from the computer's bossy order. "I know why I'm objecting, but why are you? Don't you think I can help? Or maybe you don't trust me."

"I think you know why I'm against the idea. Now, you can tell him, or I will."

"Tell me what?" Romanof asked while Angel studied Yanur. Any delay in retrieving Romanof's body increased the chances of never recovering it. Why would Yanur condemn his friend to eternity as a computer, unwilling to even make a rescue *attempt*? Romanof was willing to let her help, unless . . .

A new thought hit her. Maybe Yanur hadn't yet told Romanof she was a woman. She pinned the older man with her gaze. "You said earlier that I was brave. Don't you think I can do this?"

"It's not what I think that's important here."

So the objection would be Romanof's. Interesting, she thought. "He wants me to go."

"He doesn't know the truth."

Did that mean that Romanof would change his mind if he knew she was a woman? Well, she had grown up around men like him—men who thought women were inferior, unequal to men in intellect and skill. In fact, she had run away from men like that, seeking her independence in the only way she knew how, proving to herself and others that women were as capable of surviving the dangers of the universe as men. Romanof would never allow a *woman* to risk her life, even to save his own. He would rather spend eternity as a computer.

It would serve him right, by her thinking. And here was her chance to go home. She could confess that she was a woman, he would turn the ship around and she'd soon be free to go her own way.

The image of the man from her daydream flickered to life, then faded. Was she willing to sentence Romanof to eternity as a computer without even trying to help? And Romanof, with his primitive concepts of women, as much as drew a line in the sand and dared her to cross it.

She dared.

"I don't think we have a problem." Angel looked pointedly to Yanur. "I'll go."

The old man's mouth fell open as he gaped at her. Then he seemed to collect himself. "I can't allow you to do this. I'm sorry, Michels, but we need a man to do this job and you're not a man."

"What?" Romanof shouted.

"No. Alex, the truth is, Michels is a—"

"Boy!" Angel blurted out. "He thinks I'm a boy. But I'm not. I just look young. I'm twenty-four and I can do anything a man can do. I think I've already proven that." She glared at Yanur, daring him to expose her lie. She knew he'd be torn between protecting her and saving his friend's life. She was betting on his friend's life to win.

She cleared her expression of all emotion and watched him wage his internal moral war. The wait seemed interminably long.

"Perhaps Michels is right," Yanur finally said.

"Then let's get started." Romanof said. "Yanur, show Michels how to operate the transfer unit. When you're done, we'll go over my plan."

"Shall we?" Yanur rose from his chair and gestured to the door. Angel stood and preceded him out. "Perhaps we could stop by the galley," he added. "I find I could use a drink."

Chapter Five

After an hour of going over the operation of the transfer disc, Yanur pronounced Angel ready. Unsure what to expect as they neared the Harvestors' planet, Romanof monitored all ship-to-shore transmissions in the vicinity. Angel, who had retired to her room to rest, was summoned the moment they entered the planet's atmosphere.

When the Harvestors' Ground Control contacted them, Romanof negotiated permission to land by persuading the authorities that they had come to make a large purchase and transferring a sizable monetary "contribution" to the main bank as a show of good faith.

In return, they were given the coordinates for the landing field and Angel merged into the busy traffic pattern, descending slowly to the surface, to what appeared to be a large tarmac. As soon as they were on the ground, a stasis field enveloped the ship, pinning it to the surface. Stasis fields were not unusual, but were usually pilot-activated. Angel had issued no such command.

"Romanof?"

"Planet-activated insurance policy. Probably to make sure we settle our accounts before we leave," he deduced. "Black-market planets don't attract the most trustworthy clients."

Angel shut off the engines. "What now?"

"Time to go shopping."

"So soon?" She felt an unwelcome tremor of fear. She had reconciled herself to going out among the Harvestors, but what was the rush?

"I've been monitoring local transmissions. It's about mid-morning here and the business district is just opening. The ship we followed arrived just before sun-up, so it's doubtful they've already sold the bodies on board. I would just as soon not delay the purchase of my body."

"But I don't even know what you look like," she stalled.

"Not a problem," Romanof informed her. "Since I'll be going with you. I'll transfer to the cyber-hosted biopod for easy transportation. We'll establish communication via a concealed comm-link, which you'll wear. The ship will track my body's signal and transmit its location relative to the biopod. I'll tell you when we've located it. All you have to do is purchase it with the credits Yanur gave you.

"Yanur, you'll stay on board and monitor all transmissions. And Yanur?" He paused. "Stay alert. At the first sign of trouble, take off. Type in the command "Go Home" and the ship will transfer enough credits to get you departure clearance. That should release the stasis field. The ship will then return automatically to Earth. By the same token, if we're not back in sixty hours, leave for Earth anyway."

"I won't leave without you," the older man protested.

"If we're not back in sixty hours, we're not coming back. Ever."

Five minutes later, Angel found herself standing just inside the hatch, the pod hanging around her neck and the transfer unit, a small, flat disc, in her pocket. Yanur, being closer to her size than Romanof, had loaned her a pair of his dark pants and a shirt more in keeping with the image of a black-market trader than the uni-fit suit she'd been wearing.

She'd found a black vest in the closet that helped further mask her figure, because while there were a few female traders around, there weren't that many. Angel and Yanur decided the less attention she drew to herself, the better. She wore a black cloth, ripped from one of the large shirts hanging in her closet, wrapped around her head and tied in the back. Many smugglers sported long hair, the length being an indication of how long they'd been involved in illegal trade, and they all wore similar head cloths to keep their hair out of their way. Angel wore it for the same reason. Her final accessory, her own addition, was a small hand laser strapped around her lower arm, just under the cover of her sleeve. It was her personal version of a security blanket.

"Are you okay?" Yanur joined her in the hatch, his eyes offering a sympathetic look.

I'm going out, virtually alone, on a planet inhabited by a bloodthirsty race of aliens in order to retrieve the body of a man whose life essence is hanging around my neck and who is going to be extremely upset when he finds out I'm not the young man he thinks I am. And you ask me if I'm okay? "Sure, I'm fine," she said.

Just then Romanof buzzed in her ear. "Time to go."

Yanur nodded his head, letting her know that, although he hadn't heard him speak, he was aware of his friend's impatience. He opened the hatch and stood aside as she walked through.

Once on the other side, she paused to turn back to him.

"Be careful." He looked like he wanted to say more, but didn't dare, with Romanof able to hear everything.

Angel gave what she hoped was a smile, but probably appeared more as a grimace. "I will," she said with a reassurance far greater than she felt and waited while Yanur shut the hatch door.

The landing field was nothing more than an open stretch of barren ground; a flat surface broken intermittently by giant stasis towers standing sentry duty over a field of ships. Separating the landing field from the rest of the planet was an impenetrable perimeter-wall the height of which dwarfed even the stasis towers. There seemed to be only two ways on or off the field: by ship or through the control tower. Wanting to choose the first, Angel turned toward the second.

She should be used to this, she thought. As a courier of illegal goods, she landed on strange and hostile planets all the time. Why the Harvestors should bother her more than the usual run of scum, she didn't know. They just did. Maybe because they were like the veritable bogeymen of childhood nightmares, appearing out of nowhere on dark, starless nights to kidnap hapless victims. *I should have my head examined for doing this.*

Heading for the control tower, Angel let herself merge with the crews of two other ships headed the same way. They went inside and Angel stepped out of the crowd, giving herself time to look around. The control tower was a two-story structure, with offices running the perimeter of the second floor, but was otherwise open from top to bottom. The place had a funny antiseptic odor that fit perfectly with the sterile, plain white walls and floors. The only touch of color came from the clothes worn by the arriving and departing black marketeers, and from the artificial plants set haphazardly about the place.

Occasionally, she saw figures walk by cloaked entirely in white robes. She assumed these were Harvestors.

Near the front exit of the tower, a line had formed to gain admittance to the planet. One by one, each visitor walked past posted guards and stepped through a type of security gate. Angel took her place at the back of the line.

Without warning, a man's scream rent the air. It was followed by a hushed, unnatural silence. When the eventual drone of whispers began, it started at the front of the line, gradually working its way down to her end.

"—vaporized, damn shame."

"—regular."

"—even knew the rules."

"—tried to sneak a weapon past the guards."

"One minute, everything's fine—"

"—the next—bam!"

Angel stopped listening. And started looking for a place to dump her laser. Romanof had not mentioned anything to her about weapons being prohibited when he'd briefed her on what he'd learned about the registration procedure. She hated to lose the gun, but vaporization was not a preferred choice.

"What's wrong?" Romanof buzzed in her ear.

"Later," she hissed, not wanting to draw undue attention. Off to the side, past a grouping of artificial plants, was the vid-screen map of the city. Abandoning her place in line, Angel walked past the plants to study the map. It was a pretense that served dual purposes. The first was to gain a better understanding of the city beyond the control tower. Within moments she had memorized the basic layout of the city with the main marketplace not far off.

The second purpose was served when she returned to the line. Activating her weapon's release mechanism so the laser slid into her hand, she glanced around. Everyone's attention was elsewhere, not on her. As she passed the plants, she slowed her pace, reached her hand into the artificial leaves, and let go. The weapon dropped to the bottom of the pot, fully concealed from view. With a sigh of relief, she continued as nonchalantly as she could, to rejoin the line.

When her turn through the security gates arrived, she passed inspection without mishap. Two of the white-robed figures questioned her about her intentions, speaking in standard Terran, the language common among most trade planets, legitimate or black market. Her responses proved satisfactory, thanks to Romanof's quiet buzzing in her ear. With a final pass through a sani-ray to destroy any foreign contaminants, she followed the rest of the new arrivals through the exit corridor leading away from the building.

Outside, Angel took in the white buildings along the street, the paved roads and walkways congested with pedestrians rather than ground or air shuttles.

Looking behind her, Angel noticed that the corridor through which she'd just emerged was one-way, exit only. To her right, about a half-block away, the heavily guarded entrance to the control tower was visible. She studied the area, committing the location to memory. When the time came, she wanted to know how to find the airfield again.

"Where to?" Angel asked softly.

"I don't know. I'm not getting a clear signal. There may be

too much interference from the tower. Start walking and I'll let you know if I pick up the signal."

Remembering from the vid-screen map that the main Market Square was just off to her right, Angel headed that way, along with a large number of the new arrivals. As she walked, she grew uncomfortably warm. Looking around for a more shaded path to the square, she noticed a total absence of trees. In fact, there was no plant life to be found anywhere. No trees, no grass, no flowers. Nothing.

"How does a planet survive without plant life?" She mumbled.

"I think the answer is, it doesn't," Romanof answered in her ear. "My scan of the planet indicates that it's dying."

It saddened her to think of the planet dying, even the Harvestors' planet. She wondered if they knew, and felt sure they must.

"I think we're there," she whispered to Romanof when she reached a street lined with shops. "Are you picking up your body's signal?"

"No."

"Any suggestions?"

"Just walk around and try to look interested. But don't buy anything."

"Yes, well, I'll try to resist." Angel pushed aside the beaded entrance to the first shop she came to and froze.

Leaning against the walls were rows of standing human bodies, eyes staring vacantly in front of them, lifeless but very much alive.

"It's okay, Michels." Romanof's warm voice was calm above the furious pounding of her heart. "Don't let anyone see you're upset."

"There're just so many of them," she whispered. "I didn't realize . . ." Her words faltered and she couldn't go on.

"I know. But the worst is over for them. Remember, these are only the shells. Now, tell me what you see."

Obediently, she tried to detach her emotions, to focus on the mission. A bit mechanically, she described the barely clothed bodies in front of her.

"Males, humanoid, approximate ages between mid-forties and fifties, healthy but not what I would consider athletic."

"All of them?"

Angel scanned the walls. "Yes."

"Okay. You can leave. My body is not among these."

"Why is that?"

"Wrong profile."

She had no clue what he meant by that, but rather than ask, she left the shop and continued down the street. "You want me to try the next shop?"

"Yes, let me . . . wait . . . there! I've got a signal. It's about 750 meters north-northeast."

Angel looked around. From her current location, north-northeast would be back behind the next street where she noticed a group of traders now heading. She followed them and soon found herself on a path leading between two shops to an enclosure that looked like an outdoor theater, minus the grass and trees. Rows of chairs faced an empty stage, which was attached to a small building. Low fencing surrounded the entire seating area and the only entrance was through a registration gate.

Once again, Angel found herself waiting in line.

"Standard of credit?" The robed figure asked when she reached the front.

"Terran," she answered.

"Ship?"

"Icarus."

The man made a notation on a computer, then picked up a small electronic pad similar to the ones being carried by those inside the seating area. He checked the number on the side, keyed more entries into his computer and then handed the device to her.

"This is your bidding box. When you see a donor on which you wish to bid, enter his collar number here." He pointed to the numeric pad. "Then enter your bid amount. You will have only five standard minutes in which to place your bid. Within that time, you may change your bid amount as often as you like. A green light will mark the end of the bidding session. If yours is the high bid, a red light will appear. No light, no donor. You may bid on as many donors as you wish until the auction is over, at which time you will report back here to verify and pay for your purchase. Once payment is confirmed, you may take your donor with you or leave instructions for specific programming needs. Once you have taken possession of your purchase, there can be no returns. Any questions?"

"How soon until the auction begins?"

"About forty tocks," he said. "In Terran standard, that would be about twenty minutes."

Angel thanked him and walked into the seating area. "Are you still picking up a signal?"

"Yes, just a couple of meters from here."

"Probably in that building." Angel described the auction set-up and Romanof suggested she sit as close to the stage as possible, so he could pick up a clear signal. She selected a spot in the second row, off to the side. There were not many buyers present and Angel had no problem, even in the second row, finding a seat to herself.

"These people must have a real cleanliness fetish," Angel said, looking around. "There seem to be decontamination booths all over the place."

Romanof didn't say anything, so Angel busied herself with watching other bidders file into the area. But it was hard to stay focused and the waiting provided too much time with her own thoughts.

"Do you think anyone has ever survived the mind-swipe?"

"Not that I'm aware," he replied softly.

"You took quite a chance. There are not many people who'd be willing to try what you did."

"I did only what I felt needed to be done."

"Yanur removing your life essence from your body? That's a bit extreme, even for a noble cause."

"Child's play on some planets. It's just a matter of knowing which planets."

"Maybe, but I still think you took a big risk. You could have ended up in the organ-donation group."

"Not a chance."

"Why not?"

"As I said before, I don't fit the profile for organ donation."

"Speaking of physical profile, you want to tell me what you look like?"

"No time, the auction is starting. Keep your eyes open."

Angel watched the left stage door open and a cloaked figure appeared, leading the first donor forward. It was an alien form that Angel had never seen before. It reminded her of a large, blue blob with elongated arms, or legs, she couldn't tell which. Someone announced that the bidding had officially begun.

The first part of the auction passed in relative ease for Angel, as several different life forms, none of which resembled humans, were escorted across the stage and sold. It wasn't until the first human donor walked across the stage, a young woman Angel guessed to be in her mid-twenties, that it became uncomfortable to watch. Each successive donor, staring out at the audience with vacuous eyes, was led across the stage, completely nude except for a metallic collar worn around his or her neck, bearing a number. Angel found the sight disturbing and Romanof noticed.

"Remember Michels, they are beyond feeling, and they are beyond our help."

"I'm fine."

"I can hear your heart beating. It's interfering with my reception. Try to relax."

Angel worked to bring herself back under control. She sat and watched as male and female donors passed in front of her. By human standards, these bodies were the cream of the crop, fitting the male and female specs for physical perfection. But without the life force to animate the bodies, she could have been watching the sex-droids from Delta Sixty-Niner, an adult entertainment space station, walk across stage.

"You know, Romanof, some of these male donors are pretty good-looking." Actually, "good-looking" was an understatement. They varied in height and coloring, but they were all in the peak of health, some more chiseled than others, and all well endowed. "Maybe you should think about . . . um, how shall I put it? Trading up?"

"Trading up?"

"Sure. Forget your old body. Take one of these. I guarantee you'll never have a problem with the ladies with one of these."

"You're babbling again. And for your information, I don't have trouble with women. I like my body the way it is and I would appreciate it if you would pay attention."

"Well, at least think about it from an age standpoint. If you've been in the forces a long time, there's probably been a lot of wear and tear on your body and . . . and . . . oh God . . ."

"Michels! What's wrong?"

"Noth . . . nothing," she gasped.

"Your heart rate has increased and your body temperature is rising. What's happening?"

How could she tell him that at that very moment, a male, unsurpassed by any Angel had seen in her entire life, was being escorted across the stage? He was tall, with arms and legs so well-muscled, they stopped just short of bulging. The ends of his dark brown, almost black, hair brushed the top of his broad shoulders. A fine matte of equally brown-black hair spread in an oval across a broad chest that was mouthwatering. Her eyes followed the washboard stomach downward. As heat inflamed her face, she looked up, swallowing hard. Never had she seen a man so perfect that it left her feeling dizzy. "That's the one," she said in a daze. "I mean, that's the one."

"Start bidding, damn it." Romanof's voice blasted in her ear.

"What? You want me to buy this one?" She was sure she had misheard him.

"Of course I want you to buy it," he exploded. "It's mine."

"This . . ." she had to clear her throat. "This is your body? Your real body?"

"Yes, and if you don't bid on it, we're going to lose it!"

Boy, was she in trouble, she thought as she madly keyed in the donor's collar number. Nicoli Romanof couldn't be this Adonis before her. She refused to think about it. The bidding had already escalated to thirteen million credits. She keyed in fourteen million. "What's your credit limit?" she asked, when the current bid jumped to sixteen million. "Your body is really hot." In more ways than one, she thought.

"No limit," Alex replied tersely. Angel decided to cut to the chase and keyed in a hundred million. She didn't want to risk losing this one. Then suddenly, the green light went on and the bidding ended. Angel held her breath, waiting for a blinking red light to tell her she won.

No light appeared. Growing anxious, she studied the device, trying to figure out the problem. Then Romanof's body was led off the stage and somewhere in the crowd behind her, someone gave a whoop of delight.

"Is it over?" Romanof asked. "Did you get it?"

Angel sat there, dazed, and tried to resist the cold rain of panic as it slowly drenched her. How was she going to tell Romanof that she had just lost his body?

Chapter Six

"Michels, did you or did you not secure my body?"

"Not," Angel admitted.

"You lost the bid?" Romanof's roar of disbelief caused Angel to pluck the ear-piece out before she went deaf.

"I'll get your body," she snapped back almost as frustrated as she imagined Romanof to be. She held the ear-piece close to her ear to make sure the noise level coming through it was back to normal before putting it back on.

"How much?" Romanof's voice came to her, somewhat subdued.

She guessed it was normal to be curious. "It was at thirteen million credits when I entered my first bid of fourteen million."

"You should have bid fifty million. It would have been hard to come up with, but worth it to secure my body."

That caught her attention. "You don't have fifty million credits? You told me there was no limit."

"Be reasonable. No one has fifty million credits to spend on a donor."

"Yeah, well someone did because my last bid for your body

was a hundred million credits and I was outbid."

A gratifying silence met her statement. Up on stage, another donor was brought forward and the auction resumed. Angel left her seat and walked past the rows of people to the side table where all sales were being finalized.

"Excuse me," she said to the figure behind the desk. "Can you tell me who just purchased that last donor?"

"All sales are confidential." He raised his head to look at her, but she couldn't see his face from beneath the hood. "Will there be anything else?" His tone clearly suggested there wouldn't be.

She moved off to the side, out of the way, to think. Smugglers, traders and white-robed figures milled about, but no one paid attention to her. "Are you still picking up the tracer signal?" She asked under her breath, an idea forming.

"Vaguely. It's about nineteen meters south of our current position."

That would mean the body was still backstage. She exited the fenced area and walked around the perimeter to the back of the building.

"What are you planning to do?" Romanof asked.

"I'm going to get your body." The trick was, how? Well, maybe something would come to her.

The back of the stage building resembled the back of any other building. There were three doors exiting onto the parking area where several shuttles were parked. As Angel studied the doors, wondering if she could risk just walking through one of them, she heard the sound of an engine. She ducked back around the side of the building just before a large ground transport rumbled into the parking lot. It passed the parked shuttles and lumbered right up to the building before coming to a stop.

Angel watched two drivers, fully robed, climb out of the shuttle and walk into the building. Within minutes, a robed figure appeared pushing a bin. He did something at the rear of the transport and the back doors opened and a ramp lowered to the ground. The robed figure proceeded to push the bin up the ramp and disappear into the back of the transport. He reappeared moments later, without the bin, and returned to the building.

Unsure what to do, Angel waited. In a few moments, two robed figures emerged from the building, this time pushing a gurney between them with a body on top. The body was uncovered and nude. A donor. Angel was so close she could almost make out the numbers on the metallic collar. The drivers pushed the gurney up the ramp into the back of the transport, leaving it to return, empty handed, to the building.

A few minutes later, the scene repeated with another gurney and donor. Angel continued to watch as the robed figures loaded the shuttle. Wondering how long it would take the drivers to finish, she started when Romanof buzzed in her ear.

"The signal is moving toward us."

Sure enough, when the robed figures appeared next, the donor on the gurney was the gorgeous Adonis she had bid on earlier. It, too, disappeared into the back of the transport.

"Where are they taking it?" she mused aloud.

"I don't know, but you'd better follow."

"I will," she muttered, wondering if it would be worth the risk to steal the body but leave the life essence behind.

After the robed figures loaded Romanof's body, they stepped out of the transport. One of them disappeared into the building while the other did something to the back of the transport. The ramp lifted off the ground and disappeared under the vehicle. When the robed figure shut the back doors and walked to the front of the transport, Angel became nervous. What if he drove off? What could she do? Run and jump onto the back of it, hoping there was some way to hold on and not be seen?

But, the Harvestor merely returned inside. Angel knew she had to act now.

She ran to the transport and found the mechanism to release the back doors. They opened easily and she climbed in, hitting the button to close them behind her as she did. Now she was locked inside with the bodies.

Four donors lay nude and exposed on gurneys set side by side, two wide and two deep. Her eyes were drawn to Romanof's body and she moved to stand by its side. Of their own accord, her fingers reached out to lightly touch his shoulder as if to offer comfort or reassure herself he was in one piece.

"Start the transfer process," Romanof instructed.

"Not here. Those drivers could be back any second." She cast a quick glance out the back window and wondered how much time she really had. Think, think, she chided herself. She looked around the shuttle, hoping to find someplace to hide and saw the large bin in the corner. It was half concealed by the long white Harvestor robes hanging along the back wall of the transport. Looking inside, Angel found the bin full of clothes, but not the same white robes as were hanging up. These were off-planet clothes and she wondered if they belonged to the donors.

Just then, she heard the sound of a building door opening and then closing. Sneaking a look out the back window, she saw the two robed figures walking toward the shuttle. She was out of time. She hiked first one leg, and then the other, over the side of the bin, burrowing beneath the clothes, piling them on top of her.

She held her breath, listening for sounds of the back doors opening, but none came. The muffled noise of the front transport doors slamming shut came to her just before she felt the vibrations from the engine as it roared to life. It was with mixed feelings that she felt the transport move forward.

The trip to their destination seemed to take forever. When the transport finally stopped, Angel held very still while the drivers got out. The doors to the back opened and Angel heard the first gurney being removed. She waited until there was total silence, then cautiously peeked out.

The drivers were gone. But so was Romanof's body.

She looked toward the unknown building, visible through the open back doors. "What's the signal doing?" She whispered, knowing he would hear her.

"It's moving south."

Damn. Well, there wasn't a choice. She'd have to go in after it.

Digging herself out from under the clothes, she climbed out of the bin. She stuffed the garments back in, the way she'd found them, making sure to drape the lengths of the hanging robes over the bin. That's when the idea hit.

With a quick glance out the back of the transport to make

sure no one was there, she took down a robe and slipped it on, pulling the hood over her head. Seeing out of the fabric folds hanging in front of her face wasn't as bad as she'd thought. The loose weave of the material allowed her surprisingly good visibility. Angel felt pleased with herself. This idea might work out better than she'd hoped.

"You there," a man's voice boomed out, startling her. Angel whirled around to face the robed figure standing just outside the open shuttle doors. "Sorry, Dr. Huan'tre," the robed figure continued, sounding contrite. "I didn't recognize you."

Angel looked down at the front of her robe and saw unfamiliar lettering. Looking at the front of the man's robe, she saw similar lettering. He spoke in standard Terran, but the written words were obviously still in the local dialect. The presence of names on the robes explained how they recognized one another, but the system seemed a bit simplistic for such an advanced race. It certainly wasn't foolproof, as Angel was proving. Their loss, as the old Earth saying went.

"I'm sorry if I offended you," the figure continued, sounding worried by her prolonged silence. "I'm new. Just got my commission to Central Processing yesterday. You won't turn me in, will you?"

Angel shook her head.

"Thank you." He sounded relieved. "Smithee and Butch sent me to unload the rest of these donors."

Was that opportunity she heard knocking? Think how much time would be saved searching for Romanof's body if someone just led her to it.

"I'll help you," Angel offered, keeping her voice pitched low. She had no idea if this Dr. Haun'tre was male or female.

"Oh, okay. Thank you." The man seemed unconcerned. He stepped forward and pulled the nearest gurney forward while Angel moved to take the other end. Pushing it down the ramp, they went through the door and started down the cold, dark hallway inside.

They passed several rooms on both sides of the hall, stopping only when they reached the lift at the end. They wheeled the gurney on and the man pushed a button to go down. He didn't seem to find her continued silence abnormal, but kept up a constant chatter, for which Angel was grateful.

Romanof hadn't said anything in a while, but she knew he was monitoring everything. When the doors to the lift opened on the lower level, she helped push the gurney off. They walked by several more closed doors, all of which bore signs that Angel couldn't read.

When they reached the fourth door, they stopped.

"In here," the man said, opening the door and leading them inside.

The place looked like a morgue, filled with rows of donor bodies stretched out on gurneys. Some of them were hooked to IVs, which Angel assumed was how the Harvestors kept the bodies nourished. Countertops running along the side walls displayed various pieces of laboratory equipment. In the center of the wall at the far end of the room was a door leading into a back room and it was into this that they pushed their body. With a sigh of relief, Angel noticed Romanof's body lying not far off. Before she could think what to do about it, the robed figure hustled her out again and back to the transport to get another body.

"You're nothing like I expected," the man finally said. "I'd heard about you." He laughed and it sounded self-conscious. "Who hasn't heard about you? You're the whole reason," he looked around and lowered his voice conspiratorially, "Operation Rebirth is possible." He raised his voice back to a normal pitch. "And here you are helping me unload donors. Who's going to believe this?"

Who indeed, Angel wondered. Certainly not Romanof, who'd finally broken his silence and was setting up a low-level buzz in her ear, telling her to stop "playing around."

Fortunately, the Harvestor didn't seem to notice the noise. They pushed the second donor along the same path they'd taken before and once they reached the room, again pushed it toward the back to an empty space.

It was just as they were leaving to get the last donor on the transport that the door opened and two more Harvestors entered pushing it between them.

65

"Perrin seems anxious about this group of donors," one of the men was saying. "You know what he's like when he's this way."

"Yeah," the other one responded. "You'd think someone had just told him that he was headed for recycle, not rebirth—oh, Dr. Huan'tre!" The two men stopped when they saw her. "What are you doing here?"

Unsure how to answer, Angel kept quiet. Her companion seemed to feel the need to defend her.

"Dr. Haun'tre was helping me unload the donors."

"Helping?" the first one asked.

Angel tried to think. Dr. Huan'tre was obviously an important figure. What reason would someone like that have to be down here, she wondered? "I was inspecting the new arrivals," she offered by way of explanation, remembering to keep her voice pitched low.

The man looked at her, his expression hidden behind the hood. "Let's not mince words," he said finally. "I know why you're here. I have already explained to Perrin about the mix-up with the tags. I've been forced to recycle several of my workers and with a shrinking work pool to pull from, well, there are going to be mistakes. But I assure you, everything is under control once again and there's no need for you to come down and oversee. I'm sure you have many important things to attend to." He gestured in the direction of the door.

They wanted her to leave. Three Harvestors to one of her. And she was unarmed. As if reading her mind, Romanof spoke up. "Act like you own the place. And tell them . . ."

Angel listened as he spoke, praying he knew what he was talking about, and repeated his words aloud.

"I should not presume so much with one who is clearly your superior. I suggest you continue to do your job and allow me to do mine."

It seemed no one breathed, except the donors lying around them. The silence didn't bother Romanof and he buzzed in her ear and again, she repeated his words.

"As you said before, we've already sent more workers than we can afford to lose to Recycle. It would be a shame to lose another." Angel turned her head to look directly at each Harvestor in turn.

"Yes, Dr. Haun'tre. Your forgiveness," mumbled the Harvestor she'd originally helped as he backed out of the room. There was a muttered "your forgiveness" from the second Harvestor as he did the same. Angel almost smiled at their submissive acceptance of her words, glad the hood hid her expression. She turned to the remaining Harvestor.

"Don't say anything," Romanof instructed. "Make him break the silence first." Leave it to Romanof to know all the power plays, Angel thought, but she did as he said and waited. It seemed to take forever, but finally the Harvestor shrugged.

"Your forgiveness, Dr. Haun'tre. May I be of service?"

"No. I would like a few moments alone to study these donors."

"Very well. If you'll excuse me, I have a job to finish." He left the room and Angel relaxed a little.

"Are they gone?" Romanof asked.

"Yes. Should I take your body someplace else to do the transfer?"

"No, it's too risky. But we'd better wait a minute. Let's make sure no one comes back to check on you. Walk around and pretend to examine the bodies."

With the hood pulled low, she didn't really have to look at the donors, just appear as though she was. She waited about five minutes to see if anyone else came to the room, but when it remained quiet, she decided now was as good a time as any to start the transfer process.

She immediately walked to the back of the room to Romanof's body. Angel looked around. There were no closets or hidden corners. The room was bare except for the donors, most of whom were nude. There were, however, one or two with drapes over them. She decided to use one of the drapes to cover Romanof's body while the transfer was taking place. It was the only added protection she could provide.

Walking over to the first draped form, she pulled off the cloth. And gasped out loud.

"What's wrong?" Romaonf buzzed urgently in her ear.

"No . . . nothing. Everything's fine." The appearance of the donor caught her off guard. A jagged incision, recently made, ran the length of his torso. Blood had congealed beneath the stitches. "This one must be targeted for organ donation," she said, describing to Romanof what she saw. She walked to another draped body and pulled back the cloth. It was the same. She recovered it and went back to the first body, pushing its gurney close to Romanof's.

"I think all the covered bodies are organ donors," she said. "If I leave one uncovered and someone walks in, they'll notice."

"Okay. Here's what I want you to do. After you start the transfer process, a light will appear. Don't touch the light. Once it disappears, roll that body onto mine and cover us both with the drape. Push the empty gurney behind us so anyone walking into the room won't notice it."

"Okay. Whatever you say." Angel sounded hesitant even to her own ears.

"As soon as you've done that, I want you to leave. Go back to the ship as fast as you can and wait with Yanur."

"No. I'm not going to leave you here, unprotected."

"Michels, that wasn't a request. This room is too busy. We don't know how long it will take for my life essence to reassimilate. You can't just stand around here and wait. It's too risky. If you get caught, it will compromise my entire mission because then I'll have to worry about saving you."

Angel remained silent.

"Michels?"

"Okay, fine." She took off the robe so she had easier access to her pockets. "God, I hope this works," she prayed, as she removed the transfer disc from her back pocket.

Following Yanur's instructions, she took the biopod from around her neck and placed it on top of the disc. Some technology, which she didn't understand, held it there while she centered the whole thing over Romanof's forehead. Before she pressed the button to start the process, she leaned over to examine the metallic collar still around Romanof's neck. She looked for a way to remove it and found that it didn't go all the way around, but just encircled the front half of his throat.

Feeling around the collar with her fingers, she found the outer surface smooth. There seemed to be no obvious locking mechanism or switch. On a whim, she gave it a tug. It slid off easily in her hand.

Looking at the repulsive device for a moment, she tossed it to the floor.

It was time to start the transfer and she looked at Romanof's face and had an attack of conscience. What if he didn't survive? What if he did?

Angel stared at the disc, torn between an urgency to get this over with and reluctance for him to discover the truth about her. She had one last chance to be honest with him before it was too late.

"There's probably something I should tell you before you wake up in your body," Angel started.

"Not now, Michels. Press the damn switch."

So she did.

At first nothing happened. Then the top of the biopod opened slowly, emitting a slight hissing noise. The pulsating, bright amber light inside the tube began to seep out and gather around Romanof's body, starting with his head and spreading downward. It reminded Angel of the wispy fog hovering over the ocean's surface at the cusp of a new day. Romanof's body lay cocooned in an amber aura for a brief moment, then slowly seemed to absorb the light.

Once it was totally gone, Angel considered the best way to get the "parts" donor onto the same gurney with Romanof. In walking around to study the two bodies from all angles, she noticed a crank with a handle at the end of each gurney. She turned the crank on Romanof's cart and the bed began to rise. She reversed her direction and the gurney began to lower. She continued to crank until Romanof's body sat about twelve centimeters lower than the other donors. At this height, it was easy to roll the other donor on top of Romanof.

When they were both covered with the drape, they looked like all the other draped bodies. Now the only thing to do was to push the empty gurney behind them and wait.

Oh, she knew what Romanof had said. But in his current

state, Romanof was completely defenseless. She would not leave him unprotected.

So she waited. Occasionally, she walked quietly around the room. Other times she stood next to Romanof's body, not sure she was being a guard at duty or a mother bear watching her cub. She was just beginning to wonder at what point she should become concerned, when the doors to the outer room opened. Quickly she ducked down behind Romanof's body.

"I told you there was something wrong," she heard one of the newcomers say. "The real Dr. Haun'tre wouldn't be down here. We need to find the impostor."

"And do what with him?"

"Take him to Recycle." Angel felt the blood drain from her face. She was in trouble if they found her.

"Make sure you look under every gurney."

Angel heard the two men walk to the far side of the outer room. While they worked through the rows of bodies in the front room, she tried to find a place to hide in the back. There was nothing but row after row of lifeless donor bodies, and one empty gurney.

Damn. She started pulling off her clothes, bending close to Romanof's head as she did. "If you can hear me—lay still. Someone's coming."

It took seconds to shed all her clothes. She wadded them into a bundle and stashed them under the drape with Romanof. Then she climbed on top of the empty gurney. Feeling horribly exposed, she forced herself to lay flat, just like the other donors in the room.

She shut her eyes when the footsteps got louder. Straining her ears to catch every noise, she heard the men enter the room and walk down the aisles. So far she'd only heard the two voices. If things got bad, she could take them—maybe.

The footsteps drew closer.

Please don't find Romanof. Please don't find Romanof. Her silent prayer became her mantra. One set of footsteps stopped next to her.

"Hey, take a look at this one," a voice said above her. "Shouldn't she be in Rebirth?"

Another set of footsteps joined the first.

"Do you think someone put her here on purpose?" A second voice asked. "I mean, with those cuts and bruises, maybe she's tagged for parts."

Angel could feel their eyes on her and she tried not to think about it. She had to distance herself or she would ruin any chance to protect Romanof.

"I don't think so," the first one said. "She's not hurt that bad. She's just in the wrong room." Footsteps moved to the end of her gurney. "Grab the other end. We'll take her back."

Her gurney started to move.

"Hold it," the second voice said. "Her collar came off."

Before she knew what was going on, a collar, probably Romanof's discarded one, was placed around her throat. She concentrated on keeping her eyes shut and her breathing regular, all the while working to control her mounting fear. The gurney started to move again. It was time for action.

She counted off. One . . . two . . . three . . .

She kicked out her leg, or at least she tried to, but nothing happened. She tried again, with the same results. She twisted her head to the side, but it remained where it was. She couldn't move her arm either. Nothing worked.

She was paralyzed!

The collar! Had it done this?

The Harvestors continued to wheel her body out of the room, while she lay there, helpless to stop them.

When Romanof woke, he would figure out what happened and look for her. Her hopes soared, then plummeted. He wouldn't look. He'd ordered Michels to return to the ship. And even if he suspected that Michels had run into trouble and went in search of the pilot, he'd be watching for a man, not a woman.

Yanur could tell him the truth, but how soon would Romanof return to the ship. *If* he returned to the ship.

Face it, Angel. You could be here a long time.

Numbness started to spread over her, and her thoughts grew fuzzy. Silently, a new mantra filled her mind. *Oh God, Oh God. Oh . . .*

Chapter Seven

The first tendrils of consciousness for Nicoli were like wisps of fairyfog at early dawn on Beta Four, insubstantial and hard to hold on to. As he became more alert, he noticed that his field of awareness was limited once again to his corporeal self and what those senses could detect. And though he had enjoyed the almost omniscient awareness he'd had while interfacing with the ship's computer, he wholeheartedly welcomed the limitations of his old body.

After the transfer was complete, he continued to lie where he was, eyes closed. Systematically, he flexed and relaxed muscles, satisfied that, despite a sluggishness which he had anticipated, everything seemed to be functioning. At least so far. It was time to rejoin the living.

He opened his eyes and looked around, and saw—nothing. He blinked several times, hoping to restore his vision, but to no avail. He felt as if he were lying in the center of a cosmic void, alone. He closed his eyes while a thin thread of fear wove its way into his consciousness, foreign and unwelcome. He struggled to reclaim the cold logic on which he'd built a reputation, a career, a life.

It would seem there were some prices to be paid for the out-of-body time he'd spent. He put himself through a series of mathematical exercises, forcing the emotional side of his brain into submission and the logical side into dominance.

Concentrating, he opened his eyes again. This time, he realized his blindness was more a lack of light, not sight. Relieved, he tried to sit, but his body seemed heavier than he remembered, and the weight of it pressed down upon him. He put a hand out to his side to push himself up, but pulled it back sharply when it hit an invisible barrier. When nothing further happened, he tentatively reached out again. This time, when his hand touched the barrier, he pushed at it experimentally. It gave easily, but fell back when he lowered his hand.

On a hunch, he tried to grab at the barrier and succeeded in collecting a fistful of a heavy material. Then he realized that he was lying under a type of drape, or cover. Still clutching the material, he pulled down with all of his strength, and felt the cloth give. He released his grip and grabbed a new fistful, higher up, and pulled again. Again, it shifted. He repeated the process until the drape finally slipped to the floor.

Fresh air hit his face and he breathed it in with a welcomed relief that not even the sight of the dead man on top of him could dampen.

Nicoli began the cumbersome process of working his way to the edge of the gurney while shoving the body in the opposite direction. It took some maneuvering, but he finally made it. With an effort, he broke free of the cadaver and fell to the floor. A bit shaky at first, he pushed himself to his feet and stood there, letting his mind adjust to the fact that he was now standing. His legs were actually supporting him. Feeling more in control, he looked around.

A sea of prone, lifeless bodies surrounded him. A donor room. He remembered where he was now and felt a small rush of success that the first part of his mission had gone as planned. He was here. Not just on the Harvestors' planet, but inside one of their main processing buildings. And he was alone.

He looked around once more to make sure, half expecting a young man to appear, claiming to be Michels. It was with relief that he realized the young pilot had actually followed his instructions and returned to the ship. He hadn't been sure the boy would go.

Someone's coming. A whisper from the past fluttered, then faded. Nicoli shrugged his shoulders. He had more important things to do than try to grasp mostly lost memories.

Nicoli picked up the drape from the floor to recover the body on the gurney. When he shook it out, several things fell from its folds to the floor. He bent over to pick them up.

The first items he recognized as the transfer disc and pod. He hoped the fall hadn't damaged them. He set the pod and disc on the gurney then bent down to retrieve the other item—a cloth bundle. Carefully, he undid it, not knowing what he would find. The outer cloth turned out to be a large, white hooded robe. Inside, he found a pair of boots, a black head cloth, black shirt and matching black pants. Holding them up, he could readily see that the garments would never fit him.

Puzzled, he wondered whose they were. Another mystery he didn't have time for. He had a mission to complete.

Nicoli mentally reviewed his options. They were limited. The first thing he needed to do was get out of this room. He wanted to find the Harvestors' core of operations. From experience, he knew that no one ran an operation like this without computers. So maybe if he could find the central computer, he could uncover clues as to what made the Harvestors tick and more importantly, how to bring them down. Nicoli was declaring war on the Harvestors, but it would not be one waged with might. This war would be waged with a devious intelligence.

Knowing he couldn't very well walk around naked, Nicoli held up the hooded robe. It looked like it might fit. He slipped it on. It was a little short and his bare feet stuck out the bottom, but there wasn't much he could do about it. He wasn't planning on being seen, anyway—if he could help it.

He started to roll the rest of the clothes into a bundle and, as he did, a scrap of pale blue material slipped out. He bent over and picked up a sheer blue pair of women's panties. He took a second, closer look. They looked completely out of place down in this dungeon of the living dead. With his mind considering possible scenarios of how they came to be here, he wadded the panties, shirt and pants into a ball and stuffed them into one of the robe's large pockets. The boots didn't fit, so he left them behind.

He walked to the doorway leading into the front room and cautiously peeked in. Seeing no one, he stepped through. He walked past the rows of donors to the door leading into the hallway. With ear pressed close, he listened. When he heard nothing, he opened the door and peered out. All clear.

He moved into the corridor, closing the door behind him. He remembered that he was in the basement. The labs and offices would be on the floors above. He started along the hallway, searching for the lift, trying to remember the way he and Michels had come earlier. As he walked, he passed several closed doors. They were probably just donor rooms, but it wouldn't hurt to look. If one of these had a computer, it would save him valuable time later.

He chose a door, opened it and looked inside. It was nothing more than a storage closet. He closed the door and went to the next. He peered inside that one as well, but the light was dim, making it difficult to determine its contents. He detected no movements from within so he took a hesitant step forward, then staggered back as his senses were assaulted by a fetid, putrid smell. It was a smell he recognized. The smell of rotting flesh.

Covering his nose and mouth with his hand, he moved farther into the room, just barely making out the still forms lying atop gurneys. There were four bodies in all, and though they still wore collars, these bodies were past controlling. No pulse beat where Nicoli laid his fingertips against first their wrists and then their necks. These donors were dead and had been left here to rot. For a culture that seemed to value cleanliness, as he assumed from Michel's description of the planet and the number of decontam-units, it made no sense. It was almost as if whoever had been caring for these donors had forgotten them.

Nicoli left, taking deep breaths of untainted air after shutting the door behind him. There were two doors left. He opened the first.

It was another donor holding area, much like the one in which he'd awakened. He stepped into the outer room and glanced around. Various pieces of equipment lined the walls, but nothing resembled a computer. The air in here smelled sterile and clean and the bodies of the donors appeared to be healthy and alive, or at least as healthy and alive as they could be, under the circumstances. As he walked along, he noticed something he hadn't in the room where his body had been.

All of the bodies here shared similar build and appearance. They were large, well-muscled human males. Warriors, Nicoli concluded. He walked up to the first and studied the platinum-colored hair. Acting on a hunch, he raised the eyelid of the first man and saw the sea-green eyes he had expected. He walked down the row of bodies, checking the hair and eye color of each. Each time it was the same platinum-blond hair with sea-green eyes. Coronadians. But why were there so many? Maybe the answer would be in the computer, he thought, as he turned to leave. That's when he saw her.

She was lying on a gurney, near the back of the room. As if drawn by unseen powers, he walked over to take a closer look. Her waist-length blond hair was spread out in a wild array about her head and shoulders. She was stunning, and the thought caught him by surprise. He had known many beautiful women in his life. That he couldn't recall a single one of them at this moment had to be due to his recent transfer experience, and nothing more.

Feeling like a voyeur, his eyes flitted down her form before he could force them to study only her face. Delicately carved features were set in a complexion as pure as the finest brushed porcelain. Accenting her closed eyes were dark lashes so long they brushed the tops of her cheeks. Her chin, even in the repose of mock death, hinted that she had lived her life with an iron determination. She would not have surrendered easily to death, Nicoli thought with a possessive admiration he had no right to feel. Unable to look away, his gaze traveled down the slender column of her throat to the gentle swell of her breasts, each tipped with the same dusky pink of her lips, the same shade as the setting Althusian sun on a warm summer's night. He felt his body harden at the sight of her and fought to bring it under control.

Bruises and scratches marred the smooth complexion of her chest. They formed the pattern of a hand, each bruise the imprint of a separate finger, each scrape the width of a nail. At her side was a gash, more serious than the other wounds. Blind rage engulfed him. She had fought for her life and won this living death as her reward.

Nicoli felt the pain of his clinched fists and forced them open. Taking a deep breath, he tried to calm himself. It was imperative that he regain control of his emotions before—

"What are you doing in here?"

Nicoli spun around to face the robed figure, silently chastising himself for not being more alert. The man was Nicoli's height, though stockier, if the width of the robe was any clue. Nicoli saw the downward tilt of the man's head and knew his bare feet had been spotted.

"Who are you?" the man demanded. "Never mind. I think you'd better come with me." He grabbed Nicoli's arm, but Nicoli jerked out of his grasp.

Angered, the man lunged at Nicoli, who grabbed both of his upper arms and using the man's own momentum, swung him around, releasing him abruptly so he crashed into the nearby gurneys. Both gurneys and donor bodies tumbled to the floor.

Nicoli, dizzy from the sudden exertion, bent over and waited for the world to right itself inside his head. The Harvestor recovered first and charged into Nicoli. The two fell backwards into more gurneys and out of the corner of his eye, Nicoli saw another body fall to the floor. Belatedly, he realized it was the woman.

Drawing himself up, Nicoli stepped forward, fists clinched. As soon as the Harvestor stood, Nicoli punched in the general vicinity of the man's jaw. With the hood covering the man's face, it was hard to tell exactly where to aim. The blow connected with bone and the impact caused the man to fall back. Nicoli followed, but before he could swing again, the Harvestor rushed him, fists flying.

One of the man's hands connected with Nicoli's head, snapping it back, causing Nicoli to see dots of light behind his eyelids. His opponent was no weakling. With no time to recover,

Nicoli threw his next punch, knocking his opponent back again. The two continued to exchange blows, but the impact of each one was less damaging than the one before as both men tired. Nicoli felt close to passing out. It was now or never.

Spurred on by the thought of becoming a permanent donor, he gathered the last of his strength. The Harvestor hit first, but Nicoli was ready. He blocked the assault with his left arm and followed through with a right-handed punch. The man's head snapped to the side and his body seemed to hang for just a moment, frozen in time, then crumbled to the ground. He didn't move.

Nicoli bent over, bracing his hands on his knees, dragging air loudly into his lungs, the sense of weakness overwhelming. He must remember to tell Yanur of this unfortunate side effect of the transfer process.

As his breathing quieted and became more regular, Nicoli heard a soft moan. Turning to look at the prone body of the Harvestor, he wondered if the man were regaining consciousness. But when the sound came again, it was from further away. Turning his head this way and that, Nicoli scanned the room for the source. When he heard the whimper again, his eyes came to rest on the beautiful Coronadian female. She lay face down on the floor where she had landed during the fight.

Nicoli moved to kneel next to her, logic telling him that the noise couldn't possibly be coming from her. Nevertheless, he rolled her gently onto her back. As he did so, the metal collar, which must have been knocked loose in the fall, slipped from her neck.

Nicoli bent over her, peering into her face. When her lips parted and a soft moan issued forth, he could only stare. Then her eyelashes fluttered and opened.

Glassy and distant at first, he saw her eyes try to focus. She moved her head back and forth slightly, as if lost and trying to get her bearings. Slowly, her gaze returned to him and she blinked a few more times. Then her eyes grew round and she shrank back from him. He opened his mouth, to reassure her that everything was okay, but never got the chance to say a thing. He saw the heel of her hand just before he felt the blow.

Chapter Eight

The impact caught him off balance and he fell backwards. In that moment, the woman scrambled clumsily to her feet. The stars in his head made him dizzy and he watched with a detached curiosity as the woman ran away. She didn't get far, as she stumbled into a row of gurneys. She shied away from the first body she encountered, only to back up into another. She turned wide, fearful, accusing eyes on him, and he almost felt guilty. Before he could tell her that he wasn't the enemy, she pushed past the bodies and ran into the back room.

Nicoli raised a hand to cradle his injured nose and touched fabric instead. He'd forgotten he was wearing the robe. No wonder she had run from him, he thought pulling the hood from his head. From the back room he heard the sound of furniture or equipment crashing to the floor. If he didn't stop her soon, she'd have every Harvestor in the building coming after them.

With a heartfelt groan, he pushed himself to his feet and made his way toward the back room. He had just reached the open doorway when a pale blur barreled into him. Instinctively he grabbed her, as much to keep them both from falling backwards as to keep her from breaking free and running out into the hallway. He tried to use a firm but gentle pressure, not wanting to bruise the delicate skin he touched, but her struggling made that difficult.

"It's okay," he said. "I'm not going to hurt you."

The woman twisted violently in his arms. "Cold-blooded murderer."

"Quiet! They'll hear you."

One of her arms broke free of his grasp and started beating at his face and shoulders. With her other arm trapped between their bodies, he fended off her attacks with his free arm. Down lower, her foot kicked at his shins.

"I won't let you take me," she screamed, lifting her leg to knee him in the groin. He saw it coming, but not in time to dodge it altogether.

"Mother-*oumpf*," he swore, swallowing the words to keep from yelling. His patience fleeing with the last of his control, he laid his free arm against her throat and walked her backwards until she was pressed against the wall. He continued to press until she ceased her struggles and stared up at him, eyes round with fear, but still defiant. He pressed a little harder until her lungs labored to pull air past the constriction. With each labored breath, her breasts pressed into his chest and while she might have been oblivious to her nude state, he was not.

"I'm not a Harvestor," he growled. "But if you want to see one, keep up this racket and we'll have the whole damn room full of them. Is that what you want?" He eased his arm away from her throat slightly. "I can't hear you."

"N . . . no," she croaked.

"I didn't think so. Now, are you going to shut up or," he leaned against her throat again, "do you need more time to think about it?" She shot him a lethal look, but remained quiet. He slowly let his arm drop and took a tentative step back. They stood there, sizing up one another.

"Where am I?" The woman was the first to break the silence.

"You're in a Harvestor donor holding room."

"How did I get here?"

"I assume in the usual way. The Harvestors kidnapped you?"

Her head tilted and her look turned inward, as if she were chasing a memory. Then she frowned. "I can't remember. Who are you?" She kept a wary eye on him.

"Does it matter? Would you prefer their company to mine?"

She looked as if she were considering her options when her whole expression suddenly changed to one of shock as she brought her arms up to cover herself. "Where are my clothes?"

"I don't know. This is how I found you."

She made some reply, but he'd stopped listening. He'd heard footsteps out in the hall. Placing a hand over her mouth, he raised a finger to his lips, gesturing her to silence. When she nodded that she understood, he took her arm and led her into the back room.

"Company," he whispered, moving them away from the open doorway and off to the side. As the footsteps grew louder, he played out possible scenarios in his mind, calculating how long it would take him to reach the door and what he could use as a weapon. In all of it, the woman remained an unknown factor. He prayed that she wouldn't panic and blindly race for the exit. The sounds grew louder as the newcomer neared the outer door. Then all was silent. The door opened.

Nicoli strained to listen, trying to judge the newcomer's position from the sound of his footsteps. There was an exclamation when the overturned gurneys and donor bodies were found. Then gurneys were being pushed out of the way and Nicoli could hear the man's muttered curses. The footsteps started up and down the aisles. What would happen when the unconscious Harvestor was found?

From where he stood close to the wall, Nicoli quickly surveyed the back room. It appeared to be a work area, with countertops and small cabinets lining the walls and an open workbench down the center. Various pieces of equipment were scattered or broken on the floor. But there were no closets. There was no place to hide.

As the sound of the footsteps grew louder, Nicoli moved to stand in front of the woman. He backed up until he felt her soft curves pressing into his back and hips. He would face the enemy head on and shield her as best he could. She must have understood the danger, because wedged as she was between him and the wall, she didn't try to move away. Nicoli scanned the room again for a place to hide, hoping that something he hadn't noticed earlier would present itself. Nothing did.

He turned again to better gauge the Harvestor's position and his gaze fell on the open door. Not stopping to consider his plan, he reached behind him and placed his hand on the woman's hip. Trying to ignore the smooth feel of her skin and the quick hitch of her breath at his touch, he gently applied pressure. When he stepped sideways, she went with him. They continued, quiet step by quiet step, until they were directly behind the open door. It was scant protection, but the best he could come up with. At least he would have the element of surprise on his side, should it be needed.

The seconds dragged by as he waited for the newcomer. Of its own traitorous accord, his mind drifted to thoughts of long shapely legs topped by curvaceous hips. She was taller than most of the women he knew and pressed together as they were, he couldn't help but think how perfectly she fit against him. Then he began to notice the rise and fall of plump breasts as they pressed and rubbed against his back. As if she had just noticed the intimate contact and was uncomfortable with it, he felt her fidget. Each movement was a tortuous test of his control.

"Christ, woman, stop wiggling around. Do you think me dead?" he growled softly.

Drawing on inner strength, he forced his body to ignore the sensations and concentrate on the approaching newcomer. When the footsteps stopped just inside the door, he held his breath. He couldn't see the newcomer, but imagined him standing there, looking around. The door inched toward them, and Nicoli pressed back further against the woman, sucking in his breath to allow the door more room to move freely.

When the man's foot appeared past the edge of the door, Nicoli shoved the door as hard as he could into the man. As the Harvestor fell to the side, Nicoli moved out of his hiding spot and punched him in the stomach. Off balance, the man fell against the side countertop. When he stood again, his hand clutched a long metal pipe. Still weak from the first fight, Nicoli resigned himself to another painful bout.

The Harvestor stepped forward, swinging the pipe in an arc in front of him, preventing Nicoli from getting too close. Each step closer, forced Nicoli one step back. On the third swipe, Nicoli didn't move fast enough and the pipe smashed against his lower arm. Reacting to the pain, Nicoli bent over, pulling his injured arm close to his stomach. The Harvestor, thinking Nicoli seriously injured, changed tactics. He raised the pipe to bring it crashing down on Nicoli's head and that was his mistake.

While the man's arms were raised, Nicoli punched him in the stomach. His breath rushed out as he doubled over, dropping the pipe. Not waiting for the man to recover, Nicoli stepped forward, brought the man's head beneath his arm and with both hands, gave it a harsh twist. There was a sickening snap and when Nicoli released him, the man fell limply to the floor.

"Is he dead?" The woman's quiet question echoed in the sudden silence of the room.

"I sure as hell hope so." Then it occurred to Nicoli that she might be upset, so he forgot about the corpse at his feet and went to her.

It was a mistake. As soon as he stood before her, his mind remembered the feel of her pressed against him. His gaze wandered hungrily over her until he reached her eyes. She watched him, trapped prey regarding its predator, he thought. Nervously it seemed, she wet her lips and it was his undoing. He felt as if he were falling into the wet, rose-red tint of those lips. His body, no longer distracted by the threat of danger, reacted instantly. Mesmerized, his hands came up to gently cup her face as he slowly lowered his head.

"Please," she whispered. Confused, he paused. Please continue or please stop? Belatedly, he remembered the bruises. He was proving to be no better than the animals who had attacked her before.

Cursing, he stepped back, feeling guilty. Well, it wouldn't happen again. The woman crossed her arms to cover herself while she studied him carefully, no doubt thinking that at any moment, he would change his mind and attack her. He cursed louder and ran a hand through his hair as he looked away.

"I'm not going to hurt you," he said, his voice rough. He looked back and caught the skeptical expression on her face. She didn't trust him. "Look, sweetheart, don't get the wrong idea. You're not really my type, okay? It was just the adrenaline rush, that's all." He felt a moment's chagrin because he knew he lied.

Apparently, she believed him, because her expression grew hard and her chin jutted out. "In that case, you won't mind if I get dressed." She looked around the room, finally bringing her gaze back to him. "If you were a gentleman, you'd offer me your robe." She delivered the reprimand in a voice as warm as heated brandy.

"Well, I never claimed to be a gentleman, as the saying goes," he replied in a surly tone. "Besides, I like the way you're dressed. It might even prove handy. I could put you on one of those gurneys and push you through the halls until I find what I'm looking for. No one would suspect a thing. How about it?" He watched for a reaction, but received none. "No? Well, I suppose not. In that case," he felt in his robe pocket for the bundle of clothes he just remembered having and tossed them to her. "Try these on."

She didn't immediately move to put on the garments, but continued to watch him.

"Look, you don't have anything that I haven't already seen, up close," he snarled, but still she didn't move. "Fine, I'll leave, but hurry and get dressed. I'll be waiting."

He turned around and walked out, but not before he saw the blush start at her forehead and spread slowly downward across her chest. Once again, he muttered a curse. First, for hurting her feelings and second, for caring in the first place.

In the outer room, the unconscious Harvestor lay in the same position as before. Nicoli conducted a thorough search through the pockets of the man's robe, but came away with nothing.

He peeled off the man's hood, out of curiosity as much as anything else, and then sat back with a shock. The man's face was horribly scarred. A patchwork of skin grafts in various skin tones and textures covered it. If all the robed Harvestors looked like this, it was little wonder why they covered themselves. A gasp from behind told him the woman had joined him.

"Is he dead?"

"No. Not yet." He met her look pointedly, but didn't comment further. He stood up, bracing himself for the reaction to what he had to tell her, but instead found himself taken with how good she looked in the clothes.

"I see they fit okay." He tried to sound normal.

"Yes, um, thank you."

"Nicoli."

"What?"

"My name is Nicoli." He sucked in a bracing breath. It would take all of his legendary iron control to resist this woman's powers. "Okay, here's the deal. Neither one of us can afford to stay here too long, but I can't leave just yet. There's still something I have to do, which means I'm stuck with you for awhile. We'll just have to make the best of it."

"I don't think so," she informed him. "I can take care of myself."

"Yeah, sweetheart, you were doing one hell of a job when I walked in here. Lying unconscious on that gurney. What was that? A covert operation? Hoping to ferret out the Harvestors and take them unawares?"

"Yes. I mean, no."

He rolled his eyes at her. "Yeah, that's what I thought. You'll come with me."

"No, I won't. I'll be fine on my own."

The woman was infuriating. "I insist," he ground out between clenched teeth. "For your information, it's not just a question of your safety. I can't have you running around, letting everyone know that you somehow survived. You'll screw things up for me."

"What things?"

"That's classified."

"If I'm going to risk my life, then I think I have a right to know."

He couldn't believe they were standing there arguing over this. He gave her a cold, calculating look, hoping to intimidate her into acquiescence. She maintained her stance, never looking down or away. Damn stubborn woman. "I'm here on an S and D—search and destroy," he said finally.

"Oh," she snorted. "*That* sounds much safer. Thanks. I'll take my own chances."

"Going with me is a lot safer than lying around waiting to be turned into someone's sex slave. Unless that's what you're into? Because if it is, then I'm sure we can work something out." He made a show of looking her over casually, as if assessing her charms or lack thereof. Again he saw the blush creep into her face and felt the guilt. Something about her brought out the worst in him.

"Look, when this is over, I'll take you home, or at least I'll try to. Coronado, right?" He'd never been there, but he knew where it was. When she didn't answer, he went on. "Hey, sweetheart, I didn't mean to pry. I'll drop you wherever you want to be dropped."

She moved in agitation. "Would you please stop calling me 'sweetheart?' "

"Sure, no problem. What should I call you?"

"My name is . . ." She stopped, a strange expression coming to her face.

"What's wrong?" he asked, when the expression turned to panic.

"My name! I can't remember my name. I can't remember anything." She gave him a quiet, desperate look. "I don't know who I am!"

Chapter Nine

The woman, who had been brave enough to smash him in the nose and run away when she thought he was a Harvestor, seemed crushed under the weight of her memory loss. Despite his resolve to keep his distance, Nicoli crossed the small space separating them and gently grabbed her upper arms with his hands, squeezing until her eyes focused on his face. "It'll be okay," he said, offering her what he hoped was a reassuring smile. "It's probably just temporary. The effects of the collar, the whole experience. That kind of thing."

Frightened eyes gazed into his, but the panicked look faded. "Okay." She slowly returned his smile and if her eyes seemed a bit teary, it was easily overlooked. She didn't cry and she didn't fall apart. Remembering his own initial reaction upon first awakening, which had been unsettling, to say the least, Nicoli gave her credit. She was tough for a woman.

When he was sure she was under control, he released her arms and walked back to the prone body of the Harvestor. After a moment's thought, he bent over and grabbed the man's ankles.

"Wait here," he ordered as he dragged the body into the back room. He knew he couldn't leave the second man alive to report their presence, but he didn't want to subject the woman to anymore ugliness than she'd already seen. With a small niggling doubt as to his own humanity, he broke the Harvestor's neck and left the two bodies in the far corner of the room where they would not be easily spotted. He removed the robes and boots of both men. The taller man's boots fit Nicoli, so he put them on. He couldn't afford to draw any more attention by walking around barefoot. He carried the shorter man's boots and the robes into the outer room.

"Try these on." He held the smaller boots out to her and saw the disgust in her eyes. "Look, we don't have many choices right now. If these fit, you need to wear them. It will draw less attention."

Reluctantly, she held out her hand to accept the boots. When she had them on, she stood there like a child waiting for her parent to determine whether or not they fit. Heaving a great sigh, Nicoli bent over to feel for her toe through the end of the shoes.

"They're a little big, but not bad." He held up each of the extra robes. The one belonging to the first Harvestor was longer, so Nicoli peeled off the robe he wore. At the sound of a gasp, Nicoli looked to see what had distressed the woman and found her staring open-mouthed and wide-eyed at him. He'd forgotten he was nude beneath the robe. He felt her eyes rake over his body. His inner devil made him turn to face her, giving her a better view as he took his time putting on the other robe.

"Finished?" he asked, just before pulling the robe into place.

Her mouth snapped shut as she brought her eyes up to meet his. Then that familiar blush stole over her face and she muttered something that sounded like "sorry" and turned around.

Amused, Nicoli dug the transfer disc and tube out of the pockets of his freshly discarded robe and put them into the one he now wore. Holding up the two remaining robes to the woman, he handed her the one that was the better fit, which turned out to be the one he'd just taken off. "Put this on."

While she complied, Nicoli went to the door and opened it just enough to stick his head out into the hallway. It was empty.

"Ready?" He waited for her nod. "Okay, pull the hood over your face, like this." He demonstrated with his own robe. "Now, let's go." With Nicoli taking the lead, they stepped out, closing the door behind them. At the end of the hall, Nicoli located the lift and they took it up one flight.

The doors opened onto another long hallway at the end of which stood a large door. Nicoli supposed this was the way he'd been brought into the building. Without getting out, Nicoli let the doors of the lift shut and he punched the button to take them up one more flight.

This time when the doors opened, they were looking into a grand foyer filled with robed Harvestors. Some stood around talking while others merely walked across the foyer on their way to other destinations. Nicoli grabbed the woman's arm and escorted her off. No one paid them any attention.

"Now what?" The woman whispered.

Nicoli looked around. From this perspective, the building seemed to be shaped like a wagon wheel with this room as the central hub and hallways radiating off of it like spokes. Before he left, Nicoli was determined to explore every last passageway. "Let's see what's down here."

He walked over to the nearest spoke of the wheel and turned down the corridor. It seemed heavily populated, but no one stopped them. Nicoli found the lack of security odd. At the airfield and the marketplace, there had been at least an effort at security made. Why not here? Were the Harvestors that sure of themselves they feared no outside threat?

It was their loss, Nicoli thought. Their oversight just made his job easier.

They reached the end of the hall without anyone stopping them and stepped through the door at the end.

"Wow," the woman exclaimed, echoing Nicoli's exact thought. Stretching out to the sides and in front of them for what seemed like kilometers were rows upon rows of plants. A different variety, some bearing fruits, others vegetables, grew in each row.

"How tall do you suppose they are?"

"Easily three or four meters." He stepped up to the closest

row to get a better look. "They're not planted in dirt. I don't know what this is, but they seem to be thriving."

"What are they for?"

"Food, I would imagine. I don't remember any mention of plants growing outside. I'm not sure the planet can sustain plant life anymore. I guess this is how they survive."

The woman looked around, then turned back to Nicoli. "We seem to be the only ones here."

Nicoli started to explore the area. After a few moments, he became aware of a light hissing noise. He stepped out onto the main path and found the source.

In a section midway down the room, it was raining. Turning his attention to the ceiling, Nicoli spotted pipes running length-wise. The rain was coming from these. Letting his eyes travel along the pipes, he followed their path to their point of origin above the door through which he and the woman had entered. Next to the pipes was a small box with a series of red and green lights. As Nicoli studied the box, the green lights turned to red and the rain stopped. A second later, a few of the red lights turned green and elsewhere in the room, the rain started.

"Computer-operated," Nicoli remarked. "These people seem very dependent on their computer system."

"So? Most societies are."

"Exactly," Nicoli said patiently. "Let's go."

"Where?"

"To find a computer."

Two hours later, Nicoli found his mind drifting to images of his companion as she'd been when he first found her. It was very distracting, and certainly the last thing he needed at this juncture in the mission.

"Well?"

Nicoli ignored the question and forced his mind back to the problem at hand—breaking into the computer in front of him. Their wanderings had brought them to what appeared to be the medical wing of the building. Several of the doors on this hallway led into waiting rooms, which in turn had doors leading into back rooms filled with examination tables, lab equipment, and most importantly, computers.

They had been able to look through several of these rooms because this medical wing of the processing building was sparsely populated. It bothered Nicoli that he'd run into so few Harvestors. He doubted that the two men he'd killed had been found because he'd heard no alarms. How had these people survived this long being so careless?

It was the flip side to that question that worried Nicoli the most. The Harvestors couldn't have survived being this careless, which meant that his time for remaining undiscovered was running out.

"Well?" the woman repeated, clearly becoming impatient with her task of watching the door for unwanted guests.

"What?" he growled, trying not to look at her.

"Aren't you finished? I could've downloaded the entire USP Intergalactic Trade Agreement by now."

He cursed her under his breath as he keyed in code, hoping to find a programming language the computer understood. "How do you know about the IGTA?"

There was silence as she thought about it. "I don't know," she finally said. "Suddenly it was just there. Do you think I'll remember more?"

"Probably. Go back to the door," he bit out when he heard her footsteps coming up behind him.

"Are you kidding me?" She sounded exasperated. "Aren't you in yet?"

"No." He had to grit his teeth to keep from swearing. "It may interest you to know that it's not as easy as it looks."

"Are you sure you know what you're doing?"

He turned to gape at her. "Perhaps you'd like to take a stab at it?"

She glared at him and then reached over to slam her fist against the keyboard.

"What are you doing?" He grabbed her hand before she could do any more damage.

"It can't be any worse than that gibberish you're keying in."

"Key in the wrong command and we could have a legion of Harvestors coming for us."

"Not likely," she said. "We haven't seen a single guard in all the time we've been walking around. No one cares that we're here. Except maybe those guys you killed downstairs."

The woman was maddening. Nicoli let out an exasperated sigh. "Look Baby Girl, if you like lying around naked, waiting to be someone's sex toy, I'll be happy to accommodate you back at my ship. But not here. Right now I want you to stop messing with things you don't know anything about and go stand by the door."

She stared at him, open mouthed, for a moment. Then snapped it shut. "Did you just call me *Baby Girl*?"

"Go stand by the door."

"Did you?"

"Go stand by the door or I'll take you over my knee and bust your butt."

"You wouldn't."

He cocked an eyebrow as he stood up.

"Okay, okay." She held up her hand. "I'm going."

He waited until she resumed her post by the door before sitting back down. Feeling more than a little irritated, he ignored her and tried a new programming language. One way or another, he would hack into this system.

Baby Girl. He'd called her Baby Girl!

She spared him a glance before turning back to the door. The man was rude, domineering, irritating and obnoxious. Unbidden came the memory of his gentle look and soothing words when she discovered her memory loss. She thought back to how he'd dealt with the Harvestors, with cold military precision. And his single-minded pursuit of his mission.

And she remembered her initial fear when she'd awakened in the Harvestors' donor room. It was a miracle she was alive and she'd like to continue that miracle by remaining so. This man who called himself Nicoli was the kind of man who could go into a nest of East-Nasta vipers and walk away unscathed.

She was safe with him and if staying with him meant enduring a few insulting names, so be it.

For long moments, she stood glancing out the door, trying to be good. After awhile, though, curiosity got the better of her.

"How's it going?"

"I've accessed their global web, such as it is, and I've keyed in a program that will run all their data through a link I established with a remote site. My ship's computer will intercept the data as it transfers across and analyze it for the best method for destroying them."

"How long will it take?"

"I don't know. Depends on how much data there is and how fast their system can run the data across the link. This doesn't appear to be state-of-the-art equipment."

After a moment, she heard him stand up and start to walk around. "How's everything in the outer room look?"

"All's quiet." She turned her attention back to her small view of the waiting room through the crack in the door. It was boring, standing there, watching an empty room, and she must have closed her eyes and dozed off, because suddenly a noise jarred her awake. Opening her eyes, she saw a robed figure walking through the hallway door into the outer waiting room.

Clearing her throat, she tried to get Nicoli's attention. Just as he looked over at her, she heard the robed figure from the waiting room call out.

"Hello? Brother Nathzur? Are you back there?"

She threw a questioning look toward Nicoli and as one they turned to watch the data spilling across the computer's screen. They couldn't afford to get caught. Maybe she could stall the visitor long enough for the computer to finish. Or at least long enough for Nicoli to think of a plan.

Before she could talk herself out of it, she pulled the hood low over her face and walked out into the room.

"Ah, there you are," the male voice said the minute he spotted her. He strolled over to her and gave a gentle tug on her robe. "Please tell me you're wearing this because you find it comfortable and not because you've decided to stay behind." He chuckled when he said it.

Unsure what to say or do, she remained silent. The newcomer misunderstood her silence.

"Relax, my old friend. I want you to come with me, in whatever capacity you choose." He sighed. "It's so exciting. A new beginning—a new life. I can hardly wait." He glanced behind her, causing her to turn to follow his gaze. A screen displaying numbers hung on the wall and as she watched the numbers moved backwards.

"Time is running out," the man said. "We must hurry before it is too late. Is everything ready?" He started for the back room and she had to rush past him to block his way.

"What is it?" he asked at the door. As she struggled for the right thing to say, he pushed past her and into the back room.

She hurried after him, expecting all hell to break loose, and stopped short, staring at the sight before her.

Nicoli lay nude on the examination table in the middle of the room. A cart with some type of instrument sat next to him, flexible tubing and wires coming from the cart and seemingly fixed to various points along his body. He looked like a donor prepared for a procedure. In the corner, data continued to spiral across the computer screen. The newcomer went to stand by Nicoli.

"Nathzur." His voice held a note of awe. "He is spectacular."

She was grateful he didn't seem to expect an answer. Almost without thinking about it, she moved closer to Nicoli. Whether it was to protect him or be protected, she wasn't sure.

"He's magnificent," the Harvestor continued. He placed a finger at the top of one shoulder and trailed it down along Nicoli's arm. When he ran out of arm, he moved to the hip, continuing down a leg. Yes, she thought as she followed his finger's path with her eyes, Nicoli was truly magnificent. The man stopped mid-calf, turning toward her. Though she couldn't see his face, she felt his gaze.

"Is he for me? Or you? And don't lie. I can tell when you're lying." Before she could anticipate his move, he took a step closer and pulled off her hood.

He gasped and fell back a step. From the corner of her eye, she saw Nicoli's hands clench into fists.

"It's okay," she said, hoping Nicoli would realize the words were to reassure him.

"Okay? Nazthur, by Ha'lah, I'd say your new body is better than okay." The man pulled the hood from his face, revealing the scarred, patchwork complexion she'd seen on the other two Harvestors. He seemed oblivious to her staring as he walked around her, looking at her from all angles. "You are lovely. I'm sorry if I seem surprised. I never thought that you . . . that is to say, I know some of us had to become female. I just didn't realize that you were interested. You did this voluntarily?"

She nodded, that seeming like the correct thing to do.

"Well, then. If you're happy, I'm happy." He looked back down at Nicoli's body, then back to her. "I'm very happy. Our time at Rebirth should be fruitful, indeed." He clapped his hands together once. "Let's get started."

He walked to the far end of the lab where an empty gurney sat and rolled it to the center of the room, placing it next to Nicoli. "I find I can no longer tolerate being in this useless body that can't even respond properly to the sight of a desirable woman." He waved his arm toward the equipment lying on top of the counters. "Go get what you need. I'll get myself ready."

Tentatively, she walked across the room and made a show of riffling through the various tubes and utensils. She had no idea what equipment she was expected to gather and so looked instead for something that could serve as a weapon, if needed.

"Nathzur? This body doesn't resemble the others. Are you sure he's Coronadian?"

"What?" The familiar sounding name caught her attention, causing her to pause in her search.

"I asked if he was Coronadian? Brother Joh'nan was most specific that we only use the bodies taken from . . ."

"What is going on here?" A new robed figure stood in the doorway. His hood was pushed back and the eyes looking out of the marred face stared accusingly first at the other Harvestor and then at her. "Ibran'n, will you explain to me what you are doing in my lab with this . . . this . . ."

The newcomer walked into the room, coming over to stare at her in much the same way the first man had.

"Nathzur? I thought you . . ." Ibran'n's voice trailed off as he looked from the newcomer to her in confusion. "Who are you?" he demanded.

At that moment, Nicoli jumped off the gurney. Both newcomers looked up at him with horror in their eyes, as if they'd seen the dead rise, which from their perspective, was probably accurate.

Nicoli gave them no time to recover by rushing Ibran'n, the larger of the two men. Nathzur stood frozen in place, staring wide-eyed as Nicoli's fist slammed into Ibran'n's face with the sickening smack of flesh and bone hitting flesh and bone. The man's eyes rolled up into his head while his body slowly collapsed to the floor, unconscious.

The sound of screaming broke the sudden silence. Nazthur stood, mouth open, wailing like a woman. With her only thought to quiet the man before his screams attracted the attention of other unwanted visitors, she rushed forward. When he saw her coming, Nazthur turned to escape out the door into the waiting room.

"Oh no you don't," she muttered, grabbing two fistfuls of the man's robe and hauling him back.

When she turned him around, he cringed, throwing his arms up for protection, a quiet desperation reflected in his eyes as they darted from her face to a point just past her left shoulder.

"Now what?" she asked Nicoli, who'd come up behind her.

"Kill them."

Nazthur's eyes grew round and a sound escaped his mouth just before he sank to the floor in a faint.

She looked down on the unmoving figure. "That was effective. But seriously, now what do we do?"

"Kill them." Nicoli's tone was cold and hard.

"You can't kill them."

"Yes, I can."

"No. It's not right. I won't let you."

He stared at her, his expression daring her to keep talking. "If you're about to launch into a morality lecture, save your breath, Baby Girl. These aliens don't deserve to live."

"Have you no respect for life?"

96

"Of course I do. Just not theirs. They've killed thousands of innocent people; people who were never given a chance to defend themselves. *They* have no respect for life. Let the punishment fit the crime."

"Who are you to mete out justice?"

"Right now? For these men? I'm God."

There was no point in arguing with him. As he took a step toward the fallen man, she grabbed his arm. "I won't let you kill them."

She could almost feel the intensity of his look burning through her hand where it touched his arm. But she refused to take her hand away, even when he turned his gaze to her face. Their eyes met. His hard and cold. Hers just as unyielding, she hoped. For long seconds, they stared, neither looking away, both gauging the other's determination.

When Nicoli would have stepped around her, she moved to block his way.

"I'll fight you if I have to," she warned. In a move too swift for her to match, he grabbed her by the upper arms, lifted her off the floor and set her to one side.

"I don't fight women," he growled.

It was obvious that she could never best him in a test of wills or force, and she felt the fight drain out of her. "Please," she pleaded, not above begging.

He paused to look at her one more time, then swore under his breath. "This is a mistake." He grabbed Nathzur's still-unconscious form and dragged it to the center of the room to lay beside Ibran'n's. "Help me rip these robes into strips, so we can tie them up. I don't want them getting loose."

A few minutes later, she stood looking down at the two unconscious aliens. If either man had awaked as his wrists and ankles were being bound with the cloth strips, he'd given no indication of it. Not that she blamed them. If faced with potential death, she might feign unconsciousness, too. Ibran'n hadn't even fluttered an eyelid when Nicoli, having noticed the similarity of the man's build to his own, stripped the alien of his clothes.

The nude body of the Harvestor revealed that the patchwork

skin grafting was not limited to just the faces. There were other deformities as well—muscle atrophy in places, abnormal swelling elsewhere. There might even have been a skin rash, but she refused to take a closer look. What she saw already turned her stomach and she knew that if she were the one standing naked, she would continue to do so rather than don the clothes from any Harvestor. But Nicoli showed no such qualms. He was all business.

He gagged each man, using the remaining pieces of robe, and then dragged each one inside the closet, safely concealing them behind the closed door.

"All right, Baby Girl," he said, coming to stand behind her. "Go back and watch the door for me and let's hope no one else comes to interrupt us."

The data stopped spiraling across the screen and the results of Nicoli's query stared back at him, leaving him with a renewed sense of frustration. As he'd suspected, the entire planet was linked to a single network of computers and most primary planetary functions were operated by that system. Bringing the entire network crashing down would be as simple as installing the latest Holocaust Virus. That was the good news.

The frustration was that it didn't look like he needed the virus to bring down the Harvestors. In fact, from the history on the screen, this entire mission had been unnecessary; a waste of time. The Harvestors and their planet were dying. And from what he read, they'd been dying for so long now that few were still alive.

It would seem the Harvestors had spent several decades searching for immortality. In thinking that the key lay in fetal development, medical experiments were conducted on pregnant women. Somewhere along the line, something went wrong and the women, along with their unborn children, perished. With each new death of mother and child, the search for immortality grew stronger. But the answer was found too late. There were no female Harvestors left.

For awhile, women stolen from other planets were brought in, but all unions proved sterile and the race continued to die.

At that point, the Harvestors began replacing defective body parts and tissue as needed to keep the remaining male population alive until their self-orchestrated genocide could be stopped. To secure the organ and tissue needed, they stole bodies from other planets. This practice proved costly and the Harvestors turned to strip-mining their planet's tyrillium stores. As the leading energy source, tyrillium sales brought the Harvestors the money and power to secure black-market technology to further their experiments. When the tyrillium deposits ran low, they stole extra bodies and sold the ones they didn't keep for themselves on the black market.

It became a lucrative business, but didn't solve their problem. Time was running out and various campaigns and projects to save their people were begun. Most failed.

Only the one called "Rebirth" seemed to offer any hope. But there the information stopped and nothing else Nicoli read suggested that this last campaign had been any more successful than the others.

Feeling like he'd learned as much as he could, Nicoli set to work at the keyboard. His time spent interfaced with the ship's computer had only enhanced his already advanced programming skills and it wasn't long before he had the program for the Holocaust Virus built and uploaded. Once activated, the virus would quickly spread throughout the entire network, creating powerful electrical surges that would melt the internal circuitry of the entire system. To date, there was no known way to stop the virus. In forty-eight hours, the entire computer system would crash, permanently.

Nicoli keyed the final command to activate the virus and shut down the computer.

"Let's go," he said, turning around to find the woman still diligently watching the door.

She turned and he could see that she was growing tired. Well, it would soon be over.

"Where to now?"

"Now we go to my ship. In forty-eight hours, the entire system is going to crash and I want to be gone before then."

Nicoli led them out of the medical wing, but he had no good

idea where the landing field was relative to the building they were in. His first goal was to get them outside, which proved surprisingly easy. Dressed in the white robes, no one thought to question or stop them.

Their luck held when they took a side exit and found themselves in a type of parking lot. Five hover-shuttles stood waiting.

"Shall we?" Nicoli asked, gesturing to one.

"Do you know how to fly one of these?"

"Of course." He walked over to the first and found it locked. He tried the second and third with equal success. But the fourth shuttle's door opened easily.

They wasted no time climbing aboard. Nicoli took the pilot's seat and looked at the controls.

"Ready?" He turned to make sure she was strapped in beside him. Satisfied, he looked for the key to start the engine and found none. In fact, there was no slot in which to insert a key, even should he find it. So the question was, how did one start the shuttle?

Nicoli searched the entire console, identifying each button or lever he found with a function of the ship, none related to starting the engines. Finally, he had explained all buttons except one. So with a mental shrug, he pushed it.

Immediately, the engines roared to life. But before Nicoli could flip the lever to raise the craft off the ground, it rose by itself. At the same time, Nicoli heard the locks on the outer hatch doors engage.

He and Baby Girl exchanged questioning looks and without having to be asked, Baby Girl crossed to the doors and tried to open them.

"It's no use," she said, coming back to sit next to him. "They won't budge. Now what?"

The shuttle started to move forward at a gradually increasing pace. Nothing Nicoli tried altered the course or speed. They were not hurtling uncontrollably into space. They were not spiraling out of control. Nor did they seem in danger of crashing. What they were was trapped.

Trapped in a moving shuttle taking them to an unknown destination. And there was nothing they could do but wait and see what happened.

Chapter Ten

"Welcome. My name is Juh'ren and I'll be your Acclimation Guide." The young man standing outside the newly landed shuttle smiled and, with a wave of his hand, gestured for them to step out. Nicoli remained in the pilot's seat, studying the man through the side viewport. The man looked to be in his early twenties, with a clear, smooth complexion he'd yet to see on any Harvestor. Beneath the sun's rays, the man's blond hair shone like a halo about his head and his sparsely clothed body boasted excellent health and a superior physique. Nicoli glanced at the woman next to him in the copilot's seat, noting the marked resemblance between her and the man outside the shuttle and a horrifying suspicion started to take root.

For the past two hours, he and the woman had tried everything they could think of to regain control of the shuttle, but to no avail. It had flown along its preset course away from the city proper, across vast stretches of barren ground, until finally reaching this remote encampment. Helplessly, they waited while the shuttle approached the small airfield and landed. The engines had died and the hatch door-locks had been released.

As Nicoli had sat contemplating what to do, three men began walking toward them across the landing field.

Nicoli had braced himself for a hostile reception. The warm greeting they received instead caught him off guard.

"Please feel safe, Brothers," Juh'ren shouted, opening the hatch so he could step into the shuttle. He looked first at Nicoli and then turned to the woman, letting his gaze linger. "Very nice," he commented. "Brothers Ibran'n and Nathzur, I presume? We expected you tomorrow morning, but I can understand why you came earlier." The young man made no effort to hide his visual inspection of them, making it clear he approved of what he saw. "I assume you'll wish to be partners, but should you have a change of mind," he looked pointedly at the woman, "please don't hesitate to ask for me. I assure you, I may look young, but I get the job done—to everyone's mutual satisfaction." He walked back toward the shuttle hatch. "Now, if you'll come with me?" He stepped out and turned, clearly expecting them to follow.

Nicoli exchanged glances with his travel companion. He could tell she wasn't comfortable with the idea of leaving the shuttle. But resisting the invitation would alarm their host, and Nicoli saw this as an opportunity to learn more. If his suspicion was correct, then introducing that virus into the computer system hadn't been an exercise in overkill.

Nicoli held out his hand and waited until the woman placed her hand in his. "Shall we?" He led her off the shuttle, stopping just outside the hatch so he could scan the area. Not far from where they stood, the edge of a small village was visible. Still holding the woman's hand, Nicoli pulled her in the direction of their host, who was already several meters ahead of them.

"Who you were is no longer important," Juh'ren said once they'd caught up to him. "We ask that you not discuss your former identities while you're here. You'll be given an identification band." He held up his arm to show them the small metal circle around his wrist. "Later, you will be asked to select a new name. This is a fresh start for all of us." He smiled over his shoulder, then continued on.

They stopped at the first small building where another young man waited for them. He had the same blond hair and pure complexion as their guide and greeted them with an equally warm smile as he handed Juh'ren two bracelets.

"These are your identification bands." Juh'ren passed one to each of them and showed them how to put them on. "Please wear them at all times during your stay. We have tried to emulate the primitive environment of our new home, but it is necessary to retain some of our technology for security and tracking purposes. With these bands, you should have no trouble gaining access to all areas of the village. Should you lose your band, come back to this gate and get another.

"Now, if you'll follow me, I'll give you a quick tour before we head to the main hall for dinner. We have a special treat tonight. Brother Joh'nan will give us an update on our new homeworld. Very exciting."

Nicoli looked around, bits and pieces of what he'd learned from the computer falling into place with snatches of Juh'ren's comments. This was Rebirth. The last big endeavor the Harvestors had made to save their race. It wasn't coincidence that the villagers looked so much like the donors in the room where he'd found the woman. Yanur may have discovered how to separate a person's life essence from his body and put it back again. But the Harvestors had done him one better: They'd figured out how to put the life essence back into a different body. The villagers were donor bodies repossessed with Harvestors' life essences!

Distracted by the realization, Nicoli mechanically followed Juh'ren as they toured the small settlement. Around the perimeter of the encampment sat twelve small houses, three each on the four sides of the square. In the very center, separated by a wide, packed-dirt walkway, was a larger structure which Juh'ren identified as the main meeting and banquet hall. As a whole, Nicoli found the simple stone construction of the buildings at odds with the scattering of modern technology, like the space shuttles, security bands and lighting towers placed at the four corners of the village square.

Before he could give it further thought, they turned a corner and saw several groups of men and women up ahead.

"What are they doing?" he asked, overcome with curiosity.

"Everyone must learn his or her role in the new society. For instance, the men in this group are learning to fight." Juh'ren pointed to the first cluster of tall, well-muscled men. They were divided into two opposing teams, with each man wielding a type of three-bladed sword. Nicoli had never seen anything like it. "What type of weapon is that?"

"Warring blade." Baby Girl spoke before Juh'ren could respond.

"I see you've been familiarizing yourself with the new ways. Very commendable." Juh'ren nodded approvingly.

Nicoli turned to her, curious. "You've seen one of those before?" He spoke softly, not wanting their guide to hear.

"Yes." But she sounded bewildered. "I can't remember where, or when. In fact," she leaned closer to him so they wouldn't be overheard, "this whole place looks familiar to me. It makes me uncomfortable because I feel like I should remember, but I can't."

"It'll come. Don't try to push it."

Juh'ren led them past a second group of men. They weren't as muscular or tall as the men in the first group, and instead of swords, they carried shovels and hoes. Though there were no crops to tend, the men worked the dirt, digging and turning it. Farther down the path, a group of women dunked something into a fabricated, in-ground water source. Other women stood nearby, arms wrapped around small bundles.

"What are those women doing?" Baby Girl asked.

"Some of them are learning to wash clothes in creeks, while the others are holding babies. Not real ones, of course, they're simulated. No one has successfully given birth yet, but we keep trying." Juh'ren smiled. "As a woman, you will be trained to the best of our knowledge in the proper methods of running a home and rearing children."

"And what are they doing?" Nicoli pointed to a group where the men were yelling at the women, who stood by silently, heads bowed.

Juh'ren's face lost its smile. "That is the more unfortunate part of our program. Those are our latest recruits and they are undergoing initial acclimation training. It is difficult to understand a culture where men are in charge and women must obey unconditionally. While such an environment is hard on all of us, it is especially difficult for those citizens who have chosen to go to the New World as females. If recruits cannot learn to accept their new roles, they run the risk of endangering the entire program. So we must make sure they accept these cultural norms by subjecting them to hours of submissive-endurance training." He shook his head. "It is not a pleasant experience, but necessary."

He walked off, evidently expecting Nicoli and Baby Girl to follow.

"Here is another group of new arrivals."

Nicoli looked over at the men and women picking up dirt. "What, exactly, are they doing?"

"Why, they are learning to tolerate dirt." Juh'ren held up his hand to stall some anticipated protest. "I know it seems unpleasant, but once again, what we are doing is for a good cause. It is worth the few sacrifices we must make." They finished their tour just as the sun started to set.

At the sound of a loud gong, men and women around the village stopped what they were doing and started making their way toward the main building. Nicoli and Baby Girl followed Juh'ren, joining the throng.

As a group, they entered the building and proceeded down a long hallway, which ended in a large, open room. Standing in the middle of the room was a large banquet table capable of seating thirty.

The table already had been set and at Juh'ren's gesture, Nicoli and Baby Girl took seats near the end of one long side. Whether by design or accident, the group ended up sitting in an alternating male-female order. Nicoli counted fifteen couples in all.

At one end of the banquet hall was a large vid-screen, looking out of place among the rustic furnishings.

With Baby Girl sitting on his right, Nicoli turned to glance at the woman on his left. She favored him with a warm smile while her gaze openly roamed over his body. Taken aback by her forwardness, he glanced at Baby Girl, who had witnessed the whole thing.

"I guess the submissive attitude doesn't extend to dinnertime," she muttered.

Servants carrying large platters of food appeared through doors behind the vid-screen and Nicoli heard Baby Girl's stomach growl.

"Hungry?"

"Yes. I can't remember the last time I ate." She gave him a quick wink to let him know the play on words had been intentional.

The aroma of roasted meat and steamed vegetables wafted to him as the servants placed platters of food in front of everyone.

"I wonder where they got the meat?" Nicoli muttered.

Baby Girl's fork stopped midway to her mouth as she looked over at him. "What do you mean?"

"Have you seen any animals anywhere?"

She lowered her fork to her plate, and a look of shocked disbelief stole over her face. "You don't think these are," she leaned closer to him so she could whisper, "donors, do you?"

He didn't want to tell her that was exactly what he'd wondered. Just then, Brother Juh'ren stopped by, leaning down between them to talk. "How are you doing? I hope you're hungry because where we're going, they always serve the best cuisine." He waved his hand to take in the platters of food all around. "This was all flown in from our new home, just so you could get used to the taste. I realize you've never eaten meat before, but I think you'll discover it's not that unpleasant." He patted Nicoli on the back with one hand while letting the other rest a little too familiarly on Baby Girl's shoulder. "Enjoy yourselves." Then he walked away.

Nicoli and Baby Girl exchanged glances. "What do you think?" She looked from him back down to the piece of meat still impaled on her fork.

Nicoli glanced around at the other diners. They were all eating without reservation. "I don't know." He pierced a slice of meat on his plate and held it up. "I'll go first. That way if something happens, it'll happen to me."

She shook her head. "And get left here alone? No, I don't think so." Before he could stop her, she'd put the meat into her mouth and started to chew. "Ummm. This is good. You should try it." She smiled. Turning her attention back to her plate, she took another bite. Mesmerized, Nicoli watched her lips wrap around the meat and pull it from the fork. His throat suddenly dry, he picked up his glass and took a swallow of a pleasantly sweet liquid. Setting his glass back down, he looked across the table.

He let his mind wander as he studied the guests. He needed to know more about what the Rebirth project involved. And he needed to find a way to get back to the shuttle. Time was running out.

Picking up another bit of food, he put it in his mouth. That was when he felt the woman seated across from him watching him. When she saw she had his attention, she ran her tongue across her lips, then gave him a small smile. Surprised, Nicoli turned to see if Baby Girl had noticed, but she was deep in conversation with the man sitting beside her. From the sound of it, they were having a good time and Nicoli found that disturbing.

Then the lights dimmed and the large vid-screen blinked on. Images of green pastures and small villages resembling the encampment flashed across the screen as a voice began to speak.

"Brothers and sisters. Welcome to Rebirth. It has long been my dream to find the means by which our people can once again return to a normal life; a life where we can shed our robes and raise our faces to the sun. A life where women and children are not yesterday's memory. A life where our race will flourish and our people prosper."

The speaker paused and everyone around the table broke out in wild cheers and applause. No one noticed that Nicoli and Baby Girl were late to join in. After the noise subsided, the speaker continued.

"My family, the time for the final phase of our project is at hand. You represent the last group to cross over. Sadly, we must leave the others behind. Let us observe a moment of silence to honor their sacrifice."

Instantly, the mood in the room sobered and heads bowed. Then the voice continued. "When you have finished your period of acclimation, you will be brought to Coronado to join the others. As you know, I have secured a place of importance in the House of Scyphor. Soon the position of high counsel will be mine. Then we can begin our domination of the planet. Rest assured, everything is going according to my plan."

The speaker's voice faded into silence. Brother Juh'ren stood and walked to the front of the room. "Thank you Brother Joh'nan." He smiled at the group. "I hope everyone is enjoying their meal. When you feel ready, please continue on to the next phase of your assimilation. As usual, should you have any questions or problems, simply alert one of the servers and an instructor will be brought in to help. Private chambers are available down the hall." Juh'ren glanced quickly off to the side, to someone hidden behind the vid-screen. "It would seem we are ready to serve the second course, so I won't keep you any longer. Please enjoy."

Brother Juh'ren returned to his seat at the table. The lights remained dimmed while the image of green pastures on the screen dissolved into an abstract display of moving colors. From somewhere, soft music filtered into the room.

What had Juh'ren meant by the next phase of assimilation? Nicoli wondered, reaching for his glass. Strange, although he was certain he'd taken several drinks, his glass remained full. Across the table, he noticed several servers slipping in unobtrusively to refill glasses. As the first tendrils of numbness settled over his thoughts, he realized that he had no idea how much he'd actually had to drink.

Once again, he felt the weight of someone's stare on him and his gaze met that of the woman across from him. Odd how he hadn't noticed before how attractive she was. In fact, he thought, looking around the table, all of the women present were very attractive. Even knowing they were female donors repossessed by male Harvestors didn't detract from their looks.

Next to him, Baby Girl raised her glass to take a drink. The movement drew his gaze and he turned to watch as the sweet wine touched her lips, leaving them shiny and slick. His gaze traveled to the slender column of her throat as it pulsed with each swallow. Perhaps sensing his perusal, she turned to him as she set the glass down. She smiled back with lips glistening from the wine that still clung to them. When her tongue darted out to capture a lingering drop, he felt his body respond.

"I thought this would be horrible, you know? But it's not so bad."

Her husky voice drew his attention back to her face, which seemed flushed. His eyes followed the path of color as it swept down past her collar to disappear beneath the robe. Suddenly, images of her nude body sprang into his mind.

"I'm glad you're here with me," she whispered, thankfully unaware of his thoughts. She placed her hand on his arm, a seemingly innocent gesture that ignited his flesh where they touched. His whole body tightened with awareness as he realized how much he wanted her. The intensity of his feeling was unsettling. He grabbed his goblet and drained the contents to ease his suddenly dry throat.

Setting the glass back on the table, he looked around for anything to distract him from his thoughts and the woman inspiring them.

The couple across the table sat with their heads bent close together and it was a moment before Nicoli realized they weren't talking, but kissing. As he watched, the man trailed the back of his hand gently up along the woman's arm until his fingers grazed the side of her breast. Rather than be outraged, the woman leaned into his touch, and even from where he sat, Nicoli saw her nipples stiffen beneath the thin fabric of her blouse.

Nicoli found he could barely force himself to look away. With confusion growing in direct proportion to other parts of his anatomy, he glanced around for anything to distract him, this time focusing on the vid-screen. What had once been an abstract light show of shifting colors had evolved into a voyeuristic display of couples engaged in various sexual acts. No one else seemed to notice or care.

Down at the far end of the table, just in front of the vid-screen, a woman sat in a man's lap, facing him, her legs straddling his. Nicoli's discomfort grew worse. The warning bells in his head filtered past the effects of the wine, ringing so loudly that he almost jumped when someone's hand slid across his thigh to stroke the inside of his leg. Turning, he tried to ignore the momentary disappointment that the hand did not belong to Baby Girl.

"Shall we go to a room?" The woman sitting to his left leaned into him so her breasts pressed against his arm. At his hesitation, she rushed to reassure him. "Don't worry if it's your first time. I've done this before. I'll make sure you enjoy yourself."

"Take your hand off him now, before I remove it from your body." Baby Girl's hostile tone sliced through the air. The other woman, accurately sensing danger, backed down with a little laugh.

"That's okay, Handsome. You go with her tonight. But when you need a real woman, call me." She turned her attention to the man on her other side, leaving Nicoli and Baby Girl alone. Suddenly, his little tigress looked shy, blushing as she looked down.

"I'm sorry," she stammered. "I don't know what got into me."

Nicoli placed his finger under her chin, gently lifting it so she once again looked at him instead of the tablecloth. "It's okay."

"If you're interested in her . . ."

"I'm not." He leaned toward her, wanting to see in her eyes that she understood he was not upset. But when he would have stopped, his body just kept moving.

He pressed his lips to hers, completely unprepared for the flames of hunger that sprang suddenly to life. The contact of their lips became his only anchor, his lifeline. If he let go, he'd drown in the whirlpool of desire that engulfed him. Never had he reacted this way to a woman.

So why now? The question nibbled at him, demanding attention.

With a supreme effort, he pulled away, almost to resume the kiss when he saw Baby Girl's eyes flutter open and look at him with the same raw hunger that he felt sure was reflected in his own eyes.

A clatter of dishes dragged his attention away. Just down the table, plates, glasses and food had been hastily knocked to the floor to clear an area on top of the table for the naked couple now lying there, mimicking the actions on the vid-screen.

Nicoli had to talk to Juh'ren. Now. He got up from the table, looking for the guide and spotted him at the far end, a woman sitting in his lap. "Stay here," he told Baby Girl. About to walk off, his gaze fell to the unattached man sitting on her other side, who seemed to be showing a marked interest in her. "Never mind." He took her by the hand and helped her to her feet. "Come with me." They caught up with Juh'ren just as he stood to leave.

"Juh'ren," Nicoli bit out, catching the man by the arm, swinging him around to face them. "What's going on around here? Why is everyone acting this way?"

Juh'ren looked at him with glazed eyes that took a moment to focus. "It's the next phase," he said, as if that were explanation enough.

"Next phase? What exactly is the next phase?"

"Procreation, of course. I thought you understood. How can our race flourish if we don't procreate?"

Realization dawned. "There's something in the food."

Juh'ren looked at him incredulously. "Well, of course. You didn't think after decades of no women and not making love that you would suddenly feel the urge and remember how? But don't worry, the servers were very careful to limit the amount served to the men. After all, it wouldn't do for you to find your release before she does, now would it? Not only would that be rude, but it might be harmful to your partner."

"Harmful? In what way?"

Juh'ren leaned closer so his words would not be overheard by either Baby Girl or the woman whose hand he held. "Considering our women have been men their whole lives, even in these fine host bodies, there's going to be some initial resistance. So the women receive an extra dose of Pheromone No. 14. It will ensure you the proper . . . how should I put it? Reception?"

"Are you crazy? People have died from too much Pheromone No. 14."

Juh'ren shook his head and gave a small laugh. "I keep forgetting you're new. The oxytocins released during climax will more than counteract the harmful effects of the Pheromone No. 14. So all you have to do is make sure your partner climaxes before you do." Juh'ren patted Nicoli's shoulder. "Don't worry. We have safeguards. If you are not able to give your partner the release she needs, then we have counselors who will step in and finish for you. This process is safe and I assure you, in the state she's in," he pointed to Baby Girl, who appeared to be quite uncomfortable now, shifting from one foot to the other, "she won't care who brings her to release."

Nicoli was furious. He didn't know if he was more upset that the food had been laced, or by the suggestion that another man touch Baby Girl.

Then she clutched his arm. "I don't feel right," she said softly. She didn't complain; it was more a statement of fact. But he could see the misery, and frustration, in her eyes.

"Is there a place where we can go?" he asked Juh'ren.

"Of course. Private chambers have been prepared down the hall. Take any of the open rooms."

Nicoli led Baby Girl from the banquet room and proceeded down the long hallway. Determined that they not stay any longer than necessary, Nicoli led them past the open rooms, to the end of the hallway, hoping to find an exit from the building. His plan was to walk out and go directly to the shuttle. There had to be a way to override the preset commands. If he could, then he could fly the shuttle directly to the airfield where his ship waited.

Finding the exit locked was only a temporary deterrent, but before he could deactivate the lock, Baby Girl grabbed her lower abdomen, bent over and groaned. Every second, she seemed to be growing worse and if he didn't do something about it soon, she could die.

Giving up on the exit, Nicoli led them into the nearest open room and shut the door.

The room was small, with a bed as the central feature. A small sunken tub sat in one corner and a stand holding drinks stood in the other. The wall opposite the door had a window, with curtains pulled to hide the outside. Baby Girl tore the robe off and headed straight for the bed while Nicoli took up pacing, like a caged animal. Chivalry and honor warred with circumstance and his own discomfort. A small, pain-filled moan brought his attention back to Baby Girl, now stretched out on the bed.

"How do you feel?" He almost laughed at the idiocy of his own question. It was obvious from watching her restless movements that she was in pain. His own discomfort nagged at him, making him feel edgy. Hers must be ten times worse.

Not answering him, she squirmed, tossing her head back and forth, pressing her thighs together, trying to alleviate the growing pressure.

He couldn't allow it to continue.

He strode over to her, telling himself that he was doing this for her benefit, not his. That he would not take advantage of the situation; that he was performing a service and nothing more.

Sitting on the edge of the bed, he laid a hand gently on her arm. She cried out as if burned by his touch, but did not pull away.

"Am I dying?" she asked in a voice almost too quiet to hear.

"Not if I can help it."

She closed her eyes for a moment before opening them again to seek out his face. "It's getting worse." Looking almost as if she were afraid to ask, she whispered. "Would you hold me? Please." Unable to refuse, he leaned forward to gather her in his arms, but she shook her head. "No, lie down with me."

He hesitated for the briefest moment. It wasn't that he was reluctant to comply, but rather the opposite. He found suddenly that he wanted to lie close to her, feel her body pressed against his. It was the sudden intensity of that desire that caused him to hesitate. He was afraid that if he were to lie next to her, it wouldn't be enough. He'd want more.

He tried to think of this woman as someone's wife or mother. He would do what needed to be done to ensure her survival, but he would not take advantage of her. It was a matter of honor.

He positioned himself beside her, gathering her into his arms.

With her head resting on his shoulder, her warm breath brushed against his lower neck and chest. Then he felt the moisture of her tongue as it darted out to taste his skin, and a shudder ran down his body.

With a small groan, he tipped her face up to his so he could capture her lips with his own. His noblest intention for a chaste kiss vanished in the naïve willingness of her response. He hadn't noticed earlier at the table when he'd kissed her, but this was no experienced wife and mother kissing him back. This was the kiss of the uninitiated.

"Open for me, Baby Girl." He ran his tongue along her lips, coaxing them open. When her lips parted at his insistent probing, he rushed to take advantage, slipping his tongue inside to seek and caress hers. Pushing her onto her back, he rolled on top of her. With one arm still beneath her neck, he laid his free hand gently against her cheek to keep her head in place as he drank his fill from her mouth.

Stroking her cheek, he let his hand slide down along her body until he found the hem of her shirt. Slipping his fingers beneath the cloth, he felt the warmth of her skin. She shivered at his touch, but didn't pull away. He let his hand travel upward until he reached the gentle swell of her breast. Cupping the lush mound in his palm, he rubbed his thumb across the nipple, teasing it into a tight pebble.

A groan escaped from her throat as she arched toward him, hands clutching at his arms and shoulders.

Suddenly, the layer of clothing between them was too much. Nicoli rid them of the unwanted garments, and did so with just enough presence of mind to not rip them in the process.

Though he'd seen her naked before, he was not prepared for how the sight of her now would effect him. She was perfection. Even the scars on her body did not detract from her beauty.

Absorbed in his thoughts, he was surprised when he felt her fingers trailing across his chest to run hesitantly through the mat of hair. As he held his breath, she lifted her head to place light kisses along his pectoral line. When he could take no more, he eased her back and trailed warm kisses down the column of her throat until the path brought him to the tip of her breast.

There, he took a taut nipple into his mouth to suckle.

Beneath him, Baby Girl arched her back, offering herself to him. Her skin was unnaturally warm to the touch and Nicoli knew that he must bring her to release soon or it would be too late. He only hoped he had the strength and willpower to do what must be done without seeking his own release. Honor had never come at such a cost.

Running a hand down the length of her body, he found the apex between her legs. Already moist from passion, his finger slipped easily between the folds of her cleft. Taking her natural dew upon his finger, he massaged the opening until her sharp gasp told him he'd found her most sensitive place. He ran his finger back and forth, wanting to stoke the fires of her passion. When he felt her pressing against his hand in anticipation, he knew she was ready. Before he abandoned his resolve, he inserted his finger into her and thrust.

She called out his name and he slowly withdrew, only to slide his finger into her again. Over and over, he repeated the motion until her nails bit into his back. When her release finally came upon her, he covered her mouth with his to swallow her cries. Then he gathered her close until her shudders subsided and she lay peacefully within the circle of his arms.

Soon he heard the steady rhythm of her breathing as the increased levels of oxytocin counteracted the deadly effects of the Pheromone No. 14 and she fell into a deep sleep.

Nicoli made no effort to leave her side. He was glad he had not compromised her, but knew his current level of sexual frustration was perhaps the worst he'd ever felt. It was going to be a long, long night and he had little hope, himself, for sleep. But despite all of that, he discovered that he was content where he was.

The dawn of the new day brought with it many things. It brought a gentle light that slipped into the room past the drawn curtains to tease awake the couple lying in the bed. It brought a reminder of their purpose and the need to be gone from the encampment as quickly as they could discover how.

And it brought the full return of Angel's memory.

Chapter Eleven

Angel didn't just remember her name. She remembered everything. She knew she was an intergalactic courier for illegal goods and on the run again. She remembered fleeing Earth during the terrorist attack by stealing a ship when hers was blown up. She remembered Yanur and the computer that later turned out to be a man. She remembered the trip to the Harvestors' planet and the fight with Free Rebels along the way. She remembered tracking down Romanof's body, starting the transfer process, being interrupted and posing as a donor. And the feeling of total helplessness as the collar, placed around her throat, rendered her paralyzed and then unconscious.

As the previously disconnected pieces of her past fell into proper sequence, the events after waking in the donor room took on a distant quality. Romanof, calling himself Nicoli, had rescued her. They had tried to escape back to the ship, only to end up trapped on the shuttle destined for Rebirth. She remembered the tour, followed by the meal in the banquet hall. The food had been delicious, but the events following the meal were fuzzy.

Concentrating on the night before, she remembered a feeling of fear and urgency meshed with an unbearable sexual frustration. Images slowly appeared in her mind of Nicoli, naked, kissing her; of Nicoli's mouth and hands doing things she could hardly imagine, much less recall.

A part of her remembered that her life had been in danger. Nicoli hadn't told her, but she'd heard Brother Juh'ren talking. So what Nicoli had done, he'd done to save her life. But more than that, he'd introduced her to a part of living she'd not previously known. He'd shown her an intimacy between two people she wouldn't have thought possible and aroused a passion, and a curiosity, she didn't know she possessed. A blush stole over her at the remembrance of her own behavior; her uncontrolled reaction to everything he'd done to her body.

Behind her, she felt the warmth of Romanof's body pressed against hers, her head resting just below his chin, his arms wrapped about her. His hand lightly cupped her breast, so she dared not move, or even breathe.

She was already confused, and discovering her identity only added another layer of complexity to the situation. She had no idea how to act or what to say. Somehow, "Hi, I'm Michels, the pilot you thought was a boy, and thank you for the great sex last night" just didn't do it.

"Baby Girl, I know you're awake. Are you okay?" The whispered use of the pet name and the concern in his voice pulled at her heart. When he found out the truth, that warmth and concern would turn to anger and feelings of betrayal. It was almost more than she could bear.

"Angel." Just saying her name, her voice broke and she fell silent.

"Angel?"

She took a deep breath, ignoring how the movement rubbed their bodies closer together, and tried again. "My name is Angel. Angel Torrence."

She felt the marginal stiffening of his body. "Your memory is back?"

"Yes."

"Good. That's good." There was a moment when he paused.

"You remember who you are, where you're from, everything?"

"Yes."

"Do you remember me finding you?"

"I remember . . . everything."

"I see."

The way he said it told her he understood. The silence that followed suggested that he was as reluctant to discuss last night as she was. But something needed to be said.

"About last night," she began, wanting to choose her words carefully.

"My fault," he interrupted. "And I apologize. I never should have put you in such a dangerous situation. It was inexcusable. And I take full responsibility."

"As you should," she said heatedly, rolling over so she could look him in the face. "Especially for forcing that food and wine down my throat when I begged you not to."

"What? I didn't force . . ."

"Exactly my point. *I* ate that food. *I* drank the wine. *I* am responsible for my actions, not you." Her point made, the momentum of her lecture died away. "Look, neither one of us knew the food was laced with anything, so you can save that 'I'm responsible' lecture for someone else. Okay?" This was not the conversation she wanted to have with him. She looked away from his face, suddenly embarrassed. She couldn't continue, not with their bodies pressed so close together like this. "I need to get up." Her voice sounded a little desperate.

"Okay."

"Do you think you could look the other way?"

"Baby Girl, I mean Angel, it's a little late for modesty. Don't you think?"

"Things are different now."

"I see." She wasn't sure what it was he saw, but suddenly she was alone in the bed, as Nicoli walked away from her, taking his beautiful body and the warmth it provided with him.

He scooped their clothes off the floor, turned and tossed hers to the bed. She quickly averted her eyes, but not before discovering that her memory of him had not been exaggerated.

"Get dressed." He stood off to the side and pulled the robe

over his head. When he looked over and saw her sitting with the bed sheets pulled up to her chin, he gave a disgusted sigh and turned his back to her. "I won't look."

Angel scrambled out from under the covers and into her garments. With her clothes on, she felt more comfortable.

"About last night," she tried again.

"Are you going to tell me that you're married? I don't believe it. Not the way you kissed."

Suddenly, she couldn't remember what she had wanted to say. "What's wrong with the way I kissed?"

"Not a damn thing, once you got the hang of it. But it's pretty obvious that you're not married or involved with anyone, so there's no need to feel like you betrayed anyone's trust."

"No, I guess not." This wasn't going the way she wanted.

"And besides," he continued before she could say more, "it's not like we really did anything. Your virtue is intact."

"But . . ." She lowered her eyes, struggling to find the right words.

"But what?" Then, thinking he understood, he nodded. "You're embarrassed? Don't be. Everything you did and felt last night was because of the drugs they put into the food. It wasn't real. It didn't mean anything."

"Oh." *It didn't mean anything.* She knew he was right, but the words cut through her.

"Time to go," he announced, terminating further conversation by walking to the door.

He bent his head close, listening for sounds on the other side. Not hearing any, he opened the door. Just a crack at first, and then all the way. The hallway was empty and Angel could well imagine that everyone still slept.

Together they made their way down the hall and into the main banquet room. The dishes had been cleared from the table and the room sat dark and empty.

Outside, very few people were about. Angel and Romanof walked across the encampment without incident.

"Where are we going?"

"Back to the landing field," he said. "Maybe the shuttle that brought us here will take us back."

"Then what?"

"One thing at a time."

No one tried to stop them as they made their way to the landing field. Unfortunately, when they got there, they found the gates locked.

"How are we going to get in?" Angel asked, studying the height of the fence. It was too tall to jump, although she thought it might be possible to climb it.

Nicoli followed her gaze, then shook his head. "I don't think that'll be necessary." He raised his arm, bringing the identification band around his wrist to her attention. "We'll use these. Stay close and don't press any stray buttons."

She shot him a look, which he didn't see, and then followed him to the building where they'd first stopped after their arrival. Pressing his band against the scanner, Nicoli was able to unlock the doors.

There was nothing useful inside the building, so they proceeded immediately out back, onto the landing field.

Three shuttles sat there and Romanof went to the first. The hatch opened easily, so they stepped inside. Angel wanted to take the pilot's seat, preferring her flying abilities to Nicoli's, but he got there first. Reluctantly, she took the co-pilot's chair and helped scan the console.

"I can't tell if it's another autopilot or not," Romanoff said.

"Even if it is, any place is better than here, right?" Looking out the window, she saw movement within the building. "Company. And from the way he's waving and shouting, I'd say he doesn't want us to leave."

"Too bad." Nicoli found the switch that shut and locked the hatch doors just before the man got there.

He pounded feebly on the doors, hollering at them. "You can't leave. It's against the rules."

Angel heard Nicoli curse under his breath and turned to see what he was doing with the controls. "Problems?"

"The battery's cold. They must not have planned to use this shuttle again. It'll take a while to warm up before the thrusters kick in." He looked out the side view where the man began to fumble with the hatch controls on the outside of the ship. "If he gets the hatch open before we start moving, we won't be going anywhere."

Angel's mind raced, trying to think of something, anything to help. "We could cold-start the forward thrusters," she suggested finally.

Nicoli looked at her as if she'd sprouted a second head.

"I've done it before," she continued quickly, "but I need some way to bypass the computer's automatic takeoff program."

Nicoli smiled. "I think I can help there. You won't have long before the system detects an error in the program and shuts down."

Angel nodded her understanding. "I know how to work fast."

Nicoli's fingers flew over the keyboard as he entered commands into the computer. Angel, in the meantime, unscrewed a panel on the ship's console, exposing several wires and microchips. She sorted through the various wires until she found the one she was looking for. After pulling a length of it out, she sliced it open with a utility knife she found attached inside the cover of the panel. She peeled back some of the protective outside coating, then held the exposed length of wire close to the ignition chip for the forward thrusters.

Behind them, they heard the locking mechanisms of the hatch deactivate and the hatch door began to slowly open.

"On my mark," Nicoli said. "Now."

Angel shut her eyes and pressed the exposed ends of the wires to the ignition chip. She turned her head as sparks erupted. There was a brief moment when Angel wondered if the shuttle's engine would cooperate, but then it roared to life and the thrusters kicked in. The shuttle shot forward, the hatch doors fell shut and soon the Rebirth Encampment was left far behind.

The two-hour flight back to the main processing building was spent in silence. Nicoli was too concerned about getting from the shuttle back to his ship to worry about Angel and any upset feelings she harbored about last night.

Unfortunately, when the shuttle made its final approach and landed, it did so on the far end of the main processing building. The quickest way to his ship was through the building.

Inside, they found things were in an uproar. General confusion reigned as robed figures rushed up and down unlit hallways. To Nicoli, it was apparent that the Holocaust Virus was doing its job. They'd found an extra robe for Angel and no one paid attention to the two of them as they walked through the building. In fact, Nicoli was beginning to think that they would get back to the Icarus without incident when shouting drew his attention. Turning to look behind him, he saw a familiar figure.

"Stop them! Intruders. Call Security." Brother Nathzur stood there in the middle of the hall, pointing a finger at them and shouting. As a group, several robed figures turned.

Nicoli didn't wait to see what would happen. He grabbed Angel's hand and ran. He was grateful she was tall, for it meant she was able to match his stride. Together, they ducked down hallways, always just one step ahead of their pursuers as they zigzagged their way through the building until unexpectedly, Angel stopped before a door. She flung it open and they were outside.

"There," Nicoli said, pointing to a nearby ground transport. "Get in."

Angel ran to the passenger side as he slid behind the wheel. As with everything else, the security around the transport was nonexistent and Nicoli started the engines with a mere press of a button. He assumed this was the same transport that had brought his body from the auction and tried to remember in which direction the general marketplace lay.

As it turned out, there weren't many paved roads on which the transport could travel and after about ten minutes of driving, Nicoli spotted the landing field. He parked the transport as close as possible, without drawing attention.

"Like you own the place," he whispered to Angel, nodding his head toward the entrance to the control building. Together they walked at a leisurely pace, all the while keeping a sharp lookout for their pursuers.

There was no sign of them, but Nicoli refused to believe they were in the clear. They had almost reached the entrance, when two robed figures stepped out, each holding a .44 auto-mag Trader's Special. The armed Harvestors stood just outside the entrance and scanned the crowd. Fortunately, there were enough robed people around that Nicoli and Angel didn't immediately stand out. Nevertheless, Nicoli wasn't about to risk walking past the guards, so he took Angel by the elbow and guided her toward the building's exit corridor.

Nicoli did his best to keep them in the middle of larger groups, but even this proved to be trouble. No one else tried to enter through the exit and their effort was drawing a lot of attention. It was inevitable that, halfway to their goal, the guards spotted them.

Nicoli and Angel began to run. Like salmon going upstream, they fought their way past the exiting crowd, their progress painfully slow. When they reached the actual exit doors from the building, they found them unguarded. They easily slipped through and ran past the scanners and into the lobby. A scream brought them up short. Turning, Nicoli realized that one of the guards had unwittingly carried his .44 auto-mag through the weapons scanner and had been vaporized. The three remaining guards stood helplessly on the other side while robed figures scurried around, presumably to shut off the scanner.

Nicoli glanced outside to the landing field. The Icarus was anchored in place by the stasis field. If he didn't find a way to shut off the tower, they would be unable to take off. He stood in the middle of the lobby, looking around.

"Are we staying or going?" Angel came running up to him, having fallen behind briefly. She glanced uneasily at the commotion around the exit gate.

"Going, if I can find a way to shut off the stasis towers." He turned, looking for the main control office. It could be behind any of the doors. There just wasn't enough time to check them all.

"Can you use this?" Angel held out a small hand laser.

"Where'd you get this?" He took the weapon from her and checked the gauge. It was fully charged.

"I found it."

He didn't wait to hear more. He had what he needed. Together they ran out the back of the building.

As they approached the ship, the hatch door opened and Yanur looked out.

"Get in," Nicoli ordered. Angel scrambled to obey while he went over to the stasis tower holding the ship. Turning to Yanur, he yelled. "Is Michels aboard?"

"Yes," Yanur replied, looking a bit confused. Nicoli felt badly that he didn't have time to explain everything.

"Tell Michels to start the engines and get ready to fly. Make sure Angel is strapped in somewhere." He set the hand laser to "overload" and placed it at the base of the tower. He climbed into the ship and secured the hatch. Rushing to the bridge, he found Yanur sitting in the copilot's seat. Nicoli couldn't see Michels sitting next to Yanur, but the boy's hands were busy flipping switches, readying the ship. Not seeing Angel, he assumed Yanur had secured her in one of the cabins.

"Get ready," Nicoli yelled. "When you hear the explosion, takeoff."

They didn't have long to wait. There was a high-pitched whining as the laser's charge grew stronger. When it reached its highest point, the charge overloaded and exploded, setting off a chain reaction inside the tower. Small explosions climbed up the tower and as the stasis field shut down, the Icarus, along with several other ships, started to drift.

Immediately, Michels hit the thrusters and the ship took off. With the other vessels drifting uncontrollably, it took some maneuvering to avoid them, and it was even trickier for Michels to steer clear of the tower missiles launched at them. One glanced off the ship, blowing up a few meters past them. Through it all, the boy's flying skill proved to be as exceptional as Yanur had claimed and they were soon out into open space.

"Michels, you are one hell of a pilot."

"Thanks," came a voice Nicoli knew all too well. Placing his hands on the pilot's chair, he turned it toward him.

Angel stared back at him.

Chapter Twelve

"What the hell is going on?" The truth hit Nicoli like a super-nova. "You're Michels?"

Angel didn't say a word.

He turned accusing eyes on Yanur. "You knew Michels was a woman?"

Yanur had the decency to look guilty.

Nicoli stood so he could bend over the pilot's chair and grab the arms of it with both hands, effectively boxing Angel in. He lowered his face to hers so she wouldn't miss any part of the glare he gave her. "And just what did you think you were doing going down on that planet by yourself?"

"She was there to help you." Yanur's voice held parental censure, but it only fueled Nicoli's anger.

"Yeah, and doing one hell of a job, lying there unconscious with a collar around her neck. My God, do you have any idea what would've happened to you if I hadn't found you?"

"What?" Yanur's concern and confusion were obvious, but Nicoli was going to spare the man no quarter.

The dam broke and all of Nicoli's anger, and frustration from the night before, spilled out as he turned to Yanur. "She almost died down there. Is that what you wanted? To weigh me down with more guilt?"

"Stop yelling at him."

"Stay out of this." He whipped his head back to her. "It doesn't concern you."

"It doesn't concern me? How do you figure that?" Now Angel was shouting.

"You should never have been involved in this. If I had known you were a woman, I would never have allowed you to go."

"Allow me? You ungrateful jerk, you needed me."

"I could have found another way to achieve my goal. Without you," Nicoli argued.

"Get real. If I hadn't gone down and transferred your life essence back into your body, you'd still be living in a tube and your body would be having one hell of a time as someone's sex slave. So instead of yelling at me and Yanur, you should be thanking us."

"Alex," Yanur interrupted. "I would not have let her go if there had been another way. But Michels . . . ah, I mean Angel, is it? . . . is a rather remarkable young woman. Maybe if you got to know her better—"

"Oh, we've had time to become intimately acquainted, haven't we? Michels?" He said the name as if it left a bad taste in his mouth.

She narrowed her eyes at him. "Look, I tried to tell you the truth."

"Oh, really. When was that, exactly?"

"Well, there was that time right before I transferred you, but you wouldn't let me."

"Bad timing on your part, sweetheart."

"I know, which is why I tried again this morning, when I remembered who I was." She spoke so softly, Nicoli could barely make out the words. He remembered the moment when she woke up that morning and the conversation they'd had. She *had* been trying to tell him something, but feeling too guilty about the night before, he had misunderstood.

Nicoli pushed away from the chair, going to stand near the

open doorway. If he were honest with himself, he might admit that he was more upset with Yanur than with Angel. It would take him a long time to get over that betrayal.

As if sensing how Nicoli felt, Yanur rose from the co-pilot's seat and moved toward the door, stopping when Nicoli blocked his path. "If you'll excuse me, I believe I'll return to my room for a bit."

Nicoli stepped aside and watched him go without saying a word

"You know, he only did it because he cares about you."

Nicoli didn't want, or need, any lectures from her, so he shot her a look that he hoped conveyed that sentiment. "You're in my chair." A startled expression flashed across her face. Or maybe it was hurt. Either way, he didn't care. "Get up."

To her credit, she didn't hop right up. She turned back to the controls to make sure the ship was on auto-cruise before vacating his chair. And even then, she only went as far as the copilot's seat.

He sat down, flipped off the auto-cruise and took the steering column in his hands. It felt good to be in control. Control of his body, his emotions. Control of his ship. No one, especially a woman, was going to take that away from him.

"What's the matter, Colonel Romanof? Don't you trust me to fly your ship?"

"Nicoli. I think, after what we've been through, we're at least on a first-name basis." He fell silent, watching the stars go by, trying not to think too hard.

"You didn't answer my question." The woman was tenacious, he'd give her credit for that.

"Okay. Let's think about it. I haven't known you very long, but in that time you've managed to steal my ship and lie to me. Not exactly a strong foundation for trust, would you say?"

"Those were all extreme circumstances."

"Honey, in my line of work, those are the only kind we get."

"I saved your life. I think you owe me a second chance."

"Is that right? Well, I saved yours, so I'd say we're square. But I'll humor you. Tell me about yourself. Help me understand the kind of person you are. For instance, when you're not stealing ships, what do you do for a living?"

There was a slight pause before she answered. "I'm a pilot. I run my own courier service."

"I see." He leaned forward to type on the computer's keyboard.

"What are you doing?"

"Verifying your claim. I keep a record of all registered pilots. Angel Torrence. Isn't that the name you gave me? Or do you go under another name? Michels, for instance."

"No, I fly under the name of Angel Torrence." He heard her take a deep breath and let it out. "But you won't find my name in there. I'm not registered."

"Naturally not. And why is that?"

"Because I courier illegal goods." There was a note of exasperation to her voice.

"Aaahh. Now there's a profession to inspire trust and confidence."

"Fine, believe what you want." The expression on her face could have frozen boiling water as she glared at him. "I'm sure you're as anxious to be rid of me as I am to be gone, so as soon as we get back to Earth, you won't have to deal with me anymore."

"Fine." He snarled. "But don't hold your breath waiting to get there. We have another stop to make before we return."

"What do you mean another stop?"

He thought he detected a note of worry in her tone. That was fine with him. Let her worry about being stuck with him for awhile. Why should he be the only one to suffer?

"My mission isn't over. I still intend to stop the Harvestors. And if that means going to another planet to do it, then that's what I'm going to do."

"I don't want to spend that much time with you."

"Actually, it's not that far. Just over in the next quadrant."

Suddenly Angel grew very still. "What?"

"The planet we're going to, the planet the Harvestors are taking over. It's just in the next quadrant." He looked up from the keyboard where he'd been laying in the course. "What's the matter with you?"

"No . . . nothing. Which planet?"

"Why?"

"Damn it, Nicoli. If you're going to haul me all over the universe, you can at least tell me which planet you're taking me to."

"Coronado." He studied her face closely. Most people would not have detected the small flinch, but he saw it. She didn't want to go there. Why? "Is there a problem?"

"No," she answered too quickly.

"Are you sure?"

"Yeah." She stood up abruptly and headed for the door before Nicoli could question her further. "I'm tired. I'm going to lie down."

He watched her practically race from the bridge, then turned back to look out the front view port, glad to be alone. He needed time to think. There was a time in the not-too-recent past when logic ruled him. But from the moment he'd transferred back into his body, emotions had bombarded him. Or maybe it was the moment he'd found Angel, lying helpless in the donor room. The timing between the two was so close it was hard to tell which event triggered this emotional upheaval. But it needed to end. There was work to be done.

He sent a message to USP headquarters giving the coordinates of the Harvestors' planet. A contingent of soldiers would be sent to see that any operations still functioning were shut down and the survivors transported someplace where they could be watched and cared for. Personally, he didn't care if the whole damn race was exterminated. At least, that's what he kept telling himself.

Satisfied his message had been received, Nicoli laid in a course for Coronado and began working on a computer program to decipher all the data he'd brought from the planet. Work was what he needed now.

A few hours later, Angel woke from nightmare with a frightening sense of déjà vu. It left her feeling panicked and breathless. She sat up in bed, skin damp with perspiration, and noticed that the air in her room was stifling hot.

The scenario was too familiar. Angel didn't even bother to find her shoes before racing barefooted for the bridge.

"What's going on?" She paused to take a couple of deep breaths. "I came as quickly as I . . ." She looked around, but there was no one on the bridge.

Out the front view screen, she saw only empty space and stars. Forcing herself to listen, she heard only silence. There was no one attacking the ship; no immediate danger. Yet something was wrong.

Taking a deep breath, she forced herself to relax and in doing so, noticed the results of the diagnostic scan still on the computer screen. Everything appeared normal, until she saw the readout on the rear thrusters.

She found Nicoli on the lower level, by the thruster uptake shafts, kneeling on the floor before an assortment of tools. At her approach, he glanced up briefly.

"I saw the diagnostics on the bridge." For some reason, she felt the need to explain her being there.

"Yeah. There's a problem with the uptake. The thrusters overheated and shut down. Which is why it's so damn hot in here— no air flow."

"Oh." She hated the tension between them. Pointing to the tools, she tried to ignore it. "Can you fix it?"

"I'm going to try." He picked up a small torch and lit it. He adjusted the flame until it was no more than a bright blue light at the end of a metal shaft. Seemingly satisfied, he turned off the torch and clipped it to his belt. Looking over at Angel, he frowned. "Where are your shoes?"

"I, uh, thought we were under attack. You know, the heat in my room, the nightm . . . anyway, I didn't want to waste time looking for shoes if there was trouble."

He sighed and shook his head like a parent weary from dealing with a troublesome child. "Never mind. You won't need them."

"I won't?"

"No. Let's go."

"Go? Where?"

Nicoli nodded his head toward the shaft. "In there. I need your help."

Her eyes drifted to the shaft's opening and saw only the endless black void beyond. "No, I don't think so."

He raised an eyebrow. "Want to tell me why?"

"Well, for one thing, it's too small. We'll never both fit in there."

"Nice try. But I've already been in there and I promise you, there's plenty of room for both of us."

"Well, then, um—I don't know anything about repairing a ship. So I really won't be much good to you."

"Can you hold a flashlight?"

She sighed. "Yes."

"That'll do. There's a hole in the shaft and I need to seal it by fusing this plate over it." He held up a square sheet of metal. "One hand to hold the plate in place while the other operates the torch. That leaves me one hand short to hold the flashlight, which is why I need you. Understand?"

She nodded, unwilling to embarrass herself further. Reluctantly, she accepted the flashlight he handed her and watched as he climbed through the shaft's opening.

Almost drawn against her will, Angel took a step closer. Nicoli worked his way along the shaft and as he did, the darkness slowly swallowed him, until too soon, he completely disappeared from sight.

Angel swallowed hard. *I can do this.*

The bottom ledge of the opening was about waist high. She flipped on the flashlight's beam and after assuring herself that the beam shone strong and steady, she directed it into the shaft. Immediately the blackness disappeared and with the shiny metal of the shaft's four walls reflecting back the light, it didn't seem nearly so daunting. She could even see Nicoli's feet not far ahead.

With only a moment's further hesitation, Angel ducked her head into the shaft and began to crawl after Nicoli. She could hear him moving steadily ahead of her. Concentrating only on the task at hand, Angel moved one arm forward, then one knee, and so on. In this way, she made progress toward their goal, not daring to look behind her, knowing that if she did, she would see the darkness closing in.

Angel didn't know how long she crawled along the tunnel, but eventually she caught up to Nicoli. He waited patiently for her to bring the light so he could see the extent of the damage. The size of the hole was not large enough that Angel worried about being sucked out into open space, but the rush of air as it came through the uptake shaft and then was diverted out through the hole was daunting.

"Don't worry about suffocating," Nicoli said. He must have heard how hard she was breathing. "I've got the computer regulating the airflow in here."

"I'm fine," she lied. "What do you want me to do?"

He studied her face for a moment, as if gauging her composure. But, if like her, he thought her voice sounded unusually tense, he didn't comment on it. Rather, he addressed the business at hand. "Just focus the light here so I can see where I'm welding while I hold the plate. It won't do us much good if I accidentally hit a tyrillium cable and blow us all to kingdom come."

She did as instructed, moving the light occasionally when Nicoli progressed to a new portion of the plate. For a while, the sight of metal edges melting and fusing together distracted her. Nicoli's ability with the torch was impressive, making the entire operation seem easy and effortless.

"There," he said, after finishing the last bit and shutting off his torch. "That should hold it until we can make it to the nearest space station for repairs. Brace yourself. I'm going to have the computer start up the thrusters while we're in here to make sure they work. I don't know about you, but I'd just as soon not have to crawl all the way in here again."

Angel nodded, but remained silent.

"Computer, fire the rear thrusters."

There was a moment of nothing. Angel could almost taste the anticipation. Then everything happened at once.

The thrusters roared to life, jolting the ship violently as it shot forward. Angel, slammed against the side of the shaft, lost her grip on the flashlight and it went sailing through the air. Unable to turn easily in the narrow space, Angel could do nothing more than watch helplessly as the flashlight rolled out of view, taking the light with it. As the light faded, the walls of the shaft loomed closer. And then blackness settled around her.

Angel froze. Her pulse raced and the sound of her heart beating grew so loud she could no longer hear Nicoli's breathing beside her. She was alone. And she was trapped.

The nightmares that had tortured her for so many years assumed a dimension of reality, and it was more than Angel could take.

Chapter Thirteen

"Angel?" Something was wrong, he could tell. Her breathing had become harsh and erratic. It seemed absurd to him that this woman who had braved Free Rebels and Harvestors could be afraid of the dark. And yet . . .

"Angel?" He spoke calmly, but again, there was no answer. He wasn't sure what to do. He reached out, hoping to comfort her, but when his hand touched her, she flinched and began to whimper.

"It's okay. It's only me. You're safe. I promise you, you're safe." He tried to sound convincing as he inched his way closer to her in the shaft. The next time he touched her, she didn't flinch. But the low whimpering sounds continued.

When he had maneuvered himself alongside her, he wrapped his arms around her and drew her close. To his relief, she didn't try to pull away.

"Angel, it's okay. Whatever it is, it's okay. I won't let anything hurt you. You're safe with me."

"Not safe." The words were uttered with little more than a breath. "Never safe."

She began to struggle, a panicked flailing of her arms and legs. Afraid she would hurt herself, he held her more securely.

"Close your eyes, Baby Girl. Concentrate on my voice. We're okay. Everything's fine."

He pressed his lips to her head and continued to whisper words he hoped sounded reassuring. He wasn't used to this role of comforter. In the end, he wasn't sure what he said mattered anyway. What was important was his tone. So he kept that as soothing as he could, all the while holding her close, rubbing her back and arms with his hand.

Slowly, he felt her relax. How long they lay that way, he didn't know. Didn't care. It felt good. It felt right. And he may never have this opportunity again. Inside the shaft, there was no lying, no betrayal. Harvestors and missions didn't exist. Inside the shaft, it was just the two of them.

And though Nicoli knew it couldn't last forever, he was content for this brief time.

"Nicoli?" Her voice came softly, muffled from where her face pressed against his shoulder, her breath warm against his neck.

"I'm here, Baby Girl."

"I want to leave. Please."

"Okay. We're going." He promised. "Can you turn around?" He moved away from her, feeling bereft now that they were no longer pressed together. "Put your hand on my leg, like this." Kneeling in front of her in the shaft, he placed one of her hands on his ankle. "Just follow me. We'll go nice and slow."

The crawl seemed to take forever, with Nicoli stopping periodically to make sure Angel was okay. When they reached the opening, Nicoli climbed out first, then turned to help Angel.

For a moment they stood there, side by side, neither one saying a thing. Finally, Nicoli cleared his throat. "Are you all right?"

She didn't look up at him, seemingly absorbed in her study of the floor. "Yes, um, I'm fine, now."

"You know, if there's . . ."

Angel held up her hand to silence him. "Don't. Please don't."

"I'd like to help."

She gave a brief, bitter laugh. "Why? It's not like we're friends.

135

You don't even like me, remember?" She raised her hand when he started to argue that point. "When you're ready to share your secrets with me, then I'll share mine with you. Until then, I'd appreciate it if we could just forget this happened."

Nicoli nodded. He understood the need to keep some things to oneself. "Okay."

She cleared her throat before continuing. "If you don't need me right now, I'm going back to my cabin to change clothes. I'll, uh, come relieve you on the bridge in just a little while."

Again he nodded, but didn't say anything. She started to leave, but stopped after taking just a few steps. He waited, as she seemed to struggle with herself. Finally, she turned to look back at him. "Thank you."

"No problem." He watched her walk away.

After returning the torch and other tools to storage, Nicoli returned to the bridge. All systems were working. Well, working as normally as they could under the circumstances. He laid in a course for Delphi IV and, taking the controls, set a moderate speed out of the Darwin Zone.

Once they were safely away, his thoughts drifted to Angel, and her strange behavior in the shaft.

"Everything okay?"

Nicoli glanced at Yanur as the older man walked in and sat down in the copilot's seat.

"For now." Nicoli turned back to the vast emptiness of space looming ahead of him, and, for a time, they traveled in a companionable silence.

"About Angel." Yanur finally broke the silence.

"I don't want to talk about it."

"It?" Yanur sounded confused.

Belatedly, Nicoli realized Yanur had no idea what had happened between him and Angel. "Forget it. You had something on your mind?"

"Yes. An apology."

Nicoli nodded. "All right. I accept."

"Accept?"

"Your apology."

"Oh. No. You misunderstand me. I have no intention of apologizing to you. That girl was far more capable of saving your hide than I was, and if you stop to think about it, you'll realize I'm right."

"But you lied to me."

"Unfortunate, I agree, but a strategic necessity, which a military man such as yourself can surely understand."

Nicoli hated it when Yanur got this way. It was his "fatherly" role; the one he adopted from time to time when he thought Nicoli needed it. He supposed that Yanur considered this one of those times. Well, Nicoli didn't feel like getting a lecture right now. Things were confusing enough.

"What's the apology you were talking about? If you're not apologizing to me, then exactly who is apologizing to whom?"

"You owe Angel an apology. She saved your life—for the third time, by my count."

Nicoli stared at him open-mouthed. "You're joking. I don't owe her an apology. If anything, she owes me one. For lying to me. You know as well as I do that she should never have gone down on that planet. It was too dangerous. Had I known she was a woman, I would never have allowed it."

Yanur sighed. "Has it ever occurred to you that your views on women are archaic? I would think you'd have learned from the problems on your planet."

"Women should be protected. They are not as strong or virile as men. It is our duty to protect them."

Yanur shook his head. "Sometimes I think there's no hope for you."

They were safely out of the Darwin Zone, so Nicoli set the controls to autopilot. He had to be alone for awhile. Alone to think.

Alone to brood.

He walked to the doorway, but Yanur stopped him before he could leave.

"Nicoli. What if she was your sister? Or your mother? Wouldn't you want her to have the skills to defend herself?"

The suggestion was going too far. Nicoli felt the last thread of his patience and control snap. He stopped and pinned Yanur with his glare. "You forget, old man. My mother died because she'd been taught those skills. And because she tried to defend herself, she died a horrible death. I know. I was there."

Thirty minutes later, Nicoli stepped out of the decon-closet feeling clean, but not refreshed. Irritation rode him like a gnat on a tiger's hide. He didn't know what to think. Women should be protected. Most women wanted to be protected.

But Angel was unlike any female he'd met.

Securing the towel about his waist, he tried to push Angel from his mind. He walked over to Yanur's closet and riffled through it, looking for clean clothes. Everything hanging here was too small for him. He glanced at the clock.

Surely, by now, Angel had changed clothes and was back on the bridge. He could go to *his* cabin, retrieve clothes from *his* closet and not worry about running into her.

Feeling better, he made his way to his room. He paused outside the door, suddenly hesitant. He knocked, leaning close to listen. There was no answer. He knocked again, just to be safe. When still there was no answer, he tried the handle.

"Hello?" He pushed the door open just far enough to look inside. "Angel?"

Silence greeted him, so he walked in. It still looked like his room, everything was where he'd left it. He walked over to the closet, opened it and started searching for an outfit.

"Oh. What are you doing here?"

Nicoli turned at the sound. "I needed a . . . shirt." She stood before him, a vision, clothed in nothing more than her long blond hair and one of his shirts.

"I'm sorry. I just wanted . . . um, needed it . . . to borrow." She seemed flustered and as she spoke she waved a brush back toward the decon-unit to indicate she had just come from the shower. But Nicoli wasn't paying attention to her words. Every time her arm moved back, the shirt gaped open, revealing to him glimpses of the treasures he already knew lay beneath. He found himself thinking inane thoughts like, *lucky shirt.*

He shook himself from his schoolboy reverie. "That's okay. I have others. Keep it."

Her hands dropped to her sides as she stood facing him. Any

other woman would have looked away, frightened at the raw hunger he knew must be reflected in his eyes. He had resisted the temptation to take her before, at the Rebirth Colony, but had paid the price for it. Only now he recognized the irritation for what it was. Sexual frustration.

"Thank you," she said, and for a moment he wondered if she had read his mind, then realized she was referring to the shirt.

"It looks better on you, anyway." He smiled briefly, then forced himself to turn back to the closet. Where the hell had that statement come from? The last thing he wanted was to get involved with this woman. Taking out the first outfit he found, he closed the door and turned to leave. Angel hadn't moved.

"We'll reach Delphi IV in about two hours." He tried for a casual tone, but noticed that his voice sounded gruff. He cleared it and tried again. "I thought it might be nice to eat at the station. They don't have much in the way of amenities, but the food there is better than what we'll get out of the Cosmos-genie."

Angel nodded her head, sending light shimmering through her long blond hair. "That's fine."

Leave. Nicoli silently commanded himself, and yet his feet refused to move. *Leave.* Though in reality only a few steps away, the distance to the door seemed immeasurable. But, determined to reach it, he took the first step. Then another. But the next step, which should have carried him past her, instead brought him so close, he could feel her breath when she exhaled. *Damn.* He wanted her. From the moment he'd seen her in the donor room, he'd wanted her. Last night, being with her but not having her had almost killed him.

Raising his hand to her cheek, he looked into her eyes, and saw the uncertainty. And something else. Something more primitive.

Slowly, he lowered his head, giving her every opportunity to back away. When his lips touched hers, it was a tender promise of things to come.

He let the kiss end and rested his forehead against hers. "Tell me to go, Angel." He whispered hoarsely. "I don't think I'm strong enough to leave on my own."

"Stay."

139

It took a moment for the word to register, but when it did, it was like the breaking of a dam. With a hungry growl, Nicoli captured her lips again, only this time the kiss was urgent, almost desperate.

Dropping the clothes to the floor, Nicoli gathered her to him. He ravaged her mouth, forcing her to open to his exploration. When her arms stole around his neck, he leaned down without breaking the contact of their mouths and lifted her by the legs until she could wrap them about his hips.

Moving so her back pressed against the wall, he held her in place with the weight of his body. He throbbed with wanting her and thrust himself against the juncture of her legs. She wore nothing under the shirt, so only his towel separated their bodies. But even that proved to be too much.

Nicoli could easily have released the towel and taken her there, against the wall. But he didn't want their first time together, truly together, to be anything less than perfect. Drawing control from an inner strength, he carried her to the bed and gently set her down. With the fearful wonder of the innocent, she watched as he deftly loosened the towel and let it fall to the floor. Though he knew she'd seen him nude before, she stared at him as if for the first time. Perhaps her experience with men was limited, or perhaps it was the particulars of their association that made her seem nervous. Whatever the reason, he vowed to himself to go slow. *Please, God, help me go slowly.*

With his hands, he spread her knees where she sat on the side of the bed and knelt before her on the floor. Cupping her face with his hands, he brought her to him and captured her lips with his, demanding from her all that he gave. Undoing the last few buttons of her shirt, he slipped his hands beneath the material, wanting to feel the satiny smoothness of her skin against his palms. He cupped the gentle swelling of her breasts and squeezed. At her gasp, Nicoli broke away to trail tiny kisses down along her throat, but did not stop there. The curve of a breast rubbed against his cheek, igniting a fire where it touched. He rubbed against it, enjoying the warm feel of her soft plumpness. When he reached the cool tautness of her nipple, he turned to lave it with his tongue until it hardened into a dusky pink pebble that he took into his mouth to suckle.

Tiny moans escaped Angel's throat as he split his attentions between her breasts. He let a hand trail along the curve of her waist, down the flare of her hip to rest briefly against her thigh before moving to the delicate flesh between her legs. Already warm and moist, he parted her feminine folds with his thumb, searching for and finding the sensitive nub, which he began to stroke with slow, purposeful movements.

"Please, Nicoli," she gasped, squirming beneath his touch.

"Soon, Baby Girl," he whispered, taking her mouth again with his. He slid her shirt off completely, then eased her back across the bed. Stretched out above her, he used his arms to keep from crushing her beneath his weight. Parting her legs with his knees, he positioned himself, letting his erection tease the damp folds of her cleft until it, too, was damp and slick from her moisture.

Then he entered. Slowly at first, because she was warm and tight. So tight. He couldn't go far and had to pull back. She was wet with her own desire and he used her juices to coat his member before entering her again. This time he made it further, and then he froze.

"What's wrong?" Angel's voice was a breathy whisper.

"You're a virgin!" His voice cracked under the stress of not moving.

She looked at him and he thought he saw embarrassment flash across her eyes. Her expression, before soft and sensuous, hardened into a mask of defiance. "So?"

"So, it changes things." It took all of his self-control not to ignore the barrier and pierce it in search of his own pleasure. He had no idea where he'd find the control to just walk away.

"I'm sorry. I didn't realize my sexual status would be such a turn-off."

"A turn-off?" *Was she crazy*? "It's not a question of appeal, Baby Girl. It's a question of honor and doing what's right. On my planet, only a woman's husband is allowed the honor of taking her virginity."

"But we're not on your planet."

"No, we're not. But your first time should be with someone special."

Softly, her words came to him. "It is."

Almost afraid to believe his ears, he studied her face. "Are you sure, Baby Girl? It's not too late to stop," he lied. A more honorable man would have ignored her and walked away. But lately it seemed that Nicoli was plagued with human frailties. Especially where Angel was involved. "Do you give yourself to me freely?"

"Yes."

"You do me great honor in bestowing this gift and I offer you my life in exchange. We are bound, one to the other, *eternum*." His whispered the words to the ancient ritual, knowing he would never utter them again. "This may hurt, but I promise to make it better." He drew out. "Are you sure?"

At her slight nod, he lowered his head to capture her lips, then surged forward, breaking through the barrier of her maidenhead.

Pain momentarily pierced her senses, bringing her perceptions into sharp detail. Nicoli filled her to completeness, to overflowing, and Angel wondered that her body was able to accommodate his size. Though he held himself still, she felt the throbbing of his engorged member pulsing inside her.

"Are you okay?" he whispered.

Was that it? "Yes." She thought Nicoli had gone a little overboard with that nonsense he'd uttered about giving his life in exchange for her virginity. Maybe it had been a really long time since he'd had sex and that was his way of being grateful. Whatever the reason, she felt strangely bereft. Incomplete. Somehow, she'd thought there'd be more to it. But knowing how fragile the male ego could be, she conjured a smile.

Nicoli's breathing was more strained than before and Angel surmised that this act had taken much out of him.

"That was, uh, nice." She hoped her voice sounded sincere. She'd hate to be the one to tell him that if this was what it was all about, she wasn't missing anything.

Some of her thoughts must have shown in her face, though, because Nicoli gave a most impolite snort, just before levering himself above her.

"Nice? I suggest you hang on."

Before she had a chance to ask what he meant, he pulled back. With a sense of growing loss, she felt him sliding out. Then suddenly, he thrust forward and a rush of sensation shot through her. Before she had a chance to recover, he started to withdraw. With the next thrust, she felt the muscles of her abdomen tighten in anticipation, like pressure building just before an explosion. Again he slid out, slowly, letting her feel every centimeter of him. Then in again, never giving the tension time to dissipate.

Sensations assaulted her body. The coolness of the sheets below her and the warmth of Nicoli's body above her faded until all of her attention focused on where their two bodies joined. As if from a distance, she heard her soft cries and Nicoli's moans. Just when she was sure she could take no more, the explosion came. Stars twinkled behind her closed lids while every nerve in her body tingled, her consciousness seeming to transcend to another, ethereal plane of existence. There was no time to recover before Nicoli drove into her one last time and held himself above her, a primal cry bursting from his throat.

Both remained still as the climax slowly burned itself out and a pleasant lassitude settled over them. Still joined, Nicoli rolled to the side, turning her so they faced one another. Pulling a sheet over them, he gathered her close and held her. Angel was glad for the anchor, because her thoughts were spiraling.

It had not been like anything she could have anticipated. And she knew she'd never feel it again, and it broke her heart. She and this man had no future together. How could they?

A man who went around saving the universe didn't have time for personal commitments. And if he ever did, Nicoli was the type to want a traditional marriage and a traditional woman.

She vowed a long time ago to only marry for love and she knew full well that Nicoli, a colonel with the security forces, a man of honor, could never love someone like her. She was everything he thought a woman should not be: independent, a skilled pilot, an illegal courier and worse, a fugitive from two planets. Their lovemaking had been about lust, nothing more. Sooner or later, they would part ways. While she would have preferred it be later, it just wasn't meant to be.

143

Nicoli was going to Coronado and she couldn't go with him. Once they hit the space station, she'd have to find another ride and say good-bye.

The thought of leaving him depressed her and she allowed herself a moment of self-pity. Lying in his arms, she rested her head on his chest and enjoyed the feel of his arms about her, keeping her safe. She stayed that way until he fell asleep. Then, being careful not to disturb him, she climbed from the bed, showered again and quickly dressed.

When he awoke alone, he would mistakenly think that their lovemaking had meant nothing to her, as he was supposed to. Some lies were necessary, she thought as she walked out of the room and headed for the bridge. She just wished that after all these years, the lie-telling would come easier.

Chapter Fourteen

Angel stepped onto the space station's decking and looked around. The irony of her arrival here, at this point and time in her life, was not lost on her. The space station was still as dank and oppressive as she remembered, but it no longer frightened her as it had those many years ago when she'd first run away. After eight years of surviving on her own and piloting illegal goods, Delphi IV was just another independent station that attracted too much of the wrong element.

Right now, that suited her fine. She wasn't planning to stick around long. She'd find out which ship was departing soon and be on it. It would have been easier to get the information she needed if Nicoli had allowed her to see to the repairs for the Icarus, but he'd insisted on doing that himself. Now she'd have to get the information some other way.

"There he is." Yanur, standing beside her, pointed to the left where Nicoli could be seen walking toward them.

For a moment, Angel's heart stood still. With or without clothes, he commanded attention. Head held high, he was a man used to being in charge. Even his stride exuded raw, masculine strength.

"Shall we?" he asked, coming to stand beside her. "They'll start the repairs immediately, but it'll take a couple of hours. We have enough time to eat. There's only one establishment open at this hour, a place called Flannigan's. But I hear the food is good."

"You two go ahead," Yanur offered. "First, I want to see a man about some raw tyrillium for my medical equipment, and then maybe I'll join you."

The sound of crude laughter drew their attention to a nearby ship. The crew, appearing dirty and unshaven, disembarked and headed down the corridor.

"There's a trustworthy-looking bunch," Yanur murmured. "On second thought, it might be good for someone to keep an eye on the ship. I think I'll come back here when I finish." He gestured to the comm-link pinned to the collar of his shirt. "I shouldn't be gone long and I'll buzz you if anything is amiss. You two have fun, but be careful."

Angel and Nicoli watched the older man hobble along the corridor, then turned to go in the opposite direction, through halls lit dimly for the evening hour. The space station did not experience the rising and setting of the sun to mark its days, so the hall lights were adjusted instead. For Angel, the experience reminded her of walking through the back streets of Jupiter's Zeta Colony. It was close to midnight, and, with the exception of the crewmen ahead of them, she and Nicoli seemed the sole occupants in the connecting hallways through which they passed. Only the subtle shifting of shadows suggested otherwise. Angel flexed her wrists, taking comfort in the familiar feel of her hand laser. In this remote part of space, there were no weapon-prohibition laws.

Stepping inside Flannigan's was like entering a *Wunderland* addict's hallucinogenic trip through a virtual recreation of Earth's Wild West era. A huge mirror covered the back wall, and directly in front of it was a simulated wood bar, complete with bartender. Randomly distributed around the great room were small tables and chairs of the same simulated wood. But that's were the Wild West resemblance ended. Neon blue, green, red and yellow veins of light formed intricate patterns in the floor, branching off to various sections of the room. Their reflection, projected back into the room by the mirrored wall, made the light pattern appear three-dimensional. At one time, the embedded light veins were used to guide the service "bots." But modern technology had rendered the guidance veins of light obsolete. Still, they added atmosphere, giving the place a softer glow.

Taking the lead, Angel walked to a secluded table off to one side. From here, she could keep an eye on the entire room, and the entrance. It wasn't that she anticipated trouble, but old habits died hard.

The other ship's crew had already taken over a group of tables across the room and service "bots" were delivering their drinks. A group of women in skin-tight, low-cut jumpsuits emerged from a side door and wandered over to the crew. Angel watched in fascination as a few of the women left the gathering to sit by themselves on stools in front of the bar, leaving only the younger, more nubile women to associate with the increasingly rowdy men. Sex droids, Angel concluded. She'd been around enough bars and saloons to know that after years of professional service, only sex droids could look that young and "full of life."

"Interesting," Nicoli commented, noting the direction of her gaze.

"You find the sex droids interesting?" She didn't like the sharp edge that accompanied her tone. It was none of her business if he enjoyed the sight and company of a sex droid.

He frowned. "What I find interesting is that only the sex droids remained. Makes one wonder if the men prefer droids over real women or whether the real women prefer not to service those particular men."

"It's late. Maybe they're tired."

"Yeah, tired of getting beat up."

Angel studied the group of rowdies. "Maybe the men prefer the droids."

"I doubt it. These men get off on power and control and it's hard to dominate someone who bounces back from your worst beating looking good as new."

"Are you speaking from experience?"

147

He met her gaze, his brow furrowed. "I speak from observation."

"You don't strike me as the type who hangs out a lot in these
types of places."

"You don't think so?" He gave her a dark, self-deprecating
smile. What demons was he hiding from her?

Rather than answer him, Angel activated the menu and studied the holographic list of choices that materialized above their
table. Her stomach was a little upset, nervous about the prospect
of leaving, she guessed. But she had no idea when her next meal
would come and she knew better than to not eat. She made her
selection and then patiently waited until Nicoli made his before
deactivating the menu.

When their drinks came via a "bot," Nicoli raised his glass
and offered a toast. "To another day."

Angel touched her glass to his in silence and drank, pondering the meaning behind his words. Did he speak from a soldier's
perspective or a lover's? Her insides were tangling in knots trying to figure him out. Hell, she couldn't even figure herself out.

"Am I under arrest?" The silence that greeted her words lingered for so long, she finally looked up to see if he'd even heard.

His expression was unreadable. "No. Why do you ask?"

"I just want to know where we stand, that's all."

Nicoli looked like he wanted to respond, but instead he
pressed his lips together and remained silent. Their food arrived
and they fell into an awkward silence. As she ate, Angel tried
to sort through the many emotions and feelings assaulting her.

They had almost finished their meal when Nicoli broke the
silence. "Angel, I want you to know that you can come to me
if ever you're in trouble."

She lifted her head, chin up and met his probing look.
"Thanks, but I can take care of myself." She laid her fork down
and slid out of the chair before he could see the moisture in her
eyes. No one had ever offered to protect her before. "I'm going
to get another drink. You want one?"

"Angel, I—"

"How about a nice Martian ale? Or a Nova Zinger?" She didn't wait for him to choose, but turned and walked to the bar. She needed a chance to collect herself.

"Two Martian ales," Angel told the bartender. She watched him pour the drinks. "Place seems a little quiet tonight. Thought you'd have more ships at dock."

"That'll be fifty credits."

Angel had retrieved her money from the closet earlier and now pulled it out. With a great show, she placed one hundred credits on the counter. Before the bartender could pick it up, however, she laid her hand on top of it. "I need a ride out of here. Tonight."

He narrowed his eyes and studied her, no doubt deciding whether she was serious. Or worth the effort. "It'll cost you."

She took another hundred credits and added it to the pile. "I'd be grateful."

For a brief moment, they stared, each sizing up the other. Over the years, Angel had perfected her straight on, you-don't-want-to-mess-with-me look. She didn't have to wait long before the bartender nodded.

"There's a ship leaving in an hour, docking station Alpha-Nine."

Angel threw a quick glance over her shoulder at the group of rowdies. "That ship belong to them?"

"No. You don't want to go with them. This is an old trading vessel. Take it and you might have half a chance of leaving here alive."

Good enough for her. "Thanks." She removed her hand, picked up the drinks and carried them back to the table.

"We need to talk." Nicoli said after she sat down.

"About what?"

"About what happened earlier today."

So much had happened earlier that day. Nicoli's discovery that she was Michels, the episode in the airshaft, making love. Not love, she quickly amended. They'd had sex. That's all it had been. There was nothing to talk about. "I have to go."

"Where?" Concern etched his features.

"To the ladies room. I'll be back." Her gaze caressed his face, even as the lie fell from her lips, ripping at her heart. She couldn't let him stop her.

His gaze roamed over her and she had the distinct impression he was memorizing her features. "I'll be here, waiting for you." His velvety voice held a note of sadness. Already she missed him. How long would it take to forget him? Would she ever?

She stood to go, but his restraining hand stopped her before she could leave. "Be careful."

She cocked her head to one side and faked a smile. "I'm just going to the restroom."

"Yeah, I know." His voice sounded emotionless.

She picked up her unfinished drink, downed the rest of its contents in a single swallow and set the glass back solidly on the table. With a last look, she turned and walked away. "Take care of yourself, Nicoli," she whispered to herself, and almost didn't hear Nicoli's softly spoken parting words.

"Good-bye, Baby Girl."

Knowing he watched her, Angel ducked into the women's restroom. She'd wait here a few minutes, then sneak into the kitchen and take the back exit. Outside, the sound of raucous behavior grew louder. That other ship's crew had downed enough alcohol to float a free-trader. Angel decided to use the facilities while she waited and went into one of the stalls. The sound of the outer door opening was followed by several female voices.

"I don't know how much longer I can tolerate those jerks," the first woman said.

"Wish they'd reconsider the sex droids. I've been with these guys before, they like it rough."

"Did you see the one across the room, sitting by himself? He's a looker." A third voice spoke up.

"Yeah, for all the good it'll do him." It was the first woman again.

"What do you mean?"

"Didn't you hear Mason's crew talking? He's some kind of colonel with the USP security forces?"

"How do they know that?"

"They've run into him before."

"Oh."

"Yeah, well, it's good news for us."

"How so?" The third woman asked.

"Because tonight instead of beating on us for their jollies, they're going to beat the you-know-what out of the colonel."

The women kept talking as they fixed their makeup, but Angel had stopped listening. Nicoli was in trouble. When she heard the other women leave, she left her stall. Absently, she shoved her hands under the superclean mist, then shook them dry. Opening the bathroom door, she looked out. Nicoli still sat at the table, but his attention seemed to be focused on the glass he held, oblivious to any danger.

Mason's crew, on the other hand, seemed wound to a fevered pitch. Twelve of them, at least. There was no way Nicoli could take all of them. Angel looked at her watch. Most of her hour was up. If she stayed to help Nicoli, she'd miss her only shot off the space station.

Angel exited the bathroom and walked away.

Nicoli watched Angel slip into the kitchen. A part of him wanted her to stay, but that would have been a mistake. She was a distraction he didn't need, an emotional entanglement that could prove far too dangerous. Taking a deep sigh, he raised his glass and downed the contents.

He looked at his watch. The repairs on the ship should be complete. He tossed some credits onto the table and stood. There was nothing to keep him here now.

Leaving Flannigan's, the corridors seemed especially bleak as he walked them alone. Absorbed in his thoughts of Angel, he almost didn't hear the man behind him until it was too late. He turned just in time to keep the knife blade from piercing his back, and drove himself into his attacker.

The man was no match for Nicoli's strength and experience, and Nicoli soon dispatched him. Then he turned and found himself facing the rest of the crew that had been sitting in Flannigan's.

"If you want money, I'll give it to you." Nicoli said, realizing the futility of trying to fight all of them.

"It's not about money, Colonel Romanof. Not this time," one of them spoke. "This time, it's personal."

Well damn, he thought. He was in for the long haul. "Then bring it on. I have other things I need to do tonight."

His cavalier attitude riled the other men, as it was intended to do. An emotional fighter was a careless fighter and Nicoli needed all the advantage he could get.

Before the next man could advance on him, Nicoli bent to retrieve the unconscious man's knife. His opponents seemed content approaching him one on one, or perhaps it was that they were too drunk to consider rushing him. He met each one without hesitation, sometimes killing the other man, sometimes just knocking him out. But each man cost Nicoli energy and strength and belatedly, he realized this had been their strategy.

When the fourth man fell, the remaining crew members moved forward. Resigned to his own death, he vowed to take as many with him as he could, but before they reached him, two of the front men screamed and fell to the floor, dead. The others hesitated as wisps of smoke curled up from the bodies.

"And you thought *I* was trouble," Angel said, stepping next to him, laser in hand.

"You shouldn't have come," he growled, worried about how he could keep her safe when they were so outnumbered.

"Hi Angel, I'm glad you came back." Her voice dripped sarcasm. "Or how about, thanks Angel, for saving my life. Again."

"I'm not sure either of us will live through this," he retorted. "At least before, I knew you were safe."

At that moment, their attackers rushed forward, weapons drawn, fists flying. Angel fired, but couldn't hit all of them.

Dispatching the man closest to him, Nicoli turned. One attacker, his hand clinched around something, had slipped behind them and now stood too close to Angel, who was busy with two other attackers. As the nearly transparent blade of the crystal knife arced through the air, Nicoli leaped forward.

The blade pierced his side, slowing him temporarily. As the attacker looked on, Nicoli pulled out the blade and thrust it into the man's stomach, ripping upward as hard as he could. The man would not live to fight again.

NAME: _____

ADDRESS: _____

_____

_____

TELEPHONE: _____

E-MAIL: _____

_____ I want to pay by credit card.

__ Visa   __ MasterCard   __ Discover

Account Number: _____

Expiration date: _____

SIGNATURE: _____

*Send this form, along with $2.00 shipping
and handling for your FREE books, to:*

Love Spell Romance Book Club
20 Academy Street
Norwalk, CT 06850-4032

*Or fax (must include credit card
information!) to:* 610.995.9274.
*You can also sign up on the Web
at* www.dorchesterpub.com.

Offer open to residents of the U.S. and
Canada only. Canadian residents, please
call 1.800.481.9191 for pricing information.

If under 18, a parent or guardian must sign. Terms, prices and conditions
subject to change. Subscription subject to acceptance. Dorchester
Publishing reserves the right to reject any order or cancel any subscription.

Angel, having broken free of her two assailants, fired into the crowd. Two more fell dead while the other stumbled backward. Nicoli felt the first wave of nausea wash over him and knew he was losing too much blood. He had to get Angel to safety before he passed out.

"Let's go," he said, clapping a hand to his side. Together, he and Angel backed up.

"You're hurt," she observed, glancing at him. He knew he was covered in blood, but didn't want to alarm her.

"It's not serious," he lied.

For every step back they took, their attackers moved forward. Yet, there was enough distance between them that when he and Angel reached an intersecting corridor, they took the turn and ran.

The effort it took to maintain their pace quickly drained Nicoli of his remaining strength and his footsteps grew erratic. Darkness closed in around his vision, causing him to stumble. Angel grabbed his arm and draped it across her shoulders, holding it in place by taking hold of his hand. She holstered her laser, then wrapped the other arm about his waist, unaware that she grabbed his wounded side, sending pain lancing through him.

With each step, he leaned more heavily on her, forcing her to carry more of his weight. She was soon breathing fast and hard.

"Leave me," he ordered, thinking only of her safety.

"Forget it." Her words floated to him in a fog. "Just keep moving." Angel released his hand long enough to slap the comm-link on her shirt. "Yanur, open the hatch. Hurry."

They hit the docking bay at a pitiful run and reached the walkway leading to the hatch of the Icarus accompanied by the sounds of their pursuers' footsteps close behind. Sparing a quick glance back, Nicoli was horrified to see that the closest man was directly behind them, his knife already raised for the blow.

Then suddenly, the man screamed and fell backwards as a black burn spot spread across his chest.

Turning, Nicoli saw Yanur standing in the open hatch, laser in hand.

"Hurry." Yanur let fly with a few blasts over their heads into the oncoming group. Then he stood aside to let them board. "I've got it," he shouted, slamming his fist on the button to secure the hatch. "Get us out of here."

"Just hold on a little longer." Angel pleaded as she lowered Nicoli into a passenger seat.

He waved his hand toward the pilot's chair. "Go."

She sat down and fired up the engines. It was unlikely that the men outside could breach the hatch door, but the sooner they left, the better.

"Delphi IV Cont . . . Icarus, requesting . . . launch . . ." Angel's voice faded in and out.

Nicoli felt the pull as Angel fed the forward thrusters and heard her short laugh a moment later.

"We made it," was the last thing he heard before the darkness took him.

Chapter Fifteen

Brother Joh'nan stood on one of the many balconies at the House of Scyphor and looked out over the landscape of his people's new home. The first of Coronado's two suns was just beginning its assent over the horizon, painting the sky in wispy shades of orange, red and purple. Memories from his host body recalled hundreds of similar such mornings, but for Brother Joh'nan, it remained a novel experience. One fraught with symbolism.

For decades, his people had suffered the results of their own curiosity, paying the price for careless experimentation and lack of foresight with their very future. When it seemed there would be no salvation, Brother Joh'nan had a revelation.

The answer had been in front of them the entire time, but their weakened mental faculties refused to grasp it. They had experimented on living bodies for years, taking organs from donors as needed to replace their own, thereby extending their lives. They had sold other donors and organs on the black market, to get the funding they needed for food and to continue their experiments. It had not occurred to them to inhabit a donor body, until it was almost too late.

Once the idea was presented, transferring the life essence of one of their own into a host body had been ridiculously simple. A further refinement of the transfer process made it possible for them to access the stored memories of the host body.

This, in turn, led Brother Joh'nan to the idea of taking over another planet. For those willing to adapt to a different culture, a whole new existence became possible. Coronado, with its rich natural resources and cultural resistance to technology became the ideal choice.

Following the selection of their new home, they began abducting key personnel from that planet, transferring the life essence of one of their own into the victim's body and reintroducing them back into the world from which they were plucked. Tapping into the host body's memories, the resident Harvestor fit into his host's life with few the wiser. Those who did notice the infrequent odd behaviors ignored them, or suffered an untimely "accident."

The ultimate goal to assume control of Coronado would have been achieved more expediently had Brother Joh'nan simply taken over the high counsel's body, but the man was old and sick. So instead, Brother Joh'nan took the body of one of the high counsel's key advisors, one who was still young, and presumably healthy.

He raised his left hand and tried unsuccessfully to make a fist. He hadn't discovered the neurological disease slowly eating away at the donor's muscles until after he'd transferred to the body and re-established himself. For now, he would stay in this body. But as soon as it was possible, he planned to transfer to another. And this time, he vowed, the donor would be healthy.

A noise behind him signaled the presence of another.

"I assume you have news or you would not disturb me while I'm enjoying the sun and moonrise."

"Yes." Brother Damon spoke from behind him, his voice laced with concern. "The last group of initiates failed to arrive as scheduled."

"You contacted the Rebirth Colony?"

"No response. It's like no one's there. The little information

I've gathered from the area trading vessels seems to point to a failure with the planetary computer system."

Brother Joh'nan understood what he was being told. Without the computers, the main operating systems of the planet ceased to function. Without those, what little life remaining on their home planet would perish. In short, their planet was dead, as were all the family and friends who had remained behind.

Such was the way of things. It would have been impossible to transfer everyone to the new planet, so those left behind would have died eventually anyway as disease ate away their ability to function mentally and physically.

He nodded, accepting the news. "And our plans to build a transfer center in the village here on Coronado?"

"Proceeding as planned."

Brother Joh'nan let out his breath in a relieved sigh, then turned once again to admire the horizon.

It was the dawn of a new existence for his people.

Chapter Sixteen

When they reached open space, Angel turned to check on Nicoli.

"Oh, no." She set the autopilot and rushed to his slumped form. Pressing her fingers to his neck, she felt for a pulse. It was there, but it was weak.

"Yanur!" Where was he when she needed his help?

"Come on Nic, hang on." She ripped off one of her sleeves and held the wadded cloth against the wound in his side, which still oozed blood. She let the fingers of her free hand gently brush the side of his cheek. "Hang on, baby. You'll be okay."

His eyes fluttered open. "Where . . . ?"

"Safe. Out in open space."

"Hurt . . . you?"

"No. I'm fine."

He tried to smile, but the effort seemed too great. "Good." His eyes closed as his head fell forward.

"Nicoli!" She shouted, shaking him, afraid he'd died.

His eyes fluttered as he struggled to once again lift his head. His words were little more than a breath and Angel dropped her head close to his mouth to hear what he said. "Okay . . . to die."

Angel felt the impact of his words like a blow to the gut. He had given up; accepted death. With a sick feeling, she realized he seemed to welcome it. Well, it wasn't okay with her.

"Yanur!" She looked around for the older man as she shouted, but still saw no sign of him. *Damn.* "I'm not going to let you die, Nic. You and I aren't finished. You owe me and you can damn well pay up." Her tone was harsh with fear.

"You're . . . welcome."

"Oh no you don't! That blade was meant for me. Who the hell gave you the right to step in the way?"

". . . protect . . ."

"Yeah? Well, I don't need your protection." She wiped furiously at her face, trying to dry tears that refused to stop falling. "Don't die on me, Nic. Do you hear me? Nic? Don't you die."

"I think the people in the next quadrant heard you." Yanur hurried onto the bridge carrying his black bag.

"Where the hell have you been?"

Yanur ignored her as he dug into his bag and removed a small device. Angel recognized the triage unit as he ran it a couple of inches above Nicoli.

"How bad is it?" Her voice was almost a whisper. "Is he going to make it?"

"Normally, no." Yanur put the triage unit back in his bag and pulled out a long cylindrical tube. He opened a compartment on one side, then reached into his pocket to remove several small, greenish crystals. Angel recognized the raw tyrillium. "But I'm with you on this one. I have no intention of letting him die if I can prevent it." He popped the crystals into the tube, shut the lid and checked the gauge. Seemingly satisfied, he pressed a switch and the tube began to emit a low humming noise.

"Hold his shirt away for me," Yanur instructed.

Angel looked at the blood-soaked shirt, matted against Nicoli's side. Grabbing the front of it, she ripped it open, then gingerly peeled it back, exposing the wound. Yanur held the tube centimeters above the sliced edges, moving it slowly back and forth. Angel watched, amazed as the torn tissue knit itself together.

Nicoli's breathing became steadier, more peaceful. After a few moments, his eyes slowly opened. It seemed to take him a moment to focus, but then he saw her and gave her a weak smile.

"How are you feeling?" She smiled and leaned over him, unable to keep from brushing a lock of hair from his forehead.

"Like someone slashed me in the gut with a crystal blade." His voice sounded weak as he looked down at his side, touching it.

"Are you in pain?" Angel asked.

"Not now." He looked over at Yanur. "I guess you were able to get the tyrillium you needed."

Yanur smiled. "Yes. I thought at the time the price was a bit steep, but I've since changed my mind."

Nicoli moved in the chair and Angel put a hand on his shoulder. "What are you doing?"

"Getting up."

"No. You can sit here for awhile and rest. And you," she turned accusing eyes on Yanur. "You can tell me more about your little gismo, there."

Yanur offered her the wand to examine. "It's a Cellular Reparator."

"What exactly did it do?"

"It re-knit the torn tissue and replaced damaged cells with new ones. Any toxins introduced by the knife's blade were also eliminated."

She stared at the instrument in awe. "What else can it do?"

"It'll fuse broken bones." He gestured to his leg, which Angel suddenly noticed was no longer broken.

"Immortality," Angel breathed.

"No. That's one thing it can't do. It will heal wounds, even severe wounds. But there's a limit to what it can do. If the damage is too great, it can't heal all of it. And once someone is dead, well, it certainly can't bring him back to life."

"Useful tool to have around." Angel handed it back to him with some reluctance. "How do you get one of those?"

"You don't." Nicoli said. "Yanur invented this one and it's the only one of its kind." He gave her a pointed look. "And we keep this one a secret just between the three of us. Understood?"

Angel scowled at him. "I can see you're feeling better."

"As a matter of fact," he said, "I am feeling better. I think I'll go take a shower and wash off some of this blood." He stood up, Yanur at his side to offer support if it was needed.

When he was sure Nicoli wouldn't fall, Yanur moved back a step or two. Nicoli turned to look at Angel. His face was still an ashen color, but the spark of life was back in his eyes. "Angel, there is one thing." He gestured for her to lean toward him. When she was close enough to feel his breath warm her ear, he whispered. "*I gave me the right to step in the way.*" His lips pressed a kiss to her cheek. As she stared at him stupidly, he winked at her. Then he turned and followed Yanur off the bridge.

She watched them leave, her mind in a stunned state. When they disappeared from sight, she turned to sit in the pilot's seat. She adjusted the controls, a happy warm glow blooming within her. Feeling better than she had in a long time, she flipped off the autopilot and felt the ship's power in her hands. It was impossible to stop the smile spreading across her face.

Twenty minutes later, Nicoli reappeared on the bridge. Angel started to get up, but stopped when he sat next to her in the copilot's seat.

"You keep the controls for awhile."

"Oh, okay. How's your side?"

"Good as new."

She looked over at him, skeptical.

"Okay, it's a little tender." He smiled. "Out of curiosity, what's our course?"

"Coronado."

His eyebrows shot up. "I'm surprised. I figured you had us headed in the opposite direction."

"I did," she admitted. "But I figured you'd just turn us around anyway, so I saved you the effort." She paused a second. "Unless you've changed your mind about going?"

He shook his head. "I can't do that."

Angel shrugged. She'd known that would be his answer.

"Tell me why you don't want to go. Maybe if I understood, I could help you."

It was tempting. Not because she felt Nicoli could help, necessarily. But she trusted him. And it would be nice to finally share the story with someone.

"You were right," she said. "Back in the donor room, when you asked if I was from Coronado? I never answered you. Well, I grew up there. It's not like Earth or any of the other united planets in the system. Technology is tolerated, but only to the extent necessary to permit limited trade with other planets. Towns and villages are grouped into regions. Ruling Houses control the regions. The largest and most powerful is the House of Scyphor. The government is a dictatorship and issues between houses are settled through war.

"Equality between the genders is a foreign concept. Women must turn to the men for everything from food and shelter to protection. A woman without protection has no rights; she's an easy target. Most women whose husbands and fathers are killed in battle seek protection in other households. Virgins usually find husbands to take them. Women who are no longer virgins are lucky to find jobs as servants in another household. Those not so lucky become village whores, living off handouts from the men who use their bodies. There's no such thing as casual or premarital sex. Rape is punishable by death, but only because it represents a desecration of another man's property, not because it violates a woman. Most marriages are for political alliance, not for love." She avoided Nicoli's eyes, uncertain of his opinion on such matters. Would he find the Coronadian way as abhorrent as she? When he said nothing, she continued.

"It's all about who has the power. Of course, growing up as a child, I never knew it could be any other way. I was happy. I loved my parents and they loved me. Despite having an arranged marriage, my parents grew to love one another. My father was more liberal than most men were. He raised me to believe I was as good as the next person, even if the next person was a male. He secretly taught me to use the Coronadian warring blade and how to fight. He wanted me to be able to protect myself, if ever I needed to. He was ahead of his time, and while his views were popular with the women, the men despised him.

"My mother's father was one of those men. A man with political aspirations, he found my father to be a threat. So he plotted against him."

"How?" Nicoli's furrowed brow and scowling mouth showed his concern.

"He encouraged another man's attentions towards my mother. That man decided he wanted to marry my mother. So he *Challenged* my father."

"*Challenged*?"

"*The Challenge* is a fight with warring blades. It's a time-honored tradition for settling disputes. The victor would get my mother."

"Who won?"

"The other man." There was a moment of silence before she went on. "My father died in that fight."

"I'm sorry, Angel."

"On the day of my father's funeral, my grandfather and my mother's new husband were called away to war with another house. My mother and I walked through town following the service. An Aruebian Air Freighter had landed to do some trade. We'd never seen one that close and we were momentarily distracted from our pain. Curious, we approached it to get a better look. I'm not sure when the thought first sprouted, but almost by silent agreement, we went aboard to look around. My mother found a small closet and told me to hide.

"She said we were leaving, but first she needed to get money. She thought she could get it faster by herself. Her father was a wealthy man and she knew where he kept a stack of USP credits hidden. She would go to his house, take the money and come back before the freighter took off. Then we would start a new life together—free from my grandfather and his plans for us. For me." Angel paused, her thoughts taking her back to that day.

"What happened?" The warmth in Nicoli's voice brought her back to the present.

"My mother never returned." Angel spoke softly, as if she still couldn't believe what happened.

"She abandoned you?" He sounded incredulous.

Angel shook her head. "She was killed."

"How?"

"I don't know. I mean, I don't know specifics," she rushed on to tell him. "My grandfather's house was attacked. Very few survived. I overheard some of the freighter's crewmen talking about it. They were eager to take off."

"How old were you at the time?"

"I was fifteen years old. I haven't been home in eight years."

"How long did you stay in the closet?" From his tone, she knew he was thinking of her behavior in the airshaft earlier.

"Until we reached Delphi IV. Then I found another ship and hid again."

"And now you're afraid that if you go back to Coronado—"

"My grandfather will find me and never let me go."

Nicoli looked thoughtful. "That was eight years ago. He may not even be alive."

"I'd just as soon not take the chance of finding out."

Nicoli sat facing forward, staring out into space. After a moment he spoke again, his tone serious. "I won't let anything happen to you."

Startled at the conviction in his voice, she turned to look at him. "Thank you. But we both know there are no guarantees in life."

Three hours later, they reached Coronado. Nicoli established communications with the largest power head on the planet, the high counsel of the Ruling House of Scyphor. Nicoli hoped to convince the man that the Harvestors were a threat, but he was concerned that any culture so technologically backwards might not believe that a race of aliens was capable of taking over the bodies of their friends and loved ones.

It had been agreed that Angel would remain aboard the Icarus with Yanur while Nicoli was away. The two would monitor his whereabouts and conversations through hidden comm-links.

"Okay, I'm taking her down." Angel made adjustments to the

thrusters, and, using the guidance stick, angled the ship downward. Soon they were cruising just above the surface of the planet, slightly above tree level.

Nicoli sat next to Angel as she flew and let his gaze study her face.

"Stop it," she said.

"What?"

"Stop looking at me. I'm fine."

"I know."

"I mean it, Nicoli. You've got enough to worry about. Don't trust anyone. No one. Especially not the high counsel."

He smiled at her indulgently, tickled that she cared enough to warn him.

"Stop smiling." Angel sounded exasperated. "If you get yourself into trouble, I probably can't help you here."

"I'll be careful, Baby Girl."

A few minutes later, they landed in a field near the high counsel's palace and a contingent of guards was sent to escort Nicoli inside. Angel stayed on the bridge while Yanur walked him to the hatch.

"Testing, testing." Nicoli spoke in a regular tone.

Angel joined them a second later. "I heard you loud and clear. We'll take turns monitoring you. If something goes wrong, just say the word."

"Okay. But if something happens, let Yanur come. You," he pointed a finger at her, "stay in the ship and out of trouble." With that, he left.

"Colonel Romanof. It is a pleasure to meet you." The high counsel of House of Scyphor rose from his massive desk, walking around it to meet Nicoli halfway across the room. The high counsel was an older man, mid-seventies by Nicoli's estimate. Age had taken its toll on the man's once muscular physique, but he still stood tall and proud. They shook hands, each testing the pressure of the other man's grip. Nicoli found his grip well matched. Both men smiled.

"Your reputation is well known throughout this galaxy and the next." The man waved a hand, dismissing the guards who'd remained standing near the back of the room. They turned and left, closing the door behind them.

The high counsel offered Nicoli the chair in front of the desk, then returned to his seat on the opposite side.

"Now, tell me what brings you all the way across the universe to see me."

"High Counsel—"

"Gil'rhen, please. My friends call me Gil'rhen. I would like to think we could be friends, you and I."

The man's overt friendliness made Nicoli leery. But he acknowledged the man's request by nodding his head. "Are you familiar with the race of aliens known as the Harvestors?"

"Vaguely, yes. They kidnap residents from various planets then sell the bodies on the black market, don't they?"

"Yes. On my last mission, I infiltrated their operations."

The high counsel nodded his approval. "I'm glad to see the USP take action."

"Actually, the USP did not sanction my mission, initially. I acted on my own."

"By yourself?"

"With the two members of my crew."

"Really? What was the purpose of your mission? Reconnaissance?"

Nicoli waited a heartbeat before answering. "Annihilation."

The high counsel's expression changed from one of bored politeness to avid interest, tinged with respect. He leaned forward in his seat. "Three men against a race of Harvestors." He spoke thoughtfully, as if considering the different strategies. "And what was the outcome of your mission?"

"I believe we were successful. I've since notified the USP and they will send troops to handle any survivors."

"Excellent. Wonderful." He smiled and Nicoli could sense an old warrior's thrill of victory against overwhelming odds.

Nicoli waited for the moment to pass before he spoke again. "Gil'rhen, I didn't come here to brag about my exploits. I'm here because I've discovered the Harvestors' plan to take over another planet. Your planet."

For a moment, the high counsel stared at him, open-mouthed. "No. That can't be right," he sputtered. "You are mistaken."

"I am confident of my information."

The high counsel studied Nicoli's face, no doubt wondering if he could trust what this stranger said. "If what you say is true, they must be stopped."

"I agree, but first we must find them."

"They would have to be in the smaller villages to go unnoticed for so long."

"I agree." Nicoli looked down at his hands resting on the arms of the chair before returning his somber gaze to the high counsel. "I haven't told you the worst yet. The leader, at least, has infiltrated your household."

"What?" The high counsel practically stood up at the pronouncement. "Who?"

"I don't know, but it's someone who feels he is in line to take over your position. Until we discover exactly who it is, we must assume that no one is who he or she appears to be."

"Ready for a break?" Angel asked, walking onto the bridge to relieve Yanur. He had been monitoring Nicoli's conversation with the high counsel for almost an hour and Angel could fight her curiosity no longer.

"Absolutely." He pulled out the earplug and handed it to her as he stood up, letting her take his spot in the pilot's seat. "I need a nap."

"So, how's it going? Any problems?"

"Not really." Yanur yawned and stretched. "At first, the high counsel didn't seem to believe him, but when Alex told him about the leader being someone in his palace, he started to take it seriously."

"Okay. I'll monitor things for a while."

Yanur waved a hand, too busy yawning to speak. He walked from the bridge, leaving Angel to kick back in the chair and put in the earplug.

". . . anything unusual in the last several months?" Nicoli was asking.

"No. But then, I don't get out as much as I used to. I leave most of the travel to my two advisors."

Angel stopped listening to the words for a moment and concentrated on the sound of the high counsel's voice. It had been eight years since she'd heard it, but she would have recognized it had it been a thousand. The polite, knowing responses, spoken in rich, dulcet tones that belied the harsh nature of the man, transported her back in time. Once again she heard that same rich, calm voice telling her of her father's death.

The thrum of his voice was interrupted by a dry, grating cough, breaking the spell. Realizing she'd let herself get caught up in bad memories, she mentally shook herself and focused on the current exchange between the two men.

"I'm not familiar with your government," Nicoli said. "Perhaps you could explain it to me."

"Certainly. What would you like to know?"

"Let's start with the basic framework. You are the primary ruling body, is that correct?"

"For the Southwest region, that's correct. Each region is run by a ruling house."

"But yours is the largest?"

"Correct. We are located on the planet's largest continent."

"The Cerian Mountains fall under your domain."

"Yes . . ."

"So, in essence, you control all of the natural tyrillium deposits on the planet."

There was a moment of silence before the high counsel spoke. "I see that you are a thorough man, Colonel Romanof. You have done your research."

"I'm not the threat, Gil'rhen. The Harvestors are. But it's important for you to realize that if I have this information, so must they. If you were going to take over a planet, wouldn't you take over one with the greatest potential for future power and influence? As the USP's other tyrillium resources become depleted, Coronado stands to gain much."

After a moment, Angel heard the high counsel's mumbled agreement.

"Who else lives here at the palace? You mentioned advisors earlier."

"Yes. I have three advisors who have taken on more of my responsibilities lately," the high counsel said thoughtfully.

"Do any of them travel?"

"Well, yes, from time to time. It is often necessary for one of us to meet with the other ruling houses. But if you're thinking that one of my advisors could be a Harvestor, you're mistaken. It's simply not possible. I've known these men for years. One of them practically grew up here."

There was a pause before Nicoli continued. "You said that your family has been ruling for many generations?"

"Yes. The high counsel position is passed down from father to son."

"So, in the event of your death, your son becomes the new high counsel?"

"No." Angel detected bitterness in the high counsel's tone. "My son died thirty-four years ago."

"I'm sorry," Nicoli said. "Then your grandson?"

"No, I don't currently have a grandson."

"Then who is your successor?"

No one, Angel thought with satisfaction. Then cocked her head to the side. What had the high counsel said?

"I have a daughter, though she is very ill right now . . ."

Angel stopped listening, her mind locked on a single realization. The high counsel's daughter was alive! Could it be true?

She tore the plug from her ear and rushed from the bridge. She didn't bother to tell Yanur what she was doing—he would only try to stop her. She rushed to her cabin and undid the braid of her hair, letting it hang loosely down her back. It would be safer if she had a long skirt or robe to wear. Improvising, she took four of Nicoli's shirts from the closet, all white. She pulled one over her own top. The other three, she tied around her waist to form a rough skirt. From a distance, it might be mistaken for a dress. She had no intention of getting close enough for anyone to know differently.

The few guards left to watch the ship stood by the front hatch, so Angel walked to the back and stepped out the rear exit. She closed the hatch behind her, then carefully walked away from the ship and the palace, toward the back fields.

Once safely out of sight, she found a tree. The thought of waiting for Nicoli to help her raced fleetingly through her mind, only to be dismissed. She could do this herself. When darkness fell, she would join the workers as they returned from the fields. The crowd would move into the courtyard, taking Angel with it. And once she got close enough, she'd slip inside the palace.

Chapter Seventeen

Nicoli boarded the Icarus feeling a sense of accomplishment. While the high counsel obviously found it difficult to believe that his planet was being overtaken by Harvestors, he had nevertheless invited Nicoli and his crew to attend that evening's banquet, at which time Nicoli could observe all the members of the high counsel's staff and household for himself. Later, Nicoli and the high counsel would meet to compare notes.

Nicoli's good feeling lasted until he reached the bridge and found Yanur, pacing back and forth.

"Is she with you?" Yanur asked, his voice heavy with concern.

Nicoli's stomach plummeted. "Who? Angel?"

"She's gone."

"What?" Nicoli stepped forward. There were no signs of a fight on the bridge and Yanur appeared unhurt. "What happened? Were you boarded? Was there an attack?"

Yanur hung his head, shaking it. "No, no. I don't know what happened. When I left her, she was sitting right here, listening on the comm-link to your conversation with the high counsel. I went to take a shower and rest for a minute. When I came back to the bridge, she was gone. The front hatch was locked from the inside, but one of the back hatches has been opened." Yanur wrung his hands together. "I didn't hear anything. If the hatches had been forced, the alarms would have sounded."

"Have you searched the ship for her?"

Yanur nodded.

"Did you see any signs of a struggle? Any blood?" Angel wouldn't let herself be abducted without putting up a fight. His heart clinched at the thought of Angel hurt.

"No, nothing. In fact, everything looks the way it always does."

Nicoli searched the ship himself, looking for signs of a forced entry or struggle. After finding none, he was left to face the only possible conclusion.

Angel had left of her own free will.

She had left him. Again.

He tried not to think of it in those terms, but somehow, once the thought formed, it wouldn't be ignored.

He shook himself mentally. He'd better forget about Angel and start focusing on his mission. He went to prepare for the evening's activities, but stopped the moment he entered his cabin.

Looking around, he gave a short derisive laugh. The very idea that he could forget her was ludicrous. Every time he pulled a shirt from the closet, he'd see the image of her standing there, wearing nothing but his shirt. Tonight, he'd have to sleep in the same bed where they'd made love. Her very essence filled the room, assaulting his senses until he thought he might go mad. And when he sought to escape the onslaught of memories by going to the bridge, he found that he couldn't. Her essence was everywhere, throughout the ship.

Nicoli squared his shoulders and took his emotions in hand. When Yanur joined him a few moments later, he was focused again on the mission.

"We've been invited to dine with the high counsel tonight, as his honored guests. It'll give us a chance to study the members of his staff; see if we can discover which ones might be repossessed Harvestors."

"Can we trust the high counsel?"

"I don't think we can trust anyone."

Yanur's face temporarily brightened. "I finished the anti-toxin pills. Maybe this would be a good time to test them out. Just in case the food is poisoned."

Nicoli smiled at the older man's enthusiasm. "Bring them." Over the years, Yanur had saved his life many times over with his various medical concoctions and scientific inventions.

"And Angel?"

He looked over at his friend and knew they both would miss the feisty young woman who had come so abruptly into their lives.

"She's made her choice."

Darkness finally came and Angel slipped easily into the throng of workers going past the palace. She traveled unnoticed into the courtyard and as the group began to disperse, each headed to their separate homes, Angel walked around to the side. Not many people knew about the garden entrance.

Angel opened the door and looked into the hallway. She startled a passing servant who gave her a curious look, but quickly moved on. With the rest of the hall empty and quiet, Angel stepped inside. The tiled flooring hadn't changed much in eight years, but the hall looked different. No longer as big as it had seemed in her youth. And much of the artwork hanging on the walls was new. These observations were made on an almost subconscious level as Angel focused on finding the correct room.

It was all she could do to not run down the halls. Constantly looking about her, she turned down first one hallway then another. Would it be the same room, she wondered?

Then suddenly, she turned the corner and there it was. The door stood closed and Angel approached with caution. Would she be there? And if so, would she remember Angel? Worse thoughts crowded in. Would she hate Angel for leaving?

Afraid to find out, she refused to turn around.

She pressed her ear to the door and listened. After a few

moments, when she'd heard nothing but silence, she tested the door handle and found it turned easily.

She opened the door a crack and paused. No alarms sounded, so she pushed it open a little farther and walked in. The room appeared empty and disappointment hit her. She had felt certain her mother would be here. She decided to wait, in hopes that her mother would soon return.

Looking around, she saw that the bedroom hadn't changed. It looked exactly as she remembered, and it made her want to cry. The love she'd felt in this room, she'd not felt since she'd left. She walked over to the dresser, picking up each familiar item that sat there, silently greeting each as an old friend.

At first she didn't see her. The lighting was dim and despite the warmth of the day, many blankets were piled on the bed.

"You've come for me," a soft familiar voice said. "I knew one day you would."

Angel whirled around and focused on the woman, now visible beneath a mound of blankets. Though she looked drawn and weak, she was exactly as Angel remembered her every time she closed her eyes. With a small cry of delight, Angel rushed to the woman's side. "Mother!"

Kneeling beside the bed, Angel wrapped her arms around the frail figure. Tears coursed unnoticed down her cheek as she laid it against her mother's. "I thought you were dead. I never would have left you . . ."

"Angel?" A gentle hand at her shoulder pushed her back. Angel looked down into her mother's face as it studied her own. The voice trembled as she spoke. "Angel, my sweet Angel." She laid the palm of her hand against Angel's cheek. "I didn't mean to kill you. How afraid you must have been when the freighter was attacked. Oh Angel, I'm so sorry."

What was her mother talking about? "Mother, it's me, Angel. I'm alive. I've come to get you out of here."

Her mother's glassy eyes seemed to shift in and out of focus while her lips formed a tremulous smile. "Death is not so bad if it means we are together again."

Welcoming death? What was this? Her mother was spouting nonsense. She laid a hand against her mother's forehead and felt the fever. Her mother was suffering from delusions, thinking her daughter was a ghost sent to retrieve her upon her death.

"Mother, it's me, Angel. I'm really here. I got off the freighter at Delphi IV. I wasn't on it when it was attacked." She stroked her mother's cheek. "Please believe me." What illness did her mother have? How serious was it?

Her mother's eyelids fluttered closed again, a small smile on her lips.

Angel looked around the room. She'd been gone from the ship too long and needed to get back, but there was no way she was leaving without her mother. She had done that once, years ago, and there was no way she was doing it again. When she left Coronado, her mother would be with her. She would have to carry her; there was no other option.

Her mother was a dead weight, drifting in and out of consciousness. It felt disrespectful, draping her mother over her shoulder like a sack of vegetables, but there was no other way for Angel to carry her.

Once again, Angel checked the hallway to make sure it was empty before stepping out. Progress was slow and with each step, her burden, and her frustration, grew. She knew she'd never reach the ship.

Which is why, when she stepped outside and found a contingent of guards waiting for her, she wasn't surprised.

"So returns the prodigal child," one of the guards said, stepping forward. He gave instructions for two of his men to take Angel's mother and carry her back into the palace.

Angel gave her mother over without a fight, then turned to face the guard. "Hello, Herrod. Still doing *his* dirty work?"

The guard called Herrod did not rise to her bait. Instead, he gave her a knowing smile. "He will be pleased to know you've returned." Another gesture of his hand and two more guards stepped to either side of her. "And you've chosen a particularly interesting dress for the occasion."

Angel felt herself blush and undid the shirts at the waist and let them fall to the ground. Then she peeled off the shirt she wore. A woman in men's clothing would be frowned upon, but she wasn't interested in respecting Coronado customs. If an opportunity to escape presented itself, she didn't want to be hampered by the makeshift dress.

When she looked back at Herrod, he smiled. It wasn't a friendly smile. It was the kind of smile that made her wish she had on more clothes—or better yet, was carrying an assault cannon. He seemed pleased with her discomfort and moved closer so he could speak to her without the other guards hearing.

"An'jel, you have grown into a beautiful woman." He walked slowly around her, letting her feel his eyes roam over her body. He stopped behind her, close enough that his breath brushed against her hair when he spoke. "Tell me," he whispered, picking up a loose strand to rub between his fingers. "Are you still a virgin?"

Angel whipped about to face him, barely controlled fury in her eyes. "Stay away from me, Herrod."

Almost reluctantly it seemed, he let the lock of hair fall and took a step back, but continued his perusal of her body. Putting a finger to the side of his chin in an imitation of deep thought—because Angel was sure he was incapable of the real thing—he studied her. "I think after all these years, you're not a virgin anymore. Maybe you're married." He made a show of looking around. "But I don't see a husband, do you? No husband. No virginity. I guess that makes you a whore, doesn't it, An'jel?"

Angel ignored his taunt, turning to face him as he circled her, because she didn't trust him.

"Are you a *whore*, An'jel?" He made the word sound as filthy as he could. "Will you beg men in the streets, offer them your body in exchange for a crumb of food? Sleep with them just to have the warmth of a real bed?" He stopped walking. "Perhaps I should find out what sweets you have to offer a man. If I find you pleasing, I'll keep you for myself." He reached out his hand as if to stroke her face.

"Touch me and you're a dead man," Angel said, pleased that she managed to keep her tone even despite the rapid beating of her heart.

His hand stopped midair, then fell to his side as he laughed. "Am I supposed to be afraid of you?"

"No." Angel smiled. "You're supposed to be afraid of *him*, because if he finds out you raped me and took my virginity, he'll kill you."

Herrod's laughter stopped and the smile faded to a face gone red with anger. "If I take your virginity, then I can claim the right to be your husband. And as such, I will be the next high counsel."

Angel's laughter was genuine. "Do you really envision yourself to be *his* choice for successor? He'd probably have you killed before dinner—a minor inconvenience."

"I think not. I am the only male blood relation the high counsel has left." Herrod countered between clinched teeth.

"Your mother was a whore your father experimented with to prove he was a man. But he was weak and killed himself after the high counsel found him in his lover's bed. His *male* lover. And you think the high counsel will openly claim you as blood? You're not even good enough to be his advisor; you're a security guard."

She'd pushed him too far and didn't duck fast enough to avoid the blow to her face when it came. She fell back, stunned, eyes watering. But she lifted her head to face him. She'd gotten to him, broken his control. He'd lost and she'd won. And she wanted him to know.

The other guards pressed closer and Angel could tell that if he came at her again, there would be dissension in the ranks. They reported to Herrod, but they feared the high counsel.

Herrod stared at the guards, and for a moment, she wondered what he would do.

"Bring her," he ordered, giving her a look that promised more between them.

"Where are you taking me?" She dared to ask as he walked off, not knowing what answer she hoped to receive. But either he didn't hear, or didn't care.

He disappeared around a corner and Angel had no choice in whether she followed or not as the guards tightened their hold on her arms and led her forward.

*   *   *

Nicoli and Yanur were ushered into the main banquet room of the palace. A long table stood along the far wall, topped with food and drink. Men in formal Coronadian dress stood around, visiting with one another. Nicoli let his gaze travel across the room, and though he didn't expect to see Angel, he was nevertheless disappointed when the only women present were servants.

"Colonel Romanof, I'm glad you could make it." The high counsel stepped from the crowd, extending his hand in greeting. Behind him, two men stood patiently attentive. They wore ceremonial dress similar to the outfit worn by the high counsel, with tunics made of obviously high-quality fabric and adorned with the House of Scyphor emblem, a large black bird in flight. Below the tunics, fitted slacks were tucked into boots and warring blades were strapped about their hips. Nicoli was struck with the thought that though the outfits seemed ceremonial, they were well suited for easy movement, or fighting, if need be.

"High Counsel." Nicoli began, pausing when the old man wagged a reprimanding finger in the air. "Gil'rhen," he quickly amended. "Thank you for inviting us on such short notice. It is an honor to be here."

"I would like to introduce you to two of my advisors." The high counsel gestured to the men standing beside him. "This is Rianol D'Wintre and Pualson Metters."

Nicoli exchanged handshakes with the two men, studying each closely as he did. Both were near his own age, and resembled typical Coronadians, tall, blond and sporting warrior-like builds.

"It's a pleasure to meet you." D'Wintre said. His ready smile was smooth and easy. "I've heard much about you." His manner seemed genuine.

The other one, Metters, seemed less comfortable, but still extended his hand in greeting. "A pleasure, Colonel."

"Thank you." Nicoli politely acknowledged their words. "And allow me to introduce Yanur Snellen, crew member and good friend."

Yanur shook hands with all three men and they exchanged a few words of greeting.

"Didn't you say you had three members to your crew?" The high counsel asked, looking around the room, presumably for the errant crewmember.

"Yes. I thought it best to leave her aboard my ship for now," Nicoli lied.

The high counsel looked at him quickly. "A woman?" He nodded then. "Of course. A servant."

"No. Not a servant."

The high counsel's expression turned smug and knowing. "Of course."

Nicoli wasn't sure he liked the suggestion inherent in the man's words. The thought of Angel out there alone swept through his mind. Despite the fact that he didn't entirely trust the high counsel, Nicoli considered enlisting the man's help in finding her, just to make sure she was okay. But before he could make up his mind, the big double doors to the chamber opened and a guard hurried in.

He went directly to the high counsel and whispered something in his ear. The high counsel's face became animated as he moved off to the side and murmured something in return. Then the guard hurried back out the door.

By this time, everyone in the room had grown quiet, no doubt speculating on the situation. The doors opened again and several more guards entered. The guests crowded forward, obstructing Nicoli's view. A short distance from him, Yanur's face turned an ashen white.

With a mounting feeling of trepidation, Nicoli pushed his way through the gathered crowd until he could see. And then he felt his own face drain of color.

Angel stood, clutched between two guards, looking more defiant than scared. Her cheek was red where someone had hit her and the sight of it made Nicoli's blood boil. He *would* find who did it and make him pay.

He moved forward at the same time the high counsel did. The older man's face was still pale and he stared at Angel as if he'd seen a ghost.

"Are you all right?" Nicoli asked as he moved to stand next to her.

Neither Angel nor the high counsel seemed to notice him, their attention focused on each other.

"I never thought to see you again, An'jel." The older man spoke quietly, his voice tinged with emotion. "Welcome home." He nodded once to the guards, who released their grip on her and stepped back.

Nicoli saw her chin rise a notch as she squared her shoulders and met the high counsel's eyes.

"Hello, Grandfather."

The crowd stood in absolute silence as it absorbed the announcement. When the feeling of betrayal hit him, Nicoli shook it off. He wished she had confided in him, but after meeting her grandfather, he understood her need to keep her secrets. Now that he was here, however, he couldn't help but wonder what other surprises lay ahead.

As if in answer to his question, a commotion began in the back of the room. Acting in concert, the guests split apart, like the parting of the Red Sea, opening a path between them. A man appeared, moving forward with a calm, confident air. Nicoli judged him to be near to his own age, with similar height and build. The ceremonial outfit he wore was unlike the advisors' outfits. As he drew closer, Nicoli saw that it was identical to the high counsel's.

"Oh, no."

Hearing her quick intake of breath, Nicoli glanced sharply at Angel in time to see her eyes widen.

"What's the matter?" He whispered. "Who is that?"

"My husband."

Chapter Eighteen

Angel felt Nicoli's silence like a physical blow. She shook her head, trying to clear her thoughts, wishing she had time to explain.

"An'jel, I would like to present the counsel-elect, Victor D'rajmin. Your husband." The high counsel's tone sounded self-satisfied to her.

A man she had never met stood before Angel, staring at her with a possessiveness that startled her. "Welcome home, wife." His voice was like warm honey, dripping with sincerity. His smile transformed an already handsome face to one of such stunning masculine beauty, it took Angel a moment to compose herself.

She could not allow herself to fall into Gil'rhen's trap just because the man he'd appointed as his successor and her husband was attractive. A pawn was a pawn, no matter how enticing the other game pieces appeared.

"I am not your wife."

A gasp went up from the crowd at her announcement. The warm light in the council-elect's eyes grew cold and menacing, causing Angel to take an involuntary step closer to Nicoli.

"Do not be afraid of me, An'jel. We will suit each other well, you and I. For the last several years, I have followed, and admired, your exploits as a galactic courier. You are bright and intelligent as well as beautiful."

His speech, meant to put her at ease, had the opposite effect. "What do you mean, you've followed my exploits for the past several years?"

It was the high counsel who answered. "You didn't think that I would just let you run away, did you? My contacts on Delphi IV spotted you when you arrived. I would have brought you home immediately, but the war had just started and I felt you would be safer off the planet. So I dispatched guards to watch over you, make sure you were safe."

"No, no." Angel shook her head, absorbing his words through the ringing in her ears. Her whole life! He'd known where she was, been watching her, the entire time. Not once had she ever been free of him. She'd been living a lie and never once suspected the truth.

"The whole time?" She wasn't aware she'd spoken aloud until her grandfather chuckled.

"Up until a couple of weeks ago. We lost you on Earth during the attack on the airfield. I thought you were gone for good then. I never expected you to show up here." An inquisitive expression crossed his face. "How did you get here?

"She came with me." Nicoli spoke for the first time, drawing everyone's attention to him.

"You?" Both the high counsel and counsel-elect looked from Nicoli to Angel as if weighing the truth of the statement. Then the high counsel's expression changed to one of horror. "My granddaughter is the woman you have been traveling with?"

"Yes."

Angel watched her grandfather's face turn red as he stared accusingly first at her, then at Nicoli. Again, she was grateful for Nicoli's solid presence beside her.

"For the past eleven years, I have allowed my granddaughter to do as she pleases, wandering across the universe, all the while, discreetly following her from a distance, interfering only when I felt her life, or her virtue, was in danger." The high counsel's voice rose in volume. "I have gone to great lengths to ensure that *no man* take from her that which belongs to her husband." The words practically spewed from his mouth. "And now, I find out that the most reputed soldier of the USP has turned my granddaughter into his whore?!"

Nicoli took a step forward, bodily moving Angel until she stood behind him. In a voice laced with steel and the promise of dire things to come, he faced the high counsel. "Be very careful what you say about my wife."

Both Angel's and the high counsel's gasps were lost in the sudden murmurs of the crowd.

The high counsel spoke first. "My granddaughter is your wife? When did this marriage take place?"

"We were married a few days ago, in accordance with Althusian law."

The high counsel turned to Angel, his tone sharp. "Is this true?"

Angel looked at Nicoli, wondering what game he played. But he let nothing show on his face. She would just have to trust him. "Yes."

The high counsel remained silent and Angel knew he weighed the pros and cons of this new situation. An ambitious man, he would no doubt see the advantage of an alliance with the United System of Planets. After a moment, his expression changed to one of satisfaction. In a voice loud enough to be heard by everyone in the hall, he addressed Nicoli.

"Colonel Nicoli Romanof, do you claim An'jel ToRrenc, granddaughter to Gil'rhen ToRrenc, high counsel of House of Scyphor, for your own? Do you offer her your protection and take full responsibility for her, in accordance with our laws?"

The ceremonial words echoed across the room and Angel felt another wave of panic wash over her. Nicoli mustn't answer. "He's not familiar with our laws and customs," she protested.

"Quiet," her grandfather ordered.

"Yes," Nicoli answered at the same time.

The silence that met Nicoli's response was a death knoll for

183

Angel and she was powerless to alter the course Nicoli had set for them.

"In accordance with Coronadian law, I recognize your claim as husband to my granddaughter." Here the high counsel paused to turn toward the stunned audience. "As such, you are now successor to the high counsel position."

When Victor would have protested, the high counsel waved him to silence. "We will discuss this later, privately. In the meantime, I suggest you go change clothes."

Victor gave Nicoli a lethal look and stormed out of the room. Affecting a smile, the high counsel took a step forward to shake Nicoli's hand. "We have never had an off-worlder serve as leader of our people. It will take some getting used to."

Nicoli nodded. He had no intention of being the high counsel's successor and suspected the old man would not allow it anyway. But if he was hoping for a means to upset everyone's plans, he couldn't have arranged it any better. Victor, who had been in line for the high counsel position, became Nicoli's number one suspect for the Harvestors' leader.

Nicoli turned to Angel. Judging from the shocked expression on her face, he knew he needed to get them someplace where they could talk privately. And soon.

The bruise on her cheek stood out and Nicoli raised his hand to cup her chin, gently tipping her head to the side so he could get a better look at the injury. The outline of someone's hand was clear in the darkening skin.

"What happened?" His words were softly spoken, but he didn't bother to hide the rage burning inside him. The two guards who'd held her before, stumbled back. Nicoli saw their eyes dart toward the head guard, who, in turn, sent Nicoli a challenging look.

"I ran into something," Angel's tone was sarcastic, but her eyes begged him to let it go.

"Ah. I was afraid someone had struck you." His eyes came to rest on the head guard as he spoke and he let his tone say what his words did not. That any man who caused Angel injury would suffer the consequences by Nicoli's own hand.

By now, the guests were over their initial shock and came

forward to congratulate the high counsel and welcome Nicoli as their council-elect. Nicoli studied the face of every man whose hand he shook, trying to gauge the other man's reaction. But if any Harvestors were in this room, it was not apparent by their behavior.

Angel stood quietly beside him and he could feel the various emotions emanating off her like waves of heat off the desert. He had no doubt an interesting evening lay ahead. He was about to suggest they leave, when he heard her gasp.

"Rianol." Angel looked at the advisor with a bemused expression on her face. Then to Nicoli's surprise, she gave a shout of glee and threw herself into the other man's arms.

Rianol had the good sense to look uncomfortable under Nicoli's scrutiny and, after returning Angel's hug, stepped back to a safer distance. Angel, seemingly oblivious to the underlying currents between the men, enthusiastically rushed on. "Rianol, it's so good to see you again. Look at you, all grown up. Oh, Nicoli. This is Rianol. He and I used to play together as kids. When my father taught me to use the warring blade, Rianol was my sparring partner." There was a wistful look on her face that Nicoli found irritating.

"Colonel Romanof, please forgive my familiarity with your wife," Rianol apologized. "She is like a sister to me." Then he held out his hand to Nicoli. "Allow me to congratulate you both."

Several hours later, a serving girl showed Nicoli and Angel to a room in the palace. While Nicoli felt they would both be more comfortable on board his ship, he was willing to indulge the high counsel's request that they stay at the palace. Especially since this arrangement would give him an opportunity to study all the palace residents more closely.

After showing them around the luxurious room, the serving girl left and Angel and Nicoli were finally alone.

Standing there, Nicoli remembered how he'd felt when he came back to the ship and found Angel gone. His fear that she might run into trouble had been justified, judging from the bruise on her cheek. The thought ate at his patience. In an effort to restore his control, he walked to the bedroom door and locked it. Counting to ten, he prepared to talk to Angel in a calm, controlled tone. She never gave him the chance.

With eyes shooting flames, she started in on him. "Are you out of your mind? Did an infection from your wound rot your brain?"

"Me? What about you?" It seemed the height of hypocrisy that she should be mad at him.

"How dare you say we're married. Do you have any idea what you've done?"

He felt the dam of his control break. "If you had stayed on the ship as instructed, none of this would have happened." The reminder of the fear he felt when he discovered her gone just made him angrier. "Do you realize what could have happened to you? What if those men hadn't recognized you as the high counsel's granddaughter? What if they decided you were fair game? Were you going to fight them all? Damn it, Angel, they could have raped you." Turning away from her, he shoved his fingers through his hair, fighting for calm.

Angel grew unusually quiet and when he turned back to her, he wanted to kick himself. The fire in her eyes had been replaced with a haunted wariness. A hand, not quite steady, had strayed to her bruised cheek. Swearing at himself, Nicoli crossed the room and wrapped his arms around her, drawing her close to him. "I'll kill him," he said softly.

"I'm okay." Her words were muffled, spoken against his chest, but she made no move to pull away. "He didn't rape me, but . . ."

Nicoli tightened his embrace, trying to draw her closer, as if this were the only way he could protect her. He pressed his lips to her head and felt the warm breath of her sigh across his chest. "Tell me what happened."

She was quiet so long, he thought he might not tell him anything, but then she began. She described listening in on his conversation with the high counsel and discovering that her mother was alive.

"I had to go to her." He could hear the plea for his understanding. And he did.

"Of course you needed to go to her. But you should have waited for me. I would have helped you."

"I know, but I thought while my grandfather was with you, I could sneak in and get her." She gave a short, self-deprecating laugh. "That plan certainly backfired, didn't it?' She pulled herself from his arms and walked over to the bed, flinging her arm in the air, then letting it fall helplessly back to her side. "Married. I can't believe it. You couldn't come up with a better lie?"

"It wasn't a lie."

She whirled around to face him. "Come again?"

Nicoli sighed, knowing the worst was yet to come. "It wasn't a lie. We really are married."

She was shaking her head. "No, no, no. I think I would know if I were married." She stared at him, perhaps waiting for him to agree with her, but he said nothing. As if her knees had suddenly given out, she sank onto the edge of the bed. "Oh God. You're serious."

"I am Althusian and in my culture, a man does not take a woman's virginity unless he intends to make that woman his wife. The other day, when we made love, I accepted the gift of your virginity and pledged myself to you, making us husband and wife."

She stared at him, mouth open in disbelief. "You deceived me."

"I asked if you wanted me to stop. You said no."

"I didn't know that meant I was getting married. You conveniently left that part out." She stood up and began to pace. "Don't you see? I've spent the past eight years fighting for the right to marry who I want. I ran away from my home just so I wouldn't end up married to someone against my will. And what do you do? You go one step further. Not only do you marry me without my permission, you do it without my knowledge. And not just in accordance with the laws of your planet, but now you've done it in accordance with the same laws I've been fighting."

Nicoli's temper flared. Didn't she understand the magnitude of what he'd done for her?

"And what were you holding out for?" He sneered at her. "True love?"

"Yes." She sighed, some of the fight going out of her. "Yes. Is that so wrong?"

"Grow up, Baby Girl. There's no such thing."

She'd been looking down at the floor, but now shot him a look, some of the fire back in her eyes. "I deserve the right to find that out for myself and you took that away from me. Why? Why didn't you just walk away? Why didn't you stop?"

Why hadn't he stopped? Because he'd wanted the sex? No, Nicoli knew better than that. It had been more than the sex. But what? It was the answer to that question that plagued him. It was an answer he wasn't sure he was ready to face and he viewed that as a weakness in himself. He wasn't mad at Angel. He understood why she was upset. He was mad at himself. He'd argued that everything he'd done had been done to protect her. But it wasn't entirely true. He *had* deceived her. And he would have to make it up to her, no matter what the personal cost.

A knock at the door jerked his attention from her anguished face. Nicoli crossed the room to let Yanur in.

"I thought I'd see how everything is going." Yanur's smile quickly turned to a frown when he saw their faces. "Did I interrupt something?"

"I just told her our marriage is legitimate. She's not happy."

"You tricked me." Angel sent them both accusing looks, as if Yanur had been in on the scheme.

Nicoli didn't know why he was taking her rejection so personally, but it ate at him. "It doesn't have to be permanent. When we're finished here, I'll arrange for a divorce."

That seemed to catch her off guard. She stared at him with an expression he couldn't read. "Really?"

"Yes. But until then," he warned, "we're still married. It's legitimate and perhaps the only thing protecting us, so I expect you to act like my wife."

He followed her glance toward the bed and knew they were both thinking about the nights ahead. It would be hard, lying next to her, but not touching or holding her.

Perhaps reading his thoughts, Angel thrust her chin out in

that defiant way he'd come to recognize. "You sleep on the floor."

He sighed and she seemed to take that as agreement to her terms. She turned to Yanur. "My mother is very sick. I don't know what's wrong with her. You seem to know a lot about medicine, plus you've got that gizmo. I was wondering, maybe, if you would take a look at her?"

"Of course." Yanur said.

"Thank you." She gave Nicoli a cold look before walking toward the door. "I'll wait for you outside."

Nicoli didn't make any attempt to follow her. "Don't wander off," he ordered just before the door slammed shut after her.

The two men stared at the closed door for a moment before either one of them spoke.

"So it's true. You married her according to your ways?" Yanur finally asked.

"Yes."

There was a thoughtful pause. "Althusians mate for life, don't they?"

"Yes."

"So logically, it stands to follow that they don't believe in divorce."

"That's true," Nicoli agreed.

Nicoli felt the older man's eyes on him. "Are you planning to be the first Althusian to pioneer the dissolution of marriage bonds? I hope you realize that might jeopardize your planetary hero status."

Nicoli shot his friend a you-should-know-better look, then went to sit on the edge of the bed. An overwhelming tiredness threatened to envelop him and he rubbed his face as if he could wipe away the fatigue. "You know I never meant to marry. My lifestyle is filled with too many dangers and uncertainties. Plus, Angel has this idyllic notion about love and marriage." He shook his head, as if there were no point in trying to argue against such naiveté.

"What are you going to do?"

"When we get to Earth, I'll utter some official-sounding words and then tell her she's free to leave. When she finds someone else to marry, I won't press my claim."

"What about you? Will you remarry?"

"I will not dishonor the vows I took."

"Then why let her?"

"It is my duty, and my pleasure, to see to her happiness. If giving her this divorce makes her happy, so be it."

"What about your happiness?" Yanur asked softly.

Nicoli smiled. It was meant to be reassuring, but he knew Yanur would not be fooled by it. "Go see to the mother."

Chapter Nineteen

Ashen in color, malnourished and thin, the woman on the bed was still the most beautiful woman Yanur had ever seen. It was clear to him now where Angel inherited her stunning good looks. And though he had originally taken on the task of nursing her back to health as a favor to Angel, the task became personal the moment he set eyes on her.

He walked over to the bed to take a closer look. The woman was asleep, lying with eyes closed, her chest rising and falling in a steady pattern. She seemed perfectly at peace, except for an occasional whimper. Yanur took the triage unit out of his black bag and scanned her from head to toe.

"Well?" Angel asked, standing patiently off to the side.

Yanur bent nearer to his patient to make sure she was sleeping before he answered. "There is substantial damage to the internal organs. They are being eaten by disease." With a sudden pain to his heart, Yanur realized that if he couldn't stop the progress of the disease, she would die soon.

He set the triage unit down on the bedside table, then returned to his bag to remove the Cellular Reparator. When he turned back to his patient, quiet amethyst-colored eyes watched him.

"Don't be alarmed," he hurried to reassure her, although she didn't seem distressed by his presence. "I won't hurt you."

"I know." Her voice was barely above a whisper. "Am I dead?"

Her question made him smile. "No."

"But I am dying." Her eyes fluttered closed as she slipped into sleep again.

"Not if I can help it." He turned on the Reparator and, starting at her head, slowly ran the wand down the entire length of her body, periodically checking the instrument's battery gauge. He'd made one full sweep when the Reparator's humming stopped. The crystals were drained. Placing it back in his bag, he used the triage unit to double-check his work.

"Yanur?" Angel's quiet voice came to him.

"I've stopped the deterioration for now. But just doing that drained the crystals. I'll need to replace them before continuing the treatment." He put the triage unit in his bag and closed it. He started to leave, but Angel's hand on his arm stopped him.

"I'll go get the crystals. I know where I can find some and even though I'm a woman, I'm still the high counsel's granddaughter. I won't have any problems." Angel headed for the door, but she paused before opening it. When she turned to him, there was an uncertainty in her eyes. "Will you stay with her?"

"Of course. But be careful. Alex would never forgive either one of us if you got hurt."

After she left, he turned back to the bed. Once again, he was awed by the woman's pale beauty. Almost afraid to touch such a vision, he laid his hand across her forehead, checking for residual signs of fever. Her head felt cool to his touch.

About to step back, Yanur saw her eyes open.

"You're awake again." He smiled. "How are you feeling?"

"Better, thank you." Her voice grew a little stronger. "What did you do?"

"I've stopped the progression of the disease attacking your body."

"Am I cured?"

His smile faltered. "Not yet, I'm afraid."

"Thank you for trying." She gently gripped his arm and her fingers sent heat shooting through his system. He hoped she wouldn't notice the effect her touch had on him and silently chided himself for acting like a schoolboy with a crush. Clearing his throat, he tried to sound more professional and detached. "Don't give up just yet. I'm not finished with you. It may take some time, but I'll have you out of that bed before you know it." He hoped like hell he wasn't lying to her.

She smiled and the whole room brightened. "Would you help me sit up? I've been lying here for I don't know how long."

Yanur savored the feel of her hands braced on his shoulders as he practically lifted her off the bed. She weighed next to nothing. After he fluffed the pillows for her, she leaned back. Suddenly she frowned and ran a hand across her hair. "I must look a mess."

"No, you look beautiful." Oh God, he sounded like a love-struck idiot. He felt himself blush and quickly turned so she wouldn't see his face. When he turned back, he saw that a healthy glow graced her cheeks.

Clearing his throat, he tried to speak. "Maybe I should let you rest now," he mumbled, not really wanting to leave.

"Oh." She sounded disappointed. "Are you sure you can't stay just a little while?"

"Well, I . . ."

"Please."

He was putty in her hands. "I would be delighted." He looked around the room for a chair.

"Here." She moved her legs and patted the edge of the bed. "I'm afraid I'm still a little confused. Have we met?"

"No." He sat down, careful not to jostle the bed too much. "My name is Yanur Snellen."

"Yanur, what an interesting name. My name is Kat'rina ToRrenc."

Yanur picked up her hand and gently laid a kiss upon her knuckles in the way he'd seen it done on old Earth documentaries. "Kat'rina ToRrenc. It is a pleasure to make your acquaintance."

He was rewarded with the light tinkling sound of her laughter.

"Tell me Yanur, what brings you to Coronado? I know full well that my father would never send for an off-world physician."

"I came here with your daughter, Angel."

As soon as he said the name, she gasped.

"Angel?"

He smiled and nodded.

"My Angel? She's alive?"

"Yes, she's alive."

"Where is she?" She looked around the room as if Angel might be hiding in the room. "I thought I had imagined her. I never dared hope she was really alive."

Yanur spoke in a quiet, reassuring tone. "She will be back shortly. I know she's eager to see you feeling better."

"My father . . . does he know?" Kat'rina grew agitated. "Did he hurt her? She can't stay. He'll sell her to the highest bidder."

Yanur patted her hand, trying his best to calm her after the quick and frightened outburst. "It's okay. No one is going to hurt her, or sell her off. Not so long as Alex is around."

"Alex?"

"Perhaps I should start from the beginning." He studied her complexion, which had lost some of its color. "That is, as long as you feel up to it."

"Yes, please."

For the next hour, Yanur and Kat'rina talked. Yanur told her everything he could about Alex and Angel, while Kat'rina told him what she could about the high counsel and his advisors. Neither noticed the time slipping by until finally the door to Kat'rina's bedroom opened.

"Mother!" Angel ran across the room.

"My Angel!" Kat'rina stretched her arms out wide and Yanur barely had time to move out of the way before Angel threw herself into her mother's embrace.

For a moment, neither could speak past the stream of tears. Then suddenly, the dam burst and both women were talking and laughing at once. Neither noticed when Yanur quietly slipped out of the room.

The dinner guests had all gone home and while it was late at night, the high counsel's chambers were no less active. Despite his advanced years and failing health, Gil'rhen felt better than he had in a long time. He sat at his desk, observing the by-play between his advisors, careful not to show his amusement.

Victor ran a hand through his hair, clearly frustrated, and looked to Rianol for support.

"I believe what Victor is trying to suggest," Rianol said, "is that the people may have a hard time accepting Colonel Romanof as high counsel because he's not Coronadian. You must admit that for a man who has always touted the importance of tradition, this is an unexpected move on your part."

Gil'rhen purposely misunderstood their message. "Your concern for my granddaughter's welfare is touching. But I thought she looked happy. Didn't you think she looked happy, Rianol? Victor?"

He almost laughed as confusion distorted Victor's face. They no doubt thought he'd gone senile. After all, when had he ever cared whether anyone was happy?

"My concern is for the blood lineage." Victor tried again to press his point. "Or don't you care anymore that the succession to House of Scyphor will be passed into the hands of an off-worlder?"

Gil'rhen raised an eyebrow. "You are concerned about a dilution of the bloodline?"

"Yes." Victor heaved a sigh, no doubt pleased that finally Gil'rhen understood his concerns.

Gil'rhen waited a heartbeat before giving his advisors something to think about. "You're not viewing this situation the way I am. Don't think of Colonel Romanof as an alien. Think of him as our link to the United System of Planets—the most powerful governing entity in the known universes. And the single largest user of tyrillium. When the USP's supply runs dry, where do you think they will turn to secure more? To an unknown source? Or to their very own Colonel Romanof, who controls

Coronado, where tryillium is as common as air? I assure you, they will be delighted to pay whatever we charge."

A knock at the door interrupted further discussion and the men looked up as the doors opened and Colonel Romanof was ushered in.

"I'm sorry to bother you," he said. "I was hoping for a few minutes of your time."

"Of course, of course. We were just finished, weren't we?"

Victor frowned, obviously not pleased with the interruption. Both advisors exchanged greetings with Colonel Romanof as they passed him on their way out.

Gil'rhen offered the younger soldier a seat in one of the chairs grouped on the side of his office.

"Would you like a drink?" Gil'rhen offered, walking over to the sideboard where he kept a collection of the finest liquors. "I have both local and inter-galactic ales."

"I'll have whatever you're having."

"Very well." Gil'rhen smiled to himself as he turned his back and selected a bottle containing dark green liquid. Distilled Baneubian tree sap. Very potent, but with a vile taste. It was a favorite among his warriors, who considered drinking it a sign of strength and control. He would see what type of soldier his granddaughter had married.

He turned back around, a small glass of the green liquid in each hand. He held one out to Colonel Romanof, then sat in the chair opposite the younger man. "I'm surprised to see you at this time of night. Have you and my granddaughter tired of one another so quickly?"

Rather than hurry to give Gil'rhen reassurances, as most men would do, Romanof merely gave him a tolerant smile. "Angel is visiting with her mother just now."

Gil'rhen nodded, then took a sip from his drink. The vile liquid burned its way down his throat, but he showed no reaction.

"High Counsel, there is a matter of some importance that we must discuss."

"Please, I am at your service." He spoke, only dimly following the conversation. The rest of his attention focused on the moment when Romanof would lift the glass and drink. Would he wince? Gil'rhen wondered. Or cough as the liquid burned him? In anticipation, Gil'rhen took another sip of his own drink.

Romanof raised his glass to his lips and their eyes briefly met over the rim. Gil'rhen thought he saw the other man smile, but couldn't be certain. Then Romanof tipped the entire contents of his glass into his mouth and smoothly swallowed the liquid.

Gil'rhen struggled to keep the surprise from his face. Romanof's eyes didn't even water. His admiration and respect for the young colonel rose another notch. But he wasn't through testing the man.

"You know, Colonel . . . Nicoli. May I call you Nicoli? I have followed my granddaughter's movements for years. I'm sure she's told you much about me. Some of it is even true. But despite what she thinks, I do care what happens to her. In my own way, I have tried to protect her. And for that reason, I'm telling you this. I am a man who wields a great deal of power on this planet and I am not above using that power should I discover that An'jel was forced into this marriage. Now you may think that is hypocritical of me, as I intended to force her into a marriage of my choosing, but that is my right as her grandfather and her ruler."

Nicoli set his empty glass on a nearby table. He didn't appear the least bit intimidated. His gaze was clear and steady as he met Gil'rhen's eyes. "I would never dishonor Angel in any way." His eyes and expression took on a look of cold steel. "And I would never allow anyone to bring her harm."

The two continued to assess one another, each taking the other's measure. Then Gil'rhen nodded. He liked what he saw in this young warrior for the USP. He had a rare intelligence coupled with the strength to back it up. A valuable trait to have in an ally. Not so good to have in one's enemy.

"As we are clearing the air, I must tell you that I can't allow succession to the high counsel's position to pass to an off-worlder."

Nicoli nodded. "I did not marry your granddaughter so I could rule your house. I'm not interested in becoming the high counsel."

"Good. But we do still have one small problem. In order for the line of succession to stay in my family, the next ruler must be married to my granddaughter."

"We don't have a problem. *You* have a problem," Nicoli countered, his voice unyielding. "Because Althusians mate for life."

Gil'rhen nodded his understanding. Nicoli had passed the second test and it was a shame, because what he'd told Nicoli was the truth. He couldn't allow the high counsel title pass out of his bloodline or to an off-worlder. But he would address that problem later.

"Let us deal with one unpleasantness at a time." He forced his tone to sound lighter. "I will not allow these Harvestors to infiltrate my planet. They must be eliminated. If one or more of them has infiltrated my home, as you suspect, then naming you as my successor has threatened their plans. At some point, they will act. You must be ready."

"Rest assured, High Counsel. I will be ready—for *all* attempts on my life."

Chapter Twenty

Angel woke up late the next morning feeling tired. It had taken her a long time the night before to fall asleep. She'd returned from her mother's room to find Nicoli waiting up for her. Neither had spoken as Nicoli laid a pallet of blankets on the floor, where he planned to sleep. She'd waited a long time to see if he would change his mind about joining her in bed, hoping he might at least try. When it became clear that he wasn't going to, she'd tossed and turned for hours wondering why that upset her.

Now she looked across the room. Morning sunlight streamed through the window, targeting the empty pallet on the floor with its rays. Nicoli had awakened early, before dawn and while she'd pretended to sleep, he'd moved quietly about the room getting dressed. Just before leaving, he'd come to stand by the bed. He'd looked down at her for so long she felt certain he'd known she was awake. But then he'd turned and walked out without saying a word.

He had gone with her grandfather to search for Harvestors and she found it irritating that he hadn't invited her to go along.

Apparently, she was good enough to fight Free Rebels in open space, but not to hunt Harvestors on her home planet.

Thinking about it just made her angry, so she climbed out of bed and went into the bathroom. It had been so long since she'd showered with real water that she stood under the warm spray longer than she realized. By the time she emerged, her skin was wrinkled, but she felt better.

As she dressed, she wondered what Nicoli thought she was supposed to do all day. Sit around and wait for him to return from his great adventure? Or maybe he thought she'd seek out the other women and help them prepare food, mend clothes or something equally boring.

No, thank you.

She left her room and made her way through the halls of the palace. When Angel reached her mother's room, Yanur was already there. The two were deeply immersed in conversation and barely acknowledged her arrival. Feeling like an intruder, she turned to leave and caught sight of an object leaning against the far corner.

"Is that Father's warring blade?" She walked over to the weapon and picked it up. It was lighter than she remembered, but then, she was no longer a child.

"Yes," her mother answered. "I could never bear to give it away."

Gripping the handle with both hands, Angel raised the weapon and assumed the ready stance her father had taught her. The blade's dull gleam reflected years of nonuse and the once razor-sharp center blade felt blunt when she ran a finger along the sword's length with a feather-light touch. Memories of afternoons practicing with her father flooded her mind.

"I think he would want you to have it," her mother said, causing Angel to look toward her.

"Really?"

Her mother smiled and nodded. "Be careful."

"Thank you." She looked back at the blade as an idea formed. "If you two are okay, I think I'll go." The older pair didn't seem to notice when she slipped from the room.

*　　*　　*

Twenty minutes later, she sat in the courtyard, enjoying the sun's warmth on her back while bending over the weapon and rubbing the blades with the polishing cloth. She was lost in thoughts of her father when a shadow fell across her.

"You should be careful. One wrong move and you might accidentally cut off one of those very lovely fingers."

Her hands stilled as she cocked her head to look up at Victor. "I know what I'm doing."

He arched an eyebrow. "Is that right?"

"Yes, it is. Though I appreciate your concern," she said in a voice that let him know she didn't appreciate anything. "Don't let me keep you from going."

The smile never left his face. "Not a problem." He walked over to a nearby bench and sat down.

He looked prepared to sit all day and Angel worked to keep the irritation from showing on her face. "What happened? You draw the short straw?"

His confused expression told her that he'd never heard the expression. "It's an old Earth game of chance where everyone draws a single piece of straw from a bale of hay. The one with the shortest straw loses." She nodded to him. "Someone had to make sure I didn't run away again and you drew short straw."

The light of understanding clicked on, but the smile he gave her was far from embarrassed. It was almost suggestive. "I cheated."

That didn't make sense to her. "Why?"

"I couldn't leave to chance the opportunity to spend all day in the pleasure of your company. So I arranged for Rianol and Pualson to be busy."

"After last night, I wouldn't think you'd want to be anywhere near me."

He smiled. "I don't hold a grudge. Besides, a man always appreciates the chance to spend time with an attractive woman, especially one as unique as yourself."

Angel laughed and felt the weight of her problems with her grandfather and Nicoli lift slightly from her shoulders. The man could be charming. He also could be a Harvestor, she reminded herself. After all, who better to influence the decisions of the high counsel than his counsel-elect? Former counsel-elect, she amended. If he was a Harvestor, losing the position might make him very dangerous. Maybe she should do a little investigative work herself.

"I don't suppose *you* know how to use a warring blade?" She asked, mock innocence lacing her words.

He pretended offense. "My dear An'jel, I'll have you know that I am quite accomplished in the use of the warring blade."

"Then how about you and I go out to the practice field for a friendly clash of blades?"

"Me? Practice against a woman?"

"Don't think of me as a woman."

"Impossible." He winked at her as he rose from the bench. "But there are a couple of moves I'd like to show you."

Nicoli steered the ship to the landing site on the far side of the high counsel's palace. He had mixed feelings about the day's outing. He and Gil'rhen had visited the four nearest villages and not found a single trace of repossessed Harvestors. It wasn't that he expected to arrive and find a sign posted at the village entrance that read "Harvestors Welcomed," but he thought he would have found something. There were too many generations of ingrained cultural norms to overcome for them to blend easily into an existing community. But neither he nor Gil'rhen had noticed anything unusual at the villages they'd visited, or with the people they'd spoken to. Either the Harvestors weren't there, or they were doing one hell of a job assimilating. Neither thought comforted Nicoli.

After securing his ship and seeing Gil'rhen safely to his office, Nicoli made his excuses and went in search of Angel. He smiled, imagining how mad she must have been to discover he'd left without her. But he had already placed her life in danger too many times on this mission. He wasn't about to again.

"Angel?" He called, walking into their room. It was empty. He crossed to the bathroom, the thought of catching her coming out of the shower too good to pass up. "Angel, are you in here?" No response.

His good mood ebbed as his concern for Angel grew. Had he

made a mistake, thinking her safe inside the palace? He walked across the room, lost in the various scenarios he imagined to explain her absence when a movement outside the window caught his eye. Turning to take a better look, he felt the last of his good mood evaporate and his blood pressure rise. Angel was in the back of the courtyard with Victor and though they both had warring blades drawn, it was obvious they weren't fighting. Even as he watched, Victor lowered his weapon to the ground and moved to stand behind Angel. He wrapped his arms around her, letting his hands cover hers on the hilt of the weapon. Then, moving as one, they lifted the blade to sweep the air in an arc.

The scene bore an air of intimacy that had Nicoli gritting his teeth. It seemed much too long a time before Angel, face smiling, stepped out of the other man's embrace. Her laughter floated to him across the distance, the sound of it surprising.

He'd never heard her laugh.

It was a depressing thought that quickly turned to anger aimed equally at Victor, for making open advances toward his wife, and Angel, for seeming so receptive. He left the room, his long strides taking him quickly to the courtyard as his thoughts turned to how he would handle the situation before him.

"Colonel Romanof."

He didn't hear the servant until she stepped into his path, blocking his way. "Sorrah, isn't it?" He struggled to keep the irritation from his voice.

"Yes. I didn't think you'd noticed me."

He stared at her amazed. The serving girl had practically thrown herself at him this morning at breakfast and now she blocked his path. How could he not have noticed? Somehow taking his silence as encouragement, she smiled and took a step closer.

"Was there something you wanted?" He stared past her to the outside courtyard entrance for some sign of Angel and Victor beyond. The maid's hand on his arm brought his attention back to her. "I'm sorry, what did you say?"

"I will take care of you." From her tone he knew she wasn't offering to fix his meals. Stepping closer, she laid the palms of her hands against his chest.

Irritation warred with manners. He could hardly push the girl aside. While he debated how to rid himself of her, she took advantage of his silence, taking that last step that brought their bodies into contact.

"How can she satisfy you when you don't even sleep together?" She smiled at his confused look. "I cleaned your room this morning and saw the pallet on the floor."

"We had a fight. That's all." He shrugged, hoping to seem nonchalant, but the movement rubbed her against him and he froze.

Misunderstanding his reaction, she grew bolder. Her arms stole about his neck as she leaned up to whisper in his ear. "I know what a man needs."

Before he could stop her, Sorrah's lips pressed against his. He placed his hands at her waist and tried to gently push her away. But she refused to budge.

"What is going on here?" Victor's voice drifted across the courtyard to them.

Nicoli and Sorrah sprang apart guiltily and turned to see two equally angry faces.

The irony of the situation was not lost on Nicoli.

Angel was so mad, she could hardly see straight. Beside her, Victor had lost all semblance of the charming man he'd been all afternoon. The look he sent Nicoli was lethal and Angel wondered that Nicoli didn't die right there on the spot.

"Sorrah," he growled. "You will come with me now."

The maid's eyes grew large as she watched him stride toward her, but she did not cower or pull away when he reached her side and took her arm.

"I'm sure the colonel and his wife would like some privacy." Victor put extra emphasis on the word "wife" while pinning Nicoli with an accusing glare. After a moment's silence, he turned to face Angel. "If you will excuse us?"

He practically dragged the maid back into the palace, but Angel didn't feel sorry for her in the least. Left alone, Nicoli walked the short distance separating them.

"I can explain."

"Can you?" She didn't have to fake the frost in her tone. "All that talk about acting like a legitimately married couple." She shook her head. "I guess fidelity doesn't mean much to Althusians."

The attack hit a nerve, because he grabbed her arm and thrust his face close to hers. "And you were the model wife today, weren't you?" He sneered.

She stared at him, too stunned to speak for a moment. "*You* are accusing *me*?" She tried to jerk her arm away, but his grip was too tight.

"I saw you out there together. Don't try to deny it."

"Oh well, you caught me," she said sarcastically. "But somehow I don't think practicing with the *warring blade* is the same as *kissing*." Her words grew louder until she was shouting. With a powerful yank, she freed her arm from his grasp.

Without waiting for his response, she turned and walked out of the courtyard, not stopping until she reached the practice field. Thoughts confused by emotions of hurt and anger, she stood beside the rack of practice blades, absently clenching and unclenching her fists. Out of the corner of her eye, she caught a movement.

"What do you want?"

"We need to talk."

Angel eyed the swords lined up before her. Then grabbed one by the hilt, blades down, and tossed it to Nicoli.

"If you want to talk to me, you'll need this." She walked to an open area, satisfied to see him follow her, a confused expression on his face as he studied the weapon. She doubted he'd ever used a Coronadian warring blade. Despite the ache in her arms from the earlier practice with Victor, she raised her weapon and held it ready.

"Heads up." She lunged at him.

She caught him off guard, but he recovered quickly, blocking the downward descent of her blades. He parried with a gentler stroke of his own. She blocked his move then attacked again, swinging her weapon, letting anger fuel her strength. The impact caused Nicoli to fall back a step.

"Sorry," Angel spoke with mock sweetness. "I didn't realize

you weren't up to a real workout. I'll try to pull my strikes a bit; go easy on you."

Nicoli drew himself up to his full height and looked down at her with a thunderous expression. "No need to, Baby Girl. I can take anything you dish out."

She didn't bother to respond, but brought her weapon down. The impact of the blades clashing reverberated up her arm and left her skull ringing. Or maybe that was her temper ringing in her ear. Instinctively, she took a step back.

"Just for the record," Nicoli snarled, stepping forward, "Sorrah kissed me. I didn't kiss her."

"I don't want to talk about it." She lost more ground when Nicoli lunged and she took a step back to ease the impact of her block. Furious with herself, she swung the blade over her head and brought it crashing down. The effort cost her dearly.

"Fine. Then let's talk about what you were doing out here all alone with Victor." Nicoli blocked yet another blow that fell too hard for a practice session.

"For your information, I was investigating him." She was breathing hard and small muscle tremors made it difficult to hold the weapon steady. But she refused to stop.

"I don't want you spending time with him."

"You can't tell me what to do."

He brought his weapon up to meet hers and their blades locked together. Nicoli pressed his advantage, towering over her. "Yes, I can. I'm your husband."

Angel tried to break her weapon free, but Nicoli's strength and her own fatigue made it impossible.

"Yield." Nicoli's quiet tone hinted at more than just the sparring match.

"Never."

Lowering his arm, he forced the tip of her long blade to the ground and trapped it there. "Yield to me."

His eyes held hers hostage and the raw masculine power of his gaze washed over her, enveloping her, stealing her strength and sense of purpose until his demand became an echo of her own desire. Her resolve weakened and her fingers began to lose their grip on the blade. The slight upward tug of Nicoli's lips, the look of smug satisfaction on his face, broke the spell.

Feeling for the small button in the grip of her weapon, she pressed it.

"You first." The hilt separated from the blade and with a last burst of energy, she quickly raised her hand and placed the dagger's sharp edge against his throat.

Their gazes locked again. She struggled to keep her hand from trembling, afraid she really might draw blood. There was no fear in Nicoli's gaze.

Suddenly Angel's feet were kicked out from under her. Unable to get her arms back in time to cushion her fall, Angel hit the ground hard enough to knock the wind out of her. In the nanosecond it took to catch her breath, Nicoli pinned her to the ground with his body. She brought her hands up to beat at him, but he caught them easily and held them trapped beneath one of his, using the other for support.

Brown eyes glared into hers. The intensity in Nicoli's scowl, the anger she felt in the tenseness of his body, caused Angel to shudder. Yet she lifted her chin. Seeing it, Nicoli shook his head, a grin spread across his face. "Lesson number one, Baby Girl. Don't pull it out unless you intend to use it."

Angel concentrated on taking in air, desperately wishing his body didn't feel so good. "Get off me."

"Not before you yield to me."

"Never." She struggled against him, but the effort did nothing more than rub their bodies together. The earthy scent of crushed grass and dirt rose to mingle with the aroma of virile male, filling her senses. Her mind begged her to resist, but her body refused. Beneath his weight, her pulse quickened in anticipation.

As if reading her reaction, he gave her that knowing smile. "Yield," he whispered, his breath fanning her face.

Again, she twisted beneath him, a futile attempt. When a groan escaped his lips, she froze, noticing for the first time his arousal pressing against her stomach. For what seemed an eternity, their eyes met, searching, assessing. Anticipating.

Then his mouth captured hers and there was nothing tender in the painful pressing of his lips against hers. She tried to turn away, but he used the weight of his body to keep her pinned to the ground while he held her head still between his hands. Though she should have been frightened, she wasn't. Desire shot through her and when Nicoli's tongue demanded entry into her mouth, she opened to him.

His tongue swept inside her mouth, leaving no part untouched and she reveled in the sensations. She had never been kissed like this and it left her feeling dizzy.

A distant part of her mind whispered caution, almost too faint to be heard. Danger lay this way—danger to her heart. To her soul. But something else waited as well, just out of reach. Something she'd experienced once before with this man; something she'd never experience again once they were divorced. She would take all she could now and live off the memories later.

Passion overriding caution, Angel's hands gripped Nicoli's powerful shoulders as she matched his urgency with a hunger she herself did not recognize. Nicoli too seemed surprised, but then she felt the subtle change in his actions as his need to dominate evolved into something else.

His mouth abandoned her lips to trail tiny kisses down the column of her neck, pausing every now and then to suck gently at the tender skin. The hand at her side moved to her breast, cupping it, gently squeezing. When she arched into him, it seemed to push Nicoli over the edge and he ripped open her shirt, exposing her to the air.

She should have felt vulnerable, but she didn't. His look was one of near reverence, intense hunger, and it made her feel beautiful. Nicoli lowered his head to tease the nipple with his tongue before catching it lightly between his teeth and gently tugging. The sensation was exquisite, and low in her abdomen, anticipation grew. She moved her hips to relieve the tension and felt Nicoli's quick intake of breath as she rubbed against his swollen manhood.

Nicoli's hand moved to her waist, working to undo the fastening of her pants. Within moments he'd worked them down her legs and they lay, forgotten, to the side. The roughened palm of his hand ran along the outside of her leg, up toward her hip. He rolled his weight to one side so he could gain better access to the inside of her thighs. With a light pressure, he opened her legs to his exploration.

Using her own dampness, he moistened her feminine folds. Then with experienced deftness, his finger swept inside her. Sensation shot through her, narrowing her focus of the world to where his hand joined her body.

"Please, Nicoli," she whispered in a breathless plea, tilting her hips to meet the growing need within her.

"Yield to me, Angel," he whispered. "I won't let you fall." He captured her lips, letting his fingers probe her more deeply.

There was no need for her to speak. They both knew he'd won. The tingling sensation between her legs increased and she felt the tightening in her abdomen. Growing desperate, Angel reached down to stroke his hardened member through the fabric of his pants. He groaned into her mouth, then suddenly pulled away, leaving her alone.

Through eyes dulled with passion, she searched for him. He stood close by, shedding his clothes with a swift efficiency. Before her body could catch a chill he was back. Angel felt the warmth of his skin against hers and it was a feeling of such primal satisfaction, she thought she might burst.

Positioned above her, he opened her legs with his knees. She felt him probe the cleft of her body, a brief warning before he thrust inside, filling her completely. He gave her only a moment to adjust to his size before withdrawing. The dew of her excitement eased his second entry and he penetrated her more deeply. She shuddered in response as he held himself still, filling her, watching her.

At first, he moved slowly, deliberately, demonstrating his dominance and control. But his rhythm soon changed, each thrust coming harder and more rapidly. Now there was no gentleness in his actions, nor did she want there to be. This was a mating ritual older than time itself, driven by sheer instinct. Wrapping her legs around his hips, she held on, conscious only of the crescendo of some inner power, building until it could no longer be contained. When the explosion came, accompanied by Nicoli's primal groan of release, she soared higher than the stars in the furthest reaches of space.

How long they lay there, wrapped in each other's arms, Nicoli had no idea. He wanted to stay that way forever. In part because it felt so good, but also in part to put off facing what he had done. Funny, he thought wryly, he'd never been a coward before. Why suddenly now? Was it because he'd never taken a woman by force before? Or was it because that woman was Angel?

He shouldn't have done it this way. He'd just been so angry, seeing her with Victor. Didn't she realize how dangerous the man could be? By spending too much time with Victor, Angel risked exposing their marriage for the sham it was.

A small part of his brain called him a liar. His intentions had not been for the sake of the mission. They had been more selfish, but that was a line of thought Nicoli refused to pursue.

He looked at Angel, cradled in his arms. He had to make her understand that they must, in all ways, behave as a married couple. Nicoli had no doubt he could go through with the charade and walk away emotionally unscathed when it was over. Just because he'd told Yanur that he'd honor his wedding vows and never marry another didn't mean he loved Angel. Love? When had he ever used that word in the same sentence with anyone? This wasn't about loving someone. Uttering the words of binding back on the ship had been a matter of honor. Nothing more.

As if she felt his thoughts centering on her, Angel turned her head to look up at him. Her smile bolstered his spirits. Propping himself up on one elbow so he could look down into her face, Nicoli raised a hand to brush a strand of hair from her forehead, then let his fingertips trail softly down her cheek. "Did I hurt you?"

A small laugh bubbled forth. "No. I may be a little sore tomorrow, but it will be as much from an extended workout with the blades as anything else."

Nicoli smiled. "I'm glad. Angel, I . . ." He looked off in the distance, gathering his thoughts, unsure how to continue.

Angel placed her fingertips across his lips, silencing him. "If you apologize for what we just did, I *will* be hurt."

He leaned down, letting his lips find hers just briefly before pulling back to search her eyes. "I want you to know that no matter what happens, I never meant to hurt you."

"That sounds ominous." Angel said. "But don't worry, I know how to take care of myself."

"I know you do."

Angel twisted her head to look around the field. "We should probably get dressed."

"We need to talk."

"Ah, the four most commonly uttered words in the universe." Her smile faltered briefly. "Look. I know you don't want to stay married to me anymore than I do to you, but there's no reason why we can't enjoy ourselves for as long as it lasts, is there?"

He'd been about to suggest that very thing, but hearing her say the words left him feeling strangely hollow. He could barely formulate a response. "I suppose not. If you're sure?"

She smiled, although he thought her eyes remained a bit sad. "Okay. Good. I'm glad we agree."

"Well, then we should probably go back."

"Not yet. I have a better idea."

He helped her sit up and then handed her his shirt to put on. After scrambling to her feet, she found her pants and the tattered remains of her shirt. Tucking them under her arm, she picked up her blade and started off for the line of trees. "Come with me," she said, looking back only once to make sure he followed her.

"Where are we going?" Nicoli spotted faint traces of an old trail through the foliage.

"It's a surprise."

They walked in silence until gradually the woods opened to reveal emerald green grass surrounding a crystal clear blue pond. It was a private oasis; a place removed from time. It was his turn to look at her in surprise.

"I thought it might be nice to swim before we put our clothes back on." She didn't wait for his reply, but put down her blade and pants, took off his shirt, ran and dove into the water.

Her head surfaced and she immediately wrapped her arms

around herself, gasping and laughing. "The water's a little colder than I remembered it."

"Maybe I'll just stay here and watch you."

"What's the matter? Don't know how to swim?"

He smiled, accepting the challenge. Fixing his eyes on hers, he walked calmly into the water, never letting his expression change. Then he dove under the surface and swam toward her. He broke off the stem of an underwater plant as he swam and when he was close enough, he ran the grass up her leg.

She almost hit him in the face when she jumped, a scream catching in her throat until she realized what he'd done. He laughed so hard he almost drowned. When he came up for air, she launched herself at him in an attempt to push him back under.

They continued their play for some time until Nicoli happened to look at the sky and noticed that the first of the two suns had already begun its decent.

"We need to get back. Why don't we sit on those rocks and dry off." He looked around and saw that they were still very much alone.

"Not many people come here," Angel commented, walking up the beach to retrieve her torn shirt. "That's why I used to come here as a kid. It was one of the few places where I could be alone."

Making a point to stand with her back to him, she used her torn shirt to dry off, rubbing the cloth quickly across her body. It made him smile to think that this fierce little warrior was shy around him, especially after their earlier lovemaking and games in the water. When Angel finished, she picked up his shirt and put it on. When she turned and saw him watching, a blush spread across her face.

"What?"

"Nothing. Just enjoying the view."

"Didn't your parents teach you any manners?"

He caught her shirt when she threw it at him and used it to dry himself. "No. But Yanur has wasted many years trying to make up for the lack."

She sat on a nearby rock. "How long have the two of you been together?"

"Twenty-four years."

"Twenty-four years! That's a long time. How did you meet?"

"I was on Corrinth IV. There was a Resistance uprising and one of my first assignments after I joined the Althusian Legionnaires was to help suppress it. Yanur was a member of the Corrinth Evolution. He'd been taken hostage by the Resistance and was being held in one of their prisons. I broke him out."

"Wait a minute. Twenty-four years ago, you were a Legionnaire, on assignment at Corrinth IV during the uprising and your mission was to break a hostage out of prison? Give me a break. First of all, I'm familiar with the prisons you're talking about and they are virtually impenetrable. Second, that long ago, you would have been just a kid."

As memories flooded back, Nicoli walked over to sit beside her on the rock. "That's right. At fourteen years old, I was the youngest Legionnaire ever to be admitted." He laughed when he saw the skeptical expression on her face. There was no fooling her. "Okay, they didn't know I was fourteen. I looked old for my age, so I told them I was eighteen. Of course, *they* thought I looked young for my age."

Angel shook her head. "I can't believe your parents let you join."

His smile faded. "They didn't have much of a say. They were dead."

"I'm sorry. What happened?"

He turned his head and stared out over the water, finally daring to say aloud the words he repeated to himself daily.

"I killed them."

Chapter Twenty-one

Angel absorbed Nicoli's shocking announcement in silence. In truth, she didn't know what to say. So she sat patiently beside him and waited for him to elaborate.

"You don't seem surprised," he finally said, a hint of accusation in his eyes. "Do you believe me capable of this deed?"

"I know you've killed before. I've seen you do it. Hell, I've done it myself. But do I think you killed your family? No, actually I don't."

He seemed somewhat mollified by her answer because he nodded and then looked away, studying the horizon once more.

"So what happened?" She asked.

He was silent for so long she thought he wouldn't answer. But then he began to speak in a distant, far-off voice. "When I was ten, my planet was at war with itself. Most of the men in my village left to fight, my father included. The women and children stayed behind to run the farms and businesses. Near the end of the war, our village was attacked. Boys were particular targets of invading soldiers, so my mother hid me in a secret panel in the wall. She thought that she and my sister would be safe. You see, generations ago, our race almost died out. Women, because they could bear children, were revered and protected; respected even during times of war. There was no reason to believe their lives were in jeopardy.

"Unfortunately, because the enemy had sustained substantial losses, in a last desperate attempt to win, they enlisted the help of off-world mercenaries, who shared none of our values. It was five of these mercenaries who broke into our house and attacked my mother and sister. Though none could see me where I hid, the cracks between the panels afforded me an excellent view of the great room." He paused a moment before going on. "I stood there and watched as my mother and sister were raped and murdered."

"Oh, Nicoli. I'm so sorry."

"Don't feel sorry for me. I don't deserve your sympathy." Angel could hear the pain in his voice.

"Why do you say that?"

"Because I did nothing, Angel. I heard their screams and did nothing. I stayed where I was until long after the men left. Too afraid to come out for fear they'd be back."

"And what do you think you could've done?"

"I don't know. Something. Anything. But I shouldn't have hidden. It was my job to protect them and I failed."

"You were ten years old! A child. There was nothing you could do. If you had tried, they would have killed you. If I had a child, I would do anything to save it. And if I died doing that, at least I'd die knowing that my child was alive and safe."

Nicoli said nothing.

"What about your father?" Angel asked softly. "Was he killed fighting in the war?"

"No, my father came home shortly after my mother and sister were killed."

"He must have been so grateful you were still alive."

"No," he said. "The day he came home, he accused me of being a coward, of not doing anything to save my mother and sister. And then he walked out the door."

"He was distraught, grieving. I'm sure he didn't mean it."

"We'll never know. After he left me that day, he went drinking. By the time he headed back for home, he was so drunk he crashed his shuttle into a structure and was killed instantly."

Angel reached for Nicoli's hand, lacing her fingers through his. "Nicoli, look at me." He did as she asked and the grief she saw in his eyes shook her to her core. "You and I are so alike in some ways. We both try to control what happens to us. For years I blamed myself for my father's death, until one day I realized that sometimes, bad things happen. We can't do anything about it and sometimes the pain is so intense that you think you'll die from it. Sometimes you wish you would die. But eventually, things get better."

She squeezed his hand and held his gaze. "You can't go through life blaming yourself for things you have no control over. You didn't kill your family—those mercenaries killed them. You were left alive. Don't question your good fortune. Don't waste the gift of life by trying to throw it away. You're a good man. Believe it."

An hour later found Nicoli waiting for Angel to finish dressing in their bathroom so they could join the others in the banquet hall. He felt better than he had in a long time. It was as if a burden he'd carried had suddenly grown lighter. But he wasn't quite ready to attribute this change to Angel's words by the pond, or to figure out why they'd meant so much to him. He was saved from further thoughts of Angel by a knock on their door.

"What have you done all day?" Nicoli asked, inviting Yanur inside.

"I've been with Katrina."

Nicoli raised an eyebrow. "Katrina?"

Yanur looked abashed. "Angel's mother."

Nicoli couldn't keep the amused smile from his lips. "And you've spent all day with her? I'm sorry. That must have been tough. I'll ask the high counsel to help provide some relief so you won't have to be with her so much."

"No, no," Yanur said a little too quickly. "It's no bother, I . . . Okay, okay. I get it. You're teasing me. Well, she happens to be a very nice woman."

"I have no doubt." Nicoli laughed. He couldn't blame his friend for the attraction he felt for Angel's mother. He found himself equally drawn to her daughter, he thought, as Angel came out of the bathroom wearing a traditional Coronadian dress that left her looking enticingly feminine.

"How's Mom doing?" Angel asked Yanur.

"Medically, I've removed the toxins in her body and managed to reverse much of the damage that was done." Yanur grew silent, seemingly lost in thought.

"But?" Nicoli encouraged him.

Yanur's eyes focused once again on Nicoli. "But she doesn't seem to be getting better. Everyday, more toxins appear in her system. It's very confusing."

"Could you be leaving some of the toxin behind on accident and they're reproducing?"

"No, I thought of that. I've been very careful to remove all the toxins." He paused for a moment, giving Angel a quick glance, as if he were afraid to say more. "It's almost like she's being poisoned."

"Poisoned!" Angel gasped. "How?"

Yanur shook his head. "That I don't know. I've checked everything. I even started preparing her meals myself, to make sure no one slipped it into her food. I've monitored the air flow, the water, everything I can think of. I've even scanned the room and found no traces of the poison anywhere."

Nicoli considered Yanur's words. He could think of a number of reasons why someone might want Katrina out of the way. But who was willing to actually go as far as poisoning her? "Someone needs to stay with her all the time. Keep track of her visitors, what they do, when they come see her, all of that."

"I'll stay with her," Yanur offered.

"You can't stay with her all the time," Angel protested. "And you certainly aren't planning to sleep with her, are you?"

A blush immediately stained Yanur's cheeks. But before he could say anything, Angel continued. "I'll stay with her at night."

Nicoli wanted to object. His time with Angel was limited and he didn't want to lose even a single night. But she was right and he'd have to get used to it.

"Who's with her now?" Nicoli asked.

"Sorrah."

"What's she doing there?" Angel didn't trust Sorrah as far as she could throw her.

"She gives Katrina massages, to help maintain her muscle tone. Those long periods of immobility have taken their toll, though you'd never know to look at her." His voice drifted off as he stared off in the distance. Then suddenly, he glanced at them self-consciously as he cleared his throat. "Uh-hum. Excuse me. Well, I was just on my way to the kitchen to prepare Katrina's evening meal, but I wanted to keep you updated on her progress."

"Maybe I should take her her dinner," Angel started. "After all, you probably want a break. And you need to eat."

"No, no." Yanur's reply came quickly. "Really, I don't mind staying with her tonight. And I thought that as long as I was preparing her meal, I'd fix one for myself and keep her company. So you needn't worry about me."

Angel smiled, then walked forward and gave Yanur a brief kiss on his cheek. "Thank you."

Nicoli moved to stand beside Angel. "I guess if you're ready, we should go."

Together they walked to the big dining hall. As before when he'd arrived to dine with the high counsel, Nicoli and Angel were among the last to arrive.

"There you are," the high counsel said, coming to join them as soon as they entered the dining room. He motioned for them to precede him to the table. Taking his place at the head, he gestured to his right. "Nicoli, you sit here, next to me. An'jel, you will sit next to your husband."

As soon as the high counsel sat, the rest of the guests seated themselves around the table. Angel noticed that in addition to her, only three other women were present at the table. Each of these was the official consort of the man she accompanied. Angel would have liked to chat with them, but they sat too far away for that to be possible. With Nicoli deep in conversation with the high counsel and the man to her right obviously not interested in talking to her, a mere woman, Angel had to be content studying the gathered crowd. Further down the table, Rianol caught her eye and gave her warm smile, which she returned, no longer feeling quite so alone.

Victor sat opposite Rianol and went back and forth between an intense discussion with the advisor named Pualson, and a flirtatious chat with the woman on his other side. Angel noticed that when Sorrah walked into the room, her eyes traveled first to Victor. Angel thought she detected a flash of hurt, or irritation. Could it be that Sorrah was in love with Victor? If so, why had she made a pass at Nicoli? Was it nothing more than an attempt to make Victor jealous? Maybe capture his attention? For a brief moment, Angel felt something akin to pity for the girl.

It quickly passed as Sorrah moved around the table serving the food. When it was time to attend Nicoli, her attitude warmed. Her low-cut blouse gaped open as she leaned over him, allowing a full view of her charms. Angel felt an uncomfortable stab of jealousy, made worse when Nicoli didn't seem to mind the view. Then it was Angel's turn to receive a plate and when she looked up into the serving girl's face, Sorrah gave her a knowing smile—a cold smile—a challenging smile. Then she moved on and Angel glanced around to see if anyone else had seen the exchange.

Her eyes fell on Herrod, standing guard by the door.

The look and smile he directed her way sent chills racing down her spine. Even when she turned away, she felt his gaze boring into her. She sneaked another glance in his direction and his smile widened.

"What's the matter?"

Nicoli's quiet voice in her ear made her jump.

"Nothing," she muttered, afraid he might start trouble if he knew.

"Aren't you hungry? You're picking at your food."

"No, I've lost my appetite." Involuntarily her eyes traveled to Herrod and Nicoli followed their trajectory.

"Is he bothering you?"

"Don't worry about it, Nicoli, he's just trying to get a reaction."

"If he keeps it up, he's going to get a reaction he's not expecting."

Angel laid her hand on Nicoli's arm. "Please don't make a scene. We can't let him distract us from our purpose here."

Nicoli nodded, but didn't look happy. The rest of the meal passed slowly for Angel and even after it was over, Nicoli made no attempt to leave. Most of the guests were gone when Nicoli and Angel finally walked to the door with the high counsel.

"Thank you, Gil'rhen." Nicoli said. "The meal was outstanding."

They reached the entryway and as Nicoli shook hands with the high counsel, Angel felt Herrod's eyes like prickles across her skin. She tried to resist turning, but the temptation proved too much.

Her glance met with a knowing smirk, as if he'd known she would look. Then he pursed his lips and sent her a kiss that promised horrible things if he ever caught her alone. Angel shuddered with disgust. The threat wasn't as effective on her as it might have been on a female unused to protecting herself, but she still gave it a healthy dose of respect.

She didn't realize she'd inadvertently tightened her grip on Nicoli's hand until she heard the low growl beside her. Nicoli released her and before Herrod could react, Nicoli relieved the man of his weapon and with his arm pressed against the guard's throat, pinned him to the wall.

The other guards rushed forward to defend their captain, but the high counsel waved them back.

"Don't ever let me catch you looking at my wife again." Nicoli bit out between clenched teeth, his face close to Herrod's. "Don't look at her, don't be in the same room with her. Hell, don't even think about her. Understand?"

For a moment, Angel thought Herrod would defy Nicoli, but something must have shown in Nicoli's eyes because the guard nodded. Nicoli, almost reluctantly it seemed to Angel, lowered his arm and took a step back.

Herrod made a show of straightening his clothes. Then his eyes fell to Nicoli's hand, still holding the weapon. "What about my blade?"

Nicoli remained silent. With his free hand, he ushered Angel through the door, never taking his eyes off Herrod. Just before he stepped out of the room, he handed the blade to one of the lesser guards standing nearby. As the door shut behind them, the high counsel's voice could be heard, requesting, in a most forceful manner, that Herrod remain behind.

"Do you think he'll come after us?" Angel asked as they walked back toward their room.

"I don't think he's that stupid."

"Well, if he is, I'll be ready." She flicked her wrist and brought up her hand holding the laser. "Never leave home without it."

"Let's hope you don't have to use it. I hear the laws here are very strict, especially for women."

"That's true," she said. "Women must obey men in all things," she dutifully recited. "It's the first rule in the Coronadian Code of Social Conduct."

"Which, in the twisted logic of this culture, means that there's no such thing as self-defense for a woman."

"Don't worry about me. I'll be fine."

They reached their room and went inside. Angel had promised to stay with her mother, but now wanted only to stay with Nicoli. She wanted to lay beside him in their bed and let him make love to her. She wanted to know what it was like to fall asleep in his arms, and then later to wake in them. The memories she created now would have to last for a lifetime.

But perhaps it was better this way. The more time she spent with him, the harder it would be to walk away later. And though divorce was inevitable, the prospect seemed less appealing than it had earlier. Her emotions, her feelings, her plans, her very life had become one jumbled, confusing mess.

"I should go."

Nicoli looked at her from where he stood across the room. "Okay. I'll walk you there."

"No," she said, a little too quickly. "It's okay." She wanted to be alone, to think.

Nicoli studied her. "I don't think you should walk these corridors alone."

"I don't think anyone's going to hurt me. Not in my grand-father's palace."

He came to stand in front of her, placing his hands on either side of her face. He dropped his lips to hers in a chaste, sweet, too brief kiss. When it ended, he didn't pull away completely, but remained so close that his breath fanned her face when he spoke. "I like knowing that you're safe. Let me walk with you."

Angel smiled. "With you around, I won't be able to think." She gave his chin a quick kiss and stepped away from him, out of his influence. "Besides—as I keep reminding you—I can take care of myself."

She left the room and hurried along the hallways, wanting to be out of sight before he changed his mind and came after her. She needed to be alone, just for a little while. There was so much she wanted to sort out.

Chapter Twenty-two

Brother Joh'nan sat in a chair in his room, watching Brother Damon pace back and forth.

"We cannot let this man come in and ruin everything we've worked hard for," Brother Damon said.

Brother Joh'nan gave a small smile. "Calm yourself. I have no intention of letting that happen."

"But what are you going to do? What are *we* going to do?"

"We will eliminate him."

"How?"

Brother Joh'nan considered various choices, each having distinct advantages and disadvantages. "I haven't decided. In the meantime, I've heard that Katrina is getting better. I thought you had taken care of that."

"I did."

Brother Joh'nan looked at him questioningly until the man stopped his pacing and swung around to face him. He held his hand out in supplication, emitting a low sound of frustration. "I will. I'll take care of it."

"Okay." Brother Joh'nan let his gaze travel over the other

man's body in appreciation. "Will you stay the night?"

Brother Damon scowled, and then shook his head. "Not tonight. If you want Katrina taken care of, then I have to go make other arrangements."

Herrod turned the corner and started down another hallway, checking doors and windows as he went to make sure the palace was secure. Ever since that bitch broke into the castle without anyone noticing, he'd had to make the rounds personally. He shouldn't have to. He was a master guard, head of security.

And if that wasn't bad enough, that off-worlder had made him look like a fool in front of everyone. Most people were afraid of him, but he had misjudged Romanof. It wouldn't happen again. He turned the corner of the next corridor and stopped.

She was there, coming his way. And she was alone.

A smile crept to his lips. Now he would get his revenge.

He hid in the shadows until she drew near, then he stepped out. When she saw him, she froze. Her eyes grew large and round, like trapped prey watching as the predator closed for the attack. He gave a low laugh, smelling her fear. She took a tentative step back and he countered it with another step forward. He waited until she stepped back again, as he knew she would, and again he countered, continuing their dance.

He would have her. With that thought in mind, Herrod let his eyes stray momentarily from her face to breasts, and he licked his lips. Yes, he would have her. She would fight him, but that would only add to his excitement. Feeling his arousal pressed against his pants, he knew he could not wait.

Just before he lunged, he saw the light in her eyes change. He felt the searing hot pain across his shoulder as he was propelled backward.

He looked down and saw the small laser in her hand.

"Do you think to kill me?"

"If I have to."

He would not be a master guard if a mere woman could so easily put him off. Moving with a speed few could match, Herrod closed the distance between them and kicked the laser from her hand.

Then he lunged for her. She fought well, he thought distantly. Better than most women could. She dragged her nails across his wounded shoulder and for a moment he was distracted by the shards of pain shooting down his arm. Too late, he saw her raised knee. When it connected to his crotch, the white-hot pain sent him to his knees.

She gave him no quarter as she rammed the palm of her hand into his nose, breaking it. In blind fury, he reached out for her, pawing the air. His arms found nothing and when he could finally open his eyes, he saw that she was gone.

He lifted his hand to his nose. It was broken. Almost without thinking about it, he pressed both hands against either side of his nose, drew a deep breath and with a quick movement realigned the cartilage. The sharp pain made his eyes water and when he pulled his hands away, they were covered in blood. His blood.

He swore, reaching out to support himself against the wall until the pain in his groin subsided. A dark object caught the corner of his eye and he turned to look at it, recognizing the bitch's laser.

Still bent over, he shuffled the small distance to the weapon. He reached out, but before he could grab the weapon, another hand retrieved it.

Puzzled, he looked up. "You!"

"I told you to leave her alone or you would pay."

The last thing Herrod saw was a bright flash of light from the laser's barrel. By the time the pain in his forehead could have registered in his brain, it was already fried.

Angel was shaking when she reached her mother's room. Inside, Yanur sat in a nearby chair while her mother slumbered peacefully in bed. At Angel's entrance, Yanur looked up with a smile on his face. It quickly turned to a frown.

"What happened?" He rose from the chair and came to her. "Are you all right?"

She nodded, exhaling deeply. "Yeah, I'm okay." There would be no point in worrying Yanur. "How's Mom?"

Yanur's expression softened as he looked at the sleeping woman. "She's fine. I'm afraid I kept her awake too long today talking. She was pretty tired."

"Thank you for watching over her."

Yanur reached out and took Angel's hand, patting it in a fatherly way. "My pleasure. Will you be okay? I can stay."

"No. We'll be fine. Thank you." She watched him walk to the door.

"All right then. Good night."

" 'Night, Yanur."

Angel stood in the middle of the room and as the adrenaline left her body, she felt emotionally and physically drained. Suddenly too tired to stand, she glanced at the chair beside the bed. She plopped down in it, resting her head against the back and closing her eyes. Her mind replayed Herrod's attack and Angel realized just how close she had come to getting raped, maybe even killed. It left her feeling vulnerable and alone.

She eyed her mother's sleeping form and almost unaware that she was doing so, rose from her chair and moved to the bed. Picking up the extra blanket, she lay down beside her mother, who stirred slightly with the dipping of the mattress.

"It's all right, Momma. It's just me, Angel."

Her mother opened a sleepy eye. "Oh, my Angel. Did you have a bad dream?"

"Yes, Momma, I did."

"It's okay honey. You're safe now." She reached out a hand to brush a strand of hair from Angel's face. "Do you want to tell me about it?"

Angel knew her mother was not really awake, and maybe that was why she felt comfortable telling her. In the morning, her mother would not remember. Speaking softly, she told how Herrod had been harassing her and how she'd run into him in the hall. How they'd fought and she'd injured him and run. Finally, she told her mother how she was afraid to go back.

Angel's voice trailed off as she thought back to all the times in her life when she'd been afraid. Fear had made her stronger, but what she wouldn't give right now to have a few moments of absolute security.

Her mother's eyes remained closed, but her hand moved to pat Angel's arm as she did when Angel was young.

"Daddy can sleep in the other room. You stay with me tonight. No more nightmares, okay?"

"Okay."

Her mother squeezed her arm one last time before drifting back to sleep.

"I love you, Momma." Angel closed her eyes and let the night take her.

Nicoli stopped pacing long enough to glance again at his watch. Angel had been gone two hours and he couldn't stop worrying. He should have insisted on accompanying her to her mother's room.

Knowing he wouldn't rest until he knew she was safe, he decided to check on her himself. Leaving the room, he rapidly maneuvered his way through the labyrinth of hallways toward Katrina's room. All the while, he tried to tell himself that he was overreacting. That she was safe; nothing had happened to her. But the image of Herrod's lewd gestures refused to fade. With each step, his concern grew, until finally he swore that when next he found the man, he might just kill him.

Turning the next corner, he discovered that someone had beaten him to it.

Herrod's body lay in the hallway; a single laser shot to the forehead the obvious cause of death. His nose appeared broken and there was fresh swelling and discoloration around it. Charred blood and flesh sliced a path across his right shoulder, evidence of a second laser shot.

Nicoli felt no remorse for Herrod, but his concern for Angel's safety increased exponentially. Few others on this planet had lasers, much less weld them with such efficiency, leaving little doubt in his mind that Angel was involved in Herrod's death. But Angel was no cold-blooded murderer. She would have fought to protect herself, killing out of necessity only.

Nicoli heard the sounds of running feet shortly before he saw the four guards. Relief swept through him that he wouldn't have to attend Herrod's body long. He wanted to find Angel.

He started down the hallway when a guard's hand on his chest blocked his passage. "No one leaves the scene until the high counsel permits it."

The order chafed at Nicoli, who felt precious time was being lost. He reined in his impatience, knowing that to start trouble would only draw more attention to himself, or to Angel.

As more people drifted onto the scene, it occurred to Nicoli that the guards' appearance was unusually timely. A premonition of something bad to come settled over him and he examined the crime scene with renewed interest. The high counsel arrived and a momentary sadness flitted across his features at the sight of the body. It was quickly replaced with a mask of calm indifference.

A small exclamation off to the side drew everyone's attention. "I found the murder weapon," a guard exclaimed, bending over to pick up an object.

Nicoli watched in horror as the guard held up Angel's laser. In his mind, he remembered the conversation he and Angel had had earlier regarding women's lack of rights. The crowd grew silent as the high counsel took the laser.

New arrivals down the hall drew Nicoli's attention. He looked up and spotted Angel walking toward him, accompanied by her mother and Yanur. Even from this distance, he could see the worry and fatigue in Angel's face. Her eyes seemed haunted, brightening briefly when they met his from across the crowd.

"It's obvious that this is the weapon that killed my master guard." The high counsel made a show of addressing the crowd, but he paused to look pointedly at Angel and then Nicoli. "It stands to follow that the owner of this weapon is the murderer. The only question that remains to be answered is, whose weapon is it?"

Nicoli knew what he had to do. "It's mine."

Chapter Twenty-three

Amid the murmurs of the crowd, Nicoli heard Angel's gasp. "No."

"Colonel Romanof," the high counsel began. "Was this a case of self-defense?"

Immediately Advisor Pualson stepped from the crowd. "Colonel Romanof seems remarkably unharmed." He looked pointedly at Herrod's battered and beaten body. "I submit that it could not have been self-defense." He leveled a hostile glare at Nicoli. "I submit that we are dealing with murder."

Others in the crowd quickly took up the argument. The high counsel studied Nicoli's face, perhaps waiting to see if Nicoli would refute the accusation. But Nicoli remained quiet.

Earlier, he had contemplated killing the man to protect Angel. The man was dead, but Angel still needed his protection. "He must be punished," one of the bystanders yelled.

"He is no longer worthy to be counsel-elect," cried another.

Victor spoke then, a smug expression on his face. "His marriage to the consort-elect, granddaughter to the high counsel, must be annulled."

Nicoli watched the high counsel weighing Victor's words. Then a new voice spoke from the crowd. A woman's voice.

"Herrod attacked my daughter." Katrina, supported by Yanur, stepped forward. "Earlier tonight, he sprang on her, intent on raping her. She fought to defend herself and escaped, with Herrod alive. She came to me and has been with me since. Our laws dictate that should a protected woman be attacked, the attack is also against the man who protects her. My daughter is under the protection of two men. When Herrod attacked my daughter, he also attacked her husband, the counsel-elect. And he attacked the high counsel himself."

A low murmur settled over the crowd. Angel moved to stand beside her mother, who appeared weak from her exertion. Nicoli turned to the high counsel and almost missed the smile he quickly hid.

"My daughter speaks the truth. The penalty is death for attacking the high counsel or the counsel-elect. Herrod forfeited his life when he attacked my granddaughter, Colonel Romanof's wife. His killer exacted Coronadian justice and the matter is thus resolved. Dispose of the body before it stinks up my palace." He waved a hand and two guards swiftly moved to comply.

After they carried away the body, the high counsel turned to address the remaining members of the crowd. "Colonel Romanof and his friend Mr. Snellen will be accorded the full hospitality of my people. We owe them a debt of gratitude for returning my granddaughter to her home and for restoring my daughter's health. I would be gravely upset should any further 'unfortunate incidences' occur with regard to either of them."

With that, the high counsel moved to his daughter's side and took her hand in his. "I am much relieved to see you feeling better," he said with a small smile.

"Thank you, Father."

He gave her hand a final squeeze, released her and then walked from the scene. The rest of those assembled exchanged brief glances, and then dispersed.

Alone with Angel, Yanur and Katrina, Nicoli moved to take Katrina's hand.

"Lady Katrina ToRrenc, I am Colonel Nicoli Alexandres Romanof of the United System of Planet's Security Forces, husband to your daughter. It is an honor to make your acquaintance. I am most grateful for your timely recovery."

"Colonel Romanof, Nicoli. It is I who thanks you. I thought my daughter dead to me. I could not bear to have lost her a second time."

"As long as I am alive, I will protect your daughter."

Katrina gave him a peculiar look, then smiled. "I believe you."

"Let me walk you back to your room, Katrina." Yanur suggested. "You are recovering very quickly, but I don't want to risk tiring you too soon."

Katrina nodded.

"I'll come visit after you've rested," Angel promised, giving her mother a quick hug and kiss before she left.

Nicoli offered his arm to Angel when she turned toward him. He led her in the direction of their quarters. He wanted to make certain she was all right, and they needed to talk privately. He didn't care if she didn't like what he was going to tell her, it was for her own good. Until he could get her away from this planet, he planned to keep her with him at all times. It was the only way he knew to ensure her safety.

Brother Joh'nan paced the confines of his bedroom waiting for the knock he expected. When it came, he silently opened the door and stood back, allowing Brother Damon to enter. He closed the door as his visitor moved behind the bar at the far side of the room and began fixing a drink.

He shook his head to refuse the proffered glass of Wallachie tree ale, not wanting to dull his already dying senses with the powerful liquor. Brother Damon shrugged, then downed the contents himself. He refilled the glass to the top before corking the bottle and setting it aside.

"Well, that didn't exactly go as planned." Brother Damon's tone dripped with derision.

"What are you talking about?"

"Herrod. I saw him attack An'jel. I waited to see if Herrod would kill her for us, but she got away. When I saw her laser, it occurred to me that I could rid us of two problems at once."

"But Colonel Romanof spoiled your plan by taking the blame. Well, it doesn't matter. You should have known that the high counsel would never allow his granddaughter to be put to death." Brother Joh'nan moved away from the door, feeling every nerve in his body twitch as he walked to the bar. Even his hands shook as he placed them on the counter and leaned forward.

"Actually, that part of the plan worked fine. I counted on Romanof taking the blame, to protect her. With Herrod dead and Romanof executed for his murder, they'd both be out of our way."

"If you had consulted me first, I could have told you it wouldn't work."

Brother Damon glared across the bar at him. "There wasn't time." He picked up his drink and swallowed the remaining contents. "Joh'nan, we need to eliminate Romanof."

"I know. But we need to make sure of our method. We can't have someone come forward and throw ancient laws in our face and undermine our goals."

"Like Katrina."

"Like Katrina," he agreed. "Who looked remarkably healthy for a woman who is supposed to be dying. What's the problem?"

Brother Damon shook his head. "I don't know. With what we've given her, she should have died days ago. Romanof's friend, Yanur Snellen, must be doing something. He spends a lot of time with her. He's even preparing her meals. It's getting more difficult to administer the poison."

"Need I remind you that as long as she lives, she's a threat to our plan?"

Brother Damon took another drink from the glass, then set it purposefully down on the counter. "I'll take care of it."

Brother Joh'nan sighed and pushed away from the bar to go sit on the edge of his bed. He dropped his head into the palms of his hands, feeling like the sudden pressure and weight of it was more than his neck could support. He was so weary. The last report on the construction of the new transfer plant suggested everything was on schedule, but right now the completion date seemed interminably far away. It would be ironic if, after surviving over a hundred years, searching for the means to immortality, he died just before the dream was to be realized.

He didn't lift his head when Brother Damon spoke. "I'll take care of it, Joh'nan." This time, the words were not spoken defensively, but with a wealth of promise.

Brother Joh'nan raised his head to give his friend a smile. He knew Damon would do anything for him; as he would for Damon. For a few minutes, neither spoke.

Then Brother Damon walked over to the bed and sat down beside him. "I spoke to Brother Semuth today."

"Really?"

"Yes. It seems that the high counsel at the House of Danmoora has fallen ill. Brother Semuth feels it won't be long before he's able to step in and assume the position."

"Excellent."

Brother Damon put a hand on Brother Joh'nan's shoulder and gave it a squeeze. "Everything is coming together as you planned. These few problems," he waved his other hand generally in the air. "Minor obstacles, nothing more."

Brother Joh'nan leaned into his friend, letting his head fall to the other man's shoulder. "Damon?" He spoke wistfully. "Do you think we can keep Romanof's body alive until the transfer unit is complete? He seems healthy and you have to admit, he's reasonably attractive, in a dark sort of way."

Damon's arm moved about his shoulders and held him close. "If that's what you want."

Joh'nan took a deep breath, letting himself enjoy the moment.

"Do you want me to stay with you tonight?" Damon asked.

Joh'nan reluctantly raised his head and took a deep bracing breath. "No. I must use the rest of the night to study the old laws. There must be some way to eliminate Romanof without drawing a lot of attention to us." He raised his hand to place the side of his fingers under Damon's chin, then slowly drew the man's face close to his own. Their lips met in a familiar kiss and lingered there for just a moment. Then Joh'nan drew back and gave his lover a sad smile. "You have other things you must do. I will see you later in the day."

He stood and walked to his desk. Gazing out the window,

he didn't bother to turn around as Damon opened the door and left.

Nicoli held Angel beside him in bed. Though his body ached to join with hers, after such a long, restless night, they both needed their sleep. So instead, he held her wrapped in his arms, her head nestled against his chest, feeling that as long as they could lay like this, she would be safe. In the morning, they would talk.

He listened for the steady rhythm of her breathing that would tell him she slept, but heard nothing. "Are you all right?"

He felt her nod, but she didn't say anything.

"What's the matter?"

Then her voice came softly, almost as if she were afraid to speak. "Did you kill Herrod?"

It wasn't what he expected. "No."

"Then why did you say you did?"

"I wanted to protect you."

She pushed against his chest until he loosened his arms and raised herself until she could look down into his face. "Nicoli. I didn't kill Herrod."

For a moment, he could only stare at her. Then he realized what worried her. "If I didn't kill him, and you didn't kill him . . ."

She nodded. "Then who did?"

It was a long time before either of them slept.

The next day, Angel woke in Nicoli's arms with a feeling of such contentment she was loath to move, lest she spoil the moment.

"Morning, Baby Girl," Nicoli's soft voice washed over her. "Did you sleep well?"

"Yes." She snuggled closer to him, forgetting as she did that their marriage was a sham.

Nicoli pressed his lips to her head. "I wish we could stay in bed all day, but I promised your grandfather earlier that we would go check out a few more villages today."

"Oh." She couldn't keep the disappointment from her voice. She didn't want to be left behind again.

"So you better get dressed. We don't have much time."

Angel looked at him, afraid she had misunderstood. "I should get dressed?"

"Yes. You don't think I'm going to leave you here, do you?"

It was all the encouragement she needed.

Ten hours later, Angel wasn't feeling nearly as excited. She steered the shuttle across the planet's surface, pulling up at the last minute to clear the tops of the first group of small mountain ranges that lay between the village they'd just left and the next one on their list. She knew she was cutting her maneuvers a little close. More than once, Nicoli frowned at her from the copilot's seat, no doubt in an attempt to get her to slow their speed, but after a long, frustrating day of sitting on the ship while Nicoli and her grandfather wandered around the various villages, her grandfather's white-knuckled grip on the arms of his chair was her only source of entertainment. No way was she going to change how she was flying. This was too good an opportunity to let pass.

As if guessing the nature of her thoughts, Nicoli leaned close to whisper in her ear. "If you don't slow down, I won't bring you along on our next expedition."

"That's fine with me. All you've done so far is leave me on board. At least when I stayed at the palace, I had Victor to keep me company."

Nicoli's eyes grew dark, but he didn't say anything more. They both knew that he wouldn't leave her behind.

They had spent the entire day investigating remote villages sitting on the eastern perimeter of the Scyphor region. Angel had flown the Icarus to five different villages, and five times she had been sequestered to the ship while Nicoli and her grandfather had all the fun of looking for Harvestors. Now, at the end of the day, she was tired of the inactivity and feeling more than a tad contrary.

She pulled back more abruptly than necessary and sent the aircraft into a sharp climb over the mountains. Then, as soon as they cleared the top, she executed a steep dive. She shot Nicoli a look that dared him to say anything, and he wisely kept his mouth shut.

It had been a long, unproductive day. The two suns were beginning to set and they should have been heading back to the palace. But they'd picked up a possible lead in the last village. During one of the interviews with the townspeople, they'd learn that several members of the village had disappeared. In most cases, never to be seen again. But one young man claimed he spotted one of the missing villagers during a rare visit to the village of Queneth. But when he'd tried to talk to the man, the man had grown highly agitated and run away.

The young man had followed him and eventually caught him. But when questioned, he'd claimed he wasn't who the young man thought he was and insisted on being left alone. The young man departed and made no further attempts to contact the man. To Angel and Nicoli, the incident sounded suspicious. So instead of returning to the palace, they were flying to the village of Queneth.

Angel checked the navigrid and slowed the shuttle.

"It's going to be dark soon," she commented. "If we stay low, we can take the ship close to the outskirts without attracting too much attention."

The high counsel stretched forward, trying to get a better view of the town. "Don't expect too much. The last time I was here, the village was practically deserted. Nothing grows out here. Look around. Nothing but rock."

"Still, I think it's worth checking out," Nicoli said.

Angel landed the ship and after securing the controls, followed Nicoli and her grandfather to the hatch. "I want to go with you."

"No." Nicoli and her grandfather spoke at once. They gave each other a look that Angel interpreted as two males judging the other man's right to issue commands to *his* woman. She almost expected them to square off and start beating their chests.

At the hatch door, Nicoli paused before releasing the lock. "Angel, for once, please do what I tell you to. Stay here where I know you'll be safe."

"But what if you run into trouble? I can hold my own in a fight. You know I can."

"They would not dare harm the high counsel," her grandfather proclaimed.

Angel snorted. "If these villagers are Harvestors, I don't think they'll be impressed."

Her grandfather looked stunned, then shook his head almost sadly. "You have no respect for authority. I should never have left you out there on your own for so long."

Ignoring him, Angel turned to Nicoli. "Take me with you. You need me."

Nicoli closed the distance between them until he stood directly in front of her. He lightly gripped her upper arms with his hands so he could hold her still. He bent his head close and when he whispered, his breath sent tingles down her spine. "I do need you. And that's why you must stay here. If we run into trouble, I want to know you're safe." He lightly kissed the sensitive spot just below her ear. "Stay here." He kissed her again, this time on the cheek. "If we don't come back in an hour," he kissed her lightly on the lips, "go back to the palace and get help. I may need you to rescue me. Again." Then he wrapped his arms around her, crushing her to him. This time the kiss wasn't light and quick. His lips took hers in a long, heated, hungry kiss that made time and circumstances disappear. All her senses focused on the feel of his lips pressed firmly against hers, mouths opened wide as his tongue swept inside, leaving no place unexplored.

Then she was alone. Nicoli and her grandfather had left the ship and disappeared into the growing darkness.

Chapter Twenty-four

"Clever ruse." The high counsel sounded grudgingly impressed.

"What's that?"

"How you handled An'jel. I must remember that tactic in my future dealings with women."

Nicoli remained silent, pretending to study the landscape. He wasn't about to admit to the high counsel that his kissing Angel had not been a conscious manipulation. When she'd followed them to the hatch, he'd seen her lips set in that defiant way he'd come to know so well. At that moment, he'd wanted nothing more than to make love to her until every part of her yielded willingly, eagerly to him. The kiss was as much as he'd allowed himself to do. And he'd been sincere when he said he'd be better off if he didn't have to worry about her safety.

"The village looks smaller than the others," Nicoli said, changing the topic. "It shouldn't take long to walk the entire length and back."

As they had flown by, Nicoli had noticed that this settlement was structured as all the others. At the very center of town was a small public square from which the rest of the village spread out in concentric squares. The buildings were built predominantly from wood and rock and, he suspected, like the other places they'd visited today, there would be just enough technology to make living tolerable.

Nicoli and the high counsel walked along the main path that led into town. Over the horizon, the suns were beginning their final descent and the surrounding fields were bathed in a soft orange glow. Nicoli couldn't help but admire the pure simplicity of life these villagers enjoyed.

Nicoli stopped and looked off to his side. "I thought you said nothing grew out here."

Gil'rhen came to a halt beside him. "Is that a field of longbeans?"

"And over there," Nicoli pointed to the opposite field. "That looks like honey-melons. They look pretty healthy, too. I don't think this community is doing as poorly as you thought."

Gil'rhen looked thoughtful. "Interesting."

"Let's go on to the village and see what we can find out."

There weren't many homes along the road into town and they didn't encounter anyone as they walked. Lanterns lined the roads, casting out small patches of light, and when they arrived in the village, Nicoli was impressed with how clean everything was. He'd never seen a community so well-tended.

As they moved toward the center of town the rows of homes became more businesslike. A few townspeople appeared on the streets. The sight of two strangers seemed to attract some attention, but no one approached them. Nicoli found it a bit strange. At the other villages, the high counsel had been recognized immediately and villagers had flocked forward, eager to see to the high counsel's needs. Here, no one seemed to know him.

Nicoli exchanged looks with Gil'rhen and they continued their trek. The number of people out and about increased the closer they got to the town square.

"You should have worn a cap or something to hide your dark hair." Gil'rhen said under his breath as they passed another small group of villagers. "You coloring is unusual on our planet and seems to draw attention."

Nicoli looked around. Several of the townspeople were, indeed, staring, but he wasn't convinced they were looking at him. He slowed his pace and allowed the older man to draw ahead of him to test a theory. The staring eyes moved ahead of him.

Nicoli quickened his pace and drew even once more with the high counsel. "It's not me they're staring at, *old man*."

"Are you being disrespectful, Colonel?"

"No. Look around. I haven't seen anyone older than about forty. Nor have I seen anyone younger than early twenties. What happened to the children and the elderly?"

The high counsel's gaze sharpened. "I see what you mean. Very unusual. So you think we've found what we were looking for?"

Nicoli shook his head. "I'm not ready to jump to any conclusions yet. Let's find the local pub. Maybe we'll pick up some useful information there."

Angel finished her snack and went back to the bridge. She considered pacing the entire length and breadth of the ship, but had done it so many times already today she thought she might go crazy if she did it again.

She sat down in the pilot's chair and looked out the front view screens. There was no sign of Nicoli or her grandfather. She checked her watch and realized they'd only been gone thirty standard minutes. She leaned back in the chair, trying to convince herself to be patient, but an excess of nervous energy had her pacing the length of the bridge almost immediately.

She wasn't used to such inactivity. She wanted to be where the action was. And she was worried about Nicoli and her grandfather. Okay, maybe not her grandfather. But she was worried about Nicoli. She had grown fond of that arrogant man.

Climbing back into the pilot's seat, Angel studied the instrument panel, hoping for something to take her mind off her boredom. As she stared at the screen, she felt her eyelids grow heavy and her thoughts became less focused.

Suddenly, she jerked wide awake. The clock on the instrument panel showed that she'd only slept for a couple of minutes; ten at the most. Looking out the front view screen, she saw that the suns had fallen below the horizon and it was fully dark. It was still too early to worry about Nicoli and her grandfather, so what had awakened her?

She hadn't turned on the ship's interior lighting and was thinking of doing so, when she heard it. A faint thrumming noise.

Angel held very still, focusing all of her attention on that sound. It was not a sound heard often on Coronado, but it was one with which she was all too familiar—the sound of a spaceship.

Angel ran a perimeter scan that started just outside the ship and stretched outward until the other ship showed up on the screen. It was less than twenty-five kilometers away.

Angel tried to think what to do. She could move the ship, but what if Nicoli and her grandfather returned before she could find them. She checked the pulse cannons and found them fully charged. She would stay here. If the other ship came too close and proved hostile, she'd do her best to blow it away.

With one hand poised above the pulse cannon controls, she watched the other ship crest the last mountain range. It was too far away for her to see through the view screen, so she did what she hated most. She waited.

Fight or flight; that she understood.

The blip drew nearer, then veered off toward the village. Angel watched for another minute or two, and then the blip stopped and didn't move again. It had landed.

Dropping her hands into her lap, she sat back and released her breath in a sigh. The relief she felt was quickly replaced by curiosity. The presence of a shuttle at one of these smaller villages was highly unusual. Why would one be here, at this remote site, in the middle of the night?

There were several answers that came to mind, but most seemed far-fetched. The one she found most plausible was the one she liked the least—this was the Harvestors' village and the aliens had maintained off-world connections or activities.

If she tried contacting Nicoli over the comm-link, the other ship would be alerted to their presence. She could do nothing and wait for Nicoli to return, but the other ship might not stick around and they might miss an important clue in their search for the Harvestors. Someone needed to investigate it now, and she was the only candidate.

Nicoli's words echoed in the back of her mind, telling her once again to stay put.

"I'll go look around and come right back." Whether the words were spoken to reassure herself or Nicoli, she wasn't sure.

Excited to be doing something worthwhile, Angel studied the scan readout one last time to make sure she could find the other ship. Taking the replacement laser she'd found earlier that day during a thorough search to relieve the boredom, she opened the hatch and stepped out.

"It's time!"

The man's announcement was immediately met with a hum of excited whispers. Then everyone in the pub rose and filed outside. For a moment, Nicoli and Gil'rhen were left staring at each other in bewilderment. What was going on?

"Shall we?" Gil'rhen set the newly purchased glass of ale down and rose. Nicoli took a final drink and followed. They'd found the pub without any problems and had just settled down at a table hoping to pick up surrounding conversation when the pub doors had burst open and a man stepped inside and shouted.

Outside, it seemed the entire village populace was moving toward the same destination. Curious, Nicoli and Gil'rhen trailed after them. No one noticed the two outsiders in their excitement. Nicoli strained to overhear snatches of conversation around him, but nothing made much sense.

". . . the first to go . . ."

". . . have studied the procedure . . ."

". . . been so long . . ."

Then he heard something more familiar.

". . . how exciting for Brother Mart'n . . ."

"Careful."

"I mean Marcina, how exciting for Marcina."

"Yes, it's a new beginning for us."

Then in a hushed tone almost too quiet to hear, "Has anyone notified Brother Joh'nan?"

The whispered response came quickly. "No. He will only

want to take over. It is better if we do this on our own."

They had found the Harvestor village. Nicoli considered grabbing Gil'rhen and heading back to the ship, but curiosity won out. They allowed themselves to be swept along with the crowd down a village street, until they reached one of the many homes. Then they stopped, gathering in the front yard, excited conversations buzzing all around.

"What do you suppose is going on?" Gil'rhen leaned close to Nicoli so his words would not be overheard.

Nicoli shrugged. "I don't know. Let's wait a little while and see what happens."

He casually scanned the crowd, looking for anything that seemed unusual or might provide further evidence that this was, indeed, the Harvestor encampment.

Suddenly a woman's scream pierced the night. Nicoli tensed, ready to respond to the danger as soon as he identified its source. Around him, the crowd grew more excited.

"They don't seem alarmed," Gil'rhen said beside him.

"No, they don't."

"Perhaps the woman is being punished, or it's one of the ancient rituals."

Nicoli was disgusted at the man's casual assessment of the situation. "If a woman is being tortured inside, then I intend to put a stop to it."

The woman's scream came again and it was obvious this time that she was in extreme pain. Without waiting to see if the high counsel followed him, Nicoli pushed his way through the people toward the house, wondering who and how many he would have to fight to get inside.

The only weapon he had on him was the warring blade, strapped to his side. Unfortunately, almost every male in the village also wore his warring blade and Nicoli doubted that he and the high counsel could fight them all.

Surprisingly, no one tried to stop them when they entered the house and once they were inside, Nicoli saw why. Everyone's attention was focused on the woman lying in the center of the room. Her legs were spread wide and bent at the knees, feet flat on the floor. A man knelt between her legs and when he leaned forward, the woman screamed again.

Instinctively, Nicoli's hand went to the hilt of the blade, but before he could draw it and decapitate the man raping the woman, the high counsel laid a restraining hand on him. Nicoli looked at the older man, curious why he'd been stopped.

"Just wait," was all he said.

Nicoli would have argued, but at that moment the woman screamed again. When she stopped, the room grew unusually quiet. Something was about to happen and Nicoli tensed in preparation.

Then a new sound filled the silence. The sound of a newborn's cry. It was met by a collective gasp from the crowd and then there was a mix of laughter, cheers and more crying.

The man kneeling between the woman's legs stood and turned. In his arms, he held an infant. He turned so all could see it and in that moment, Nicoli got a look at the woman on the floor. Her head rested in the lap of another woman, while two others held her hands. All the women were weeping, but they seemed to be tears of joy. Then the mother raised her hands up to receive her child.

"Marcina," the man holding the baby said. "You have delivered to us a fine, healthy baby girl—the first child to be born to our kind in over a hundred years."

The happy cheers of the gathered villagers drowned out anything else the man would have said. Nicoli allowed Gil'rhen to pull him through the crowd, back outside.

"Now is the time to strike, while they are preoccupied with the new birth."

Nicoli stared at the high counsel. The same thought had occurred to him when he'd realized he'd found the Harvestor village. But that had been before he'd seen the sight of the newborn child and the happy faces surrounding it. These people weren't concerned with taking over a new planet, or annihilating an alien race. These were people rediscovering what it meant to live, to have neighbors and family. What it meant to have children who would ensure the survival of their race.

"No," he said. "These people are not our enemy. It is their

leader we must find. Let's go back to the ship. I need time to think about this."

Nicoli started down the street. The high counsel grabbed his arm and jerked him to a stop.

"Colonel, need I remind you that this is my planet and my region. I will not allow this race of . . . of aliens to take up residence here."

"High Counsel, now is neither the time nor the place for this discussion. The destruction of this village will accomplish nothing. The real danger is in allowing the Harvestor leader to continue with his plans to take over your planet. Right now, we don't know who that is. By the same token, he doesn't know we're looking for him. Destroying this village tips our hand and makes our search that much harder. Once I've found the leader and taken care of him, what you do to these villagers is your concern."

Unless I choose to make it mine, he added silently.

It took Angel almost fifteen minutes to find the spot where the shuttle landed. Her trek had taken her out of town, across several fields to the top of a small escarpment. With the suns newly set, she stood in the shadow of the night looking down into a ravine where a cargo shuttle stood next to a large building.

The lights in the building shone through the windows placed high on the walls. They provided enough illumination that Angel could make out the shapes of several people unloading something from the shuttle.

Curiosity soon had her picking her way cautiously down the steep embankment. The darkness provided her the perfect cover, but it also made her descent more dangerous. It was hard to distinguish safe hand- and footholds in the sharp, jagged rocks. Several times, her foot slipped, causing her to slide for a meter or so, arms flailing while a shower of smaller rocks skittered down the mountain ahead of her. Each time, she regained her balance and froze, waiting to be discovered either from the sound of the rocks she'd dislodged or the pounding of her heart.

When she reached the bottom, she crouched low and waited in the shadows, pondering her next move. A small part of her knew she should have gone back to get Nicoli, but now that she was this close, she wasn't about to turn back. She watched two men walk from the large building to the cargo ship. They talked as they approached the ship and disappeared inside. A few moments later, they reappeared.

Between them they held opposite ends of an anti-gravity pallet bearing what looked to be small, computerized machines. Angel couldn't tell the specific nature and purpose of the devices, but looking at them, they appeared far too advanced for any of the surrounding villages.

As the men disappeared inside the building once again, Angel crept up to the ship. It was impossible to tell from where she crouched if there was anyone else on board. It was a chance she'd have to take. Staying low, she walked the length of the ship. The markings on the vessel were nondescript. There was no name or call letters printed on the outside, which was common for ships of illegal couriers. Even hers hadn't sported a name or call letters.

So Angel had to wonder, what was a ship doing here illegally and what was being carted into the building?

She rounded the front just as the two men she'd seen earlier exited the building. Shrinking back, she waited until they had reboarded the ship. When she heard the sound of the engines firing, she knew she had to take a chance and run to the side of the building. If she stayed where she was, the heat from the thrusters would scorch her at takeoff.

Not giving herself a chance to think about it, she raced the distance from the ship to the building, staying as close to the side wall as possible and hoping to blend into the shadows once she got there. She watched until the shuttle lifted off and disappeared into the night sky.

For a moment or two, Angel stood there considering her options. She could always return to her ship and find Nicoli. Together, they could come back and discover whatever was going on inside. But she was here now and it galled her to waste time unnecessarily. The fact that the men from the shuttle hadn't turned out the warehouse lights was a blessing, but it bothered her. Why leave the lights on? Was there someone else inside? Or were the men planning to return?

Angel searched the night sky and found it clear and open. Satisfied, she walked silently to the warehouse door. Again, she paused, listening for any sound on the other side. When she was met with continued silence, she stretched out her hand and tried the door handle. It turned easily.

Slowly, she pushed open the door, hoping that anyone standing on the other side might not immediately notice. When no alarm sounded, Angel stuck her head around the edge and peeked inside. A feeling of déjà vu swept over her as she found herself looking at an open foyer with hallways branching off in the pattern of spokes in a wheel. There was no one visible, so Angel left the safety of the open doorway and stepped into the building. Well lit, the place had the clean, white sterile feel of a medical facility—which made the small trail of dirty footprints stand out even more.

Angel followed the footprints down one of the hallways and eventually into one of the rooms. When she stopped to look around, her heart slammed into her chest. She was in an outer room and the footprints clearly led to another doorway at the far end. But Angel wasn't able to move.

All around her stood empty gurneys just like those she herself had laid on back at the Harvestors' main processing building. Thankfully, these gurneys were empty. But for how long?

Still looking about, Angel followed the dirty footsteps to the far door. She pressed her ear close to listen for noise. When she heard only silence, she tried the knob and again, found the door unlocked.

Pushing it open, she stepped inside. The walls were lined with counters, on top of which sat a vast array of equipment. It looked familiar and then she remembered where she'd seen it before. The lab she and Nicoli had been in when they'd found the computer. This was life-essence transfer equipment!

She had to tell Nicoli. Not caring that her footprints joined the others, leaving evidence of her visit, she hurried out of the room, into the foyer. She pulled open the door a crack and looked outside.

There was no shuttle. She sprinted across the open area to the escarpment and began climbing. She ignored the scratches and scrapes as she groped for handholds to support herself while her feet fumbled for toeholds. She wanted to be far from here before the shuttle returned, as she felt positive it would. She was certain that by now Nicoli and her grandfather would have returned to the ship and noticed her absence.

When she reached the top of the bank, Angel crawled to her knees and sat, trying to catch her breath. She stared into the night, hoping to pierce the total darkness, but to no avail. In fact, the darkness seemed to mock her efforts and the more she strained to see past it, the harder it became. A wave of dizziness washed over her and for a fraction of a second, she lost her sense of direction all together. In that moment, she was afraid to do more than breathe. Afraid that even a single step would send her flying down the steep cliff to her death.

The memory of hiding in a small closet waiting for her mother to return assailed her. She fought back the panic. She would not succumb to her fears; fears that belonged to the young girl she no longer was.

Taking a deep breath, she closed her eyes and thought back over her trek here. When she had first reached the edge of the escarpment, the warehouse had been slightly to her right. She had climbed back up the escarpment directly in front of the building, so she only had to head off to her left to be back on the correct path.

She opened her eyes again and the darkness no longer seemed as intimidating. Rising to her feet, she took her first tentative step forward. Only the ground wasn't where it was supposed to be and when her foot finally met the bottom of the crevice, the impact knocked her off balance and she fell, twisting her ankle in the process.

Pain lanced up her leg and prickled the palms of her hands where she had scraped them. Perched at an awkward angle, she realized that her foot was stuck in the crevice. Gritting her teeth, she used her hands to push herself into a standing position. Her ankle was almost too sore to move, but she tried anyway. Turning it this way and that, she tried to find the position that would allow her foot to be pulled out. But it wouldn't budge.

She threw her hands up in the air in a gesture of helpless frustration. *Could things get any worse?*

As soon as the thought formed, she knew she'd jinxed herself. Any number of things could still go wrong. Not the least of which would be that when she finally caught up with Nicoli, he would be furious.

Then she heard something that caused her greater alarm. Off in the distance came the sounds of the cargo shuttle approaching. They would use the ship's perimeter lighting to help them land in the valley beyond the escarpment and she was standing too close to the edge for them not to see her.

With renewed vigor, she pulled at her foot, trying to free it. She bent over and ignoring the pain, clawed at the rocks. Almost too soon, the first beam of light hit her with an intensity that blinded her.

Instinctively, she threw her arms up to shield her face and realized with a sick, sinking feeling that it was too late to escape.

Chapter Twenty-five

The light vanished as quickly as it had appeared, leaving Angel to face the pitch-black night around her. She froze and focused her full attention on the night sounds, and what she heard sent adrenaline coursing through her veins.

She wasn't alone.

Before she could think what to do, a form loomed out of the darkness. "Good God, woman. You'll be the death of me yet."

Angel's knees almost buckled from her relief. "Nicoli?"

"What are you doing just standing out here?"

"My foot's stuck in these rocks." She heard Nicoli's sigh but couldn't see his face.

"Okay. Let me see."

"No. Don't turn on the light." Angel looked up to scan the horizon. No sign of the aircraft was visible. Yet.

"Are you worried about that ship coming in?"

"Yeah, I am." She could tell from the sound of his footsteps that he was close. She needed to keep talking so he could focus on the direction of her voice. "We definitely don't want to be here when they return." She started pulling on her foot again, trying to dislodge it, but had no luck. In the distance, she heard the low thrum of the ship's engines.

"Who is it?"

"Illegal couriers."

Nicoli was in front of her now and she felt, rather than saw, his response to the news. "What're they doing here?"

"As near as I can tell, flying in equipment."

"I don't know what's more irritating, that equipment is being flown in, or the fact that you know about it after disobeying my orders to stay put." Nicoli knelt before her and slid his hands down her calf to her ankle, exploring first one leg and then the other, until he determined by touch which foot was stuck. Despite the gravity of their situation, she thrilled to the warm roughness of his hands.

"Any idea what the equipment is for?"

Nicoli's hands left her foot to explore the surrounding rock, leaving her to feel bereft and cold. "I'm pretty sure they're building another transfer facility."

In the resulting silence, the sound of the approaching aircraft grew louder.

"Is there any place to hide around here?" Nicoli's voice sounded strained and she felt his hands working feverishly to dislodge rocks from around her foot.

"There's an escarpment about five meters behind me and a line of trees about fifty meters to the left. Not much else."

"How steep is the descent on that escarpment?"

"Steep enough, especially in the dark." She glanced up once more to check on the ship's progress. "Hurry, Nicoli!" The ship's lights were visible now. It wouldn't be long before they were directly overhead and out here in the open, she and Nicoli made easy targets.

"Nicoli," she warned, then suddenly he tugged on her foot and it came free.

"Come on." He grabbed her arm and started off toward the edge of the escarpment. She tried to follow, but when she put weight on her newly freed foot, intense pain shot through her ankle and it refused to hold her weight. Stumbling, only Nicoli's grip on her arm kept her from falling. Draping her arm around his neck, Nicoli held on to her hand with his in a hold that paralleled the one she'd used on him at the spacestation. He shoved the searchlight into her free hand, then wrapped the arm closest to Angel about her waist.

He moved surprisingly fast toward the cliff, practically carrying her. When they reached the edge, they stopped. The lights from the warehouse were visible below but their illumination didn't reach up the escarpment. The first few meters were treacherously hidden in shadow.

Nicoli grabbed the searchlight from Angel's hand and, directing it downward, turned it on. The brilliant beam of light was blinding and Nicoli snapped it off immediately. How he saw anything in those few moments, Angel had no idea. But they were out of time.

The drone of the ship's engines was loud enough that Angel didn't need to see the ship's lights to know how close it was. But she turned anyway. The ship's landing lights cut a serpentine path across the surface of the field; each sweep of light just a little closer than the last.

Then suddenly, Angel was pulled off balance, over the edge of the cliff. Her scream lodged in her throat, she threw out her arms to brace her fall and somehow landed on her feet with Nicoli's body pressing her into the face of the cliff. A gust of wind buffeted them as the ship roared overhead.

Angel closed her eyes and waited for disaster.

The ship continued past them, down into the ravine where she heard it land. Slowly, she noticed that Nicoli was no longer pressed against her, but had taken a step back. She opened her eyes and looked around.

Together, she and Nicoli watched the ship's hatch open, spilling more light into the basin. With some of the darkness banished, Angel could just make out Nicoli's features. Turning her attention back to the ship, Angel watched the same two men she'd seen earlier emerge. Once again they carried equipment balanced on an airlift between them as they walked to the warehouse and disappeared within.

"You shouldn't have gone inside." Nicoli's whisper brushed warmly against her ear. "You should have waited for me."

"There wasn't time. And FYI, the transfer units look to be almost complete."

Nicoli only nodded, his eyes still watching the activities below.

"We found the Harvestor village, didn't we?"

"Yeah." His tone suggested there was more to tell.

"What's the matter?"

He glanced at her in surprise, but didn't pretend that everything was okay. "Something about my trip into the village is bothering me. But we'll talk about it later. Now, I need to decide what to do."

"Go back to our ship?" Angel asked hopefully.

"Not just yet. If, like you say, the units are almost finished, then any time now they could resume their old tricks and start killing people. I can't let that happen."

"Okay?" She drew the word out as she spoke, making it a question.

"My chief concern is that we still don't know who the Harvestor leader is."

"Victor?"

"Probably, but we can't be positive. We only know it's someone at the palace. If we expose the village, the leader has a chance to disappear in the ensuing chaos. There are more villagers than I'd first anticipated and there's no way to contain and deal with them quickly and quietly. No, I need some way to flush out the leader. Force him to do something rash, and expose himself."

Nicoli's voice drifted off as he fell into thought. Angel's thoughts turned to her ankle, which throbbed painfully. Afraid to move, lest they draw attention to themselves, they remained where they were and watched until the men below finished unloading the ship.

This time, they shut off the warehouse lights.

"I guess they're not coming back," Angel observed.

As the ship lifted off, Nicoli and Angel knelt against the face of the cliff, making themselves as small a target as possible and waited until the shuttle disappeared into the night.

They remained in that position until they no longer heard the ship's engines and the night grew quiet once more.

"Did you take the laser from the ship?" Nicoli's words seemed unusually loud in the sudden stillness.

"Yes."

"Let me have it."

She released the weapon from its holder and gave it to him.

"What are you going to do?"

"Shake things up." He flipped on the searchlight and started down the escarpment. "Stay here," he ordered. "I'll be right back."

Angel's foot and ankle hurt too much to protest, so she eased herself into a sitting position and resigned herself to wait. With each step down the steep embankment, Nicoli took the light farther away. When he reached the bottom, Angel saw him try the doorknob. When it opened, he glanced back, then disappeared inside. As the door fell shut, the night enveloped her.

Once or twice while she waited, Angel pressed her fingers against her ankle in an attempt to relieve the pain. Each time she did, her ankle seemed more swollen, leaving her to dread the long walk back to the Icarus. The only thing she looked forward to less than that journey was Nicoli's lecture on disobeying his orders that was sure to accompany it.

It seemed a long time before the warehouse door finally opened and Nicoli stepped out. He switched on the searchlight and climbed up to where she sat.

"Time to go." He offered her a hand up, then glanced at her face in apparent concern when she put her sore foot on the ground and flinched in pain. When he directed the light to her ankle, she saw that it had swollen to about twice its normal size.

"Can you walk?" His voice was laced with doubt.

"I'll try."

"Come on. I'll help you." Handing her the searchlight, he once again draped her free arm around his shoulders, put an arm around her waist and started up the escarpment. Nicoli moved quickly as he maneuvered them upward and by the time they reached the top, despite the cool breeze blowing, he and Angel were both sweating.

"Can we rest a minute?" Angel asked, trying to catch her breath. Nicoli had to have heard her, but he remained quiet, seemingly lost in thought. Without stopping, he started them across the rocky surface at a brisk pace.

Though Nicoli practically carried her, Angel still put weight on her sore ankle and after they had gone several meters, the pain became excruciating. "I can't go on, Nicoli. I have to rest."

"There's no time, Baby Girl." His tone was affectionate but urgent. "We have to get farther away."

"Why? I don't think the shuttle is planning to return tonight."

"No time to explain." Nicoli swept her up into his arms and strode across the field as she clung to him.

They left the rocky terrain around the escarpment and reached the grassy field.

When the explosion came, it shook the mountain. Nicoli fell to the grass and covered Angel with his body. Rocks and debris hit the ground like a small meteor shower against the side of a ship.

Nicoli remained on top of Angel for several minutes until the sound of falling debris subsided. Then he pushed away and let Angel roll over. Their eyes met and for several heartbeats, neither spoke.

"Are you all right?" Nicoli finally asked, concern reflected in the tender note in his voice.

Angel just nodded, taking the hand he offered and letting him pull her to her feet.

"Angel?" He looked down into her face as he brushed her cheek with his fingers in a gentle caress. "Are you all right?"

"You owe me another laser."

"I heard an explosion."

Nicoli ignored the high counsel, pushing past the man in order to carry Angel to his cabin. He set her down on the edge of the bed and bent to remove her shoe. Even though he'd carried her most of the way, he worried that the walk back had done serious damage to her ankle. He undid the fastener, but couldn't remove the shoe because of the swelling. Crossing to his desk, he opened the drawer and took out a knife.

"I'll have to cut it off," he said, coming back to stand before Angel.

She looked up at him, her eyes wide. "My foot?"

He smiled. "The shoe."

"Oh. All right."

Nicoli knelt before her and propped her foot on his knee to

give him better access to the shoe. "Once the shoe is off, your foot will probably swell even more. When we get back to the palace, I'll have Yanur look at it."

"We have a palace physician." The high counsel spoke from the open doorway. "He will see to my granddaughter's injury."

"No." Nicoli didn't trust the palace physician.

"Nicoli, we need to get out of here before anyone comes to investigate." Angel sounded tired.

"I'll see to this first." He inserted the tip of the knife into the side of her shoe and applied pressure outward, neatly slicing through the material. He did the same on the other side and then cut the top of the shoe open. Slowly he peeled it from her foot and tossed it in the corner.

"Okay. Shoe's off. I'll be okay, just get us out of here." Angel reached out to touch his hand as he stood next to her. He didn't want to leave her alone. As unsettling as the thought was, he actually wanted to stay and take care of her.

"Go," she ordered when he hesitated. He knew she was right.

He leaned down to speak softly in her ear. "I won't be gone long. I'll get us on course and then come back and check on you." He pressed his lips to hers in a kiss too brief to get him into any real trouble, then walked to the bridge with the high counsel hot on his trail.

Sitting in the pilot's seat, Nicoli fired up the engines. A quick look at the perimeter scan revealed no other ships nearby. *So far, so good.* It would be nice to get back to the palace before the news broke. Then he'd get to see Victor's reaction. The sooner he ended this mission, the sooner he could get Angel away from this place.

"What was that explosion?" The high counsel spoke from behind him, reminding Nicoli of a gnat that wouldn't go away. "I deserve to know what happened," the gnat continued, sitting in the copilot's seat.

Nicoli sighed. "We found a warehouse where the Harvestors were building a transfer facility. I thought I might get the Harvestor leader's attention if I blew it up."

"Without consulting me?"

"I didn't consider that necessary."

"You didn't consider it necessary?" The high counsel's voice rose. "Need I remind you that *I* am the high counsel?"

"I don't particularly care." And he didn't. Nicoli was physically tired from carrying Angel all the way back to the ship and had done his best to control the anger and fear still simmering from when he'd returned earlier and found her gone. He just didn't have the energy to be polite anymore.

He barely looked up when the old man stormed off the bridge. Nicoli was glad for a moment to himself while he set a course for the palace.

Only after they were safely away from the village did Nicoli activate the autopilot. With the perimeter scan set to sound the alarm if company should appear, Nicoli felt he could leave the controls to return to Angel.

Halfway down the hall, he heard the unmistakable sound of flesh striking flesh. Running to his cabin, he found Angel sprawled across the bed, a hand pressed to her reddened cheek. But what he noticed the most was the way her eyes, glistening with unshed tears, stared up at the high counsel in childlike fear.

"You will not disobey orders again," the high counsel shouted, raising his hand. Nicoli took the last step needed to reach the old man and, grabbing his wrist in an iron-tight grip, Nicoli twisted the arm back at a painful angle.

"Don't ever touch her again, do you understand?" He growled the words in the other man's ear.

The high counsel grimaced, but did not cower. "Unhand me this instant. I am the high counsel. She was instructed to stay on board and she chose to violate those orders. She must be disciplined."

"Not by you."

"I am the high counsel. And I'm the oldest living male member of her house. It is my duty to see to her punishment." The high counsel twisted his head to glare at Nicoli in defiance.

"Perhaps you didn't understand me." Nicoli spoke slowly and distinctly. "Touch her in any way again and I'll kill you. Now do you understand?" He retained his hold on the old man's arm, afraid that he might carry through with his threat anyway. It took great discipline to hold his anger in check and remember that the high counsel was old, and very powerful. When he was certain that his point had been understood, he slowly released his grip, remaining alert to any sudden movements the older man might make.

The high counsel glared first at Nicoli and then at Angel. He turned and walked to the door. "We have found the Harvestors and I will deal with them. Your services, and your presence, are no longer needed."

After the high counsel left, Nicoli went to Angel's side. "Are you all right?"

She gave him a sad kind of smile. "You seem to be asking me that a lot lately."

He smiled and reached out to brush a strand of hair from her face, letting his fingers run through the long, silky lengths as he did so.

"He just caught me off guard," Angel went on. "I wasn't ready for it, and then as soon as he hit me, it was like I was a kid again and suddenly I couldn't think straight."

Nicoli knelt beside the bed, pulling her into his arms and letting her head rest against his shoulder. "I'm sorry I wasn't here to protect you."

"You couldn't have known he would do that. He's been so different lately. I thought he had changed. You know, softened with the years." She sighed. "I guess he was just using you." She lifted her head so she could look into his face. "We can't trust him. You know that."

"I know," he agreed.

"I'm afraid you made an enemy of him. He's not going to want you to be my husband anymore." Nicoli saw her lips tremble and his anger with the high counsel tripled.

"Let's go back to the palace, get Yanur and my mother and leave."

Nicoli shook his head. This wasn't over as far as he was concerned. "I can't. The Harvestor threat can't be eliminated until we discover their leader. I'm sorry, Baby Girl, but I need to stay a little longer."

Angel sighed. "I knew you'd say that."

He smiled and stood. "I have an idea. Why don't you come to the bridge and keep me company?"

Chapter Twenty-six

At the palace, Damon walked into Brother Joh'nan's room and found his friend sitting in a chair, staring out the window into the pitch-black night sky.

"You've heard the news?" Damon knew he had when Brother Joh'nan didn't even acknowledge his presence. "You haven't given up have you? Because we can rebuild the transfer unit. It's true that much of the equipment was destroyed, but I've already contacted Jennins."

Brother Joh'nan finally turned from the window to look up questioningly. "Jennins?"

Damon felt another stab of concern. "You know Jennins. He's the black market trader."

Joh'nan nodded. "Yes, I remember him now. From time to time, my mind grows fuzzy."

Damon offered a comforting smile. Joh'nan was the most intelligent man he'd ever known. He was the one who discovered the way to save their people and had shown the rest of them. It wasn't right that their survival came at the price of his life. If only for the chance to make things better, Damon wanted to hurry the takeover of the Coronadian government. He crossed the room to put his hand on Joh'nan's shoulder. "It will be okay. Jennins said there is still equipment to be bought on Vega. We'll rebuild the unit and find a new donor body. But Joh'nan, we must eliminate those standing in our way and we must do it now. We are out of time."

"Always so anxious, my friend. Everything comes in time." Joh'nan smiled and raised his hand to lay it on top of his friend's. "But you will be pleased to know that I have found a solution to our problem."

Damon's shock was immediate and he bent so he could look into Joh'nan's face. "You have? What?"

"Oh, yes. I found it buried in the ancient laws. A contest of sorts. It requires the endorsement of a Quorum, but I don't see that as being a problem."

"What about the high counsel? Can he stop it?"

Joh'nan seemed to consider the question. "He could, but he won't. I don't know what game the high counsel has been playing, but I assure you that he has no intention of allowing Colonel Romanof to be his council-elect."

Damon pulled an extra chair over, turning it so he could sit facing the other man. "Tell me more."

"Should we succeed, the House of Scyphor, and all the power that goes with it, will be ours. But this solution I've found is not without great risk to one of us."

Damon nodded his understanding. "Then we must take measures to ensure there is no risk at all."

Joh'nan smiled and nodded. "And I know just how to do that."

It was the middle of the night when Victor returned to his room after secretly meeting with the individual high officials of the House of Scyphor. Their ignorance of life off Coronado and elsewhere in the universe was exceeded only by their paranoia over what an off-worlder, such as Colonel Romanof, might do to their life on the planet, should he become high counsel. A few carefully phrased suggestions had made it easy to secure the endorsement he needed to carry out his plans.

Sitting on the edge of his bed, he looked at his watch. It was too early to execute the next phase of his plan and he was too excited to sleep, so when the knock came at his door, he welcomed the interruption.

He rose and crossed the room. He knew who stood on the other side of the door before he opened it, and so the smile he pasted on his face was not altogether false.

"I have missed you so." Sorrah threw herself into his arms, sighing into his mouth as her lips met his.

He returned her kiss with an enthusiasm that still amazed him. To think that after all these years, a lifetime in fact, without a woman, he could find pleasure in a woman's touch or in a woman's body.

Sorrah pulled away just enough to look into his face. "Tell me again," she whispered.

He smiled indulgently. "I love you as I have never loved another woman." He took perverse pleasure in the truth of his words. He had loved many men, but never a woman.

"How much longer must we wait?"

Though he felt his body responding to her, he didn't pretend to misunderstand what she meant. "Not much longer now. I promise."

She rewarded his answer by rubbing her body against his. "Good. When you are high counsel, I will be the perfect high consort for you. I will see to all of your needs." She pressed her lips to his, suggesting just how she might see to his needs. When she pulled back, she seemed almost shy.

"What is it?"

"Do you think I could have my very own maid?"

"Of course." Brother Damon laughed for her benefit and felt a slight twinge of guilt flutter through him. He would miss Sorrah after he killed her. She had been useful, and loyal, in fulfilling her duties to him. All of her duties. He thought she might even be willing to kill for him, though he'd never asked her to. That kind of loyalty was hard enough to find, much less replace.

An'jel would not be as cooperative, nor as blindly loyal. She had spent too many years away and had grown independent as a result. Such independence could threaten his plans. And while everything he did was for the good of his people, Victor couldn't help but wonder if there might be something, or someone, he could keep for himself.

Taking her by the hand, he led her to his bed. With gentleness born of familiarity, Victor removed her clothes until she stood before him in her feminine perfection. She was indeed lovely and he took pleasure both in the sight of her and his own body's reaction.

He devoted much time to their lovemaking, not stopping until they were both well satisfied. And even then, he held her in his arms for a while longer.

"Sorrah, my love. Are you awake?"

"No."

He smiled and kissed the top of her head where it rested on his chest. "I wish we could spend the night together, but I have things yet to be done tonight."

She sat up and looked at him. "What could be so important that it can't wait until the morning?"

He touched the tip of her nose with his forefinger in a playful gesture. "Your future as high consort, unless of course you wish to continue being a maid?"

She smiled and gave a sigh of pretend indulgence. "Well, I suppose if you must go."

It was his turn to smile. "Actually, *you* must go. Back to your room." He threw off the covers and got out of bed. His clothes lay in a pile on the floor and he bent to retrieve his pants. Sorrah followed his lead, albeit reluctantly, climbing out of bed to dress.

After he finished putting on his shirt, Victor walked over to his desk and picked up the small vial he had placed there earlier. Turning, he saw that Sorrah was dressed. "I want you to take this vial. At breakfast tomorrow, put four drops into Colonel Romanof's morning drink—without him knowing of course. Will you do that for me?"

She took the vial and looked at it suspiciously. When she looked up at him, he saw the doubt and concern reflected in her eyes. "If you don't wish to do it, I will understand," he said, reaching to take the vial back.

She clutched it tighter and moved it away from him. "No, it's just that, well, I've never killed anyone."

Victor smiled his most tender smile and brought his hand up to cup her cheek. "These drops will do nothing more than make the colonel tired. That's all."

"Really?" Her voice sounded hopeful.

It was ridiculous to him how a few simple words could be so reassuring to her. "I would never ask you to kill the colonel." He watched her tuck the vial into the pocket of her skirt and returned her kiss before she walked out of the room. He closed the door behind her and leaned against it, a sense of satisfaction settling about him. "No, Sorrah. I would never ask you to kill the colonel. I only ask you to drug him so that I may have that honor."

Angel woke to a loud crashing noise.

"Angel!" Her mother shouted from the open doorway. "Something's happened. You have to wake up."

In one movement, Angel flung back the sheets and comforter and jumped out of bed, forgetting her ankle in her haste until the searing pain shot up her leg. Instinctively, she looked around for a weapon as she fell back against the bed, fearing her mother was in danger, or being attacked.

When no threat materialized, she looked from the dent in the wall where the door had hit when her mother barged in, to her mother, who now stood in front of her, staring at her foot.

"What happened to your foot?"

"Nothing. What's going on?"

Her mother's gaze snapped to her face and the shocked expression turned to one of grave concern. "It's Nicoli."

"Is he okay? Has something happened to him?" Angel looked at the bed, remembering how he had laid beside her until she'd fallen asleep.

Her mother rushed to the closet and rummaged through it, pulling out a change of clothes and tossing the garments at her.

"Yes and yes. Hurry and put these on. Oh here, let me help you."

"Mother, please." Angel tried to control her frustration as her mother began to assist her out of her nightclothes and into the new outfit. "What's going on?"

"Your grandfather has called for a Quorum."

Angel paused in the process of buttoning her shirt. "A Quorum? Now?" Angel's hand fell to her side, the buttons on her shirt forgotten as she considered this new information. A Quorum was only called for extremely important matters. "It's the middle of the night. Are you sure?" As her thoughts raced, her mother finished buttoning her shirt.

"Yes. One of the maids told me." The shirt finished, her mother looked at her, a grave expression on her face. "Gil'rhen summoned Nicoli to appear."

"Oh, God." It couldn't be good. Whatever the reason, it couldn't be good. "I have to get there."

"Of course."

Angel didn't bother to put on shoes. She slipped her arm around her mother's shoulders and together, they made their way through the halls to the high counsel's chambers.

The doors were closed when they arrived, but Angel no longer bowed to ceremony. She opened the doors and hobbled in.

Eight high officials from the House of Scyphor sat, four on either side of her grandfather. Victor stood before the group on the right, wearing his formal attire. His head was bent in quiet conversation with Pualson, a smug expression on his face.

Nicoli stood before the group as well, with his back to Angel so she couldn't see his face. Something serious was taking place. Not even her barging in had drawn so much as a head turn from anyone except Rianol, who stood just off to the side. He wore a grave expression, like a man with too much responsibility to bear. Seeing him, Angel felt her alarm grow. If Rianol was this concerned, the situation had to be bad.

When he saw her, Rianol walked over to offer his support. Smiling her thanks, she placed her hand on his arm, releasing her mother who immediately moved to the other side of the room where Yanur watched the preceedings, his face grim.

"What's going on?" She asked Rianol, leaning close so she could whisper in his ear.

"Victor is protesting his displacement as your husband and council-elect."

"Politics," she muttered disgustedly. "Well, it's too late. Nicoli is my husband and Victor had just better get used to it." Even as she said the words, she feared the reality of her world was about to be jarred.

"An'jel." Rianol's tone was sympathetic and she knew she didn't want to hear what he had to say. Inside, she screamed at him to remain quiet, hoping that if he didn't say anything more, they could all go back to bed and everything would return to normal. But that wouldn't happen. She couldn't stop the events about to unfold.

"Victor has issued *The Challenge*."

An unnatural silence descended around her and her perception took on a surreal quality. Her voice, when it finally worked, came out almost a squeak. *"The Challenge?"*

"I'm sorry, An'jel."

"No," she shook her head. "There's been a mistake."

Angel turned to look at Nicoli's back, ramrod straight, powerful in appearance. He was the embodiment of authority, military leadership and expertise, honor and integrity, bravery and courage. He was everything she was not and in that moment, she would have done anything to protect him from her planet's archaic laws.

"No." She shouted and all heads turned toward her. Pulling at Rianol so he would walk with her, she moved closer to the center podium. "Don't allow this to happen, Grandfather. You, yourself, have already blessed our union."

Her grandfather's eyes were cold when they turned to her. "Silence, woman. Know your place. If you can not control your tongue, I will have you thrown out of the room."

Shocked, Angel moved closer to Nicoli. "Please," she begged him. "Don't agree to this." She leaned closer to whisper in his ear. "Tell him we're not married. Tell him anything so you won't have to fight. We can leave the planet."

Nicoli just stared at her, disapproval written across his face. "I will not run."

"Colonel Romanof." The high counsel's voice boomed over the room, halting all other conversations. "In accordance with our ancient laws, Victor D'rajmin challenges your claims to be husband to An'jel ToRrenc and to the title of council-elect. He calls into question your strength and ability to defend these two privileges. What say you? Do you agree to meet Victor on *The Challenge* field? Or do you relinquish your claims?"

Angel held her breath, waiting for the miracle that never came.

"I will meet Victor D'rajmin on *The Challenge* field." Nicoli's voice rang clear and strong throughout the chamber.

"No." Angel cried. "You don't understand."

Nicoli turned to her. "Everything will be okay."

She wouldn't allow him to console her. She gripped his arms with her hands. "You don't understand." She enunciated each word, hoping to make him understand. "*The Challenge* is a fight to the death."

Chapter Twenty-seven

"It is done." The high counsel's voice rang out over the council chamber. "Tomorrow at noon, Victor D'rajmin will meet Colonel Nicoli Romanof, here in my chambers, for *The Challenge*. They shall fight with the warring blade until one man lies dead. The Right of Claim for my granddaughter, An'jel ToRrenc, belongs to the survivor, as shall the title of council-elect. At any time before noon tomorrow, either party may withdraw from the fight and in doing so, forfeit his Right of Claim." The high counsel looked first to Victor and then to Nicoli. "Do you both understand?"

"Yes." The men spoke in unison while Angel looked on. Never had she felt so powerless.

The high counsel continued to talk, but Angel tuned him out. She needed to think of a plan; a way out of this mess. There was no doubt in her mind now that Victor was the Harvestor leader. Just as there was no doubt in her mind that he would find some way to cheat in tomorrow's fight. She and Nicoli had hoped the leader would expose himself, but they hadn't counted on this.

When the Quorum adjourned, Angel's mind still puzzled over possibilities. Silently, she joined Nicoli, her mother and Yanur as they walked out of the council room.

No one spoke as they made their way to Yanur's room. When Nicoli helped Angel to a chair, she surfaced from her thoughts, glanced up and for the first time, noticed Yanur's face. The old man seemed suddenly years older. His haunted eyes and grim expression reminded her of her mother's face so many nights ago when Angel's father faced *The Challenge*. Then, as now, it was a matter of honor to not back down. Angel didn't see much value in honor if you weren't around to enjoy it.

Yanur moved to the corner of the room where he took his small black bag from the closet. Carrying it to Angel, he knelt before her, opened the bag and removed the Reparator. When he activated the beam and ran it across her ankle, she felt the tingling that accompanied the regeneration of healthy cells and watched in amazement as the swelling subsided and the colorful bruises slowly turned to a healthy glow.

When the ankle was fully restored, Yanur switched off the machine. He held it suspended in the air and Angel found she couldn't look away. The Reparator had saved Nicoli's life once before. Why couldn't they use it again? She tore her gaze from the Reparator to look at Yanur. As if he read her thoughts, he shook his head.

"To the death," he whispered.

"Once a person is dead, it will not bring him back to life." She quoted his words, spoken outside the space station; each syllable a death knell.

Yanur nodded and turned to place the Reparator back in his bag. But Angel still saw the single tear escape his eye to roll down his cheek, and knew its twin coursed down her own.

Nicoli came to help Angel stand. Looking up into his face, she knew she could no longer deny the truth. She loved him.

The sheer amazement of her discovery left her in a state of shock and she had to look away, before he saw it in her eyes.

"What is it?" There was concern in Nicoli's voice.

She quickly masked her expression and shook her head. "Nothing. Shall we go?"

Taking a few tentative steps, she stopped and turned to Yanur. "Good as new, thank you."

"You're welcome." He gave her a sad smile as he watched her walk around. Her mother moved to his side and slid her arm through his. Knowing he must feel a pain equal to her own, she was glad her mother was with him.

Still holding her hand, Nicoli pulled Angel to the door. "We'll talk tomorrow," he said to Yanur.

The older man nodded and Nicoli turned and led Angel out into the corridor. As they walked along the passage leading to their bedroom, Angel's thoughts turned once again to the fight. The weight of her misery made her head seem too heavy to hold up and, beside her, Nicoli's silence was deafening.

Back in their room, they prepared for bed, going through the normal, routine motions with a surreal calm. Angel tried to pretend that this was like any other night, but the effort proved too much.

Tossing the pants she had just folded onto the floor, she whirled around to face Nicoli. "How can you act like nothing is happening?"

With that calm, unhurried air so typical of him, he finished taking off his shoe, then looked at her from where he sat on the side of the bed. "How would you have me act?"

"I don't know." She threw her arms up in the air as she paced toward him. "Get mad, slam something around. Yell. Do something."

"Why?"

Exasperated, she stopped mid-stride and stared. "Tomorrow, you're going to fight Victor."

"Yes, I know."

"It's a fight to the death."

"I'm aware of that."

"Damn it, Nicoli. One of you isn't going to survive."

"You're worried about Victor?"

"Aargh!" She yelled. The man was impossible. "Of course I'm not worried about Victor. I'm worried about you."

"Thanks for the vote of confidence."

Angel stared at him in disbelief. "Do you really want to die so very much that the possibility of it doesn't bother you?"

"I will not forfeit the fight and leave you to face Victor and your grandfather alone."

"We could leave—you, me, Yanur and my mother."

Nicoli shook his head. "Running away is not the answer."

"Sometimes staying isn't either. You know as well as I do that Victor is going to cheat to win."

"Probably."

"So what will you do?"

"Are you asking me if I will cheat to beat him?"

"Yes."

He didn't even pause to consider his answer. "No. I won't cheat."

Angel let her head fall forward in defeat. "Death before dishonor," she mumbled. She raised her head and pinned him under her stare. "Well, you know what Nicoli? Good only triumphs over evil in the storybooks—not in real life."

"I'll be fine." He moved to her side and wrapped his arm around her shoulder. She let him lead her to the bed to sit beside him.

"I pray to God that tomorrow you *are* fine, but I can't help being afraid for you." Angel stroked her hand along his cheek. "I don't want anything to happen to you. I couldn't bear it. I've already lost too many people I love. If I lost you too . . . ."

She kissed him then. Kissed him as if it were their last kiss, conveying in action the feelings she was too afraid to put into words. It was the desperate kiss of a starving woman and Nicoli returned it with equal fervor.

Somehow they ended up stretched out, naked, pressed against each other. She basked in the feel of his hard chest rubbing her breasts, their legs intertwined and hands clasping each other's heads as lips devoured lips and tongues danced with each other.

Angel wanted this moment to last forever. But more than that, she wanted it to happen again.

"Nicoli," she pleaded, pulling her head away as she grasped for one last small thread of sanity to hold on to. "Stop."

"Why? You want this as much as I do."

"You're right, but we have to plan. Tomorrow—"

"SShhh." Nicoli placed a finger to her lips. "Angel, just for tonight," he whispered, "let there be no tomorrow." He kissed her again and the thread snapped, leaving her wanting only to feel him inside her.

He didn't make her wait, taking her in strokes so fast and powerful, all she could do was hold on until they both found their release.

The second time they made love, they took their time, and the reward was no less satisfying.

Afterwards, bathed in the afterglow of such loving, Angel settled herself against Nicoli's side, her head resting on his chest. Never before had she felt so cherished and safe. As the steady rhythm of his heartbeat lulled her to sleep, she smiled to herself. She had spent her entire life running from her grandfather and the arranged, loveless marriage he would force on her. She had wanted more from life. She had wanted to find true love. And now she had.

"I love you, Nicoli," she whispered into the darkness. "You're the only one I'll ever love."

Her declaration met with silence. Perhaps he was already asleep and hadn't heard her.

Or maybe, a small part of her brain chimed in just before she fell asleep, he'd heard but didn't feel the same.

Nicoli didn't consider himself a coward, but nothing scared him more than those four simple words Angel had uttered. "I love you, Nicoli."

At first his heart had leapt for joy, then a lifetime of conditioning had kicked in and he shut the door on his emotion. He couldn't afford to love anyone, because of his job, because of the kind of person he was. The old arguments slipped easily into place. Angel could do so much better, he had no right to keep her. To hell with the Althusian laws. Hadn't he broken enough of them already in his life? What was the real reason he wouldn't divorce Angel?

The answer to that question kept him awake the rest of the night. When the first ray of light peeked past the window curtain, Nicoli eased himself from Angel's arms and left the warmth of their bed.

As quickly and quietly as he could, he dressed. There was much to be done today and he shouldn't have stayed up so late, making love to Angel. But oh, it had been worth it. If he died today, it would still have been worth every second he'd spent with her.

Nicoli left the room and headed for the kitchen, intent on dealing with adversity on a full stomach. To his surprise, Sorrah was already up and preparing the morning breakfast.

"Good morning," she said as he walked in. "You're up early."

"Big day."

She smiled, a friendly smile that lacked the seductive innuendoes of their earlier encounters. "So I heard." She waved at the various foods cooking on the stove. "Are you hungry? Sit down. I'll fix you something."

Nicoli looked around, on the verge of refusing her. Hunger warred with his desire to be alone with his thoughts.

"You'll need your strength today," she reminded.

"Okay." A table sat in the middle of the kitchen and he started around it, about to take a spot on the far side when she stopped him.

"No, no. Sit here." Sorrah laid a plate on the side closest to her. It seemed curious to him, but before he could ask, Sorrah was already explaining. "It's just easier to be able to turn around and hand you the food, that's all."

Nicoli took the seat she indicated and she began to fill his plate with eggs and meats. She placed a bowl of fruit in front of him. "Would you like some wineberry juice or hot-brew?"

"Hot-brew, thanks."

Nicoli ate a forkful of eggs and was glad he'd opted to eat. As he ate, he noticed Sorrah's reflection in the side of the fruit bowl. He saw her take a mug from the cabinet and then glance over her shoulder at him. Something about the gesture made him suspicious, so he pretended to be absorbed in his food, all the while keeping an eye on her movements through her reflection. She reached into her apron pocket and pulled out a small vial. Then her hands disappeared in front of her. But Nicoli had no doubt that she had just slipped something into his drink.

She turned and set the hot-brew on the table. "If it's not warm enough, I can heat it."

"I'm sure it will be fine." He pushed away from the table and stood up. "I'll take it with me."

He left the kitchen, mug in hand and made straight for Yanur's room. He knocked on the door, then pushed it open, not waiting for Yanur's invitation.

"Yanur, are you—oh, I'm sorry. Please excuse me." Suppressing a smile, Nicoli quickly backed out of the room and shut the door. Yanur and Katrina looked as if they had spent the night much in the same way he and Angel had, only apparently they had slept longer.

Scuffling noises came from within the room and then a few minutes later, a sheepish looking Yanur opened the door.

"You can come in now."

Nicoli walked in and found Katrina standing on the far side of the bed, dressed but with an embarrassed flush staining her cheeks. She'd made an attempt to comb her hair, which was more than he could say for Yanur, who looked like he'd never seen a brush in his life.

"I'm sorry, Katrina. I didn't mean to barge in." Nicoli was at a loss for the right words. In all the years he'd been with Yanur, he couldn't ever remember catching his friend in bed with a woman. That this particular woman happened to be his mother-in-law just made the situation that much more uncomfortable. "I, uh, I didn't know." He let his words trail off.

Katrina seemed to relax when she saw how flustered he was. "It's all right, Colonel."

"Nicoli, please. Or Alex. Yanur always calls me Alex."

"Alex, then." She smiled when she said it and walked over to stand by Yanur, who took her hand in his and held it.

"I didn't mean to sleep so long, Alex," Yanur said, then looked at the mug in Nicoli's hand. "Is that for me?"

"No." Nicoli walked over to the potted plant in the corner and emptied the contents into the dirt. "It's been doctored, with what exactly, I don't know. I didn't care to find out."

"You two probably have things you need to discuss," Katrina said. "I should be going."

Almost shyly, she kissed Yanur and started for the door. She stopped when she came even with Nicoli, placing her hand lightly on his arm. "I wish there was something I could say to convince you not to fight, but I know I can't. It is a matter of honor for you, and I understand that. I want you to know how much I appreciate your taking care of my daughter, and bringing her back to me. I couldn't have asked for a better son-in-law and I'm glad you're a part of my family." She raised herself on tiptoes to place a kiss on his cheek and when she pulled away, Nicoli saw her eyes glisten with unshed tears. Something strange and mysterious clutched at his heart like an iron band. He heard her sigh deeply before giving him a smile. "Please be careful this afternoon. Now, if you'll excuse me, I think I'll see if I can sneak in and out of my room before that horrid woman finds me and insists on giving me one of her massages." She turned her head to give Yanur a parting smile and then walked out of the room.

"Horrid woman?" Nicoli asked, perplexed.

"Sorrah." Yanur said as if that were explanation enough.

"Interesting."

"It is?"

"Yes. Sorrah's the one who doctored my drink, not fifteen minutes ago."

"Didn't you say you thought she and Victor were close? This is his doing, I'm sure."

Nicoli smiled. "Won't he be surprised when he discovers his little ploy didn't work?"

"Should we do something about Sorrah?"

"No. If we do, Victor will know he didn't succeed and he'll try something else. We're better off this way."

Yanur looked down, suddenly too interested in his feet or the floor. "There is another option."

With a sense of déjà vu, Nicoli shook his head. "I will not forfeit the fight."

Yanur heaved a heavy sigh. "I know."

"I wanted to ask you a favor."

Yanur's eyebrow shot up. "Of course, anything."

Nicoli took his time, not exactly sure how to ask. "Should something go wrong this afternoon, and I don't make it, will you take Angel away from here? I need to know she'll be safe if I'm not around to protect her."

Yanur stared at him, as if seeing him for the first time.

"Will you do that for me?" Nicoli asked.

"Of course, Alex. You know I will." Yanur crossed the room to stand in front of Nicoli. "Did I ever tell you how proud I am of you? Because I am, you know."

Nicoli gave a half-hearted smile. "Thanks. You've always been there for me. You've been both a father and a friend. I appreciate it."

"You've been a good son, Alex."

The two men exchanged awkward hugs before Nicoli walked out, leaving Yanur to stare at the door, a puzzled expression on his face. Over the years, he'd watched Alex risk his life many times. But Yanur had never seen him so worried over the possibility of his own death.

Preoccupied by these thoughts, Yanur retrieved his black bag and left his room.

Chapter Twenty-eight

"Care for some company?"

Angel skipped another small stone across the lake before looking up. "Do you remember when we used to come here as kids? I used to get so frustrated because I could never make my stones skip as far as yours."

Rianol smiled. "I see you've been practicing."

Angel managed a small smile. "Anytime I found myself near a lake, I always skipped a few stones across it. Over the years, it just sort of developed into a habit. Now it helps me think."

"Is that why you came here? To think?"

"Partly." She let her fingers brush against the grass along the bank where she sat. "And to get away for a while."

"Would you like for me to leave?" Rianol offered.

"No, actually I think I'd like the company." She patted the ground beside her. "Want to pull up some dirt?"

Rianol gave the ground a speculative look. "Maybe we could take a walk instead?"

Angel shook her head. "*You've* sure changed. I remember getting in trouble with my parents for coming home covered in mud because *you* said it would be more fun if we slid down the muddy side of the bank into the water." She studied him to see if her mild teasing had the desired effect. He still looked determined to walk. "You're sure you don't want to sit and toss stones?"

"I'm sure." He stretched out his hand to help her up.

"Thanks." She brushed off her clothes and then together, they began to stroll along the path circling the lake.

"I would have thought you'd be with your husband."

Angel felt the same stab of disappointment she had felt when she awakened earlier to find Nicoli gone. "He's off preparing for the fight—I . . . I didn't want to get in his way." She still wondered if he'd heard her confession last night, if that had anything to do with why he sneaked out. "But I also couldn't sit around in the room and watch the clock until noon, so I came out here." She turned to study him. Buried beneath the man's face, she saw traces of the boy he once was. Today, his face appeared more gaunt than usual and she wondered what stress this fight was causing him.

"How are you doing?"

He looked surprised that she would ask. "Me?"

"Yeah. This can't be easy. After all, Victor's your friend."

"Well, um, yes. I've known Victor a long time." He looked at her with uncertainty. "I have a great deal of respect for Colonel Romanof, as well. This whole thing," he waved his hand in the air. "It's just unfortunate."

"Understatement of the century, Rianol. Today, one of us is going to lose someone very close. It's more than unfortunate. It's asinine." She let her breath out in sigh of resignation. "And I don't know how to stop it."

"The colonel doesn't strike me as the kind to forfeit a fight."

"No, you're right. He's not. But what about Victor? Do you think if I went to him, he'd call it off?" She knew he wouldn't, not if he were the Harvestor leader as she suspected, but she wanted to hear Rianol's thoughts.

Rianol shook his head. "No. Even if Victor decided to forfeit, there'd always be someone else. The high counsel, for as long as he continues to live, will see that Colonel Romanof meets with a continual string of challengers. No matter how good he is, he can't beat them all. Sooner or later, one of them will win and you'll find yourself with a new husband—and no say in the matter."

Angel shuddered and gave a shaky laugh. "Are you trying to cheer me up, because if you are, I want to tell you—you suck at it."

Rianol stared at her in shock, then burst out laughing. "You are full of surprises. Life with you would never be dull, that's for sure." He took her hand in his and pulled her to a stop so he could face her. "The colonel is a lucky man."

"Thank you," she said sincerely.

"Listen, the fight will start soon. I spoke to the high counsel and he agreed to bend the rules and allow you and Mr. Snellen to be present during the fight. But An'jel, you can not interfere. If you do, you'll be thrown out. That was the best I could do."

The rules stated that only the high counsel, the members of the Quorum and the fighters could be present. She had been dreading the long wait to hear the results of the contest. She wasn't sure now whether she could handle watching it, but she'd rather be there with Nicoli in some capacity, than sitting around waiting. She threw her arms around Rianol and hugged him. "Thank you."

Rianol hesitated before awkwardly hugging her back. Thinking about it, she couldn't remember seeing Rianol with a woman. Nor had he ever spoken about someone special to her. How lonely that must be. Suddenly, she felt very sorry for him.

"I just want you to know that I'm here for you, if you need anything," he whispered in her ear.

At high noon, the chimes from the large clock sounded, resonating off the walls of the high counsel's chamber and marking the commencement of *The Challenge* fight. Emptied of all furniture, the large rug on the floor had been removed to reveal blood red tiles set among the darker ones, forming a large circle. Within this circle, Victor and Nicoli stood, facing one another. The high counsel and members of the Quorum lined the back wall while Yanur, Angel and Katrina stood together off to the side. Across the room, Rianol stood alone.

Victor and Nicoli wore form-hugging black pants. Neither shirts nor shoes were allowed, to avoid the possibility of concealed weapons. If the situation weren't so grave, Angel might have enjoyed the high level of testosterone on display. The scene was reminiscent of the slave auction back on the Harvestors' planet.

She and Nicoli had not talked prior to the fight. He had seemed preoccupied, with good reason, and she'd been loath to break his concentration with something as trivial as her feelings. When they had arrived at the chamber, he'd nodded to Yanur and given her a kiss. With a whispered "this won't take long" and a wink, he'd walked confidently into the ring to meet Victor.

Angel's over-strung nerves virtually buzzed with tension when the high counsel stepped into the ring. "This fight is for the title of council-elect and for the Right of Claim for my granddaughter, An'jel ToRrenc. Once the fight begins, it will not end until one of the contestants lies dead. Does either party wish to forfeit?"

Both Victor and Nicoli shook their heads no.

"Very well. Let the fight begin." The high counsel stepped quickly from the ring, as if expecting both men to lunge, but neither did. Like dancers, they moved in tandem, circling but always opposite one another, sizing up each other. When Victor's face moved into view, Angel saw his predatory smile and her heart grew cold with fear.

At that instant, Victor lunged. Nicoli knocked the other blade aside easily, then thrust his own blade forward. Victor parried the attack.

It continued in this manner—lunge and parry, lunge and parry—each forward or downward thrust harder than the last, until Victor's breathing grew hard. It finally seemed to dawn on him that Nicoli was not as winded, and the smug smile he'd worn from the beginning, faded to a frown. His plan to cheat was an obvious failure.

It quickly was apparent to all that Nicoli was the better blades-man. For the first time since *The Challenge* was issued, Angel felt a spark of optimism. Maybe there could be a happy ending for her and Nicoli after all.

Nicoli drew first blood when the tip of his blade connected with Victor's upper arm, slicing into it. Victor stared at the wound in horror, as if for the first time realizing he might be the one killed today. Now fighting for his life, his thrusts grew wild and desperate. Heedless of wasting energy, he swung his blade faster and faster, trying to beat Nicoli down. Nicoli raised his blade to block the blows, but the impact drove them out of the circle, toward the side where Angel and Yanur stood watching.

Both men had sustained numerous cuts, and blood flowed freely down their bodies, painting a grim picture of impending death. Victor labored for every breath he took and even Nicoli sounded winded. As the men tired, the blows came less quickly. Finally, the wait between each thrust grew so long that when Victor next raised his blade, Nicoli stepped closer and slammed his fist into the other man's face. Victor's head snapped back and he crumpled to the floor.

Angel held her breath as she waited for Nicoli to deliver the killing blow, but it didn't come.

"I have won," he announced. "There is no need to kill this man to prove myself."

"You must kill him or the fight is not finished," the high counsel demanded.

"I refuse."

Nicoli gave Victor a final look, then lowered his blade, turned and walked toward Angel. Too elated to remain standing, Angel ran and threw herself into his arms, unconcerned about the blood. "I told you to have a little faith in me," he whispered before kissing her. Then he let her go so he could shake hands with Yanur.

Standing to the side of Nicoli, Angel caught a flash of movement from the corner of her eye. She turned. Victor had recovered and now, with his warring blade leveled at her, charged forward. An inhuman howl issued from his throat. Though her mind screamed to move, her body refused. She froze, and waited for the blade to pierce her heart.

Angel closed her eyes. Nothing happened. Opening her eyes, she saw Victor hovering before her, a look of shocked disbelief on his face. When he looked down, she followed the direction of his gaze. From his stomach protruded Nicoli's blade. For the second time, he crumpled to the ground. This time, dead.

With a feeling of relief, Angel turned to Nicoli. And felt her world upend itself. Victor's blade had found its mark. Grunting with the extreme pain, Nicoli pulled the blade out and dropped it. Before she could wrap her arms about him, his legs buckled and he slumped to the ground.

Someone screamed, over and over and she realized it was her. "Oh, God, no. Nicoli."

Her hands hovered around the wound, unsure what to do. It was Yanur who pulled off his shirt and used it to stanch the flow of blood.

She knelt there helplessly as Yanur examined Nicoli. When he looked at her again, it was to shake his head slightly.

"No. You're wrong," she sobbed. Leaning over Nicoli, she laid her hand against his face. "Hang on. You'll be okay."

Nicoli's eyelids fluttered, then opened. He seemed to have trouble focusing on her, but he gave her a weak smile. "My Angel," he whispered.

Her smile felt wobbly through her tears.

"Victor?" He asked.

"Dead."

"Good. Then you are safe." He coughed and blood trickled from the corner of his mouth. Angel quickly wiped it away with the corner of her shirt.

"Shush, my love, don't talk. Save your energy. We'll talk later."

"Both know this is the end." She heard the blood gurgling in his lungs, making speech difficult. "Funny. Spent my life, looking for death." He coughed and she held him until the tremors stopped. When he spoke again, his voice sounded much weaker. "Now, when I finally have a reason to live, death finds me." He raised an unsteady hand to wipe away the tears streaming down her cheeks. "Wanted to spend my whole life with you. Not enough time. Want you to know . . . I love you, Angel. Never doubt that I love you . . . more than life itself."

Releasing one last shuddering breath, his arm slipped to his side and silence stole over him. Angel sat in shock, unable to believe he was gone. How could he be dead? This was the love she had searched her whole life for. There could never be another.

Overcome by grief, her head dropped forward and the tears fell unceasingly. She didn't even notice when her mother led her from the room.

Chapter Twenty-nine

Three days following Nicoli's death, Angel emerged from the black hole that had become her life. Having fallen into such sorrow and despair, she wondered that the emotions didn't kill her. At her lowest moment, she prayed they would, wanting to be with Nicoli in any way she could.

During that time, her mother slipped in and out of the room, bringing food that went untouched, and sleeping pills that had to be rationed, lest she succumb to temptation and swallow too many. She cried until her swollen eyes were incapable of producing moisture, and then cried some more. Finally she fell into a deep sleep and when she awoke, she knew it was time to move on.

Her world had ended, but life had not and though she'd toyed with the notion of killing herself, it wasn't in her nature. She was a fighter, and she would survive.

She managed to pull a brush through her hair, but it took all her energy just to remove the tangles, so rather than braid it, she left it loose. Next she held a rag soaked in cold water against her face in an attempt to reduce the swelling around her eyes. Her efforts proved unsuccessful.

Finally, she left her room and headed for the kitchen. She wasn't hungry, but knew on some basic level that she must eat. It was late morning and the kitchen was full of workers. Some were clearing away the last remains of breakfast while others started preparations for the noon meal. When she entered, they ceased their activities to stare, making her feel self-conscious.

She stood, facing the looks of curiosity, sympathy and pity, unsure how to handle them. When Sorrah walked into the kitchen from the other doorway, there was no sympathy or pity in the look she gave Angel. Raw hatred and anger glared at her from behind eyes as swollen as her own. Any other time, Angel might have glared back, or confronted the woman, but not now. She knew all too well what it felt like to lose someone you loved, as she was sure now that Sorrah had loved Victor.

Angel abandoned all thoughts of eating and left the kitchen to go to her mother's room. She found it empty. Yanur's room was vacant as well and somewhere in the fog of the last couple of days, she remembered her mother saying that Yanur had taken Nicoli's body and left the planet. A part of her didn't blame him for leaving, though she wished he'd at least said good-bye. She would miss him, but maybe it was better this way.

After spending so many days in her room, the thought of returning to it was inconceivable, so she walked outside with the intention of becoming hopelessly lost in the maze. It was there that Rianol found her a short time later.

"Am I intruding?"

"No." She gestured to one of the benches placed along the path of the maze. Sitting at one end, she left room for him to join her. She tilted her head back, letting the warmth of the two suns wash over her face. The sky shone a crystal blue and somewhere nearby, birds chirped their staccato songs. Time seem to hold still and Angel felt a momentary peacefulness settle over her. It was the kind of moment that left one thinking that today was a good day to be alive. The irony stung.

"Life's funny," she observed. "Sometimes it seems that no matter how hard or fast I run, it's never hard or fast enough, you know? I spent most of my life trying to get away from here only to end up where I started. And when I finally find the one thing I was looking for . . ." Her throat grew too tight to speak and tears welled up in her eyes. She blinked rapidly to clear them. She would not cry. But when Rianol put his arm around her shoulder to offer comfort, she didn't pull away.

"I'm sorry," he whispered. "I'm sorry it turned out like this."

"I'm sorry, too," she whispered back. "I'm sorry because you lost a friend as well. Victor's dead but I can't find it in me to feel bad about that. He killed the man I loved." She felt him stiffen beneath her head. "Do you hate me?" She wasn't sure she cared if he did or not.

"No. I understand." They sat together in silence, watching the leaves on the bushes rustle in the gentle, warm breeze. Noises from the palace drifted to them then faded. Angel thought that if she held very still and quiet, the rest of the world and all of its horrible realities might vanish from existence, at least for a little while.

She wasn't sure how long they sat there before Rianol broke the silence.

"What will you do now?"

"I don't know. I hadn't thought about it."

"You could leave."

She raised her head to look at him. "You mean the planet?"

He gave her a weak smile. "I'll help you. I'll find a ship for you, but you'll need to leave soon, An'jel. Your grandfather isn't going to sit around and mourn Victor's loss. If I know him, he's already lining up the next Council-elect. In another couple of days, you'll be married again."

"Oh, God." He was right. The knowledge was a sledgehammer-strength wake-up call.

Nicoli was dead. Nothing could change that. She could leave; go back to Earth—to Dugan and Skeeters. She could become a courier again. She'd take her mother with her, and find Yanur. They could start a new life. This time, she'd have to do a better job of evading her grandfather. It wouldn't be for long. He was old and dying. He wouldn't live much longer.

But then what? What happened to all the people who looked to him for protection from the other Houses? The people who counted on the House of Scyphor for their livelihood? Would they really be better off with whomever her grandfather found to be the next high counsel? Wasn't their future well-being as much her responsibility as his?

These were the questions Nicoli would ask. She knew it as well as if he were sitting here voicing them. Nicoli, who made it his life's mission to take care of and protect others, no matter what the cost to him personally. If she had learned nothing else from him, maybe she had learned at least this one thing. She couldn't run from her responsibilities or problems.

She shook her head. "No, I'm not going to leave. I have a responsibility here, to these people. Somehow, I have to find a way to change things, make them better."

Rianol looked at her, an uncertainty in his eyes. "I have a suggestion, but I'm not sure if you'll like it."

Angel raised her eyebrows, encouraging him to continue.

"Marry me." Before she could say anything, he held up his hand to silence her. "I know you don't love me. I don't love you, either, but we're fond of one another and I think we'd suit each other well. Well enough to rule a planet—together. The way it's supposed to be done. I'm offering you a marriage of convenience, An'jel; protection from your grandfather. And I'm offering you a chance to make changes, by ruling by my side, as an equal."

Angel studied Rianol's face. For a Coronadian man to suggest men and women be equals was revolutionary, amazing. He almost made her think it could work, but was she brave enough to try?

She turned to Rianol. "What about my grandfather? Do you think he'll go for it?"

"No. That's why we marry without his permission."

"How?"

"We sleep together."

"What?" Angel pulled away in surprise. She didn't want to offend Rianol, but she wasn't going to sleep with him. "No, I'm sorry. I just don't think I can . . . this soon . . . ever."

"It's okay, An'jel. I should have explained better. I didn't mean we had to actually, you know, physically consummate the relationship." He shuddered beside her. "One of the ancient laws specifies that if a man and woman consummate their relationship and then publicly proclaim themselves to be man and wife, then they become so by law. It's called the Rite of Consummation. We spend the night together and the next morning we stand in the public square and tell everyone that we're married."

Angel wasn't sure she liked the sound of that. "It seems too easy."

"It is. As long as no one stakes a prior claim, and they shouldn't with Colonel Romanof dead, then we'll be recognized as husband and wife and there's not a damn thing the high counsel can do about it."

The whole idea of spending the night with Rianol left her feeling queasy, but she fought against it. Nicoli was dead and this was the only way she could protect herself if she wanted to stay. "Okay. Let's say this works, what's to stop my grandfather from initiating another Challenge fight?"

Rianol shook his head. "The Quorum won't go for it. The only reason they agreed before was because your grandfather convinced them we couldn't have an off-worlder as high counsel. He can't use that argument with me. Besides, the members of the Quorum know and like me. It won't be a problem."

Angel took a deep breath. Things were moving too quickly for her. "When?"

He looked at her as if he'd already thrown a lot at her and didn't want to press his luck. "Tonight."

"Tonight!" Her husband had just died.

"Or tomorrow, but the sooner we do it, the safer you'll be. I'm sorry An'jel. I know it seems too soon. We just don't have a lot of time."

Angel shook her head and took a deep breath. "You're right. We'll do it tonight."

Taking both of her hands in his, he stood up. "I'll leave you now to think about this. If later this evening, you still want to go through with it, then come to my room. Everything will work out fine. You'll see." He leaned over to press a chaste kiss to her cheek.

Angel mentally shied away from the contact. It didn't feel right. Maybe it never would.

She continued to sit in the maze long after Rianol left. She thought about everything that had happened and about what she was going to do. She could think of many reasons not to go through with the marriage to Rianol, but all were selfish.

Finally, her stomach started growling, so she wandered back to the kitchen. Maybe now that she had a plan of action, her stomach would settle down and she could eat.

It was after the midday meal and the kitchen was empty. Preparations for the evening meal wouldn't begin for another hour or so. Angel walked in, glad to have the place to herself. She gathered the makings for an old-fashioned sandwich and was cutting the bread when her grandfather walked in.

"What are you doing here?" she muttered.

"I saw you come in here, so I followed you." He walked to the far side of the table and sat down facing her. "I thought you would have left by now. Run away."

"Well, I didn't." She set the bread aside and picked up the meat to start cutting a slice. She paused in mid-slice. "Would you mind telling me why?"

He looked at her, eyebrows raised.

"Why you were so against Nicoli? He would have made a great leader. He wasn't afraid to stand up and do what was right. Is that why you felt threatened? Is that why you didn't stop the fight?"

"Victor issued *The Challenge*."

"Don't." Angel stabbed the knife into the cutting board. "Don't even pretend you had no control over what happened. You and I both know the truth. You didn't want Nicoli as your successor because he was better than you. A better leader. A better man. A better everything."

"You shouldn't speak to me with such disrespect," the high counsel warned. "I am still the ruler of this house. And your grandfather."

"You have to *earn* respect." She pulled the knife out of the cutting board and busied herself with cutting a piece of cheese. She slapped it on the bread, followed by the meat she'd sliced earlier. When her sandwich was done, she looked up to find her grandfather studying her.

"I'm dying," he said, sounding truly old and sick.

She sighed. "It's probably no less than you deserve." But she said it without rancor in her tone.

"It's over. You won."

"Did I?" She gave a half-laugh. "Somehow I thought winning would feel better." She picked up her sandwich and walked to the door, stopping when she heard his sigh.

"Victor would have made you the perfect husband and leader. I don't know that I can find someone that perfect again."

"Victor wasn't as perfect as you thought."

He cocked his head. "What do you mean?"

"He was a Harvestor. And he found you, not the other way around. Nicoli wasn't just protecting *me* in that fight. He was protecting you and the rest of the planet from the Harvestors. Think about it." She turned and walked out.

The rest of the day passed slowly, but eventually the two suns set and Angel found herself knocking on Rianol's door.

"Come in." Even from the other side of the door, he sounded nervous. "My quarters are not as big as yours," he apologized after she walked in. "But I think we'll be comfortable here to-night." She came to a stop in front of the bed. Large enough for at least three people, it had head- and footboards made of Co-ronadian knotty wood. "We'll have to share the bed, just in case anyone happens to barge in on us, or checks the room later. It needs to at least look as if we slept together."

Angel nodded and took a leisurely stroll about. There wasn't much to the room. A desk, a couple of chairs and a wet bar, with a bathroom off to the side. She'd have to talk to Rianol later about separate quarters. For now, she just wanted to get through the night.

"How about a drink?"

"Sure," Angel answered. "Martian Ale?"

Rianol smiled. "One Martian Ale coming up." He washed his hands at the wet bar sink, then poured the neon blue liquid into a glass. She took it from him with a nervous smile. She wasn't really thirsty, but hoped it would soothe her nerves. She took a couple of sips as she finished circling the room.

It was a short trip, so when she completed her tour, she went over to the desk and sat in one of the chairs beside it. "What do we do now?"

He shrugged. "I don't really know. I guess we could talk." He picked up the drink he'd poured himself and took a swallow. When he took the glass away from his mouth, his hand shook.

"Rianol, are you okay? Don't tell me I make you nervous," she joked, looking at him while reaching out to put her drink on the desk. She missed and the glass slipped off the edge and onto the floor. The blue liquid spilled everywhere.

"Oh, I'm sorry." She scooted off her chair to stoop by the mess. "Rianol, do you have a towel or something . . . Rianol?"

He stood trembling, mesmerized by the liquid seeping into the carpet. He didn't seem to hear her when she spoke.

"Rianol?"

"You spilled." He sounded aghast.

"Yes, I did. I'm sorry, but I'll clean it up if you'll toss me a towel or something."

"No. I'll do it," he snapped. Picking up a rag, he whipped by her and started to dab the liquid from the carpet. "You'll have to be more careful." He sounded as if he were speaking through clenched teeth.

"Sorry, Rianol. I didn't mean to upset you."

As if just realizing how absurd he was acting, Rianol looked up at her. "I'm sorry. I like things clean and neat."

"I understand," Angel said, trying to sound as if she really did.

He finished wiping up the excess liquid, then walked back to the wet bar. He washed his hands after throwing the soiled cloth into the trash bin.

"I'll fix you another drink."

"No, that's okay. I'm not really thirsty."

"I think you should have one anyway. To calm you for the rest of the evening."

She wanted to protest, but didn't want to argue with him when he already seemed so upset. "Okay, fine." She picked up the fallen glass from the floor where he had overlooked it and started to hand it to him.

He had already poured her drink into a new glass and was standing with his back to her. She saw him reach into his pocket and pull out a small vial. Warning bells started ringing in her head. She couldn't see what he was doing with the vial, but knew he was putting some of its contents into her drink. Did she confront him? Or pretend she didn't see and just not drink it?

She stood up just has he put the vial back into his pocket and turned around. "Rianol, I think maybe we're rushing things."

His eyes narrowed and she could almost see the thoughts racing around in his head.

She waved a hand toward the door, trying to act casual. "I'm going back to my room. I just need a little more time." She started for the door.

Rianol set down the glass and started to walk toward her. "I don't think we should wait."

"I do. It's just too soon for me."

Then he was there, beside her, and before she knew it, he punched her in the jaw and everything grew dark.

Chapter Thirty

Consciousness, when it came, slammed into her with a force equal to the blow that had knocked her out. She noticed the pain in her jaw, but ignored it. It was her inability to move her arms or legs that demanded her attention. She tried to assess her situation without opening her eyes. She was lying on something soft, which she assumed was the bed. Her arms were stretched above her head and metal cuffs fastened around her wrists held her secure. Her legs were shackled, as well.

"I know you're awake, An'jel. I didn't hit you that hard. Can't hit anything that hard." Rianol's tone sounded bitter.

Angel opened her eyes to see him standing to the side of her, legs spread and arms crossed over his chest.

"Why?"

"Haven't you guessed by now?"

"Are you working for my grandfather?"

He threw his head back and laughed. There was a manic edge to his laughter that she hadn't noticed before and when he looked at her again, it wasn't with the eyes of the Rianol she'd come to know. This man was crazy. Or . . .

"You're a Harvestor."

"We prefer the term Magdatians, but yes."

"I, we, thought Victor was the leader."

At the mention of Victor's name, Rianol's eyes grew solemn. "No. Victor was not our leader. I am."

"Did you kill Herrod?"

"No, Victor did. He saw you two fighting and took advantage of the situation. I believe he hoped to eliminate Colonel Romanof." Rianol shook his head. "Victor never had the patience to wait and plan things through. Oh, well. Victor's last act of sacrifice proved his worth. With Colonel Romanof out of the way, I can continue as planned."

"You won't succeed. I'll stop you." Angel stretched her head back, trying to see how her hands were secured. Rianol had locked her into a pair of handcuffs with a special chain that allowed them to be secured to the headboard. She pulled it to test its strength while Rianol stood by and watched without apparent concern that she would free herself.

"Struggle all you want. The more you do, the more the bed will look slept in." Rianol came forward and ran a finger down her cheek. Then as if the touch of her skin was offensive, he rubbed his fingers together. "After all, tomorrow we'll want to look convincing."

"I wouldn't marry you if you were the last man—"

"I wouldn't be so hasty to offer threats." Rianol shouted over her. "Unless, of course, you have no concerns about your mother's safety."

An unnatural calm settled over her. "Where is my mother?"

"Oh, I imagine she's enjoying a quiet meal right about now. With Sorrah, who's been most helpful after I discovered her involvement in the colonel's demise. And then tomorrow morning, when it's time for us to make our little announcement, she'll stand with your mother in the crowd. Sorrah will have a tiny hypo in her possession, containing a deadly poison. One wrong word from you and your mother will die. Very painfully, I might add. So, before you do anything rash, you might wish to reconsider. You just buried a husband. Are you so willing to bury your mother, as well?"

* * *

Between her discomfort from being chained to the bed and her fear of what Rianol might do should she fall asleep, Angel fought to stay awake all night. By morning, she was exhausted. When Rianol finally released her, Angel felt too stiff and too tired to do more than glare at him.

"Get undressed," he ordered.

Angel rubbed her wrists, trying to work circulation back into her arms. "Why?" As she watched, he stripped off his shirt.

"We're about to have company." He smiled at her. "Don't worry, I won't take advantage of you. You're not my type."

"Why's that? Too independent? Too Coronadian?"

"No. Too female."

Angel gaped at him. "Victor was your lover."

"Very astute of you. Now take off your clothes or dear old mom gets a hypo for breakfast."

Somehow, knowing he had no interest in her sexually made it easier. As Angel stood and did as he ordered, a thought occurred to her. "You poisoned my mother? How?"

Rianol spared her a quick glance. "Tainted massage oils. Now climb into bed and get under the covers."

Her tired brain fought against her fatigue, searching for possible ways out of this predicament. Finding none, she followed his instructions, pulling the covers up to her chin in an effort to cover her nudity. As she did, she cast a glance at Rianol and gasped. She hadn't realized how thin and frail Rianol was beneath his clothes. As he walked to the bed, she noticed the slight twist of his right foot.

Perhaps feeling her eyes on him, Rianol glowered at her. "Don't worry, my dear. I find this decrepit body as disgusting as you do. But thanks, no doubt, to your and Romanof's efforts, it will be a while longer before I have the new transfer unit up and operational."

Rianol crawled in beside her, but didn't look any happier about being there than she did. He'd barely tucked his legs under the cover when a knock came at the door.

"Come in." Rianol shouted, quickly draping an arm around Angel's shoulders, pulling her close.

"What is so urgent that I had to come here . . ." Her grandfather's voice fell silent as he stepped into the room and saw them. For a moment, his face mirrored his shock. Then he pulled himself together. "What's the meaning of this?" He demanded of Rianol. "What are you doing with my granddaughter?"

"We're invoking the Rite of Consummation," Rianol replied smoothly, squeezing Angel's arm to no doubt remind her to keep quiet. As if she would risk her mother's life, she thought disgustedly. "As you can see," Rianol continued. "We spent the night together, as man and wife, and need only make a public declaration to legalize our marriage."

"Is this true?" Her grandfather glared at her.

Angel could only nod.

Her grandfather seemed to age before her eyes, all the fight going out of him. "Very well. I will make the necessary arrangements. Be at the square in an hour." He didn't look at either of them before leaving the room.

Rianol jumped out of bed and crossed the room, apparently unconcerned about his lack of dress. He shut the door and turned to give her a smile. "That went well, don't you think?"

Yanur stepped to the outer fringes of the crowd gathered in the village's public square. The tracer tag embedded in the necklace he'd given Katrina indicated she was here. He'd told her he'd come for her, as soon as he took care of Nicoli's body. Had she believed him?

He surveyed the faces in the crowd, feeling the anticipation and excitement in those gathered there. And his concern grew.

Then he spotted her. She would never hear him over the noise, so he pushed his way through the crowd, until he stood behind her.

"Katrina." Her name was a prayer on his lips.

At the sound of his voice, she turned to him and her eyes lit up with joy. Then, so quickly that he wondered if he'd mistaken her initial reaction, her eyes clouded and her expression grew solemn.

"Hello, Mr. Snellen."

Mr. Snellen? What was this? "Katrina, I'd like to talk to you."

He looked pointedly at her companion, recognizing Sorrah, the maid Katrina hated. "Alone."

Katrina's glance darted to the maid before turning to him. "I'm afraid that's not possible."

For a moment, he doubted himself. Had he been wrong thinking there was more to what they shared than mere friendship? Then he saw it, a flicker of emotion in Katrina's eyes. Fear.

"Very well," he said to her. "I'll leave."

He saw the desperation in her eyes when he turned to move away, but he didn't go far. Reaching into his pocket, he pulled out the neuro-tazer. He pressed it to the maid's neck and she crumpled into his waiting arms, unconscious. The crowd, too distracted by what was about to transpire at the podium, didn't seem to notice as he dragged her off to the side and set her against a tree.

When he turned around, Katrina was there. For a moment, she stood and stared at the unconscious maid. Then a smile broke across her face and she threw herself into his arms.

"I knew you'd come back. Your timing, as usual, is very good." The look of love she showered on him left him breathless.

"You really need someone to watch over you," he scolded.

"Are you applying for the job?"

Yanur looked deep into her eyes. "Yes, I am." He lowered his head, touching his lips to hers, putting his heart and the promise of a lifetime into a single kiss.

Angel approached the square in a dreamlike state. Fatigue and frustration dominated her emotions and thoughts. She was barely aware of the villagers, gathered in the square, their eyes turned expectantly to the small group walking across the stage to the podium.

With Rianol on one side, clutching her arm, and her grandfather on the other, Angel scanned the crowd for her mother. She was nowhere to be seen.

"Good villagers of Scyphor," Rianol began. "Hear me now. In accordance with the Rite of Consummation, I swear before all of you that An'jel ToRrenc and I, Rianol D'Wintre, did consummate our marriage and stand before you now as husband and wife. Let any with prior claim speak now or forever remain silent."

Angel prayed for a miracle, knowing none would come. Angel longed to remove the confident smile that crossed Rianol's face as he looked out over the people. Then a voice shouted from the crowd.

"I lay prior claim."

A buzzing started in Angel's head, playing games with her mind. The voice she heard was a figment of her imagination; wishful thinking but nothing more. A low murmuring of voices began in the crowd and grew louder. Then the onlookers parted and a figure stepped forward.

"Nicoli." The name rushed from her lips on a whisper as she gripped the podium with both hands to steady herself. How could he be alive? It was a miracle. She wanted to race into the crowd, throw herself into his arms, but her mother's life lay in the balance.

"Colonel Romanof," Rianol said with a sneer. "You're a hard man to kill."

"I doubt you will be," Nicoli responded. "Step away from my wife."

Rianol smiled. "I'm afraid that you were declared legally dead at *The Challenge* fight. Your claim is forfeit. But don't worry." Rianol brushed the back of his hand down Angel's cheek in a mock show of affection. "An'jel waited at least a day or two after you died before coming to my bed."

Nicoli stared at her, confusion and doubt evident in his gaze. "Angel?"

She wanted to cry out, deny Rianol's claims, profess her love for Nicoli, but she remained silent, dying a little inside. When Nicoli turned to go, she looked away, unable to watch, and spotted someone waving on the far side of the gathering.

She looked closer and gasped. Her mother stood, smiling, beside Yanur. Sorrah was nowhere to be seen "Nicoli, wait . . ." The laser Rianol pulled from beneath his jacket and now held to her side caused the rest of her cry to die into silence.

A gasp went up from the gathering, drawing Nicoli's attention. He turned back.

"You couldn't stay quiet, could you?" Rianol growled at Angel, one hand grabbing her hair close to the scalp to hold her in place while the other hand brought the laser to her head. He jerked her hair roughly as he shouted. "You tell them we spent the night together."

Angel gritted her teeth against the pain, her eyes tearing involuntarily. "Never," she ground out between clenched teeth. "I wouldn't sleep with you if you were the last man in the universe."

A hush fell across the crowd while Rianol stared about, wild-eyed, as if unsure what to do.

"It's over," Nicoli shouted, training his own laser on Rianol. "Let her go."

Rianol pushed Angel in front of him as a shield. "You'll have to kill me first," he shouted, firing the laser at Nicoli. People screamed and fell, en masse, to the ground, as the shot missed its target. Rianol backed off the stage, pulling Angel with him. He fired three more bursts erratically into the crowd, then turned and ran toward the palace gardens, taking Angel as his hostage.

"There's a shortcut that way," Katrina said breathlessly, rushing up to Nicoli and pointing to the far side. "Cut through the trees."

Nicoli didn't wait. He sprinted as if his life depended on it, because it did. Angel made him want to live again. Without her, his life meant nothing.

He barely noticed the sting of the tree branches as they scraped his arm when he pushed his way through the woods. All he could think about was getting there in time.

He reached the spot where the maze opened up just as Rianol emerged with Angel.

"You can't stop me," Rianol shouted, pulling Angel in front of him again as he faced Nicoli. "I won't let you destroy my dream."

There was a wild look to Rianol's eyes and Nicoli feared pushing him over the edge. "You picked the wrong way to go about it, Rianol." Nicoli tried to sound calm over the pounding of his heart. "It's over."

"No. I'll kill you both if I have to." Rianol's laser wavered dangerously back and forth. "Drop it," he said, nodding toward Nicoli's weapon.

Nicoli knew he was dealing with a madman. With no shot open to him, Nicoli lowered his laser to the ground.

Then suddenly, Angel went limp. Unable to hold her, Rianol's arm dipped under the weight and Angel fell to the ground. In that instant, Nicoli lunged, knocking Rianol off his feet. He grabbed the hand holding the laser and the two men wrestled for it.

Rianol pulled the trigger. A single shot fired and Angel screamed.

In a blind rage, Nicoli twisted Rianol's arm and the laser fired another shot, this time striking Rianol in the head.

Leaving the body there, Nicoli rushed to Angel's side, scooping her up into his arms, mindful of the laser wound in her side. Her eyes fluttered open as she whispered his name. "Nicoli?"

"I'm here, Baby Girl." He held her close, pressing his lips to her forehead, praying he could get her medical attention before it was too late.

"Rianol?"

"Dead." Nicoli looked at the body in disgust before turning back. A tear escaped her eye to roll down her cheek. "I saw you die."

"Don't talk," Nicoli urged, looking around for Yanur, willing his friend to suddenly appear.

"Tell me how," she whispered.

"After the fight, Yanur let everyone believe I was dead. He transferred my life essence back into the biopod, then took my body to the ship where he used the Reparator to heal me. We moved the ship so no one would interrupt us."

"You could have told me."

Nicoli heard the pain in her voice and his heart ached. "I'm sorry, Baby Girl. There wasn't time."

"I understand." She raised a hand to caress his cheek, then

let it fall limply back to the ground. Her eyes drifted shut and she grew still.

"Angel!" Fear made his voice sharp. He couldn't lose her. "Please don't leave me," he begged. "I don't think I can live without you. I love you, Angel."

She smiled, slowly opening her eyes. "I'm not dying. I'm just tired. It was a long night."

Nicoli could hardly believe it. "You're okay?"

"Yeah. It's only a flesh wound. I've had worse." She raised her hand to cup the back of his head and pulled it down to hers. "Now shut up and kiss me."

Epilogue

Skeeters Bar, Earth
One year later

"I thought I told you not to come in here during peak business hours," Dugan shouted from his office doorway. "The customers don't feel comfortable when there's a USP Security Forces colonel hanging around. Scares 'em away."

"Give it break, Dugan." Angel responded, making straight for the bar and collapsing onto a stool. "Nicoli hasn't been with the Security Forces for almost a year now, and you know it."

Dugan cast a dubious look at Nicoli, who merely smiled as he leaned against the bar next to Angel's stool. "You're still scaring away the customers."

Without raising her head from where it throbbed in her hands, Angel mumbled. "It's mid-morning. There are no customers. And if you aren't nice, we're going to leave."

"What's with you this morning?"

Nicoli came to her defense. "She's not feeling well."

Dugan's attitude changed immediately to one of fatherly concern. He had slipped easily back into his familiar role when Angel returned to Earth, a new husband in tow. And while he didn't act thrilled with the idea of having a government agent as a pseudo son-in-law, claiming it was bad for business and all, Angel knew that he secretly admired her husband.

"You drink too much Martian Ale last night?" Dugan stood close to her now. "I told you to go easy on that stuff."

"No. I didn't even drink last night," Angel argued, fighting another wave of nausea as it roiled in her stomach. "Ask Martin if you don't believe me."

She peeked up at the bartender, who always seemed to be wiping the counter.

"That's the truth, Dugan. Not a drop for our girl, here. Wasn't feeling too good last night, either, as I recall."

"I think she might have picked up a bug over on Zeta Prime," Nicoli offered by way of explanation. "It's the middle of the rainy season there."

"What were you doing in that God-forsaken part of the quadrant?" Dugan asked.

"Just debugging a computer program," Nicoli replied casually.

Angel snorted. "We had to steal it back from the Wathuilies first."

"Well, yeah. We had to do that, too." Nicoli replied.

"That's it." Dugan slammed his fist down on the counter. "Sorry," he said when Angel groaned. "You're not going on any more of these missions, do you understand?"

"We're not?" Nicoli sounded amused, and Angel hoped he would humor Dugan. She wasn't sure she could handle one of their "debates" on the dangers inherent in her and Nicoli's new line of consulting work.

"Actually," Nicoli continued. "We're going to Coronado for a few months. Angel's mom is due to deliver in a week or so and Yanur, who can bring the dead back to life, suddenly doesn't feel capable of delivering his own child."

"Oh." Angel heard the disappointment in Dugan's voice. "When were you planning to leave?"

"That kind of depends on you," Nicoli said.

"I don't follow."

Angel raised her head to look first at Dugan, then at Martin. "Well, to be honest, I was hoping you two would go with us. Mom and Yanur would love to have you visit. And you said the other day that you wouldn't mind checking out the place."

Dugan and Martin exchanged surprised looks, then a slow smile spread across both faces. "You want us to go with you?" Martin asked.

"Unless you don't feel like you can leave." Angel said, knowing full well that both men had enough money put away that they could afford to take off indefinitely.

"What about those Harvestors?" Martin sounded a little dubious.

"There are no Harvestors left on Coronado," Nicoli reassured him. "Rianol, I mean Brother Joh'nan, achieved his goal better than he realized. He saved his people. The entire village of initiates has been fully indoctrinated into the Coronadian society. They are living happy, healthy, normal lives—or at least as well as anyone could on that backward planet."

"Hey, that's not fair. Mom and Yanur have done a lot to turn things around. Everyone has accepted Yanur as the new high counsel and Mom said they're getting fewer complaints about her attending the council sessions.

"And the Harvestors did bring an aptitude for technology with them, so in another fifteen years, when Yanur and Mom retire and it's our turn to run the planet, Coronado will be practically state-of-the-art."

There was a shared moment of silence, then Angel bolted from her stool and ran into the bathroom, where she emptied the contents of her stomach into the waste disposal. When she was sure nothing else would come up, she wet a cloth and wiped her face. This morning ritual had grown too familiar of late.

She emerged from the bathroom to two gawking male faces, and a very troubled-looking Nicoli.

"What?" She felt a little on display. At that moment, her stomach growled and she looked over at Martin. "Got any food in the place? I'm famished."

"I thought you didn't feel well," Dugan said suspiciously.

She shrugged her shoulders. "I'm feeling better now."

Dugan turned to Nicoli. "How long has this been going on?"

"About three weeks, near as I can tell."

A slow smile spread across Dugan's face. "Interesting. Well, by all means, Martin and I will go with you to Coronado."

Martin looked surprised. "We will?"

Dugan chuckled. "I wouldn't miss this for the world."

Angel looked at Dugan. He knew. It wasn't fair. It was her body and even she wasn't sure. Before she could say anything, he walked back to his office.

"Be sure to pack enough clothes," he shouted to Martin when he reached the doorway. "At least enough for eight or nine months, maybe longer." He shut the door and they heard him laughing on the other side.

Martin rushed around the counter and gave her a hug. "Congratulations, girl. I gotta go pack." He walked to the front door, locked it and placed a "Closed" sign in the window. Then he disappeared upstairs.

Nicoli had been unusually quiet during this exchange and Angel found she was afraid to look at him. They'd never talked about having kids. After the childhood experience he'd had, she wasn't sure he wanted any. She felt, rather than saw, him step closer.

"Angel? Is it true?" He whispered as if speaking louder might shatter the moment.

"I think so." She turned hopeful eyes up to study his face. "I was going to ask Yanur to scan me when we got to Coronado."

A smile crept across his face and he gathered her into his arms.

"Are you okay with this?" she asked. "I mean, we never really talked about it."

"Am I okay?" He gave a nervous laugh. "I'm not sure I know how to be a father. But, yes, I'm okay. I want kids."

She looked up amazed. "You do? I didn't know that."

He smiled. "I've wanted kids since the moment I saw you."

She laughed. "The first time you saw me, I was lying naked on a gurney in the middle of the Harvestors' processing building. Somehow I don't think having kids was on your mind."

"True, but the thoughts I had were along those lines."

"Oh, really?"

"Yes. Shall I tell you all about them?"

"No. I'd rather you show me."

He reached down and lifted her into his arms.

"Where are you taking me?" she asked, resting her head against his shoulder as he headed for the stairs.

"To the stars and beyond."

CONTACT
SUSAN GRANT

A BEAUTIFUL CO-PILOT WITH A TERRIBLE CHOICE.

"After only three novels, Susan Grant has proven herself
to be the best hope for the survival of the futuristic/
fantasy romance genre." —*The Romance Reader*

A DARK STRANGER WHO HAS KNOWN NOTHING BUT DUTY.

"I am in awe of Susan Grant. She's one
of the few authors who get it." —*Everything Romantic*

A LATE-NIGHT FLIGHT, HIJACKED OVER THE PACIFIC.

Shadow Crossing
Catherine Spangler

Celie Cameron spent her youth as a smuggler, skirting the law. But though she's given that up, she misses the adrenaline rush of danger. Then a routine delivery goes haywire, throwing her into the arms of a handsome pilot—an android, or so she thinks—and Celie suddenly finds herself embroiled in a galaxy-spanning intrigue and deception.

Rurick is a miracle creation. But though he attracts her as no human ever has, his secrets threaten all Celie has ever believed. She resists his allure . . . until she learns to trust her heart. Then they will challenge the evil that threatens the Verante quadrant, and love will bring light to the dark expanse of space known as Shadow Crossing.

- -

RAVYN'S FLIGHT
PATTI O'SHEA

Ravyn Verdier is on a mission to test the habitability of Jarved Nine. Damon Brody is sent to rescue her when the rest of her team is mysteriously killed. Trapped on a planet that harbors an unimaginable evil, they have only each other.

An abandoned city holds the key to their survival, but what they find behind its ancient walls defies all their preconceived notions and tests the limits of the bond that has formed between them. To succeed, they will have to cast aside their doubts and listen to their hearts. For only when they are linked body and soul—when they realize love is their greatest weapon—will they be able to defeat the force bent on destroying all life.

LORD
OF THE
DARK SUN
STOBIE PIEL

Ariana awakens a captive. Her ship has been disabled and her friends hurt, and she is to blame. She cajoled them into braving the outskirts of space. And now they are to be transported to a non-Intersystem planet where they will be slaves.

The world is bleak and shadowy, as are its inhabitants. And though these men are slaves as well, that hardly makes them less dangerous. Yet one rises above the others, and Ariana sees in him nobility. This is a prince in a barbarian's body, one who can teach her how to be wild. On this planet with its dark sun, Ariana knows he will help her survive. And she will show him a love that will last through whatever follows.

- -

Spellbound
KATHLEEN NANCE

As the Minstrel of Kaf, Zayne keeps the land of the djinn in harmony. Yet lately, he needs a woman to restore balance to his life, a woman with whom he can blend his voice and his body. And according to his destiny, this soul mate can only be found in the strange land of Earth.

Madeline knows to expect a guest while house-sitting, but she didn't expect the man would be so sexy, so potent, so fascinated by the doorbell. With one soul-stirring kiss, she sees colorful sparks dancing on the air. But Madeline wants to make sure her handsome djinni won't pull a disappearing act before she can become utterly spellbound.

WHISPERS ON THE WIND

JUDY GILL

In a secluded cave amid the Canadian Rockies Lenore finds Jon: the lover of her dreams, a man quite literally from another world. In a desperate bid for survival he has sought her out telepathically. Injured and separated from his crew, Jon's success, the future of his planet, his very life depends on Lenore. She denies him nothing, sharing her home, her knowledge, her strength, and eventually her heart. Until what had begun as mere caresses of the consciousness progresses to a melding of not only bodies, but souls.

___52435-X $4.99 US/$5.99 CAN

ATTENTION
BOOK LOVERS!

Can't get enough of your favorite **ROMANCE**?

Call **1-800-481-9191** to:

* order books,

* receive a **FREE** catalog,

* join our book clubs to **SAVE 20%!**

Open Mon.-Fri. 10 AM-9 PM EST

Visit **www.dorchesterpub.com**
for special offers and inside
information on the authors you love.